Kingdom of Power, Power of Kingdom

Kingdom of Power, Power of Kingdom

The Opposing World Views of Mark and Chariton

ROB STARNER

With a Foreword by Mikeal C. Parsons

☙PICKWICK *Publications* • Eugene, Oregon

KINGDOM OF POWER, POWER OF KINGDOM
The Opposing World Views of Mark and Chariton

Copyright © 2011 Rob Starner. All rights reserved. Except for brief quotations in critical publications or reviews, no part of this book may be reproduced in any manner without prior written permission from the publisher. Write: Permissions, Wipf and Stock Publishers, 199 W. 8th Ave., Suite 3, Eugene, OR 97401.

Pickwick Publications
An Imprint of Wipf and Stock Publishers
199 W. 8th Ave., Suite 3
Eugene, OR 97401

www.wipfandstock.com

ISBN 13: 978-1-60899-008-5

Cataloguing-in-Publication data:

Starner, Rob.

Kingdom of power, power of kingdom : the opposing world views of Mark and Chariton / Rob Starner ; with a foreword by Mikeal C. Parsons.

xx + 218 pp. ; 23 cm. Includes bibliographical references and index.

ISBN 13: 978-1-60899-008-5

1. Bible. N. T. Mark—Criticism, Narrative. 2. Chariton. De Chaerea et Callirrhoe. I. Title.

BS2585.2 S71 2011

Manufactured in the U.S.A.

To George R. Stotts, Dean, Mentor, Friend
Who taught me the honor of giving the "last full measure of devotion"
to Kingdom service

To George F. Paul, Teacher, Mentor, Friend
Who modeled genuine interest in students and made me believe
I could be a teacher

To Lynn Anderson, Bibliothécaire Sans Egal, Friend
Who selflessly and sacrificially has helped me personally and professionally

To The Memory of My Grandfather, Leo
Who taught me the indispensable nexus between prayer and exegesis

To The Memory of My Father, Roger
Who encouraged me by identifying with the divine approbation:
"This Is My Beloved Son in Whom I Am Well Pleased"

To the Memory of My Uncle Jim
Who first gave me opportunity to teach the Bible and
Who from first to last encouraged me therein

To the Memory of My Brother-In-Law, Derek
Who impacted me by his life and his death

To My In-Laws, Eugenia and Jozef
Who model relational evangelism

To My Mother, Carmella
Who taught me to love books

To My Wife, Maja
Who sacrificially
supports my
writing

To Our Children, Kali and Kaleb
Who are our first ministry and foundation for the future

Contents

Acknowledgments

A WORK OF THIS nature never leaves the writer without a large debt of gratitude for assistance received in various aspects of the project. Special thanks are due Jerry Camery-Hoggatt not only for his willingness to listen to the gist of my proposal and offer sound direction of approach, but also for recommending starter resources, one of which (his own, as it happens) afforded the foundational grid that I used to ascertain how Mark's and Chariton's readers would respond to their respective narrative cues. Additionally, for their sound academic counsel, I wish to thank my *Doktorvater*, Mikeal C. Parsons, and primary readers, Naymond H. Keathley and Stephen R. Todd. Their oral and written observations stimulated my thinking and prompted me to greater clarity. I am particularly grateful to Dr. Parsons for writing the kind foreword to this book.

Several other individuals also command my deep appreciation. I would like to acknowledge the generous aid of my former colleagues Stephen A. Badger and Kevin O. Patterson, who not only read extensive portions of my manuscript and engaged me in critical dialogue, but also offered timely assistance with computer tasks related to the installation and fine-tuning of software used in the display, printing, and analysis of Greek texts. Special thanks are due also to K. C. Hanson, Chris Spinks, Christian Amondson, and the rest of the editorial staff at Wipf and Stock for kindly agreeing to make this book available to a wider audience, to Jordan Daniel May for his speedy and thorough skill in putting the entire manuscript into the publisher's format, and to my New Testament students, Mandi Mendoza, Nick Tangco, and Tim Martinez for their gracious labor in compiling the indices.

I wish to thank also my friends, who have patiently endured the many occasions on which this project precluded social interaction, and who, in spite of this, have faithfully offered encouragement. My deepest appreciation, however, goes to my family: to my wife, Maja, for her willingness to share firsthand all the sacrifices concomitant with an academic endeavor of this magnitude; to my parents, Roger and Carmella Starner, for their tireless, unflinching financial and emotional support; and to my parents-in-law, Eugenia and Józef Baluczynski, for their unceasing prayers on our behalf. Their support of someone else's goals—without thought of a personal return on their investment—is indeed one illustration of thinking "the things of God."

Finally, I owe profound gratitude to God, who enabled me to fulfill the rigors of academic research and writing, provided strength to endure long days of labor and nights without sleep, and comforted me through seasons of isolation necessitated by this project. *Sola Gloria Dei!*

Foreword

IN 1955, THE GREAT Harvard don Henry J. Cadbury made an off-handed observation regarding the study of the Acts of the Apostles: "I do not know where one can get so many illustrations of the idiom and ideas of the author of Acts in 150 pages as in the love story of his near contemporary, Chariton of Aphrodsia" (*Book of Acts in History*, 8). Cadbury's comment went virtually unnoticed until Richard Pervo's 1979 Harvard dissertation, "The Literary Genre of the Acts of the Apostles" (published in 1987). Since that time, however, a spate of studies has been published that explore various dimensions not only of Acts, but also of the canonical Gospels, in light of the ancient Greek novels. Much of that work has been associated with the Ancient Fiction, Early Christian and Jewish Narrative Group (now "Section") of the Society of Biblical Literature, which began in 1992 (see e.g., the two volumes of collected essays published in the SBL Symposium Series, in 1998 and 2005). Among those contributors one might mention especially Ronald Hock for making singular contributions through a series of essays and presentations (Hock also chronicles other recent scholarship on the novels and the NT in two issues of the *Petronian Society Newsletter*, which are archived at http://www.ancientnarrative.com/PSN/index.htm).

To the growing body of literature on early Christian literature and the ancient novel, this work of Rob Starner is a welcomed addition. In this volume, Starner explores the vexing issue of Mark's narrative order—a problem recognized as long ago as Papias—in light of the narrative sequencing of Chariton's novel. Using a combination of narrative criticism (especially the work by Genette and Perry) and reader-response analysis (especially Iser), Starner shows how both Mark and Chariton use the literary devices of, among others, prolepses, analepses, anachronies, and gaps to advance the plot of the story. In both cases, the narrator's point of view or ideology is clarified by these shifts in narrative order. Starner argues that the reader is drawn to emulate "the things of God" perspective in Mark and to reject the "things of man" point of view. For Chariton, on the other hand, the ideological perspective focuses on power (or powerless) relations between and among human characters, between and among the gods, and between and among the interactions of gods and humans. In both cases, the texts' meaning is illuminated in compelling and clarifying ways. Furthermore, Starner has gone a step beyond Cadbury to show that not only do the idiom and ideas of the novel illustrate the idiom and ideas of the NT writer, but also that the fact that the ideas of Chariton are communicated *through and by means of* the idiom, in this case of narrative sequencing, which brings into bold relief the way this same interaction functions in the Gospel of Mark. For this, Starner has put all of us in his debt.

Mikeal C. Parsons
Professor and Macon Chair in Religion
Baylor University

Preface

THE INVESTIGATION CHARTED IN the following pages employs a literary analysis designed to test the hypothesis that Mark's Gospel should be interpreted in light of its generic affiliation with ancient romance novels of Hellenistic popular literature, a thesis I first encountered in Mary Ann Tolbert's *Sowing the Gospel: Mark's World in Literary-Historical Perspective.* I admit an initial predispositional disinclination for understanding any of the biblical materials in the same vein as fictional literature (as if Jerusalem truly had nothing to do with Athens!), but this perspective betrays a cultural myopia whose fuzzy rendering of things distant obscures the thoroughly religious character of the NT world.

The fact that analysis of genre must give attention to the literary features of the text is hardly revelatory. The question for me was, what sort of literary features would afford a manageable database with which to make the comparison? In the course of my investigation, I stumbled upon a work whose intriguing title charted the path: *Clumsy Construction in Mark's Gospel*, by John C. Meagher. In view of the high esteem the writers of Scripture have commanded in the church for nearly two millennia, these words had an irreverent and almost bellicose ring, issuing a challenge that I believed should not go unanswered.

Meagher's denigration of Mark's Gospel was based, among other things, on Mark's frequent repetition of words, phrases, and, in his judgment, entire episodes, all of which he interpreted as needless redundancy most naturally attributable to the ineptitude of the writer. But context is a critical adjudicating factor here, particularly with regard to Mark's audience. If an audience is pressed for time and somewhat disinterested in the message, then repetition is an unwelcome annoyance to be sure; but if an audience is concerned to apprehend important information for later use, repetition is a fully appreciated heuristic device. When it comes to the deployment of both Mark's Gospel and Chariton's *Chaereas and Callirhoe*, the respective *Sitze im Leben* likely are far less akin to a dreaded committee meeting than to an infant CPR class. To put the matter plainly, Meagher's assessment assumes Mark's audience was as disinterested in Mark's narrative and as disappointed by its redundant and disordered presentation as he himself is.

The present volume operates under the premise that Mark's literary features, particularly repetition (frequently through flashbacks and foreshadowings) and the oft-noted disordered arrangement of narrative events, are more rightly and profitably understood as intentional rhetorical strategies than unwitting slip-ups. The force of this point is compounded when we realize that the original audiences were undoubtedly *auditeurs*, not readers. In other words, critiquing these works by the canons of literary criticism without first considering their fit with the organizing principles of oral performance is a risky enterprise that may lead not only to a mistaken view of the composer's acumen, but also to a distorted understanding of composition itself.

In addressing the issue of Mark's narrative "disorder," my investigation took foundational cues particularly from the work of Gerard Genette (*Narrative Discourse: An Essay In Method*), Menakhem Perry ("Literary Dynamics: How the Order of a Text Creates Its Meanings"), and Meir Sternberg (*Expositional Modes and Temporal Ordering in Fiction*). These narratologists understand the ordering of events in a narrative as an instructive design by means of which authors guide their readers in making sense of their works.

Convinced that the sequential arrangement of events in a narrative was one of the ways that authors helped readers process their works, I began to probe the reading process. Wolfgang Iser's *The Act of Reading* prompted me to consider seriously the reader's role in the author-text-reader transaction, and Jerry Camery-Hoggatt's *Rhetoric of Text, Rhetoric of Sermon: A Reader-Response Approach to the Business of Preaching* (a manuscript later published as *Speaking of God*) provided a grid (gleaned from Camery-Hoggatt's research in cognitive psychology) with which I postulated the effect that specific narrative arrangements have on readers from various social locations.

The result was for me an exciting journey into two story worlds that likely shared a common historical-cultural setting. Analyzing the narratives of Mark and Chariton from the vantage point of narrative sequence identified two conflicting worldviews: For Chariton the world is controlled by the goddess Aphrodite, who serves as a powerbroker distributing political, economic, and sociological power to agents who use that power for self-serving ends, but whose fate she herself ultimately determines. For Mark, the world is governed by an omnipotent God who surprisingly operates from a position of weakness, inviting (not coercing) humans to accept his rulership and urging them to adopt the self-sacrificial, service-oriented life principle that he himself modeled in the sacrificial life and death of his own Son.

In spite of the stylistic, thematic, and telic similarities between Mark's Gospel and Chariton's novel, the two works have significant differences, differences that should caution us against reading Mark's Gospel as an ancient romance novel. To be sure, both romance novels and gospels were entertaining ways of inculcating and disseminating cultural ideals and mores, but that point of convergence alone is not sufficient to establish generic equivalence.

Finally, the emergence of this book is somewhat like uncovering an archeological artifact; for apart from minor stylistic modifications, the work is in essence the doctoral dissertation I presented to the faculty of Baylor University nearly two decades ago. In spite of this temporal distance, the methodological approach and the overarching theme are as relevant today as they were upon its completion—and arguably more so. Whether it comes as a "lost treasure" or merely as a "clay pot" is for the reader to decide.

Rob Starner
Professor of Greek and New Testament
Southwestern Assemblies of God University

Tables

Abbreviations

AARAS	American Academy of Religion Academy Series
AERJ	*American Educational Research Journal*
AJP	*American Journal of Philology*
BDAG	W. Bauer, F. W. Danker, W. F. Arndt, and F. W. Gingrich, editors, *Greek-English Lexicon of the New Testament and Other Early Christian Literature*, 3rd ed. (Chicago, 2000)
BDGL	Bibliothek der griechischen Literatur
BLS	Bible and Literature Series
BR	*Biblical Research*
BSer	Bollingen Series
BTB	*Biblical Theological Bulletin*
Budé	Collection des Univeristés de France
BZ	*Biblische Zeitschrift*
CBQ	*Catholic Biblical Quarterly*
CGTC	Cambridge Greek Testament Commentary
ChrCent	*Christian Century*
CogPsy	*Cognitive Psychology*
ExpTim	*Expository Times*
FF	Foundations and Facets
FFFor	*Foundations and Facets Forum*
GBS	Guides for Biblical Scholarship
GR	*Greece and Rome*
HTKNT	Herders Theologischer Kommentar zum Neuen Testament
IDB	*The Interpreter's Dictionary of the Bible*, edited by George A. Buttrick, 4 vols. (Nashville: Abingdon, 1962)
Int	*Interpretation*
JAAR	*Journal of the American Academy of Religion*
JBL	*Journal of Biblical Literature*

JBR	*Journal of Bible and Religion*
JEdP	*Journal of Educational Psychology*
JEP	*Journal of Experimental Psychology*
JETS	*Journal for the Evangelical Theological Society*
JR	*Journal of Religion*
JSNT	*Journal for the Study of the New Testament*
JSOTSup	Journal for the Study of the Old Testament Supplement Series
JTS	*Journal of Theological Studies*
JVLVB	*Journal of Verbal Learning and Verbal Behavior*
LEC	Library of Early Christianity
MemCog	*Memory and Cognition*
NIBC	New International Biblical Commentary
NIDNTT	*New International Dictionary of New Testament Theology*, edited by Colin Brown, 4 vols. (Grand Rapids: Zondervan: 1975–78)
NLH	New Literary History
NovT	*Novum Testamentum*
NTS	*New Testament Studies*
NUSPEP	Northwestern University Studies in Phenomenology & Existential Philosophy
PGC	Pelican Gospel Commentaries
PMLAA	*Publications of the Modern Language Association of America*
Proof	*Prooftexts: A Journal of Jewish Literary History*
PRSt	*Perspectives in Religious Studies*
PsyRev	*Psychological Review*
PT	*Poetics Today*
RevExp	*Review and Expositor*
SBLDS	Society of Biblical Literature Dissertation Series
SBLSP	*Society of Biblical Literature Seminar Papers*
SNTSMS	Society for New Testament Studies Monograph Series
STL	*Studies in the Literary Imagination*
TBT	*The Bible Today*
TDNT	*Theological Dictionary of the New Testament*, edited by Gerhard Kittel and Gerhard Friedrich, translated by G. W. Bromiley, 10 vols. (Grand Rapids: Eerdmans, 1964–76)

Th	*Theology*
Them	*Themelios*
ZPEB	*The Zondervan Pictorial Encyclopedia of the Bible*, edited by M. C. Tenney (Grand Rapids: Zondervan, 1975)
ZTK	*Zeitschrift für Theologie und Kirche*

1

Introduction

Mark . . . wrote accurately, though not in order, all that he remembered of the things said or done by the Lord.

—Eusebius, *Ecclesiastical History*

THE DISORDERED NATURE OF the Gospel of Mark cannot be chron-
icled among the discoveries of modern literary inquiry. Indeed,
as Eusebius's quotation of Papias shows, awareness of disarrangement
in Mark's Gospel reaches back into history almost as far as the Gospel
itself.[1] Not surprisingly, therefore, the Gospel of Mark has presented a
challenge to modern scholarship, which holds the systematization of
data to be a *sine qua non* of critical research.

The apparently indiscriminate arrangement of Mark's narrative
material has given rise to numerous attempts to fit these materials into a
logically structured grid. Joanna Dewey recently remarked: "Of making

1. Papias's οὐ μέντοι τάξει has engendered a wide array of interpretations. One
proposal holds that the phrase refers not to the extant Gospel but to Mark's notes on
Peter's teachings (as, e.g., Kennedy, "Classical and Christian Source Criticism"). This
view, however, does not explain the disorder and compositional vulgarity that characterizes the Gospel itself. Most interpretations of Papias's enigmatic phrase fall in
two broad categories. The phrase describes either the Gospel's lack of chronological
order (as, e.g., Hengel, *Mark*, 48) or its departure from some recognized literary, artistic,
or thematic pattern (as, e.g., Colson, "τάξει in Papias"). Disorder in Mark's Gospel is
widely recognized but variously interpreted. According to Hengel, "the complaint about
inadequate 'order' does not in fact relate to the literary arrangement . . . but to the historical and chronological arrangement of the material" (Hengel, 48). Bultmann (*History
of the Synoptic Tradition*, 349) faults Mark on both counts: "The ordering of the material
is often determined on quite accidental grounds. . . . So it is a misconception to infer
from Mark's ordering of his material any conclusions about the chronology and development of the life of Jesus." For analysis of other understandings of τάξις, see Guthrie,
New Testament Introduction, 70; and Rigg, "Papias on Mark."

outlines of the Gospel of Mark there is no end, nor do scholars seem to be wearying of it. Yet we have been unable to agree on a structure or outline for Mark."[2] The variety and complexity of recent attempts to outline the Gospel of Mark is sufficient to illustrate the intricate nature of its structure.[3]

This plethora of suggested outlines for Mark's Gospel may be partially attributed to the disjunctures in the Gospel's chronological scheme and the lack of temporal references from which a tenable historical sequence can be discerned. D. E. Nineham assesses the Markan materials in typical form-critical fashion. According to Nineham, Mark

> consists of a number of unrelated paragraphs set down one after another with very little organic connexion.... These paragraphs are sometimes externally related to one another by a short phrase at the beginning or end, but essentially each one is an independent unit, complete in itself, undatable except by its contents, and usually devoid of any allusion to place.[4]

2. Dewey, "Mark as Interwoven Tapestry," 221. According to Dewey, the search for a single linear structure for Mark's Gospel is doomed to failure since "Mark does not have a single structure made up of discrete sequential units but rather is an interwoven tapestry or fugue made up of multiple overlapping structures and sequences, forecasts of what is to come and echoes of what has already been said" (224). Noting that this style is characteristic of aural narrative, Dewey writes: "Mark is telling a story for a listening audience, not presenting a logical argument. Arguments may be clouded by the lack of a clear outline, but stories gain depth and enrichment through repetition and recursion" (224). These observations are significant for the approach and conclusions of the present investigation.

3. See, e.g., Lohmeyer, *Evangelium des Markus*; Faw, "Outline of Mark"; Cranfield, *Mark*; Nineham, *Mark*; Taylor, *Mark*; Schweizer, *Mark*; Perrin, *New Testament*; Culpepper, "Outline of the Gospel"; Hedrick, "What Is a Gospel?"; Hurtado, *Mark*; Myers, *Binding the Strong Man*; Waetjen, *Reordering of Power*. The outlines of Taylor, Cranfield, and Hedrick take a geographical approach to the structure of Mark's Gospel; Schweizer, Faw, Perrin, Culpepper, Myers, and Waetjen follow a thematic scheme; and Lohmeyer balances themes and geography. Nineham and Hurtado appear to treat the Markan materials as a concatenation of autonomous pericopae. Even more ingenious are the suggestions of Carrington (*Primitive Christian Calendar*) and Farrer (*Mark*). Carrington holds that a synagogue lectionary formed the basis for Mark's arrangement; Farrer sees OT typology and numerical schemes behind the Markan arrangement. For a comparative analysis of the outlines proposed by Lohmeyer, Taylor, and Perrin, see Kee, *Community of the New Age*, 62–64.

4. Nineham, *Mark*, 27–28.

Responding to C. H. Dodd's argument that Mark relied on an outline of Jesus' activity preserved by the early church,[5] Nineham writes:

> It seems clear that by the time [Mark] wrote, it will no longer have been possible to recover the *historical* order of events, except in the most general terms. What is more, the earlier history of the material, as we have traced it, suggests a doubt—surprising perhaps to a modern reader—whether St Mark was *interested* in the historical order.[6]

The jumbled temporal arrangement of the Markan materials has led some scholars to conclude that Mark's Gospel "defies any definitive structural model."[7]

While Mark's structural awkwardness has long been recognized, programmed analyses of this attribute have appeared only recently. Two such works especially important for the present context are H. A. Guy's *The Origin of the Gospel of Mark* and John C. Meagher's *Clumsy Construction in Mark's Gospel*.

Guy and Meagher give impetus to the present investigation since both tend to view the Gospel as story and embrace a rather low assessment of Mark's literary quality. Guy identifies various types of disorder in Mark, such as interruptions, repetitions, haphazard arrangement, and lack of topical or logical connection between successive statements. Meagher describes Mark's literary character as "very ordinary, homely, untrained prose, full of the same stylistic sloppiness and clumsy mismanagement of basic storytelling techniques that one expects to find in unsophisticated writing. . . ."[8]

Meagher extends his charge of negligent mishandling of the Gospel materials beyond the Gospel writer to the antecedent stages of the text's production, namely, the oral transmission of the materials and the redaction that the materials underwent prior to being arranged in their final

---

5. Dodd, "Framework of the Gospel Narrative."

6. Nineham, *Mark*, 28–29 (emphasis original). Cf. Bultmann, *History of the Synoptic Tradition*, 338: ". . . analysis shows that Mark has nowhere used a source which itself had already portrayed a thoroughly coherent life of Jesus which could have been described as a Gospel."

7. E.g., Dewey, "Mark as Interwoven Tapestry," 224; Myers, *Binding the Strong Man*, 109.

8. Meagher, *Clumsy Construction*, 57.

form.[9] Denying the possibility of producing a precise history of forms and affirming the likelihood of inappropriate or mistaken contributions by redactors, he finds the assumptions and conclusions of both form and redaction criticism unacceptable.

Meagher succeeds in providing a model for understanding the transmission of oral materials and in demonstrating the weaknesses of form- and redaction-critical approaches.[10] Nevertheless, he despairs of finding a more serviceable methodology. Thus, his work provides special motivation for this study; his negative assessment of past hermeneutical approaches and failure to offer a solution in their place issue a challenge to find legitimate procedures for reading Mark's Gospel.

JUSTIFICATION FOR THE STUDY

Jerry Camery-Hoggatt well illustrates a major weakness of methodologies that focus on extra-textual issues. He recounts a conversation with his preschool daughter in which she related her version of the story of "Little Red Riding Hood"—a version in which she added the qualifying words "biscuits and wine" to the "basket of goodies" in the original story. He describes his reactions:

> Now mention of biscuits and wine caught my ear. . . . Suddenly I found my interest shifting. Rather than listening to the story, I was listening for other clues about the version she had taken over. Had she heard it at school? Was its diction British? In a sense, I was listening *through* the story, rather than to it. . . . By focusing

9. This is seen in the title and contents of Meagher's earlier article, "Die Form- und Redaktions*ungeschickliche* Methoden (emphasis added to title). Meagher plays on the word *geschichtliche* ("historical") by substituting the term *ungeschickliche* ("awkward" or "unskillful").

10. The model Meagher offers is oral humor. He describes pitfalls in the telling of a joke, thus: "When their tellers try to reconstruct them from their experienced but imperfect memories, and even when they attempt to insert creative improvements, they often forget or distort crucial information, import irrelevant motifs or formulas from the general tradition, bungle important lines of development and make careless substitutions for particular elements of the original version" (*Clumsy Construction*, 5). Meagher's model well illustrates several destructive processes involved in the transmission of *a* type of oral tradition. However, his assumption that the Gospel materials (stories told for moral and spiritual orientation) and jokes (stories told for amusement) were handled in the same fashion is highly suspect. Moreover, many of his observations about stylistic awkwardness betray an ignorance of the function of ancient narrative devices and an unwillingness to take the Gospel on its own terms (see, e.g., Williams, *Gospel against Parable*, 223–24).

on the matter of sources, I had permitted myself to lose track of the story itself.[11]

"Los[ing] track of the story itself" is precisely what the discipline of narrative criticism seeks to avoid.[12]

Historical questions related to a given text (e.g., sources, original audience, and setting) have their proper place. At issue, however, is the status of that place.[13] Using history to elucidate the biblical text is always legitimate.[14] But the same cannot be said of the converse, for supplying answers to historical inquiry is not the primary concern of the biblical

---

11. Camery-Hoggatt, *Speaking of God*, 48 (emphasis original).

12. Barton, "Mark as Narrative," 231: "If we attend only to the *archaeology* of the text, devoting all our time to reconstructing the layers of tradition which lie concealed beneath it, we may miss what is most obvious: namely, the text as it stands" (emphasis his).

13. Determining whether and why Matthew or Luke borrowed from, added to, altered, or omitted some pericope or saying in Mark or Q, or why Mark operated in like fashion on Matthew and Luke, has occupied the attention of scholars from the time of the quill pen to that of the notebook computer (see, e.g., the fine historical survey of scholarship on the Synoptic problem by Reicke, "History of the Synoptic Discussion"). At the 1984 Jerusalem Symposium on the Interrelations of the Gospels, three primary solutions to the Synoptic problem were posited: the two-source hypothesis, the two-Gospel hypothesis, and the multiple-stage hypothesis. These were championed by F. Neirynck, W. R. Farmer, and M.-É. Boismard, respectively. B. F. Meyer, in "Objectivity and Subjectivity in Historical Criticism," characterized the tenor of this conference, *vis-à-vis* "criteria for historicity judgments on Gospel traditions," as one of "confusion and disagreement" (546). "New Testament scholars," he observes, "draw on ostensibly common methods and are bewildered by the chaos of conflicting results" (Meyer, "Afterword," 565). Noting Morna D. Hooker's recognition of subjectivity in matters of historical inquiry (in her "Christology and Methodology" and "On Using the Wrong Tool"), Meyer argues for an epistemological shift ("critical realism") that recognizes the necessity and value of subjectivity ("Afterword," 565). Eta Linnemann no longer is kindly disposed to the subjectivity in the assumptions and results of the historical-critical method. She recently launched a scathing critique of historical criticism in general (*Historical Criticism of the Bible*) and its application to Synoptic studies in particular (*Is There a Synoptic Problem?*), referring to the historical-critical method as a "pseudo-science" (*Synoptic Problem*, 210). Narrative-critical approaches offer a way around the issue of sources.

14. See, e.g., Beavis, *Mark's Audience*. Beavis reacts against ahistorical approaches that bracket the ancient reader and the ancient reading process and that regard "'the text itself' as the self-contained locus of meaning" (13). "Mark," she writes, "is not just a literary text, but a *hellenistic* literary text, and as such, it must be understood against the background of Graeco-Roman (and hellenistic Jewish) reading through the study of education and literary culture in the first century, and in terms of some *model* of the *use* of the Gospel in the Marcan Community" (10; emphasis original).

writers.[15] Referring to the Jesus-sayings material, Robert C. Tannehill rightly cautions:

> When the scholar uses these texts as sources of information about historical events, persons, or views which lie behind them, he is forcing concerns which are subordinate in the text into a dominant position.[16]

The results of such approaches have lead Meagher to a conclusion that represents one way of dealing with the disordered nature of the Markan materials: attribute it to the ineptitude of the writer. Meagher is neither the only nor the first scholar to take such a despondent stance.[17] Nevertheless, in the current trend of viewing the Gospels as intentional narrative constructions, Mark increasingly is being regarded as a writer of considerable literary acumen.[18] This study seeks to demonstrate that

15. Using the text to uncover historical circumstances surrounding author, text, and audience is, however, a common approach. Scholars frequently affirm the text's connections with history on the basis of the author's purpose, which they typically identify by isolating redactional elements from source material. See, e.g., Achtemeier, "'He Taught Them Many Things.'" Achtemeier's concern is to identify "something of the religious dimensions of the community from which and for which Mark wrote" (465). He faults Kee (*Community of the New Age*) for "assum[ing] that we can derive valid insights into the nature of the Marcan community from all of the material in Mark, without careful differentiation of the apparent intention of that material in the Gospel itself" (467 n. 4).

16. Tannehill, *Sword of His Mouth*, 7.

17. Dehn (*Der Gottessohn*, 18) declared that Mark was "neither an historian nor an author. He assembled his material in the simplest manner thinkable"; Bultmann (*History of the Synoptic Tradition*, 350) wrote: "Mark is not sufficiently master of his material to venture on a systematic construction himself"; Trocmé (*Formation of the Gospel*, 72) charged that Mark was a "clumsy writer unworthy of mention in any history of literature." But see Alter's "How Convention Helps Us Read." Alter issues a general offensive against "much of biblical scholarship" for "concluding . . . that the ancient text is redundant, defective, incoherent, or 'primitive,' out of a failure to recognize the distinctive literary conventions that have shaped it" (116). Recent emphasis on oral composition and hermeneutics also offers a more positive understanding of Mark's apparently haphazard arrangement. Joanna Dewey ("Oral Methods"), e.g., holds that Mark's Gospel was composed for a listening audience. Applying the conclusions of Havelock (*Preface to Plato* and "Oral Composition"), Dewey argues convincingly that Mark's structure is wholly in accordance with the oral compositional techniques of his time: it consists of visible happenings not abstract thought; its order is paratactic, not logical (cause and effect) or chronological; and it features numerous retrospections and prospections that suggest connections between episodes and facilitate memorization (Dewey, "Oral Methods," 35–42).

18. "The broad result of recent literary-critical studies has been to strengthen the view that Mark is a generally well-constructed narrative with evident and successfully-

attributing the narrative "disorder" to an intentional literary scheme offers a more fruitful way of dealing with the Markan materials.

Narrative-critical approaches that propose to look *at* the text for the ways it addresses its readers rather than *through* the text for primarily historical data represent a relatively recent phase in NT scholarship, a phase that has generated fresh, holistic views of the biblical narratives. Nevertheless, both the techniques by which the biblical narratives have been analyzed as well as the extra-biblical materials with which these biblical narratives have been compared have been drawn largely from the modern period.[19] The legitimacy of such an approach is rightly being questioned.[20]

In his 1989 survey of Markan scholarship, Larry Hurtado concludes: "there is increased emphasis that Mark should be analyzed in light of Jewish and pagan literary traditions of the Greco-Roman era."[21] Steven

---

executed authorial purposes and emphases" (Hurtado, "Gospel of Mark, 48). One of the earliest scholars to hail Mark's literary achievement was Enslin ("Artistry of Mark"). Petersen ("'Point of View,'" 97) describes the Gospel of Mark as "a carefully and integrally composed narrative." Best (*Mark*, 130) and Boomershine ("Mark the Storyteller") characterize Mark as a good storyteller. Grounding his argument on the presence of catchwords, Von Wahlde ("Mark 9:33–50," 50) speaks of the "skill and art" of Mark's arrangement of 9:33–50. Fowler ("Using Literary Criticism on the Gospels," 629), discussing the feeding episodes in Mark's Gospel, writes: "When the second feeding incident begins to unfold, it is narrative artistry and not careless editing that makes the disciples say, 'How can one feed these men with bread here in the desert?'" See also Fowler's *Loaves and Fishes* and *Let the Reader Understand*.

19. A few notable exceptions are Pritchard, *Literary Approach*; GBilezikian, *Liberated Gospel*; Lang, "Kompositionsanalyse"; and Standaert, *L'évangile selon Marc*.

20. According to Kelber ("Gospel Narrative and Critical Theory," 132) the "application of modern Western aesthetics to the Gospels has been persuasive in turning the ancient Gospel narrators into our literary contemporaries, creating the illusion of identity. It marks a hermeneutical achievement in its own right. But it also suggests a reading through the distorting lens of a cultural bias." Alter ("How Convention Helps Us Read," 116) agrees that the use of modern literary techniques as a grid for analyzing ancient texts is vulnerable to the criticism of producing "no more than a particularly modern form of midrash, a willful and imaginative wrenching of the text from its own historical context into that of the interpreter." Nevertheless, he offers two strands of countervailing data: "elements of continuity or at least close analogy in the literary modes of disparate ages" and "the self-conscious sense of historical perspective which is part of our modern intellectual equipment."

21. Hurtado, "Mark in Recent Study," 50. Beavis does precisely this in "Trial before the Sanhedrin," "Women as Models," and *Mark's Audience*. Other works that attend to the Greco-Roman literary environment are Burch, "Tragic Action"; Kennedy, *New Testament Interpretation*; Aune, *New Testament*. Papers presented at the 1992 and 1993

Sheeley stresses this same caveat in his treatment of the Gospel narrators. Commenting on the future of narrative-critical research, Sheeley admonishes:

> The character of narrative criticism as a recent development must be balanced by a renewed interest in the popular literature of the ancient world. Ancient romances, histories, and biographies provide one with a social and literary milieu for the gospels. One's analysis of the gospel narrators must be challenged and controlled by one's experience of other ancient narrators and their techniques.[22]

The hypothesis proposed by Mary Ann Tolbert is a prime example of a counter approach. Tolbert argues that the Gospel of Mark is best understood from the perspective of its affinities to the ancient romance

---

annual meetings of the Society of Biblical Literature testify to the recent interest in the Greek romances. Houck ("Why New Testament Scholars," 4) sees the romances as a "virtually unparalleled, if little used, source for a wide range of social and intellectual institutions in the Greco-Roman world during the New Testament Period."

22. Sheeley, "Narrator in the Gospels," 223. One important difference between modern and ancient narrative theories has to do with where each falls on a cognitive-affective continuum. Modern analysts view narratives as having primarily a cognitive function, while ancient theorists regarded them as primarily emotive (see, e.g., Tompkins, "Reader in History"). The distinction between cognitive and emotive cannot be sharply drawn. More and more modern narratologists are focusing on the emotive nature of the Gospels. Tannehill (*Sword of His Mouth*, 6) rejects the notion that the primary purpose of the Gospel texts is to convey information. Von Wahlde ("Discipleship," 67) argues that Mark's purpose is not primarily *informational*, but *formational*. But *transformational* is the most appropriate description, since it recognizes that the reader has an established form before encountering the text. Wuellner ("Where Is Rhetorical Criticism Taking Us?" 460–61) credits rhetorical criticism with moving "from a traditional message- or content-oriented reading of Scripture to a reading that strengthens ever-deepening personal, social, and cultural values." "Rhetorical criticism," he argues, "makes us more fully aware of the *whole* range of appeals embraced and provoked by rhetoric: not only the rational and cognitive dimensions, but also the emotive and imaginative ones." Moore ("Narrative Commentaries") criticizes one approach that focuses on the cerebral aspect of the reading experience: "But if it is a wholly cognitive role of reading which has been charted, can [one] be said to have adequately connected with this ancient author's intent?" (49). For an approach that accounts for both cognitive and emotive elements see, e.g., Boomershine, "Mark 16:8." Boomershine concludes: "The impact of the ending, therefore, is to appeal for repentance from silence in response to the commission to announce Jesus' messiahship after his resurrection. The effect of the ending could be called a purging of the fear [emotive] associated with the apostolic commission. Thus, the ending is a climactic reversal of expectations [cognitive] in the central Marcan motif of the messianic secret" (238).

novels of Hellenistic popular literature.[23] Several scholars have analyzed the narrative techniques evidenced in many of these works,[24] but none of them has compared these devices with the corresponding narrative devices found in Mark's Gospel.

PROPOSAL

Since Tolbert and others have rightly judged the reader's understanding of a work's genre to be one of the most important guides to its interpretation,[25] this study tests Tolbert's association of Mark's Gospel with the ancient romance novels of Hellenistic popular literature by comparing Mark with Chariton's *Chaereas and Callirhoe*,[26] using the temporal aspect of narrative sequence as the primary standard of comparison.

The remainder of this chapter treats methodological matters and includes brief examples drawn from the narratives of Mark and Chariton. Chapter 2 outlines the reading theory used in the analysis of the Gospel of Mark (ch. 3) and *Chaereas and Callirhoe* (ch. 4). The final chapter compares and contrasts Mark and Chariton in terms of how each handles narrative sequence and considers the implications for reading Mark's Gospel as Hellenistic popular literature.

METHODOLOGY

The procedure for the present investigation falls under the general rubric of literary criticism. The selection of this methodology arises from the conviction that the Gospels may legitimately be read not only as compilations of loosely related tradition complexes, that is, as "windows" through which one can see the first century world, but also as particular stories, that is, as "mirrors" that reflect a specific religio-philosophical

23. Tolbert, *Sowing the Gospel*, 55–79.

24. B. Perry, *Ancient Romances*; Heiserman, *Novel before the Novel*; Hägg, *Novel in Antiquity*; Holzberg, *Antike Roman*.

25. Tolbert, *Sowing the Gospel*, 48. Tolbert regards genre as "the single most important guide." See also Kent, "Classification of Genres," 1–2; S. Mailloux, *Interpretive Conventions*, 126–39; and Hirsch, *Validity in Interpretation*.

26. Chariton's novel was selected since most scholars believe it to be the earliest (100 BCE–50 CE) of the extant ancient novels. Two ancient novels that share similar themes are Achilles Tatius's *Leucippe and Clitophon* (150–200 CE) and Xenophon's *An Ephesian Tale of Anthia and Habrocomes* (50–150 CE).

worldview and challenge their readers to evaluate themselves in light of it.[27] More narrowly, this study may be placed under the headings of narrative criticism and reader-response criticism, since its objects of study (Mark's Gospel and Chariton's *Chaereas and Callirhoe*) are properly narrative material and since it emphasizes the dynamics of the text in precipitating the reader's response.[28]

Credit goes to Hans Frei for substantiating biblical scholarship's failure to take seriously the narrative form and function of the Gospels.[29] Where meaning is held to derive from "ideational, historical and existential referentiality," readers are likely "to focus less on the narratives themselves, and more on what they [are] assumed to be referring to."[30] In reaction to this, some biblical interpreters adopt a literary approach that focuses exclusively on the internal structure of biblical narratives.[31] Kelber notes deficiencies in both models:

> While the referential model focused our attention upon realities behind or beyond the narrative, the formalist model drew our interests to the narrative *per se*, divorced from author and readers, objectified in print and secured in neutral space. Neither paradigm encouraged attention to our activity as readers. . . . Both paradigms took the reader for granted as objective scholar analyzing an autonomous text.[32]

27. Krieger applied the metaphor of the window and mirror to written texts in *Window to Criticism*, 3.

28. The label "reader-response" is applied to a variety of contrasting and conflicting approaches that share a common interest in the role of the reader. Suleiman and Crosman (*Reader in the Text*) suggest six major divisions: rhetorical, semiotic and structuralist, phenomenological, psychoanalytic and subjective, sociological and historical, and hermeneutic. For other discussions that treat these distinctions, see, e.g., the essays in Tompkins, ed., *Reader-Response Criticism*; Mailloux, "Reader-Response Criticism?"; idem, "Learning to Read; idem, *Interpretive Conventions*; Fowler, "Who Is 'the Reader'?"; idem, *Let the Reader Understand*, esp. 7–59. Fowler notes three elements common to most reader-response approaches: (1) they focus on the reader and the experience of reading; (2) they view reading as a concrete, temporal experience rather than abstract perception; and (3) they understand meaning as event rather than content.

29. Frei, *Eclipse of Biblical Narrative*. For a summary analysis of Frei's contribution, see Placher, "Hans Frei."

30. Kelber, "Critical Theory," 131.

31. See Poland, *Literary Criticism*.

32. Kelber, "Critical Theory," 132.

Reader-response criticism offers a rhetorical model that possesses the strengths of the referential and formalist models while avoiding some of their pitfalls.[33]

The means by which a text conducts its readers have been the subject of considerable scholarly examination.[34] Since these textual devices are too numerous to afford comprehensive treatment here, the present research is restricted to the domain of narrative time and, more specifically, the temporal ordering of narrative events.

Recent years have witnessed increased scholarly interest in narrative time. In his most comprehensive and frequently cited work, *Narrative Discourse: An Essay in Method*, Gérard Genette draws the distinction between the time of the story and what he calls the "pseudo-time" of the narrative.[35] He argues that this distinction can be observed in the order, duration, and frequency of events.[36] Tomas Hägg applies to the ancient Greek romance novels several aspects of narrative time that also can be placed under these headings.[37] Tzvetan Todorov's classic *Introduction to Poetics* includes a chapter that considers the aspects of time and order.[38] Meir Sternberg contributes a rather technical treatise on a variety of aspects related to narrative time,[39] and Paul Ricoeur speaks of a narrative's "refiguring" of time.[40]

The element of narrative time has also kindled the interest of biblical scholars. Robert Funk devotes an entire chapter to narrative order and shows how temporal elements in biblical texts can be used to determine narrative units.[41] David Rhoads, both in his article "Narrative Criticism and the Gospel of Mark" and in his joint venture with Donald Michie, *Mark as Story*, gives attention to the order in which events are

33. For a balanced critique of literary approaches in general, see Longman, "Literary Approach". See also Wuellner, "Rhetorical Criticism."

34. See, e.g., Chatman, *Story and Discourse*; Funk, *Poetics of Biblical Narrative*; Rimmon-Kenan, *Narrative Fiction*; Sternberg, *Poetics of Biblical Narrative*.

35. Genette, *Narrative Discourse*.

36. The first of these three categories will be used as the organizing matrix for the present investigation.

37. Hägg, *Narrative Technique*.

38. Todorov, *Introduction to Poetics*, 13–59.

39. Sternberg, *Expositional Modes*.

40. Ricoeur, *Time and Narrative*. Ricoeur uses the notion of narrative time to show that "history" and "fiction" are in some sense good neighbors (see esp. 3:180–92).

41. Funk, *Poetics of Biblical Narrative*, 187–207.

presented in the Gospel of Mark.[42] R. Alan Culpepper, drawing upon the work of Sternberg and Genette, applies the categories of order, duration, and frequency to the Gospel of John.[43] And Norman Petersen, in his *Literary Criticism for New Testament Critics*, includes a chapter entitled "Story Time and Plotted Time in Mark's Narrative."[44]

The distinction between "story time" and "discourse time" provides a serviceable means of assessing how a text influences its readers. In view of our focus on narrative sequence, Genette's discussions on "order" are an appropriate starting point. By "order," Genette calls attention to the fact that the chronological order in which events occur ("story time") often does not coincide with the order in which they are imparted to the reader ("discourse time" or "narrative time"). He labels these discordances "anachronies." Narrating an event that took place earlier Genette calls "analepsis," while narrating an event that will take place later he labels "prolepsis." Genette further refines these categories by labeling those analepses and prolepses that refer to events occurring entirely before or after the time of the narrative as "external," those that refer to events entirely within the narrative as "internal," and those partially in both domains as "mixed." Multiple analepses and prolepses that refer to the same event are differentiated as "repeating" (conveying the same information) and "completing" (referring to the same events but filling in gaps found in the previous narration by providing new information).[45] The goal of this type of analysis is to identify all of the anachronies in the story and assess their effect on the reader/hearer.

The Gospel of Mark is replete with prolepses. The cluster of repeating/completing prolepses centered on the passion-resurrection motif, though not treated extensively in the present study, serve as examples. The first clear instance is in Mark 8:31. The key elements of this prolepsis ("suffer," "rejected by the elders, chief priests, and teachers of the law," "killed," "three days," and "rise again") are found several other places in the narrative. Mark 9:33–34, for instance, is a completing prolepsis that, in addition to reiterating several elements from 8:31 (chief priests, teachers of the law, death, three days, rise again), provides more detail regarding the suffering (mocking, spitting, flogging) and adds the ele-

---

42. Rhoads, "Narrative Criticism; Rhoads and Michie, *Mark as Story*, 42–43.

43. Culpepper, *Anatomy of the Fourth Gospel*, 51–75.

44. Petersen, *Literary Criticism*, 49–80.

45. Genette, *Narrative Discourse*, 33–85.

ment of betrayal. Other prolepses mention only part of this complex, some literally (14:8, death; 9:9, 14:28, rising from the dead), and others metaphorically (2:20, bridegroom will be absent; 9:39, "cup" and "baptism" of Jesus; 12:1–12, parable of the tenants).

Mark's Gospel also gives ample evidence of analepsis. The beheading of John the Baptist in 6:17–28 is a clear example, since Herod (6:16) and the narrator (6:17–19) relate an event that took place earlier (story time) than this point in the narrative.[46]

Chariton utilizes these same narrative techniques. In *Chaereas and Callirhoe*, however, prolepses serve primarily as general headings for the following scene or series of scenes. For example, after describing a costly funeral, Chariton writes: "That which seemed to have been done to honor the dead girl set in motion the beginning of greater events" (1.6.5). This type of prolepsis functions to thrust the reader forward but provides few plot details in advance. The introductory section of book 5 is one example of the more numerous and extensive analepses that provide a synopsis of the major events transpiring to that point in the narrative.[47]

NARRATIVE SEQUENCE AND IDEOLOGY

Time is the arena in which both story (the thing told) and discourse (the telling) play themselves out. Nevertheless, the temporal dynamics operative in each of these domains do not produce the same effects. Since events in the story world are subject to the constraints inherent in chronological time, they have a natural and predetermined order imposed on them. But the narrative world offers the possibility of presenting the events of a story in a sequence motivated by rhetorical intention (*invention*) rather than chronology. Shimon Bar-Efrat writes:

> The shaping of time within the narrative is functional and not random or arbitrary, making a genuine contribution, in coordination and cooperation with the other elements, to the character, meaning and values of the entire narrative.[48]

Menakhem Perry argues convincingly that the sequential arrangement of events in a narrative plays an important role in the production

---

46. Petersen, *Literary Criticism*, 59.

47. Also 1.14, 2.5, 4.3, 4.4, 5.5, 6.1, 8.7, and 8.8.

48. Bar-Efrat, *Narrative Art in the Bible*, 142.

of its meanings. Since the events of a story can appear in a variety of sequences, and since each sequence has a unique effect on the meaning apprehended, any given sequence of events is able to "induce the reader to opt for the realization of certain potentialities (e.g., impressions, attitudes) of the material rather than others . . ."[49]

Robert Bergen also addresses narrative order. He argues that the order in which information is presented to the reader is a discourse-grammatical feature that can help determine authorial intention.[50] According to Bergen, the sequential arrangement of story events is one of the hints that the author drops to "help the audience figure out which portions he considers to be more significant."[51]

Norman Petersen carefully analyzes the sequential arrangement of narrative events in Mark's Gospel[52] and later suggests that narrative order is used to transport the narrator's ideology:[53]

> It is . . . only in the plotting of the episodes and the motivations imputed to the actions of characters that the full extent of Mark's ideological point of view can be seen. For in the plotting of incidents we can detect the formal manner in which the narrator successively discloses information to his reader, and sequentially

---

49. M. Perry, "Literary Dynamics," 40. Perry affirms: "Literary texts may effectively utilize the fact that their material is grasped successively; this is at times a central factor in determining their meanings" (35). This is no less true when the sequence of presentation happens to follow the chronological order according to which the events transpire in the story world. Perry expresses it thus: "It is erroneous to consider that only the 'distortion' of a 'natural' order can have rhetorical effects" (42).

50. Bergen, "Text as a Guide."

51. Ibid., 331.

52. Petersen, "Story Time."

53. Petersen, "'Point of View,'" 108. Novak ("Narrative and Ideology" 73) offers a helpful definition of ideology that is appropriate for the present context: "*Ideology is a guiding vision of future social action*" (emphasis original). He distinguishes between the subjective and objective aspects of ideology. The former refers to the "vision, horizon, and intentions of the person who holds it." The latter refers to the "active forces in the social world around that person that provide the arena of human action." "Ideology" is used here in the broad sense of "worldview" (as, e.g., Uspensky, *Poetics of Composition*, 8), and yet more specifically, as the organizing principle of life (Novak's subjective element), but not in its restrictive political sense (Novak's objective element; see also Myers's, *Binding the Strong Man*, where the phrase "All Narrative Is Political" is part of the title of one subsection [1.D.iii., 26]). Culpepper (*Anatomy of the Fourth Gospel*, 32) describes the function of the Johannine narrator as "facilitat[ing] communication of the implied author's ideological or evaluative system to the reader."

relates items of information to one another, creating thereby a
world of values as well as of events.[54]

The work of Bar-Efrat, Perry, Bergen, Petersen, and others suggests
the following analogy: just as a conductor's baton is the means by which
musicians are given the cues necessary to sound out a musical score,
so the narrative text is the means by which readers are given the cues
necessary to sound out the author's ideological score.[55]

The author's ability to steer, persuade, and even seduce the reader
is explained in part by two correlative axioms: the fact that the text re-
leases its information sequentially, and the fact that the reader does not
wait until the end to start making sense of the data.[56] Indeed, from the
opening sentence, the reader attempts to organize the fragments of narrative material into a grid that creates maximum coherence in the data
encountered to that point.[57]

Perry proposes that the meanings conveyed by a narrative are not
limited to the "conclusions reached by the reader at the end-point of the
text continuum." Instead, he argues that

> the effects of the entire reading process all contribute to the
> meaning of the work: its surprises; the changes along the way;
> the process of a gradual, zig-zag-like build-up of meanings,
> their reinforcement, development, revision and replacement; the
> relations between expectations aroused at one stage of the text
> and discoveries actually made in subsequent stages; the process

54. Petersen, "'Point of View,'" 108.

55. The fact that narratives convey ideologies is widely recognized. See, e.g.,
Uspensky, *Poetics of Composition*, 137: "In a work of art, . . . there is presented to us
a special world, with its own space and time, its own ideological system, and its own
standards of behavior"; Keegan, *Interpreting the Bible*, 97: "Becoming an implied reader
involves . . . becoming a slave of the ideology involved in the text"; Kingsbury, *Matthew
as Story*, 2: "When one reads the Matthean narrative, one . . . enters into another world
. . . which possesses its own . . . system of values"; Tannehill, *Narrative Unity*, 8: "The
message of Luke-Acts is . . . the complex reshaping of human life, in its many dimensions, which it can cause." See also Sternberg, "Ideology of Narration"; Booth, *Rhetoric
of Fiction*, i; and Rhoads and Michie, *Mark as Story*, 43–44.

56. M. Perry, "Literary Dynamics." Bar-Efrat (*Narrative Art*, 141) affirms an author's
ability to "exploit the reader's temporary ignorance in order to heighten interest and
tension."

57. Perry, "Literary Dynamics," 45. Perry notes three principles according to which
the reader constructs these grids: (1) preference for frames that link the highest number
of disparate items; (2) preference for the frame connecting the items most closely; and
(3) preference for the "simpler, more conventional, typical" frame.

of retrospective re-patterning and even the peculiar survival of meanings which were first constructed and then rejected.[58]

Best comments on the significance of Mark's arrangement:

> Thus, by drawing the incidents together and adapting them into a larger unity Mark has given to each incident a new flavour, he has produced new meaning from it, a meaning to suit his purpose.[59]

CONCLUSION

Using narrative texts as windows to supply answers to historical questions assigns them a function uncorroborated by their contents. A mirror is a more appropriate metaphor since narratives reflect a specific image of the world and invite readers to evaluate themselves in light of that world. The Gospel of Mark and *Chaereas and Callirhoe* are rhetorical documents; they are designed to evoke some response from the reader. In literary terms, they solicit their readers to adopt the narrator's ideological viewpoint.[60]

Scholars such as Bar-Efrat, Bergen, Perry, and Petersen argue convincingly that the narrator's ideology can be detected in, and is in part responsible for, the sequencing of narrative events. The connection between ideology and narrative sequence is apparent in but not limited to departures from a chronological presentation.

---

58. Ibid., 41.

59. Best, *Mark*, 128.

60. In order to give these narratives a legitimate hearing, one must give attention to the fact that in the ancient world "the chief function of language [was] pragmatic or rhetorical and intended to persuade or somehow affect the hearer" (Fowler, *Let the Reader Understand*, 23). Mack and Robbins (*Patterns of Persuasion*) interpret Synoptic pronouncement stories as ancient Hellenistic *chreia*. Robbins writes: "Primarily, the author pursues his own rhetorical goals. His degree of submission to an oral or written version available to him depends on many factors, including his own personal inclinations. He develops or alters the rhetorical dynamics of the story and imposes his own style and length on the unit as these dimensions further his rhetorical goals. . . . [H]e will not hesitate to compose it according to his own style and rhetorical interests" (19). Derrett (*Making of Mark*, 1:2) criticizes previous scholarship on Mark's Gospel: "The leaven of optimism and the warmth of imagination have worked for nearly two centuries on the dough of ignorance; and we have an inflated mass of conjectures which is indigestible and unpalatable." The "new start" he proposes explains the rhetorical strategy behind the selection and arrangement of the Markan materials as an effort to "tell the story of Jesus as parallel to, and step by step analogous with, the story of Moses and Joshua" (1:24).

Careful examination of the texts of Mark and Chariton identifies many instances of narrative anachrony, each of which exerts a particular influence on the reader. The primary objective of the present investigation is to ascertain the nature of that influence. This task requires an awareness of the salient characteristics of language and an understanding of how the brain processes linguistic units.

Although this study focuses on the literary features of the selected narratives and on how readers process narrative data, the historical perspective is not ignored altogether. The present methodology is thus distinguished from those narrative-critical approaches that cling unreservedly to the naïve notion of the autonomy of the text and therefore bracket all components having to do with extra-textual referentiality (e.g., real author, real reader, authorial intention, and so forth).[61]

Thus, while the present approach intentionally avoids using either Mark's or Chariton's text to answer historical questions, it occasionally appeals to the historical context of author and audience in order to interpret the function of their narrative materials. As the discussion in chapter 2 shows, some awareness of the real reader's social context is critical for understanding what effects the sequential arrangement of narrative events has on the implied reader.[62] Therefore, we shall make reference to the sociocultural repertoire shared by the real author and

61. Myers (*Binding the Strong Man*, 24) faults literary criticism for divorcing itself from historical questions: "Anxious to overcome historicism, [the literary critical approach] has in many cases tried to liberate the text from all historical referentiality whatsoever." He agrees that "historical criticism betrays the narrative integrity of the text," but contends that "literary criticism betrays its historical integrity" (25). His methodology combines both approaches in order to allow each discipline to provide crucial correctives for the other.

62. Wilder (*Bible and the Literary Critic*, 29–30) cautions: "If narrative is ultimately 'intentional' and 'suasive,' this undercuts any strict view of the autonomy of the text.... That 'no narrative can be transparent on historical fact' does not mean that all links with our human experience, all resonances, are excluded. The very act of reading involves a correlation of text and life and therefore some prior referentiality of the text. The issues here become specially acute with the recent critical school, which deepens the gulf in question by urging the sedimentation of all our inherited frames of perception and interpretation, and beyond that by its radical epistemological skepticism." Robbins (*Jesus the Teacher*, 1) faults source, form, and redaction criticism for "fail[ing] to keep in touch with basic social and cultural phenomena in the Mediterranean world that created the environment in which Christianity lived and moved and had its being." For other studies of Mark's Gospel that give attention to its Greco-Roman context see, e.g., Standaert, *L'Evangile selon Marc*; Beavis, *Mark's Audience*. On the social world of the Gospels, see Theissen, *Gospels in Context*.

his first century audience whenever this sheds light on the rhetorical strategies displayed in the text.

How a text influences its readers is a complex operation. Literary critics have proposed a number of theories to explain the various mechanisms involved. In the following chapter we examine five salient characteristics of language and the role they play in the processing of narrative texts. In doing so, we arrive at a model that informs our treatment of the anachronies found in Mark's Gospel and Chariton's *Chaereas and Callirhoe.*

2

A Model for Reading

Interpretive Conventions

As a literary text can only produce a response when it is read, it is virtually impossible to describe this response without also analyzing the reading process.

—W. Iser, *The Act of Reading*

INTRODUCTION

THE TERM "READING" REFERS primarily to the process of apprehending written language. Disciplines that deal with the literary analysis of texts, however, frequently employ the term in a technical sense to describe a particular way of understanding a given text. The titles or subtitles of many books confirm this assertion. A few examples from the field of biblical studies are Fernando Belo's *A Materialist Reading of the Gospel of Mark*, Ched Myers's *Binding the Strong Man: A Political Reading of Mark's Story of Jesus*, Bruce Vawter's *On Genesis: A New Reading*, and John Wilcox's *The Bitterness of Job: A Philosophical Reading*.[1] Each of these works illustrates a way of reading that approaches the text in question with an admitted bias.

An interpreter's analytical agenda is a direct function of the controlling factors ("predispositions") that bring her or him to the task. These predispositions include both the interpreter's purposes in undertaking the investigation and the results that he or she hopes to find. Biblical scholars, for example, approach their materials from a variety of methodological perspectives (e.g., form criticism, source criticism, redaction

---

1. Belo, *Materialist Reading*; Myers, *Binding the Strong Man*; Vawter, *Genesis*; Wilcox, *Bitterness of Job*.

criticism, text criticism, literary criticism, structuralism) and presuppositional slants (e.g., demythologization, new hermeneutic, sociology of knowledge). And this accounts for only part of the multiplicity. Indeed, the situation is far more complex, for within this variety of methodologies lies an equally important diversity of theological and ideological perspectives (e.g., fundamentalism, liberalism, dispensationalism, feminism, liberationism, materialism) from which these methodologies are executed.

Denying the contribution that any of these programs makes to a proper understanding of the biblical materials would be foolish. Nevertheless, a common vantage point is needed from which to adjudicate between the conflicting conclusions that inevitably arise when differing methodologies are applied to the same data. One solution may be found in an element long taken for granted but only recently subjected to critical scrutiny: the reading process itself.

In his defense of a reader-oriented perspective on literary theory, Wolfgang Iser tenders the following criticism of approaches that ignore the reading process:

> So long as the focal point of interest was the author's intention, or the contemporary, psychological, social, or historical meaning of the text, or the way in which it was constructed, it scarcely seemed to occur to critics that the text could only have a meaning when it was read.[2]

For Iser, meaning derives from the process of actualization. He urges that the interpreter pay more attention to the process than to the product.[3] Therefore, as a vantage point for this variety of hermeneutical methodologies the present study proposes a theory of reading that takes account of the cognitive processes involved in the reading experience, for a "*theory* of reading provides . . . a standard against which individual assertions about reading can be calibrated."[4]

---

2. Iser, *Act of Reading*, 20.

3. Ibid., 18. Iser advises: "Far more instructive will be an analysis of what actually happens when one is reading a text. . . . It is in the reader that the text comes to life . . ." (19).

4. Camery-Hoggatt, "Rhetoric of Text."

PRESUPPOSITIONS

"Authors play games with readers, and the text is the playground."[5] Iser's clever aphorism expresses the notion that reading involves four essential elements: author, reader, text, and purpose. Moreover, since the game metaphor involves competition, the statement well depicts the notion that reading is an experiential and cognitive activity that pits the world of the author over against the world of the reader.[6] In his description of the reading transaction, Terence Keegan highlights general effects that authors intend their works to have on their readers:

> Authors deliberately create artistic works that will involve the activity of the reader, that will tantalize the reader, tease the reader, challenge the reader, upset the reader, and force the reader to get into the text and do something with it.[7]

In the business of reading, then, the reader's world is confronted by the literary world molded by the author. The medium for this confrontation is the text. The object of the game is, in Iser's terminology, not meaning-assembly (winning or losing) but a text-guided, reader-produced aesthetic object, a reorientation effected by the interaction of the reader's habitual orientation with the role he or she voluntarily assumes as reader.[8] The rules of the game are the technical requirements of language.

Understanding the dynamics of language is important, since language is the means by which the author's world is brought to the reader.

---

5. Iser, *Prospecting*, 250. See Hutchinson, *Games Authors Play*.

6. McKnight, *Postmodern Use of the Bible*, 260–63.

7. Keegan, *Interpreting the Bible*, 84.

8. Iser, *Prospecting*, 63–65. Iser postulates that a split occurs because readers, on the one hand, "slip into the role mapped out by the text," but on the other "cannot completely cut [them]selves off from what [they] are . . ." In the resolution of this tension, the reader experiences a transformation that, to my mind, has occurred even if the reader returns to her or his habitual orientation. A reader may return to habitual orientation (contra Iser, 64), but he or she will do so via a new perspective. The term "reorientation" aptly describes this transformation. Thus, the reading "game" should not be viewed as winning or losing, i.e., apprehending or misunderstanding the author's meaning (contra Hutchinson, *Games Authors Play*, 7; who sees its emphasis "on the pleasure which is derived from analysis and recognition, on the pleasure of *mastery* over a text which has been presented as a specific form of challenge" [emphasis original]). But see Iser, *Act of Reading*, 4: "In discovering the hidden meaning, the critic has, as it were, solved a puzzle, and there is nothing left for him to do but to congratulate himself on this achievement."

Robert Bergen discusses several assumptions about communication that are important to the present context.[9] Firstly, since the mind can consciously process only a limited number of items simultaneously, a considerable portion of the communication process takes place at the subliminal level. That a reader often is not consciously aware of the cognitive processes involved in reading makes her or him vulnerable to the shocks and surprises that a given textual configuration can bring. Secondly, the writer and reader must share a set of equivalently understood symbols (code).[10] Thirdly, the language code operates within the constraints imposed by genre. Fourthly, language is hierarchical.

Jerry Camery-Hoggatt surveys literary criticism, cognitive science, and sociology and notes four common boundaries in their view of language. All affirm: (1) the importance of a language's natural environment; (2) the functions of language to persuade, alienate, assimilate, confuse, and entertain; (3) the ability of language to transport meaning on multiple levels—emotional, cognitive, social, and personal; and (4) the necessity of language's psychological and sociological context for accurate comprehension.[11]

Before considering the role these play in the business of reading, a fundamental distinction between initial and subsequent readings of the same narrative must be noted: only with the initial reading can one assume the reader's ignorance of subsequent events in the discourse.[12]

CHARACTERISTICS OF LANGUAGE

Camery-Hoggatt probes five features of language that are integral to the present treatment of Mark and Chariton: selectivity, ambiguity, polyvalence, aurality, and linearity.[13] Since these elements have a direct bearing

9. Bergen, "Text as a Guide."

10. Alter ("How Convention Helps Us Read," 115) notes that "every culture, even every era in a particular culture, develops distinctive and sometimes intricate codes for telling its stories ..." For a general discussion of codes, see McKnight, *Postmodern Use of the Bible*, 115–66.

11. Camery-Hoggatt, *Speaking of God*, 80–82.

12. Kennedy (*New Testament Interpretation*, 6) holds that the NT texts "were originally intended to have an impact on the first hearing ..." Yet even here one is faced with the problem of the extent of the reader's knowledge of the story of Christ (to set aside Mark's telling of it) assumed by the narrator.

13. The outline of this section follows Camery-Hoggatt, *Speaking of God*, 51–56. Although some of these categories are not directly related to narrative sequence, their

on how an author guides a reader through a given text, we shall examine each of them and describe its influence.

Language Is Selective

The complex nature of the cause-effect chain that interconnects all events predetermines that the whole of a story can never be told. *Ipso facto*, a storyteller leaves certain details out of his account. This creates narrative "gaps" that must be negotiated by the reader.[14]

Often these omitted details relate to unstated causal connections between two or more events. A reader's natural compulsion to "impose maximal plot-coherence on a set of narrative events" assures that she or he will assume the existence of a causal linkage between any pair of narrative events, "unless otherwise instructed."[15] Sternberg cites a lyric that illustrates this tendency:

> Every day, that's the way
> Jonathan goes out to play.
> Climbed a tree. What did he see?
> Birdies: one, two, three!
> Naughty boy! What have we seen?
> There's a hole in your new jeans![16]

---

utility for describing the rhetorical effect of the anachronies treated in chs. 3 and 4 warrants their inclusion here. For other discussions of these features, see Ingarden, *Cognition of the Literary Works*; van Dijk, *Text and Context*; van Dijk and Kintsch, *Strategies of Discourse Comprehension*; Iser, *Act of Reading*; Hutchinson, *Games Authors Play*. For a reading model less dependent on psycholinguistics see Fowler, "Critical Model of Reading." Fowler's emphasis on reading as a temporal experience and meaning as event are important for the present context.

14. Iser (*Act of Reading*, 167–69, 171–72, 174–79) describes a reader's handling of narrative gaps as "filling." Fowler (*Let the Reader Understand*, 46) suggests that the reader may "bridge," "bypass," or "leap over" gaps. Sternberg ("Gaps, Ambiguity") offers a concise discussion on theory (186–90), which he then applies to selected episodes from the Hebrew Bible (190–229). For an excellent treatment on the processing of narrative gaps, see Camery-Hoggatt, *Speaking of God*, 59–73, 74–85.

15. Moore, "Narrative Commentaries," 42–43. Fowler (*Let the Reader Understand*, 137) writes: "In a logical, rational world, *post hoc, ergo propter hoc* is a logical fallacy, but in the world of narrative, *post hoc, ergo propter hoc* is the reigning presupposition, unless we are told otherwise." See also Sternberg, *Poetics of Biblical Narrative*, 189.

16. Sternberg, *Poetics of Biblical Narrative*, 187.

Of the numerous possible explanations for the torn jeans, the reader holds tree climbing responsible because this hypothesis links this element to the hole in a causal relationship. Sternberg writes:

> This hypothesis offers the simplest and most probable explanation for the coexistence and unfolding of the different givens in the text: it creates maximal relevance among the diverse features and levels . . . and brings together more elements than the alternative hypothesis (the hole was already there before the boy climbed the tree).[17]

Narrative gaps are evident not only in missing information (what is left unsaid) but also in departures from a chronological time scheme. Shimon Bar-Efrat distinguishes chronological time from narratological time. The latter, he notes, "is subjective and expands or contracts according to the circumstances; it is never continuous, being subject to gaps, delays and jumps."[18] Thus, narrative gaps are an inevitable and significant feature of any narrative. According to Iser, they "function as a kind of pivot on which the whole text-reader relationship revolves."[19]

At first glance, these gaps appear to be a negative feature, fraught with hindrances to swift and accurate communication. They require additional time and energy, and they engender ambiguity. Nevertheless, as the following example shows, this quality can be used to produce powerful rhetorical effects:

> A man woke up terrified and reached for the matches so he could light a candle. The matches were put into his hand.[20]

This brief British folktale easily evokes the terrifying image of an unwelcome intruder (human or spectre) intent on doing harm to an unsuspecting man. What creates the anxiety is not so much what the story *says* as what it leaves *unsaid*. What it leaves unsaid is supplied—more often than not, unknowingly—by the reader.

That readers fill narrative gaps is certain. How they do so in a given case, though not certain, is nevertheless predictable, for the choices a reader makes in filling narrative gaps are neither unlimited nor arbitrary. The writer has a vested interest in how the reader fills the gaps in his nar-

---

17. Ibid.
18. Bar-Efraht, *Narrative Art*, 142.
19. Iser, *Prospecting*, 34.
20. Quoted in Camery-Hoggatt, *Speaking of God*, 59.

rative. Indeed, this interest plays a part in the narrative choices that she or he presents to the reader. Sternberg's comments are instructive:

> Literature is remarkable for its powers of control and validation. Of course, gap-filling may nevertheless be performed in a wild or misguided or tendentious fashion. . . . But to gain cogency, a hypothesis must be legitimated by the text.[21]

Gap-filling is controlled by a number of factors. The most obvious of these is what *is* said in a narrative. That is, the details that *are* included influence the way a reader will fill in the details that are not included. Let us return to the British folktale. A man (apparently alone) wakes up terrified (Did he hear a prowler? Is he really alone?) and reaches for the matches so he can light a candle (a light source that gives only a meager amount of light and produces shadows in which someone may remain hidden). The scene is set: the man is alone and frightened. He reaches for some matches to light a candle in order to assure himself that he is alone and thus free from danger. But the very act he hoped would alleviate his worst fear instead confirms it: someone (or something!) put the matches in his hand![22]

Context also influences the filling of narrative gaps. If our British folktale is told around a campfire on a damp drizzly night under a full moon with wolves howling in the background, the effect of the story is certain to be intensified. If, on the other hand, the tale is told in a hospital or any institution where others are usually nearby, the man's terror may be taken merely as a bad dream and the gap may be filled as a companion's kind effort to calm the man.

The context in which a narrative is encountered and the details that it supplies are important factors that influence how a reader fills the narrative gaps. Yet these components represent only external constituents of the gap-filling enterprise. For an adequate understanding of the entire transaction one must give attention to a central, internal

---

21. Sternberg, *Poetics of Biblical Narrative*, 188. Sternberg (189) treats several factors that control the process of hypothetical reconstruction: (1) the nature of the materials (e.g., actional, thematic, norm-structuring); (2) the language and poetics of the materials; (3) the generic features of the materials; (4) laws and regularities of the world projected by the materials; and (5) "basic assumptions or general canons of probability derived from 'everyday life' and prevalent cultural conventions." Some of these are treated below.

22. The passive construction of this sentence heightens the uncertainty of the agent (person? ghost? demon?) placing the matches in the man's hand.

ingredient, namely, how the mind stores, accesses, and utilizes linguistic information.

Although scientific investigations of semantic memory are still in their formative stages, a fundamental consensus is emerging: "semantic memory is not stored as discrete units, but as hierarchies of features clustered around central organizing nodes."[23] These hierarchies have been labeled variously as "schemata," "scripts," and "frames of reference."[24] The present investigation follows Camery-Hoggatt in taking "schema" as the encompassing term and the latter two terms as specialized forms of schema.[25]

The hierarchical ordering of schemata appears to be based on experience rather than logic.[26] Since the brain seems to access first those schemata that are most typical, learning is properly understood as a linking of new data with that which is already known. According to Morton Hunt,

23. Camery-Hoggatt, *Speaking of God*, 61–73, 77. See also Bergen, "Text as a Guide." "The idea of some basic scaffolding or armature that determines the 'essence' of things," writes Gombrich (*Art and Illusion*, 132–33; quoted in Iser, *Act of Reading*, 90), "reflects our need for a schema with which to grasp the infinite variety of this world of change."

24. The use of "schema" in connection with memory processing goes back at least as far as Bartlett, *Remembering*. This term is similarly employed in Rumelhart and Ortony, "Representation of Knowledge"; and Rumelhart, "Schemata." The term "frame" is used in Minsky, "Framework for Representing Knowledge"; Winston, *Artificial Intelligence*; Hrushovski, *Segmentation and Motivation*; and Funk, *Poetics of Biblical Narrative*. The term "script" is used in Schank and Abelson, *Scripts, Plans, Goals*. Van Dijk and Kintsch (*Strategies of Discourse Comprehension*, 309) describe scripts as *ordered* sets of actions. For a historical overview of these concepts, see Tannen, "What's in a Frame?" For a review of approaches that apply schema theory to the structure of discourse, see Thorndyke and Yekovitch, "Critique of Schema-Based Theories." Such include: Thorndyke, "Cognitive Structures"; Mandler and Johnson, "Remembrance of Things Parsed"; Kintsch and van Dijk, "Toward a Model"; and Graesser, *Prose Comprehension*.

25. For general discussions on schema theory, see Crawford and Chaffin, "Reader's Construction of Meaning," 4–11; and van Dijk and Kintsch, 47–49.

26. On the former, see Collins and Loftus, "A Spreading-Activation Theory of Semantic Processing," 407–28; and Hunt, *Universe Within*. On the latter, see Collins and Quillian, "Retrieval Time from Semantic Memory," 240–47. Van Dijk and Kintsch (*Strategies of Discourse Comprehension*, 310) affirm the conclusion of Abbott and Black (*Representation of Scripts in Memory*) that script actions activate their superordinates in the script hierarchy, but not vice versa. Van Dijk and Kintsch use the classical "restaurant" script of Schank and Abelson to illustrate: "when we encounter the word *restaurant* in a text, we do not think of 'ordering,' 'eating,' and 'paying,' but if we hear these words which are subunits of a script, the script label 'restaurant' will be activated."

new material is added to this network by being plunked down in a hole in the middle of an appropriate region, and then gradually is tied in, by a host of meaningful connections, to the appropriate nodes in the surrounding network."[27]

A linguistic unit may call forth multiple schemata of the same kind or a variety of different kinds of schemata: "lexical" (another word), "frame of reference" (stereotyped situation), "script" (activity that follows a predictable sequence), and "world knowledge" (knowledge acquired formally rather than experientially). As the various schemata are accessed, this information is used to fill in gaps.

Language Is Ambiguous

That several different schemata often are associated with the same linguistic unit illustrates the inherent ambiguity of language. On the surface, this feature appears to be wholly negative. In reality, however, ambiguity is a necessary component of the reading experience. Iser affirms:

> As what is meant can never be totally translated into what is said, the utterance is bound to contain implications, which in turn necessitate interpretation. Indeed, there would never be any dyadic interaction if the speech act did not give rise to indeterminacies that needed to be resolved. . . . [I]ndeterminacy is a prerequisite for dyadic interaction, and hence a basic constituent of communication.[28]

Thus, ambiguity is both a catalyst and an obstacle for the reading process. Since the human mind is not equipped to retain all the ramifications of all possible schemata and, at the same time, evaluate freshly encountered data, the reader must have "some sort of switching mechanism, some way of directing traffic, that lets some units pass and diverts others to side streets."[29] This mechanism is described by cognitive psychologists as forming a "gist" (roughly equivalent to Iser's "theme").[30] That is, instead

27. Hunt, *Universe Within*, 107–8.

28. Iser, *Act of Reading*, 59.

29. Camery-Hoggatt, *Speaking of God*, 90–91.

30. According to Iser (*Act of Reading*, 96–97), a narrative text contains a whole system of perspectives that are continually interweaving and interacting. Thus, Iser writes: "It is not possible for the reader to embrace all perspectives at once, and so the view he is involved with at any one particular moment is what constitutes for him the 'theme'" (97). Numerous studies have shown that in prose narrative, the gist of a sentence is

of retaining conscious, verbatim knowledge of what was read, the reader carries forward only the gist of it.[31]

Cognitive science suggests two different, but complementary, models for the gist-making mechanism: "bottom-up" and "top-down" reading strategies.[32] These models appear to have arisen as a way of explaining how the placement of a word in a sentence or text facilitates the reader's perception of that word.[33] The two models can be differentiated by the general direction of their approach. Bottom-up constraints describe reading as a movement from the parts (letters, words, sentences, etc.) to the whole. Top-down constraints picture a reader starting with some knowledge of the whole and moving to an understanding of the parts.

Most cognitive scientists agree that reading is the result of the interaction between top-down and bottom-up strategies. Teun van Dijk and Walter Kintsch, for example, affirm that reading

> is not simply a sequence of processes starting with feature detection and letter identification, and continuing through word recognition and sentence parsing to more global discourse processing. Instead of a sequence of bottom-up processing, we have a situation in which higher level processes affect the lower ones; that is, we have top-down effects with which to contend. . . . [S]everal authors have proposed two-process theories, where a bottom-up, data-driven analysis process interacts with a top-down, knowledge-driven hypothesis-testing process.[34]

more easily remembered than exact wording. See, e.g., Brewer, "Memory for Ideas"; Sachs, "Memory in Reading"; Anderson, "Verbatim and Propositional Representation"; Begg and Wickelgren, "Retention Functions"; Brewer and Lichtenstein, "Memory for Marked Semantic Features."

31. The reader is seldom aware of this activity. See Bergen, "Discourse Criticism," 328: "Because the human mind can consciously process only a small number of the elements involved in the communication event, the greatest number of language variables must be processed subconsciously." Speaking of language strategies performed by the reader, van Dijk and Kintsch (*Strategies of Discourse Comprehension*, 71) affirm: "those strategies in most cases will not be preprogrammed, intended, conscious, or verbalizable by the language user. Rather, we should say, they are strategies of the cognitive system, usually beyond the conscious control of the language user."

32. See, e.g., van Dijk and Kintsch, *Strategies of Discourse Comprehension*, 22–27; and Camery-Hoggatt, *Speaking of God*, 91.

33. The first study to test the effect of sentence context on word recognition was Tulving and Gold, "Stimulus Information." For an experiment testing the effect of longer contexts on word recognition, see Wittrock et al., "Reading as a Generative Process."

34. Van Dijk and Kintsch, *Strategies of Discourse Comprehension*, 22–23.

BOTTOM-UP READING STRATEGIES

Bottom-up reading strategies include the lexical, syntactical, textural, and gesticulative aspects of communication. At the lexical level, the reader sets out to access the proper schema for each word. To speed up the process, the mind partially activates clusters of "target" words suggested by the previously encountered material, thus narrowing down the field of schemata to be accessed.

Syntax also plays a role in delimiting the schematic possibilities. Because syntactical and lexical features are inextricably conjoined, such typical syntactical markers as affixes, word order, and function words may all serve to delimit lexical possibilities as the following sentences illustrate:

1. The old salt sailed seven seas.

2. The old dog is running faster than the young boy.

3. The old dog is running for President.[35]

In the first sentence the positioning of "the" and "old" anticipates the typical article-adjective-noun syntactical pattern. The number of possible nouns that could follow this particular pattern ("The old . . .") is, for practical purposes, infinite. Since "salt" in its most frequently used sense is rarely linked with the adjective "old," the reader reassesses the combination "old salt" and recognizes this as a colloquial expression for a sailor. The remainder of the sentence assures the reader that he or she has now accessed the proper schema.

The second sentence, "The old dog is running faster than the young boy," uses all linguistic units in their most frequent senses. Specifically, it replaces the third element of the article-adjective-noun complex with a noun that is modified frequently (and reasonably) by the adjective "old" and qualifies the verb "is running" with the adverb "faster," evoking its ambulatory sense.

The third sentence, "The old dog is running for President," appears to use the noun "dog" and the verb "is running" in their most usually employed senses. The phrase "for President," however, necessitates a reassessment of the verb "is running" and the noun "dog": "running" is no longer "rapidly ambulating" but "candidating for a political office"; and

---

35. The structure of these examples and the type of analysis they are given here were prompted by Camery-Hoggatt (*Speaking of God*, 93–96).

"old dog" is no longer a neutral term for an aged canine but a pejorative term for a human being. Thus, this triad of sentences illustrates that while lexical and syntactical schemata can accelerate the rate at which narrative material is processed (esp. sentence 2), the reader's initial projections occasionally are overturned (as in sentences 1 and 3).

Although primarily germane to the aural aspect of language, texture (e.g., modulation, tone, rhythm, intensity) and gesticulation (hand movements, facial expression, etc.) also aid in disambiguating. These elements are especially relevant to the Gospels.[36]

TOP-DOWN READING STRATEGIES

Top-down reading strategies describe a way of comprehending the constituent parts of a linguistic unit. This understanding is informed by some prior knowledge about the entire unit, particularly such items as context, genre, and theme. Context includes within its scope a broad range of features that frequently are interrelated: historical, geographical, cultural, and literary settings.

Setting is an essential component of all communication. As Iser put it, "All utterances have their place in a situation, arising from it and conditioned by it. Speech devoid of situation is practically inconceivable."[37] Those features of setting that concern general world knowledge may be viewed as a filter through which readers (or hearers) process all incoming linguistic stimuli.[38] For example, the complaint, "I'm having trouble with the old man again," would be taken in one sense if snarled by a teenager on a street corner, another if lamented by a middle-aged woman in a laundromat, and still another if confessed by an elderly man in a pastor's office.[39]

Context speeds up disambiguation in the lexical arena by ruling out certain schemata. Van Dijk and Kintsch note:

36. On Mark, see Kelber, *Oral and Written Gospel*, esp. 44–90.

37. Iser, *Act of Reading*, 62.

38. Cognitive scientists argue that knowledge of context is the critical backdrop that illumines freshly encountered stimuli. See McLelland, "Stochastic Interactive Processes," esp. 4–6.

39. The basic structure of this example is from Camery-Hoggatt, *Speaking of God*, 103.

... If we hear on the radio

(13) *Three masked gunmen robbed a bank yesterday.*

we are not aware of the alternative meaning of *bank* as river bank. If someone says in the supermarket

(14) *These brown ones over there, they are cooking bananas.*

we are not aware of an alternative parsing with *are cooking* as the verb and *bananas* as the object. This suggests an intelligent word recognition mechanism that somehow uses the context in (13) to retrieve the right meaning of *bank* without even considering alternatives. In parsing (14), the fact that *they* is deictically identified as brown objects immediately precludes the alternative parsing of the syntactically ambiguous second phrase requiring an animate subject.[40]

In its literary aspect, context encompasses the options and constraints presented by the linguistic material that has preceded the unit in question. Antecedent material predisposes or "primes" the reader to interpret subsequent material in a certain fashion.

Priming impacts the cultural context as well. Camery-Hoggatt notes:

> The cultural repertoire we bring with us to the reading can prime our reading in one direction or another, in the process blinding us to other schematic possibilities which would have been perfectly clear to the reader for whom the text was originally prepared.[41]

The priming effect of background on comprehension is made clear in the following piece of narrative prose:

> Rocky slowly got up from the mat, planning his escape. He hesitated a moment and thought. Things were not going well. What bothered him the most was being held, especially since the charge against him had been weak. He considered his present situation. The lock that held him was strong but he thought he could break

---

40. Van Dijk and Kintsch, *Strategies of Discourse Comprehension*, 33.

41. Camery-Hoggatt, *Speaking of God*, 113. In one description of the reading process, Iser accents the role of a reader's background: "the structure of the text sets off a sequence of mental images which lead to the text translating itself into the reader's consciousness. The actual content of these mental images will be colored by the reader's existing stock of experience, which acts as a referential background against which the unfamiliar can be conceived and processed" (*Act of Reading*, 38). Gender also predisposes the reader to construct schemata in specific ways (see Flynn "Gender and Reading").

it. He knew, however, that his timing would have to be perfect. Rocky was aware that it was because of his earlier roughness that he had been penalized so severely—much too severely from his point of view. The situation was becoming frustrating; the pressure had been grinding on him for too long. He was being ridden unmercifully. Rocky was getting angry now. He felt he was ready to make his move. He knew that his success or failure would depend on what he did in the next few seconds.[42]

This passage intentionally activates two possible schemata: breaking out of jail and breaking free from a wrestling hold. Richard Anderson and his colleagues presented this narrative segment to a music class and a wrestling class. The result was not surprising. The music students used the jail schema, while the wrestling students chose a wrestling match for their interpretive schema.

Thus, the reader's background is a key factor in determining how she or he processes narrative material. The closer the reader is to a particular schema, experientially, the more likely he or she will be to invoke that schema. How this passage would be interpreted, say, by anyone who has spent time in prison occasions no uncertainty.

Genre, a second top-down reading constraint, governs reading by providing cues as to what to expect and establishing imaginative boundaries.[43] Umberto Eco describes the cues given to the reader by the well known genre signal "Once upon a time . . ." According to Eco, this phrase establishes

> (i) that the events take place in an indefinite nonhistorical epoch,
> (ii) that the reported events are not "real," (iii) that the speaker
> wants to tell a fictional story.[44]

Owing to the genre-clues afforded by this expression, the reader not only knows what to expect, but also is more prone to accept elements that otherwise for her or him would lie beyond all plausibility.

Knowing the theme of a linguistic unit also aids the reader in disambiguating.[45] The reader usually arrives at a theme through a trial-and-error process in which a guess based on clues provided within the text is tested for coherence with the linguistic material. This process is repeated

---

42. Anderson et al., "Frameworks for Comprehending Discourse," 372.

43. See McKnight, *Postmodern Use of the Bible*, 219–21.

44. Eco, *Role of the Reader*, 19.

45. See McKnight, *Postmodern Use of the Bible*, 234–41.

until a satisfactory fit is found. The following paragraph, used in a 1974 study by J. D. Bransford and M. K. Johnson, illustrates the importance of a knowledge of theme to the reading process, since it does not offer sufficient clues for the reader to determine a satisfactory motif:

> The procedure is actually quite simple. First you arrange things into different groups. Of course one pile may be sufficient depending on how much there is to do. If you have to go somewhere else due to lack of facilities that is the next step, otherwise you are pretty well set. It is important not to overdo things. That is, it is better to do too few things at once than too many. In the short run this may not seem important but complications can easily arise. A mistake can be expensive as well. At first the whole procedure will seem complicated. Soon however, it will become just another facet of life. It is difficult to foresee any end to the necessity for this task in the immediate future, but then one never can tell. After the procedure is completed one arranges the material into different groups again. Then they can be put into their appropriate places. Eventually they will be used once more and the whole cycle will then have to be repeated. However, that is a part of life.[46]

This paragraph was given to two groups of subjects. One group was given the paragraph as transcribed above. The second group was given the identical paragraph, but with the heading "Washing Clothes." Reading the paragraph with the theme in mind makes all the details perfectly understandable. Subjects in the first group recalled only a minimum of details, while performance of this same task was measurably improved in the second group.

Camery-Hoggatt has posited seven mutually interactive and corrective constraints that enable the reader to overcome the natural ambiguities of language and process a narrative unit: context, genre, theme, lexical range, syntax, texture, and gesticulation.[47] "When all the

---

46. This experiment is discussed in Bransford and McCarrell, "Sketch of a Cognitive Approach," 206; and in Camery-Hoggatt, "Rhetoric of Text," 106–7.

47. All of these are subsumed by what Iser (*Act of Reading*, 69) refers to as the "repertoire" shared by text and reader: "The repertoire consists of all the familiar territory within the text. This may be in the form of references to earlier works, or to social and historical norms or to the whole culture from which the text has emerged...." According to Sykes (Grammar of Narrative," 122), experimental psychologists "point out that there is a grammar of narrative which consists of a setting, a theme, a plot, and a resolution. Conformity to this grammatical sequence is a condition of a story's capacity to be re-

constraints are in alignment the redundancy of information enables the reader to focus in on the specific schemas and nodes of information that the speaker intends."[48]

Language Is Polyvalent

Although alignment of reading constraints makes the intended meaning of a given narrative unit more clearly and more readily discernable, such unanimity is not required—and often is not desired. This is especially apparent in literary works in which clarity and speed are subordinated to other aims (e.g., intrigue, suspense, surprise).[49] When the reading constraints generate conflicting messages, the resulting interference compels the reader to review the material and check for errors.[50] This retrospection and repair routine is illustrated in the following linguistic unit:

> I was afraid of Ali's powerful punch, especially since it had already laid out many tougher men who had bragged that they could handle that much alcohol.[51]

Camery-Hoggatt describes the interpretive process:

---

called." Sykes relates this pattern to the Christian life: "To live in the Christian pattern is to see one's life in a particular *context*, the dealings of God and humanity, given a particular *theme*, human redemption, set in a *plot*, the story of Christ and the church, and anticipating a *resolution*, namely the last judgment" (124; emphasis original).

48. Camery-Hoggatt, "Rhetoric of Text," 168. On the disambiguating function of redundancy *within* as well as among the various reading constraints see, e.g., Carpenter "Stylistic Redundancy"; Cherry, *On Human Communication*; Pierce, *Signals, Communication*; Suleiman, "Redundancy"; Wittig, "Formulaic Style"; and Anderson, "Double and Triple Stories." Anderson writes: "Redundancy increases predictability by decreasing the number of possible alternatives. This reduces uncertainty and facilitates the communication process (82; ref. Cherry, 18). Suleiman classifies various types of redundancy.

49. See Alonzo-Schoekel, "Hermeneutics." The author writes: "Literary language shows a preference for multiplicity and complexity, it . . . makes use of connotation, allusion, suggestive ambiguities . . ." (380).

50. The phenomenon of interference was demonstrated in the famous study by Stroop, "Studies of Interference." This study drew attention to interference between the verbal and visual processing systems by exposing the difficulty of reading the names of colors that had been printed with an opposing color (e.g., the word "red" printed in blue ink). For a survey of other studies that explore the "Stroop Effect," see Spoehr and Lehmkuhle, *Visual Information Processing*, 242–45.

51. Clark and Clark, *Psychology and Language*, 81.

Contextual signals ("Ali") prime the reader to target one meaning for the word "punch," and this appears to be confirmed by the reference to "tougher men" being "laid out." At the end of the sentence, though, a disambiguating term calls for retrospection and repair.[52]

The polyvalent nature of language means that it strikes the reader/hearer on different levels creating a kind of "double exposure" effect in which one frame is overcoded on top of a different frame. The resulting interference causes the reader to ambivalent between the two frames, considering the ramifications, first of one and then the other. At times, the immediate context tips the scales and one frame wins out over the other. At other times the frames are held in balance until a more appropriate moment when the subsequent information will resolve the interference in a way that produces a certain effect on the reader. Occasionally the tension between frames is left unresolved by the narrative.[53]

Language Is Aural

The aural aspect of language has to do with the way what is spoken makes its impact on the listener's ear. For example, the tone in which something is said clearly is a significant factor in communicating a speaker's interests. Stress given to certain words by changes in volume, pitch, or articulation can reinforce or betray a speaker's intentions. When communication takes a written format, however, these features become difficult to recover.

In recent years scholars have given considerable attention to the differences between oral and written communication.[54] Several have sought to apply the results of such study to the biblical materials. In

52. Camery-Hoggatt, *Speaking of God*, 119.

53. The Gospel of Mark illustrates this last case. The portrayal of the disciples is alternately positive and negative throughout the narrative. When the Twelve seem irremediable, there are others, whom Rhodes and Michie call "little people," who follow Jesus. Nevertheless, at the end all have fled in fear. This conflicts with the "call" frame where Jesus promises to make the disciples "fishers of men," a tension that is not resolved in the narrative.

54. See, e.g., Horowitz and Samuels, *Comprehending*; Green and Morgan, "Writing Ability"; Gumpez-Cook and Gumpez, "Oral to Written"; Lord, *Singer of Tales*; Ong, *Presence of the Word*; idem, *Interfaces of the Word*; idem, *Orality and Literacy*; Scribner and Cole, *Psychology of Literacy*; Tannen, "Oral and Literate Strategies"; idem, "Relative Focus."

particular, the theory that the Gospel materials were originally transmitted in an oral format has given rise to recent investigations that address their aural nature.[55] While much of the emphases given in an oral setting (e.g., matters of tone) is unrecoverable, scholars point to devices such as *inclusio* (perceptible in oral and written formats) to illustrate ways of stressing particularly salient points.

In addition to tone, however, the very texture of the words themselves plays an important role in the meanings and emphases they convey. This is most clear when meaning is understood in both its cognitive and affective senses. In a study conducted by Wolfgang Koehler, subjects were given two nonsense words, "maluma" and "takete," together with two sketches similar to the ones featured below and asked to label the sketches with the appropriate word:[56]

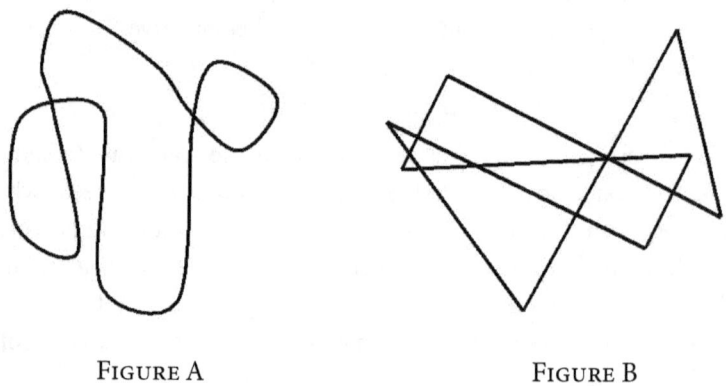

FIGURE A   FIGURE B

Koehler explained the preponderant tendency to pair "maluma" with Figure A and "takete" with Figure B by appealing to the similarity of "feeling" produced by the visual and auditory stimuli. "Maluma" is the more round sound and "takete" the more sharp, or to use another visual analogy, the sounds making up the word "maluma" change more gradually than "takete" just as the direction of the lines changes more gradually in Figure A than in Figure B. Thus, the link between texture and visual imagery is apparent.

55. See, e.g., Dewey, "Oral Methods"; Gerhardsson, *Memory and Manuscript*; Keck, "Oral Traditional Literature"; Kelber, *Oral and Written Gospel*; Lord, "Gospels as Oral Traditional Literature."

56. Koehler, *Gestalt Psychology*; cited in Camery-Hoggatt, "Rhetoric of Text," 213.

In addition to texture's power to intensify visual imagery are its abilities to confirm genre and facilitate memory. Such features as rhythm, meter, assonance, and alliteration make a narrative passage more easily memorizable. The sounds of the words or combinations of characters aid the memorizing process by creating associative links with meaning.

Language Is Linear

Discussing the process by which readers apprehend—and are apprehended by—texts, Iser notes that a "text cannot at any one moment be grasped as a whole."[57] According to Iser, this feature distinguishes texts from objects, which, as he claims, "can generally be viewed or at least conceived as a whole."[58] This comparison, however, overlooks the fact that one is equally unable to apprehend a physical object as a whole, since only one side of it can be seen at any one moment. Nevertheless, that physical objects share this characteristic with texts does not destroy Iser's claim. Indeed, his point is made stronger by acknowledging this similarity between texts and objects and drawing the argument from the lesser to the greater: since a person is unable to apprehend the whole of a physical object at any one moment, how much more is a reader unable to apprehend a literary text at one moment? This approach has greater force, especially in light of Iser's later contrast between text and object:

> We always stand outside the given object, whereas we are situated inside the literary text. . . . instead of a subject-object relationship, there is a moving viewpoint which travels along *inside* that which it has to apprehend. This mode of grasping an object is unique to literature.[59]

Since the "angle" from which the reader views the text continuously changes throughout the reading, he or she apprehends only certain aspects of the text at any one moment. Iser writes:

> Apperception can only take place in phases, each of which contains aspects of the object to be constituted, but none of which can claim to be representative of it. Thus, the aesthetic object

---

57. Iser, *Act of Reading*, 112.

58. Ibid., 108–9.

59. Ibid., 109 (emphasis original).

cannot be identified with any of its manifestations during the time-flow of the reading.[60]

Even at the end of the reading the reader is not able to conceptualize the entire text, only a manufactured gist. What the reader does experience is the effect of the exchange. She or he has been moved through a series of viewpoints to a new viewpoint, but the interchange that has accomplished this cannot be replicated even if replayed.

The linear characteristic of language sets the course along which this text-reader interchange proceeds. Moreover, since previous information affects how readers respond to subsequent information and since subsequent information often causes readers to reevaluate their understanding of previous narrative data, linearity gives powerful rhetorical potential to the sequential arrangement of narrative events.

Mary Ann Tolbert cites a humorous scene from the American television series *M*A*S*H* that illustrates the importance of narrative sequence:

> An unexploded bomb had landed in the hospital compound and surgeons Hawkeye and Trapper John were attempting to disarm it while Colonel Blake read out the instructions sent by the Army. Blake read, "Now cut the two wires leading to the timing fuse," and then looked up. The two doctors carefully cut the wires. Blake looked back at the instructions and read, "But first remove the fuse." At that point, panic ensued, everyone ran for cover, and the bomb—a dummy, as it happened—exploded.[61]

Thus, language is selective not only with respect to the events a speaker or writer chooses to relate but also the order in which she or he chooses to relate them.

Narrative material is fundamentally a selection of characters that, when placed in a certain sequence, form words that, when placed in a certain sequence, form phrases that, when placed in a certain sequence, form sentences, and so on. Even in those languages where grammatical structure is more dependent upon inflection than succession, the narrative material of any given text is nonetheless encountered in one and only one sequence.

---

60. Ibid., 108–9.

61. Tolbert, *Sowing the Gospel*, 7n13.

While inflection-based languages offer a more flexible word order within sentences, the larger linguistic units are equally subject to a sequential arrangement.[62] By evoking in a particular sequence specific elements from the interconnected web of schemata, the narrator guides the reader in deciding which schemata to access and which to ignore. The following sequence of statements is used to illustrate:

1. John was on his way to school.

2. He was terribly worried about the math lesson.

3. He thought he might not be able to control the class again today.

4. It was not a normal part of the janitor's job.[63]

The name "John" suggests a genre of stories whose details are commonly experienced. The link with "school" confirms this notion and specifies the experience. The reader now has accessed a schema that sees John as the schoolboy on his way to school. The second sentence further confirms the typicality of the experience, since fear of math class is a common part of students' academic lives. The third sentence, however, is anomalous to the schema accessed thus far. Since controlling a class more appropriately fits the teacher schema, the reader retrocedes to the earlier sentences to evaluate the possibility that John is a teacher. Since nothing in the sentences precludes the identification of John as a teacher, this readjusted schema is carried forward to the next piece of information. Here, the reader finds a statement that again overturns the schema that he or she has built to this point: John is neither a student, nor a teacher, but a janitor!

But the reader's task is not finished. He or she must review the previous information and test the schema of John as janitor for its fit with the antecedent information. The reader can envision a situation where all these details fit. In fact, all the difficulties are cleared up if the whole group of sentences is prefaced with something like:

---

62. Bergen, "Discourse Criticism," 331, rightly notes that any deviation from conventional syntactical or semantic arrangement draws the attention of the reader, a phenomenon that Bergen labels "order-based highlighting."

63. This series of statements is found in Sanford and Garrod, *Understanding Written Language*, 114; cited in Camery-Hoggatt, *Speaking of God*, 146.

> In light of the shortage of substitute teachers, the administration of Central Dauphin East High School asked John, the school janitor, to fill in for Mr. Paul's Basic Math class for two days. His first day was, in his mind, a complete fiasco.

With this preface the sequence of information becomes:

1. John is a Janitor.
2. John is asked to teach two days of math classes.

If the original sentences are read in this light, the difficulties are resolved. Moreover, since changing the order of presentation eliminates the former difficulties, the retrospection and repair activity was demonstrably necessitated by the sequence in which the reader encountered the details of the text. Thus, by arranging the sequence according to which the details of a narrative are presented, the author influences the reader's perception of the narrative material.

CONCLUSION

We have examined five characteristics of language (selectivity, ambiguity, polyvalence, aurality, linearity) and shown that each of these qualities plays an important role in how a text affects its reader. The approach has portrayed reading as a transaction between the text and the reader in which both play an active role. Thus, a proper understanding of the act of reading includes what the reader does to the text as much as what the text does to the reader.

Nevertheless, while we must take seriously the role of the reader in the narrative transaction, we must also avoid the error of aggrandizing it. The act of reading effects a confrontation between the reader's world and the literary world created by the author. The text is the initiator and constant guide; the ideal reader is the respondent and faithful follower.

The reorientation produced by the interaction of the reader's orientation and the role voluntarily assumed as reader is text-guided at every point. The text requires readers to fill gaps, but predisposes them to fill these gaps in a certain way. The text introduces ambiguities, but provides readers the tools (for example, bottom-up and top-down reading strategies) to disambiguate them. The text induces multiple schemata but influences readers toward a specific schema. The text draws and/or intensifies readers' attention to specific viewpoints by the very sound of the words employed. And finally, by sequential arrangement of narrative events the text steers readers through a series of viewpoints, predisposes their reaction to subsequent data by antecedent data, modifies their understanding of antecedent data by subsequent data, and challenges them to accept the narrator's ideology.[64]

We have argued that the reader produces a framework that organizes antecedent textual information and controls the processing of subsequent textual data. Often freshly encountered material necessitates a modification of the framework; occasionally the framework collapses altogether and must be replaced by an entirely different grid. Narrative sequence is an important factor in this process. Chapter 3 examines the sequential organization of narrative events in Mark's Gospel and describes the effects of this arrangement on the reader.

64. When readers are required to assemble meaning, they are more inclined to adopt the resultant viewpoint since they themselves have participated in its construction. This concept is particularly significant for Mark's Gospel because readers are consistently constrained to "put the pieces together" themselves. Moreover, the labor involved in the process entrenches the viewpoint more firmly in the reader's memory.

3

Narrative Sequence in the Gospel of Mark

More attention must be paid to the relation between the structure of Mark's thought and the structure of his text. Though it is
much easier to select a theological theme to analyze in Mark, it is
much more fruitful and doubtless more accurate . . . to investigate
Mark's theology through the ordering of *all* the material.

—Leander E. Keck

INTRODUCTION

THE LINEARLY DIACHRONIC NATURE of language described in chapter
2 explains two important strictures: the first assures that no text can
be read *tout d'un coup*; the second requires that a text be apprehended
in the sequence in which it is presented. Unlike a film—which can be
run backwards, frame by frame, or a musical score, which can be played
backwards, note by note—a text cannot be read backwards and remain
a text.[1]

As described in chapter 2, the reading experience is a repetitive
process of constructing hypotheses on the basis of preceding data and
later modifying these conjectures in attempts to account for subsequent
data.[2] The reader is reluctant to abandon an established framework.[3]
Data that challenge the reader's established framework often indicate a
central feature of the author's agenda. Perry remarks: "The more difficult

1. Genette, *Narrative Discourse*, 34.

2. Iser (*Act of Reading*, 11) describes reading as a "continual interplay between
modified expectations and transformed memories." The text-reader transaction is thus
an evolving process of anticipation, frustration, retrospection, and reconstruction.

3. Perry ("Literary Dynamics," 45) describes the logic behind frame production.
According to Perry, the reader prefers frames that (1) are more conventional, (2) link
the highest number of disparate items, and (3) connect the items most closely.

it becomes to match fresh items with a frame constructed at the beginning of the text, the greater the attention commanded by these items."[4]

The potential of narrative sequence for promoting the narrator's ideology and the reader's iterative process of fitting freshly encountered narrative material into an incipient grid play a key role in the meanings a text induces. So every link in the narrative chain enlarges to some extent the text's overall impact on the reader. Thus, any treatment of narrative sequence in Mark's Gospel cannot be exhaustive but must be selective.

Even if one considers only those places where the narrative arrangement departs from chronological order (analepses, prolepses), the number is unmanageably large. Therefore, since the goal of the present investigation is not to explicate every instance of anachrony but to compare how Mark and Chariton each handle narrative time, and since the temporal ordering of narrative events influences the meanings produced by the text-reader exchange, the scope of chapters 3 and 4 is confined to those narrative segments considered to have special value in demonstrating that narrative sequence is a vehicle for the narrator's ideology.

The general approach is to examine each selected narrative segment in its immediate context, giving primary attention to any link with what directly precedes and follows it. To assess accurately the contribution each of these narrative segments makes to conveying the narrator's ideology, however, requires a preliminary description of that ideology as seen from a holistic view of the Gospel.

THE IDEOLOGY OF MARK

Markan scholars increasingly are giving deserved attention to the function of the Gospel's prologue. While they do not always agree on its precise extent, they seldom deny its importance.[5] Frank Matera, for example,

---

4. Ibid., 19.

5. Precisely which verses constitute the Markan prologue remains a matter for debate. The most frequently tendered arguments terminate the prologue either with 1:13 (e.g., Lightfoot, *Gospel Message of Mark*, 15–20; Matera, "Prologue as Interpretative Key," 15; Tolbert, *Sowing the Gospel*, 108; and Funk, *Poetics of Biblical Narrative*, 218–27) or 1:15 (e.g., Keck, "Introduction to Mark's Gospel"; Pesch, *Markusevangelium*, 71; and Boring, "Mark 1:1–15"). For an excellent discussion on the function of narrative introductions and a helpful bibliography on the topic, see Parsons, "Reading a Beginning"; idem, "How Narratives Begin." For a careful evaluation of the Markan introduction, see Boring, "Mark 1:1–15." Boring outlines and carefully examines the arguments for various suggested endpoints (1:8, 11, 13, 15) to the Markan prologue. He concludes that the

argues that the "hermeneutical key to Mark's Gospel is the information supplied in the prologue."[6] Specifically, he finds three interpretative keys in Mark's introduction:

> First, John the Baptist is the promised Elijah, Jesus' precursor. Second, Jesus is the Spirit-empowered Son of God, the one in whom the Father is pleased. Third, Jesus has confronted Satan in the wilderness and has not succumbed to his temptations.[7]

The validity and function of each of these elements is examined later in the present analysis. Of significance here is the fact that none of the characters (except Jesus) shares this information with the reader. This condition strengthens the bond between the reader and the narrator and, from the beginning of the narrative, inclines the reader to accept the narrator's (= Jesus') point of view.

The first words of the Markan Jesus introduce Mark's central organizing principle of life: the kingdom of God.[8] Mark does not explicitly define this expression; rather, he allows the contexts to imply the appropriate schema. The reader discovers that God's kingdom is not a geographically demarcated suzerainty but is everywhere that God reigns and his will prevails.[9] This "territory" can include that part of the human psyche in which the power of deliberate action or choice operates.

For Mark, the response to God's rule is the most important decision every individual must make. Near the climax of his narrative, Mark shows Jesus rebuking Peter for setting his mind on τὰ τῶν ἀνθρώπων rather than τὰ τοῦ θεοῦ (8:33).[10] He underscores these two conflicting ideologies not only by placing them immediately after the recognition

---

introductory section ends with 1:15 and functions to focalize the narrative, introduce its main characters and themes, and relate it to the time of the readers.

6. Matera, "Prologue as Interpretative Key," 15.

7. Ibid., 9.

8. Some manuscripts have Jesus proclaiming "the good news of the *kingdom* of God" in v. 14.

9. Goppelt (*Theology of the NT*, 1:70) draws this from the first three petitions of the Lord's Prayer (Matt 6:9–15; Luke 11:2–4). In a later part of this chapter we show how this is demonstrated in Mark's narrative.

10. The ideologies presented in Mark's Gospel fall into two opposing categories: "thinking the things of God" and "thinking the things of men." Petersen ("'Point of View,'" 108) writes: "For the narrator . . . there are two ways of perceiving things, two perspectives from which to construe them; one is right and the other is wrong; one divine, and one human. . . . [T]he right way is that taken by Mark and Jesus."

scene, but also by juxtaposing them. Nevertheless, the meaning of these phrases is as indeterminate as their presence is conspicuous. What specifically is intended by "the things of God" and "the things of men"? In his typical fashion, Mark does not directly state this for the reader,[11] but he does provide clues. The rhetorical strategies he employs encourage the reader to adopt the "things of God" perspective.[12]

Mark directly confronts his reader with the question of allegiance immediately after the first of Jesus' three major passion predictions.[13] Jesus denounces Peter's perspective, τὰ τῶν ἀνθρώπων, (8:29c, military Messiah?) as being in opposition (ἀλλὰ) to God's. In the next breath,[14] he calls people together and proclaims God's perspective (8:34). "Thinking the things of God" means self-denial and sacrifice on behalf of others. The choice is not trivial; the person's soul is at stake (vv. 35–37).

Mark follows the second passion prediction with an episode that provides material for the "things of men" schema. Jesus asked his disciples what they were arguing about while they were "on the way," but the disciples "were remaining silent" (9:34a). Why? Because "on the way" they had been arguing (analepsis) about who was the greatest ("the things of men"). Jesus immediately called them and sat to signal the importance of what he was about to teach: "If anyone wants to be first, he must be the very last and the servant of all" (9:35). Being "slave of all" is a position of weakness and humiliation, not power and status.[15] Mark punctuates this by recounting the episode of the disciples trying to stop an unknown

11. Fowler (*Let the Reader Understand*, 163) describes Mark's narrative strategy as a "rhetoric of indirection." "The language," he writes, "is figurative, that is, it needs to be figured out. It is not straight-forward or direct; it resists being taken at face value."

12. For an overview of a number of narrative strategies operative in Mark, see Fowler, *Let the Reader Understand*; Tolbert, *Sowing the Gospel*; and Rhoads, "Narrative Criticism." On the rhetorical function of Markan irony, see Camery-Hoggatt, *Irony in Mark's Gospel*. On narrative order in Mark, see Funk, *Poetics of Biblical Narrative*, 187–207; and Petersen, *Literary Criticism*, 49–80.

13. See Tannehill, *Sword of His Mouth*, 106–7. Regarding Jesus' teaching on discipleship, which follows each of his three major passion predictions, and which emphasizes servanthood and sacrifice on behalf of others, Tannehill argues that the repetition and antithetical pattern (8:35; 9:35; 10:43–44) combine to give the teaching its greatest possible force. "This is necessary," he says, "because . . . it is not easy to hear words that challenge our fundamental view of life and wish to replace it with another" (107).

14. The connection between the two events is simply καὶ. Nothing indicates that a time gap intervened.

15. Ibid., 104.

follower of Jesus from exorcizing demons in Jesus' name because he was not of their group (9:38). Jesus disapproved. In God's kingdom, name and status are not important. Doing the will of God identifies one as a member of Jesus' family (3:35).

After the third passion prediction, Mark shows the disciples requesting the positions of power and authority (the things of men) when Jesus comes into his glory (10:37). Jesus calls them together, condemns the Gentiles' way of lording authority over people, and tells them that everyone who wishes to be great must be a servant, and the one who wishes to be first (greatest) must be the slave of all (things of God; 10:43–44). Significantly, the blind beggar Bartimaeus receives his sight and follows Jesus "on the way" (10:52). And since "following Jesus on the way" is a metaphor for a self-sacrificial, service-oriented relationship with humanity,[16] society's liability is transformed into its benefactor— a *taker* becomes a *giver*.

Mark's Gospel ultimately concerns a person's relationship to the rule of God. Accepting the rule God requires doing the will of God. With Jesus as the primary model, Mark urges his readers to reject the "things of men" approach (desiring self-aggrandizement and overpowering others to attain it) and woos them to adopt the "things of God" mode (desiring the welfare of others and sacrificing one's own to improve theirs). For Mark, doing God's will means joining God in his mission for the world. And this can be accomplished only one way—by following Jesus.

NARRATIVE SEQUENCE AND MARK'S IDEOLOGY

Acknowledging the relationship between narrative order and ideology provides a way to narrow the scope of our narrative-time comparison of Mark and Chariton. More importantly, it takes seriously the rhetorical function shown to have been a central feature in the first-century literary milieu. This chapter and the next attempt to show that sequence is a vehicle for the narrator's ideology. Chapter 5 compares Mark and Chariton in terms of the operation and ideological output of their narrative order.

---

16. Jesus' own mission statement (or at least the narrator's evaluation of Jesus' mission) introduces the blind man episode: "For even the Son of Man did not come to be served, but to serve, and to give his life as a ransom for many."

Yahweh's Messenger: Mark 1:2

The first instance of anachrony in Mark's Gospel occurs in the initial sentence of the narrative proper:[17]

καθὼς γέγραπται ἐν τῷ Ἠσαΐᾳ τῷ προφήτῃ ἰδοὺ ἀποστέλλω
τὸν ἄγγελόν μου πρὸ προσώπου σου, ὃς κατασκευάσει τὴν ὁδόν
σου. (1:2)

This verse offers both a backward and a forward projection: the reference to Isaiah the prophet is an external analepsis that anchors the narrative in the Hebrew Scriptures;[18] the quoted prophecy functions as an internal prolepsis since it refers to a figure who is to come and a messenger sent as his forerunner. This makes possible a nexus between these personages and the narrative's protagonist.

Mark does not directly state the connection between Jesus and the figures mentioned in 1:2; instead, he requires the reader to deduce it on the basis of the information he subsequently supplies. Narrative sequence sets up specific associations among the actants. The primary characters

17. Mark 1:1 is properly taken to be a heading or title either for the entire narrative (so Boring, "Mark 1:11–15") or at least for vv. 2–13 (so Cranfield, *Mark*, 34–35). This view amplifies the importance of the opening words and the entire narrative; it not only identifies the protagonist of the narrative but also affirms a connection with "good news." The ambiguity of the genitive Ἰησοῦ Χριστοῦ makes the translations "good news about Jesus Christ" and "good news proclaimed by Jesus Christ" equally valid— and not mutually exclusive—interpretations. This is only the first instance of ambiguity in a Gospel that makes full use of the narrative strategy of indirection. See esp., Fowler, *Let the Reader Understand*, 155–227. Boring ("Mark 1:11–15," 50–53) makes a good case for taking εὐαγγελίου as a reference to the story of Jesus (what is told, i.e., the good news about and/or brought by Jesus) and as a reference to the Markan narrative itself (the telling of the story). Rejecting the suggestion that ἀρχή indicates the "introduction" (of a book or section) as indemonstrable anywhere in Greek literature, Boring correctly focuses on the term's relation to a "rule," "standard," or "first principle." Thus, the title claims that Mark's narrative is the governing standard for all proclamation of the good news about and/or brought by Jesus. Cf. Keck ("Introduction," 359): "*What Mark is about to tell* as the ἀρχή of the gospel of Jesus Christ refers neither simply to John as the forerunner nor simply to Jesus' own preaching (*ipsissima verba*) but to the Christian gospel that has Jesus as its content and starting-point" (emphasis added). In Mark 1:1 τοῦ εὐαγγελίου Ἰησοῦ Χριστοῦ refers to the salvation that Jesus proclaimed and brought to the world.

18. Mark 1:2 has long been recognized as problematic since it is not found in the extant writings attributed to Isaiah. It is likely a conflation of Mal 3:1a ("See, I am sending my messenger [Messiah?] who will prepare the way before *me* [Yahweh]") and Exod 23:20 ("See, I am sending an angel ahead of you [ancient Israel] to guard you along the way and to bring you to the place I have prepared").

in vv. 2–11 are diagrammed in Tables 1 and 2 at the end of this chapter. The identifications among the figures in this section will be understood differently according to whether or not the reader has prior knowledge of the Hebrew Scriptures quoted by the narrator. Table 1 outlines the associations likely to be constructed by a reader unfamiliar with these quoted prophecies, while Table 2 offers the same analysis assuming the reader's knowledge of these writings.

The configurations in Tables 1 and 2 show the typical connections that readers make between the characters in the prophecy and those in the Markan narrative, especially the identification of the messenger with John the Baptist. Before making the case for this association, however, we give deserved attention to Mary Ann Tolbert's contention that the prophecies adapted and adopted in Mark 1:2–3 are "intended to describe primarily Jesus...."[19]

Tolbert's argument begins with an observation directly related to this chapter's theme:

> The only character in Mark introduced to the audience to whom the Scripture could refer is Jesus: Jesus is named in 1:1, then comes the Isaiah passage in vv. 2–3, and only afterward is John presented in v. 4.[20]

Part of the difficulty here relates to the identity and competence of the reader. If the reader is not familiar with the Hebrew Scriptures, then, *from the vantage point of v. 1*, identification of the messenger with Jesus is the most natural inference to draw from v. 2 (see Table 1).

Even in this case, however, the identification is overturned when the reader encounters John the Baptist performing the stated activities of the messenger (1:4). But the image of Jesus as messenger is not dead; it is only dormant. The primacy effect assures that the reader will subconsciously retain vestiges of this initial parse that are likely to be reinstituted later in the narrative.[21]

In the case where the reader is sufficiently familiar with the original contexts of these quotations, to recognize that the first part of the quote

19. The arguments that are summarized and evaluated here are found in Tolbert, *Sowing the Gospel*, 240–48. Tolbert does admit a secondary reference of the Isaianic prophecy to John the Baptist (240).

20. Ibid.

21. See, e.g., Mark 1:12, where Jesus appears in the desert, and soon (v. 15) is found preaching a repentance message.

is actually a conflation of Exod 23:20 (LXX) (καὶ ἰδοὺ ἐγὼ ἀποστέ–
λλω τὸν ἄγγελόν μου πρὸ προσώπου σου . . .) and (with alteration)
Mal 3:1 (MT) ("See, I will send my messenger, who will prepare the way
before *me*"), the identification of the messenger may remain indefinite
(see Table 2).

In Exod 23:20, the speaker is Yahweh; the messenger is an angel
of Yahweh; and the recipients are Moses *and*, by synecdoche, the entire
Hebrew nation. Thus, on the basis of the intertextual association of Mark
1:2 and Exod 23:20 and the information supplied in Mark 1:1, the reader
could identify the speaker of Mark 1:2 as Yahweh, the messenger as Jesus
(the only character mentioned thus far), and the recipient as him- or
herself. The grid, however, is not tightly closed. Since Moses is the direct
recipient of Yahweh's words in the Exodus citation, Jesus could be the
direct recipient of the similar words in the Markan context, in which
case the identity of the messenger would remain open to question.

The speaker in Mal 3:1 is Yahweh;[22] the messenger is Elijah (cf. Mal
4:5); and the one before whom the messenger is sent is—Yahweh! If the
reader brings this information to bear on Mark 1:1–2, her or his previous
identification of the messenger with Jesus will be called into question.
Identifying the messenger as Elijah forces the reader to associate Jesus
with the recipient ("you"). This opens the reader to the identification of
Jesus with Yahweh, since the "me" (referring to Yahweh) of Mal 3:1a has
been changed to "you" (referring to Jesus) in Mark 1:2. In this case, the
question of the messenger's identity is also left open.

That the reader would have the energy or the competence to complete this circuitously complex cerebration is certainly questionable.
Nevertheless, the scenario presented does account for the possible data
that could be utilized in this narrative exchange and the sequential program according to which these data would be taken into account.

Tolbert adds several other objections to taking John the Baptist
as the referent of the Scriptural quotations in Mark 1:2–3. First, she
maintains that taking John as the messenger makes Jesus the one before
whom John is sent and therefore involves a confusing switch of nar-
ratees from the reader (1:1) to Jesus (1:2). This is true if one sees καθὼς
γέγραπται as a clause connecting 1:1 with 1:2. If, however, 1:1 is seen
as a title (either to the entire book or to the initial section), the switch

---

22. Malachi identifies Yahweh as the speaker in 1:1, 4b, 6c, 8d, 9, 10, 11b, 13a, b, 14b;
2:2, 4, 8b, 16a, b; 3:1c, 5c, 6, 7b, 11b, 12b, 13, 17; 4:1d, 3b.

presents no such difficulty for the reader who, in this case, is permitted to eavesdrop on the conversation between God and Jesus.[23]

Second, Tolbert argues that identification of the messenger with John suggests that Jesus is the recipient of the prophecy and thus yields an unusual interpretation of prophecy since it has a prophet speaking for God to God's Son rather than to the people or the leaders of the people. This argument does indeed make identifying Jesus with the messenger more likely than identifying him with the recipient of the prophecy. But even if the messenger is taken to be John the Baptist, the identification of Jesus as recipient of the prophecy is not required. The references to σου in v. 2—in spite of being singular—can be identified equally well with the reader.[24]

Third, connecting these quotations with John the Baptist requires that v. 2 start with καθὼς γέγραπται, a phrase that, when used to introduce a scriptural quotation, "*never* appears at the start of a new sentence."[25] Robert Guelich maintains that the function of this introductory phrase "consists in forming a bridge between what has preceded and the quotation that follows. The formula and quotation *always refer back and never forward* in the context."[26] This also is a tenable argument in favor of the reader's initial tendency to identify the messenger as Jesus. But nothing in this argument precludes the possibility that καθὼς could begin a new sentence. Boring, for example, argues that "the clause begin-

---

23. As Boring ("Mark 1:11–15," 60) puts it: "The reader gets to overhear the voice of God addressing *Jesus*, the one whose way is to be prepared, and . . . this one is then called κύριος, a title never given to Jesus in the body of the narrative. . . . [T]he reader knows that Jesus is the Lord in the Messianic sense, from 1:3 onward, but the characters in the narrative do not know this" (emphasis original).

24. Tolbert (*Sowing the Gospel*, 242) argues that the singular "you" can appropriately refer to the audience on two possible grounds: (1) the authorial audience may be taken as a "corporate personality, a communal singularity in which the part represents the whole (synecdoche)"; or (2) the author may have "imagined the gospel message to be aimed at individuals." Tolbert presents Mark's widely recognized "wink" to the reader, ὁ ἀναγινώσκων νοείτω (13:14) as "the only possible evidence to decide the issue. . ." (ibid.). It may be objected, however, that although a singular "reader" is addressed here, the substantive, ὁ ἀναγινώσκων, may refer not to the audience, but to the one who reads the narrative to the audience. On this, see Fowler, *Let the Reader Understand*, 83–85; Kennedy, *New Testament Interpretation*, 5–6; BDAG, s.v. ἀναγινώσκω; and *Oxford Classical Dictionary*, s.v. "anagnostes" and "recitatio."

25. Guelich, "Beginning of the Gospel," 6 (emphasis original).

26. Ibid. (emphasis added).

ning with καθώς is best construed with what follows . . ."[27] He excuses the awkwardness of the καθώς construction as Mark's attempt to keep John the Baptist subordinate to Jesus even though the Baptist appears on the scene first. This "complicated and somewhat awkward opening sentence," according to Boring,

> allows Jesus the κύριος, "Lord," to be addressed "offstage" by the transcendent voice of God before the plotted narrative begins. The result is that when John appears in 1:4 his identity and significance are *already* determined by his relation to Jesus, not vice versa.[28]

Fourth, as a corollary to her previous argument, Tolbert adds that separating καθώς γέγραπται from v. 1 makes ἀρχή, that "always pertains either to the immediate introduction of a literary work or the actual beginning of the main section,"[29] a title for the whole narrative.[30] Though meritorious, this argument does not take sufficient account of the semantic range of ἀρχή, that "always signifies 'primacy,' whether in time: 'beginning,' *principium*, or in rank: 'power,' 'dominion,' 'office.'"[31] From the perspective of time, it can mark the point in a temporal sequence at which something new commences,[32] or it can convey the origin or source of something (as a kind of "first cause").[33] From the perspective of rank, it can denote "powers," "authorities," "rulers," or it can suggest fundamental or foundational principles (i.e., "groundwork," "elementary teaching").[34] Assaying these senses of ἀρχή in the context of Mark 1:1 is sufficient to show that ἀρχὴ τοῦ εὐαγγελίου Ἰησοῦ Χριστοῦ υἱοῦ

---

27. Boring, "Mark 1:11–15," 50.

28. Ibid., 60 (emphasis original).

29. Guelich, "Beginning of the Gospel," 8. Cf. Boring ("Mark 1:11–15," 51): "'introduction' (of a document or book) is not among the definitions of ἀρχή given in Liddell and Scott (1953)." See also ibid., 70 n. 14.

30. Tolbert, *Sowing the Gospel*, 243. See also Aune (*New Testament*, 17): "Ancient literary parallels indicate that Mark 1:1 is not a book title ('beginning' means the point at which the narrative starts)." However, he offers no supporting evidence.

31. Delling, ἀρχή, 1:479.

32. Ibid.

33. Bietenhard, "Beginning," 1:166.

34. Ibid.

Θεοῦ need not be taken as a title to the whole narrative, even if the καθὼς γέγραπται clause is separated from v. 1.[35]

Finally, if John is the messenger and Jesus is the one before whom he is sent, then the "crying voice" and the "Lord" are also John and Jesus respectively. But, according to Tolbert, the identification of Jesus with "Lord" is an

> odd assumption . . . , for in every other scriptural quotation that employs κύριος ("Lord") in the Gospel, the referent is clearly God in distinction from Jesus (e.g., 11:9; 12:11, 29, 30, 36, 37).[36]

Tolbert's observation is significant. Nevertheless, Jesus as "Lord" is not an unthinkable schema for Mark's implied reader. Cranfield claims:

> By the time [Mark] was writing . . . Κύριος was a regular title for Jesus, and O.T. passages in which Κύριος represents the Tetragrammaton were being referred to Jesus (e.g., Joel ii.32 in Rom. x.13).[37]

Moreover, the very configuration of vv. 1–3 could be explained as a rhetorical ploy that moves the reader to consider the possibility that Jesus is Lord.

Tolbert is to be commended for her treatment of the opening verses of Mark's Gospel. Many would hesitate to challenge the timeworn association of the "messenger" in v. 2 with John the Baptist. Especially noteworthy for the present context is the fact that this interpretation stems from a narrative approach, and, in particular, one that gives attention to narrative sequence.

In view of the preceding arguments, how did John the Baptist become so firmly identified with τὸν ἄγγελον of Mark 1:2? The answer

---

35. E.g., Isaiah's prophecy may be seen as the origin or foundational principle behind the good news about and/or brought by Jesus. But this kind of argument is not nearly as reasonable as that of Boring. Boring sees ἀρχή and κανών as close relatives. If ἀρχή is seen as "rule" or "standard" and describes Mark's telling of the story (εὐαγγέλιον, i.e., God's action in Christ), then 1:1 would be an appropriate title for the whole narrative. "It is clear," says Boring ("Mark 1:1–15," 53), "that Mark composes a narrative which he intends to function as a normative statement for preaching the εὐαγγέλιον Ἰησοῦ Χριστοῦ, and that his way of doing this is to narrate the events that form the ἀρχή of this preaching, i.e., their beginning and foundation. He expresses this by carefully choosing as the first word of his title for his whole composition a word that means not only 'beginning,' and 'first principle,' but 'rule, norm.'"

36. Tolbert, *Sowing the Gospel*, 245.

37. Cranfield, *Mark*, 40.

lies partly in the influence of the later Gospels[38] and partly in what follows in the Markan narrative. Our interest lies primarily in the latter.

The quotation from Isa 40:3 (in 1:3) helps the reader to fit the pieces together. The "messenger" is described as a "crying voice in the desert" calling for repentance. This makes clear the link with John the Baptist, who in the following verse is found "in the desert" preaching a repentance-baptism. The reader thus identifies the messenger of v. 2 with John the Baptist. This identification is strengthened by vv. 5–7 where John is described in the prophetic mode of Elijah and fulfills the essential prediction related in v. 2.

The "you" of v. 2 is paralleled with the "Lord" (v. 3), the "mightier than I" (v. 7), and the "Coming One who will baptize with the Holy Spirit" (v. 8). The appearance of Jesus immediately after the prediction in v. 8 strongly suggests him as the fulfillment of the predictions in the previous verses. This identification is strengthened by the appearance of the Holy Spirit in connection with Jesus at the latter's baptism in v. 10.[39] Finally, the appellative "Son" in v. 11 points back to the heading in v. 1 and thus reminds the reader that Jesus stands in a special relationship with God.

By now it should be apparent that Mark does not intend to spell out everything for the reader. Rather, he has left a number of clues that enable the reader to navigate amidst a rubble of ambiguities and invite the reader to accept the narrator's (= protagonist's) ideology. In terms of the grid-making process, the reader has taken the narrator's bait by construing Jesus as the messenger in v. 2, only to have this schema overturned by four clear parallels to John the Baptist: he is in the desert; his dress and diet parallel Elijah's; he is crying out; and he is preaching a repentance-baptism (vv. 4–6).

As soon as the reader's grid has been adjusted to fit these data, however, he or she encounters Jesus, the original choice for messenger, preaching repentance in the desert. The hints are more subtle here, and while they are not sufficiently dominant to cause the reader

---

38. For a brief but helpful treatment of the influence of the later Gospels, see Tolbert, *Sowing the Gospel*, 241, esp. n. 7.

39. That Mark's Jesus nowhere baptizes in the Holy Spirit illustrates the rhetoric of indirection. Uncertainty as to whether he will fulfill this role is allowed to linger in the reader's mind. Nevertheless, the very appearance of the Holy Spirit with Jesus points in that direction.

to rework the grid, they are commanding enough to color the remainder of the narrative with the notion that Jesus is in some sense a messenger from God.[40]

But the effect of these anachronies may go deeper. The "good news" *about* Jesus Christ and the "good news" *brought by* Jesus Christ are linked to a time outside of the story world of Mark's narrative. The quotation from Exod 23:20 concerned a promised messenger who would provide direction and protection en route to the Land of Promise. The quotations from Isa 40:3 and Mal 3:1 concerned a messenger who would bring judgment. Is the coming messenger bringing deliverance or judgment? The ambiguity allows the reader to form a schema that includes both possibilities. Thus, at the outset of the narrative, we can see a distinction between "insiders" and "outsiders." This frame colors the interpretation of the entire Gospel.

The positioning of these anachronies at the beginning of the narrative produces an initially positive and powerful image of the protagonist.[41] Beginning, as he does, *in medias res*, Mark never pictures Jesus at the weakest, most helpless moment of his life; the infant in a feeding trough (Luke 2:12, 16) simply has no place in his narrative.[42] Rather, Jesus is "the Mightier One" (1:7), divinely affirmed to be the Son of God in his introductory scene (1:11).

In his survey of critical theory on narrative beginnings, Mikeal Parsons notes the power of the primacy effect:

> Giving or withholding information can be used to create certain
> first impressions and the primacy effect of those first expressions

40. Mark's narrative sets up a polyvalence that lingers in the reader's mind: If Jesus is the messenger, he is the one sent to prepare the reader's "way"; if John is the messenger, he is the one sent to prepare Jesus' way. If Jesus is the recipient of the message from the voice of God, then John is the messenger and parallels Elijah in function and Jesus is one before whom the messenger is sent and parallels Yahweh.

41. Tolbert (*Sowing the Gospel*, 111) argues that the aural features of Mark's opening lay stress on its importance. Noting the recurrence of the -ου termination in vv. 1–3, she writes: "The whole unit is given stately, liturgical tone through the use of rhyming devices. . . . Such rhyming enhances the formality of the narrator's opening address to the reader and intensifies the distanced, authoritative weight of the words themselves."

42. The closest Mark comes to showing a "weakness" of Jesus is in 6:5 where he relates that οὐκ ἐδύνατο ἐκεῖ ποιῆσαι οὐδεμίαν δύναμιν, but even here he hastens to add εἰ μὴ ὀλίγοις ἀρρώστοις ἐπιθεὶς τάς χεῖρας ἐθεράπευσεν. Moreover, the idea that the problem with healing is due to some weakness of Jesus is not at all clear. Indeed, Mark offers another factor in the next sentence: ἁμαρτίαν αὐτῶν.

insures that the reader will cling to those first thoughts as long as the narrative will possibly allow.[43]

In the case of Mark's narrative, the opening presents a powerful Jesus, and nothing in the remainder of the narrative overturns this notion. Even when Jesus undergoes humiliating death on a cross, he is not pictured as weak in himself; he has voluntarily and courageously chosen this course. The predictions of Jesus' passion in the narrative world prepare the reader just as these same predictions in the story world were intended to prepare the disciples.

The point is clear. Although Jesus is powerful, he operates from a position of weakness, servanthood, and self-sacrifice. He calls disciples, but not to enhance his ego; he performs miracles, but not to achieve wealth or fame; he outwits law scholars, but not to display his acumen. Rather, he lives to bring people wholeness of life. His life is the quintessential paradigm for operating in the "things of God" mode.

Prophecies of "Isaiah," John, and Jesus: Mark 1:2, 8, 17

The opening section of Mark's Gospel contains other anachronies. Norman Petersen notes that although each of the three figures appearing in Mark's opening verses utters predictions ("Isaiah" in v. 2; John in vv. 7 and 8; and Jesus in v. 17), only the predictions of Isaiah and John find fulfillment in the plotted time of the narrative. As Petersen puts it,

43. Parsons, "Reading a Beginning," 20. Parsons notes that the label "primacy effect" was coined in psychological studies and later adopted by Sternberg, Perry, Rimmon-Kenan and others, who do not necessarily base it on the actual experience of "flesh-and-blood" readers (Parsons, 21, 27 n. 3). Marrou's classic, *A History of Education in Antiquity*, esp. 160–70, 277–81, underscores the keen attention that Greek and Roman education devoted to character analysis. This approach was not only applied to the classics, but to historiography as well. Weeden, who uses the Greco-Roman emphasis on character analysis as a foundational principle for the approach he employs in *Mark: Traditions in Conflict*, reminds his readers that as early as the fourth century BCE Greek historians were writing "not so much in the interest of accurate information as in the interest of guiding the reader to a moralistic interpretation of the world. In this way history was used to inspire him to emulate the lives of the virtuous and to disdain the lives of the corrupt" (15). Sternberg (*Expositional Modes*, 96) notes how the primacy effect operates *vis-à-vis* character portrayal: if initial representations of a character are positive and negative qualities appear only later in the story, the reader is likely to view him as "a good fellow with some human frailties"; if the identical character representations are given in reverse order, the same character would likely appear as "an ugly customer surprisingly possessed of a few attractive or redeeming traits." This kind of analysis is instructive in the case of Jesus and the disciples.

> Isaiah predicted something and John's appearance fulfilled it;
> John predicted something and Jesus' appearance fulfilled it; Jesus
> predicted something and . . . and what?[44]

Petersen has rightly identified a narrative gap that creates suspense, but his analysis oversimplifies the textual data. John's immediate appearance does fulfill Isaiah's prediction of a coming messenger. Likewise, Jesus' sudden appearance fulfills John's prediction of the coming of "one mightier than he." The ordering of these prolepses and the immediate narration of their apparent fulfillment sets the reader up to expect a similarly prompt fulfillment of the third. The narrative, however, overturns this expectation and leaves the reader hanging.

But the narrative strategy is not as clean as Petersen makes it. John also claimed that the Coming One would baptize with the Holy Spirit (1:8),[45] and although the scene that immediately follows includes Jesus, the Holy Spirit, and a baptism, Jesus is himself baptized in water rather than baptizing others with the Holy Spirit. Thus, John's prediction is at least partially unfulfilled.

Moreover, Petersen's schematic diagram of 1:1–15 treats Jesus' affirmation, πεπλήρωται ὁ καιρὸς καὶ ἤγγικεν ἡ βασιλεία τοῦ θεοῦ· μετανοεῖτε καὶ πιστεύετε ἐν τῷ εὐαγγελίῳ (v. 15), as a prediction. But the rules of grammar do not require it to be taken in a future sense. The meaning of ἤγγικεν ἡ βασιλεία τοῦ θεοῦ has long been a matter for critical debate.[46] Part of the reason for this controversy may be attributed to the ambiguity in the verb ἠγγίζω, which has both a present ("has arrived") and future ("has drawn near," that is, "is imminent") sense. Although Dodd's proposal to translate it in the former sense is linguistically a remote possibility, the dual sense of this verb gives rise to an element of uncertainty. Even if ἠγγίζω never carried the sense of "has come," ambiguity would remain since the proximity implied by the translation "has drawn near" may be spatial as well as temporal.[47] All this demonstrates that in terms of prediction fulfillment this "predic-

44. Petersen, *Literary Criticism*, 53.

45. Petersen notes this prediction earlier (ibid., 51), but does not include it in his schematic plotting of 1:1–15.

46. For an overview of research on this topic see, e.g., Goppelt, *Theology of the NT*, 1:51–55.

47. Kümmel ("Naherwartung," 31–46) argues that the perfect tense ἤγγικεν denotes "it has drawn near" in all NT contexts that employ it.

tion" of Jesus is not tightly closed. Indeed, its open-endedness kindles the reader's curiosity regarding God's kingdom.

Jesus' invitation to Simon and Andrew, Δεῦτε ὀπίσω μου, καὶ ποιήσω ὑμᾶς γενέσθαι ἁλιεῖς ἀνθρώπων (v. 17), however, does, with v. 18, amount to a clear prediction. Jesus promises that he will make Simon and Andrew fishers of men *if they will follow him*.[48] The narrator immediately adds καί εὐθὺς ἀφέντες τὰ δίκτυα ἠκολούθησαν αὐτῷ (v. 18), fulfilling the condition related in the implied protasis. But nothing is said of fishing for men! The reader is left hanging.

Both the meaning of "fishers of men" and the precise nature of the fulfillment of Jesus' prediction are mysteries that the reader can fit into her or his incipient grid only with the subsequent information provided by the text. Thus, Petersen's basic point stands: suspense is achieved. But the suspense is at least as much related to the baptizing with the Holy Spirit and the fishing for men as it is to the coming of the kingdom of God.[49] Thus, the predictions of Isaiah, John, and Jesus display a pattern of increasing open-endedness.

The concept of fishing for men fits well with the narrative's emphasis on discipleship and may receive uptake at a number of points in the remainder of the narrative (e.g., the appointing of the Twelve [3:13–14], the testimony before governors [13:9], the proclamation of the gospel [13:10; 14:9], the sending out of the Twelve "two by two" [6:7], and even the sowing of seed [4:3–20, 26, 31]).

The appointing of the Twelve (3:13–15) gives the reader the first glimpse of what Jesus has in mind for his followers since his promise to make Simon and Andrew "fishers of men" in 1:17. Thus, 3:13–15 expresses literally what was expressed metaphorically in 1:17. And since 3:13–15 describes Jesus' intention for his disciples, it also functions as a prolepsis pointing to a future time when Jesus' disciples will in fact preach and drive out demons.

---

48. See Robertson, *Grammar*, 1022–23. Robertson treats this verse under the heading of "implied conditions." Thus, in 1:17, "the imperative is used where a protasis might have been employed" (1023).

49. Spirit-baptism, kingdom-citizenship, and people-fishing are important features that the Markan narrative presents to the reader for processing. Any quest for *the* central theme of Mark must not overlook the intimate solidarity among them. On these themes, see particularly Best, *Following Jesus*; Kelber, *Kingdom of God*; Mansfield, "*Spirit and Gospel.*"

The scarcity and covertness of references to the actual evangelistic activity of the disciples serve only to intensify the reader's curiosity regarding Jesus' prediction that the disciples (specifically Simon and Andrew)[50] would be fishers of men. Mark 6:7–13 and 9:18 are the only places in the narrative where disciples actually engage in what might be called "fishing for men." Even in these cases the activity takes place off-stage. In Mark 6:7–13, the reader is *told* that they went out and preached and drove out demons, but he or she is not *shown* the action in process. In 9:18, the reader learns via an analepsis of the disciples' attempt and failure to expel an unclean spirit, but this activity is neither shown nor told.[51]

The remaining allusions to the evangelistic activity of the disciples (13:9–10; 14:9) are prolepses that find no fulfillment in the narrative. Nevertheless, these references do keep alive the reader's curiosity regarding Jesus' prediction and serve to intensify the effect of the ending in 16:8b: καὶ οὐδενὶ οὐδὲν εἶπαν, ἐφοβοῦντο γάρ. Thus, the reader is invited to take up the role abandoned by the disciples and become the ideal disciple.

The utter abandonment of Jesus at the narrative's end is not incomprehensible. The narrator frequently relates incidents of opposition that come on the heels of Jesus' calls to discipleship. The one place where the reader is clearly informed that the disciples engaged in evangelistic activity (6:12–13) is immediately followed by the analepsis regarding Herod and John (6:14–29). John preached that Herod should repent (6:18; cf. 6:12) and was horribly executed. What lies in store for Jesus' disciples?

The execution scene is immediately followed by an analepsis that informs the reader that the disciples had been evangelizing: Καὶ συνάγονται οἱ ἀπόστολοι πρός τὸν Ἰησοῦν, καὶ ἀπήγγειλαν αὐτῷ πάντα ὅσα ἐποίησαν καὶ ὅσα ἐδίδαξαν (6:30). Thus, the anachrony relating the death of John the Baptist is intercalated into a context describing the disciples engaged in evangelization. The effect of this narrative arrangement is intensified by the account of the feeding of the five

---

50. The text does not reveal the content of the appeal made to the other disciples. With no evidence to the contrary, the reader fills the gap by incorporating the "fishing for men" schema from the Simon-Andrew call.

51. On mimesis ("showing") and diegesis ("telling"), see Funk, *Poetics of Biblical Narrative*, 134–61. For fuller treatments of the distinction, see Genette, *Narrative Discourse*, 161–211; idem, *Figures of Literary Discourse*; Chatman, *Story and Discourse*, 32–34 and chs. 4–5; Rimmon-Kenan, *Narrative Fiction*, 71–85, 106–16.

thousand, where emphasis is placed on the responsibility of the disciples to meet the needs they observe (6:34–44).[52] This narrative arrangement implies (1) that disciples have the charge of ministering to people's needs and (2) that their ministry may result in persecution.

Mark frequently links the call to discipleship with allusions or illustrations that warn the reader of the consequences of responding positively to that call.

Jesus himself, the ultimate model for discipleship, is opposed in the incident that immediately follows 3:14–16. Specifically, his family says he's out of his mind (3:21), and the religious scholars say he is possessed by Beelzebub (3:22). When he performs other actions that are to be part of the ideal disciple's role, he again encounters resistance. In 5:2–17, he frees a man from demon possession and the townspeople plead with him to leave their region. He later heals a woman of a hemorrhage (5:34) and restores life to a dead girl (5:41), but the reactions he gets are far from complimentary ("they laughed at him" [5:40] and "they took offense at him" [6:3]). Thus, even before Jesus begins to talk directly about the suffering nature of his task (8:31), the reader is aware of the association of suffering with discipleship.

Mark offers three primary prolepses in the prophecies of Isaiah, John the Baptist, and Jesus. They are narrated in a sequence that displays increasing open-endedness. Isaiah predicts a coming messenger; John's appearance fulfills the prediction. John predicts the coming of "One mightier than he"; Jesus' arrival fulfills the prediction. The fulfillment of Isaiah's and John's predictions primes the reader to expect the fulfillment of Jesus' promise to make the disciples fishers of men. The fact that the disciples do not fulfill this promise encourages the reader to fulfill it. The text thus solicits the reader to think the things of God, using Jesus as the model.

John the Baptist: Mark 1:14

The reference to John's imprisonment in Mark 1:14 is an internal analepsis that looks back to an event in the story world not previously related in the narrative world. Both the narrative gap it follows and the narrative gap it creates illustrate the selective characteristic of language discussed

---

52. Note esp. the ὑμεῖς in Jesus' command, δότε αὐτοῖς ὑμεῖς φαγεῖν (v. 37). Though unnecessary for grammatical sense, ὑμεῖς suggests emphasis on the responsibility of the disciples.

in chapter 2. What effect does this narrative arrangement have on the reader?

Mark 1:14 immediately follows the narrative segment that informs the reader that Satan tempted Jesus. However, regarding the details (and outcome!) of the temptation, the narrator is completely silent.[53] Mark's reader will negotiate the gap in one of two ways. The reader familiar with the story of Jesus will give greater attention to *how* Jesus defeated Satan, whereas the reader unfamiliar with the story of Jesus will be concerned to find out *if* Jesus defeated Satan.[54] For the former, the Gospel is primarily didactic; for the latter, evangelistic.

But the disjuncture at 1:14 creates a narrative gap of its own. Nothing in the narrative prepares the reader for the incarceration of John. The reader unfamiliar with the story of Jesus is completely taken by surprise. The narrator alludes to John's imprisonment, but gives no details regarding its cause or outcome. This information is delayed until 6:14–29 where it is more directly linked with the activity and fate of the disciples.[55]

53. Even in the Markan absence of a declaration of victory (cf. Matt 4:1–11 and Luke 4:1–13, which clearly *show* Jesus as victor, although Luke hints that the issue is not settled: . . . ὁ διάβολος ἀπέστη ἀπ᾽ αὐτοῦ ἄρχι καιροῦ [4:13]), ascertaining the outcome of the temptation scene is not an insurmountable challenge for Mark's reader, esp. a first-century reader. In Mark's account the temptation scene is immediately followed by Jesus' proclaiming the εὐαγγέλιον τοῦ θεοῦ. Friedrich ("εὐαγγελίζομαι," 710) demonstrates that εὐαγγελίζομαι predominately was used to proclaim news of victory: "The εὐάγγελος comes from the field of battle by ship . . . , by horse . . . , or as ἡμεροδρομήσας, as a swift runner, and proclaims to the anxiously awaiting city the victory of the army, and the death or capture of the enemy . . ." Friedrich claims that "εὐαγγέλιον is a technical term for 'news of victory'" (722) and is often found with σωτερία (711). Keck ("Introduction to Mark's Gospel," 362) observes that in Mark's presentation πειρασθῆναι carries the forensic sense of "trial" or "testing" rather than the moralistic connotation of "temptation" that it carries elsewhere (cf. Matthew and Luke). For Keck, "Mark regards Jesus' encounter with Satan . . . as a power-struggle in which Jesus is victorious" (361). The point of all this is that the outcome of the "trial" is not explicitly stated in Mark; the reader is required to deduce this from the subsequent narrative clues.

54. Modern broadcasting of a boxing match may provide a helpful analogy. One who watches a videotaped replay of the match after having learned the outcome is more attentive to the strategies that brought victory to the winner and the errors that brought defeat to the loser. The one who watches the match live looks for clues that will help predict the outcome.

55. See below. This point is significant even for the reader who has heard previously the story of the Baptist's death. The fact that its narration is delayed until after the narration of the sending of the Twelve makes likely the connection between the fate of the Baptist and the fate of the disciples.

The immediate effect of the allusion to the Baptist's imprisonment is to move John offstage and Jesus to center stage, a position that he occupies for the remainder of the narrative. Nevertheless, since the narrator has already established a close connection between the roles of Jesus and John, a certain degree of suspense regarding John lingers in the background.

As an actor in the story, John is never heard from again. Nevertheless, he is kept in the mind of the reader by brief references at significant points of the narrative. These occur both before (2:18) and after (8:28; 11:30, 32) the reader learns of his death (6:14). The effect on the reader differs accordingly.

The first of these references maintains the suspense regarding the Baptist's fate, and, linked with Jesus' response (2:19) to the question of why his disciples did not have the habit of fasting (2:18), may even hint at his demise. Jesus argued that disciples do not fast when the teacher is with them. This response not only explains why Jesus' disciples were not fasting, but also hints that John was no longer with his disciples, since the questioners affirmed that John's disciples were fasting.

Although death is not the only possible explanation for John's separation from his disciples,[56] it is probable in view of Jesus' subsequent prediction, "the time will come when the bridegroom will be taken from them, and on that day they will fast" (2:20). This internal prolepsis, though veiled, is the first of Jesus' predictions of his passion, the culmination of which is not narrated until 15:37.

The references to John that follow the Herod incident remind the reader of the Baptist's death.[57] The first of these (8:28) functions as an internal analepsis pointing back to the same triad of responses to the question of Jesus' identity narrated in 6:14–16. The repetition of these labels for Christ shows Jesus' identity to be a central issue for Mark.[58] The Herod-Baptist analepsis highlights the Baptist's death and, since the close link between the roles of Jesus and John has already been made in the introductory section of the narrative, suspicion regarding the destiny of Jesus increases.

---

56. Imprisonment itself involves separation, yet it is likely that John had some contact with his disciples even when he was in prison.

57. Cf. 6:14 where Herod thinks Jesus is John the Baptist raised from the dead.

58. Hurtado, *Mark*, 134.

The two-stage healing of the blind man (8:22–26) that immediately precedes this recognition scene metaphorically parallels a growth in understanding [59] and sparks the reader's expectation that the dim-witted disciples will finally catch on to Jesus' identity and mission.[60] Peter's response to Jesus' first open prediction of his passion shows a literary parallel with the first stage of the healing of the blind man. In 8:29, he affirms that Jesus is the Christ, but his balking at Jesus' passion prediction shows that he did not fully understand the role of the Christ. He saw Christ in his kingly role, but was blind to the necessity of his suffering. His understanding of Jesus was as cloudy as the eyes of the blind man before the second stage of his healing.

The remaining references to John the Baptist (11:30, 32) not only remind the reader of his connection with Jesus but also call to mind his brutal execution. Verses 27–33 introduce the parable of the vineyard and supply information vital to its interpretation. Specifically, the placement of these analepses primes the reader for seeing John, who received a head wound (6:27: καὶ ἀπελθὼν ἀπεκεφάλισεν αὐτὸν, cf. 12:4: κἀκεῖνον ἐκεφαλίωσαν) and was treated shamefully (6:28: καὶ ἤνεγκεν τὴν κεφαλὴν αὐτοῦ ἐπὶ πίνακι, cf. 12:4: κἀκεῖνον . . . ἠτίμασαν), and Jesus (1:11: υἱός . . . ἀγαπητός, cf. 12:6: υἱὸν ἀγαπητόν) as the natural referents of key characters in the parable that follows.[61]

In summary, the analepsis to John's imprisonment in 1:14 is the first of a series of analeptic references to him. The contexts in which these occur and the parallels drawn between John and Jesus provide the

---

59. See Mark 8:17–19, where a clear link is made between understanding and physical sight. This sets the reader up for taking the blind man's recovery of sight as a metaphor for the opening of one's understanding.

60. The disciples' participation in the feeding miracle in 6:35–44 makes their incomprehension of the second feeding incident in 8:1–9a, the pinnacle of their stupidity. They are as ignorant of Jesus' identity as the blind man of the following scene is of Jesus' physical appearance.

61. Houck ("Why New Testament Scholars," 10–12) analyzes Mark's presentation of Jesus and John from the standpoint of narrative sequence. In view of the witness of the other Gospels, which present the ministries of Jesus and John as contemporaneous, Hock views Mark's narration of the Baptist's ministry first as born of a conscious decision. He compares the roles of John and Jesus to those of Astylos and Dionysophanes (in Longus' *Daphnis and Chloe*) and argues that "by placing the activity of John before that of Jesus, and both before the expected judgment of God, Mark has presented their activities as analogous in the divine sphere to the human roles of slave messenger and son who precede the visit of a householder to his estate" (11).

reader with data to construct the schema of τὰ τοῦ θεοῦ. The individual acclimated to the "things of God" operates from a position of weakness, as reflected in the suffering that both John and Jesus endured. Again, these temporal disjunctions serve to highlight and promote the narrator's ideology.

Binding the Strongman: Mark 3:27

Mark 3:27 provides another interesting example of anachrony: ἀλλ οὐ δύναται οὐδεὶς εἰς τὴν οἰκίαν τοῦ ἰσχυροῦ εἰσελθὼν τὰ σκεύη αὐτοῦ διαρπάσαι ἐάν μὴ πρῶτον τὸν ἰσχυρὸν δήσῃ ..." The inflection of αὐτοῦ admits τοῦ ἰσχυροῦ or τὴν οἰκίαν as possible referents. Accordingly, the first part of this sentence concerns the plunder either of *his* (that is, the strongman's) goods or *its* (that is, the house's) goods.[62] Both senses are appropriate for the chronological sequence of the first two elements (entrance—plundering), but the latter more clearly so, since one must enter a house in order to remove its contents.

The logical arrangement in which entrance precedes burglary is disrupted by the displacement of the third element (the binding of the owner). Entrance must precede burglary. Nevertheless, having entered a house, a thief must first bind the owner; only then can he plunder his possessions.[63] In the narrative order, however, the plundering of possessions appears first and only afterwards is thought given to the fact that the house may be occupied. Thus, taken together, the three segments of this brief episode appear in an order that is neither logical nor chronological.

At first, this inverted order seems to place emphasis on robbing the goods rather than subjugating the strongman. But such is not the case. Indeed, the phrase that immediately follows rectifies the order: καὶ τότε τὴν οἰκίαν αὐτοῦ διαρπάσει. But why does Mark add it? It supplies no new information. Should we view this redundancy as an illustration of the "clumsy construction" of which Bultmann, Meagher, Trocmé, and others have spoken? Or is Mark employing a literary device designed to highlight a critical point? The latter hypothesis is preferable.

---

62. That the *house* is plundered in the redundant phrase, καὶ τότε τὴν οἰκίαν αὐτοῦ διαρπάσει, may support the latter of these alternatives.

63. It is unlikely that a householder would stand idly by and watch his goods being carted off, and far less likely that he would assist the burglar in packing up his goods.

In the absence of modern conventions for emphasizing selected portions of written materials (for example, bold-facing, italicizing, underlining, quotation marks), ancient writers occasionally sandwiched materials they wished to emphasize between similar words or phrases, employing a narrative technique known as *inclusio*. In Mark 3:27, the expressions for plundering (τὰ σκεύη αὐτοῦ διαρπάσαι . . . τὴν οἰκίαν αὐτοῦ διαρπάσει) form an *inclusio* that focuses the reader's attention on the intervening material (ἐὰν μὴ πρῶτον τὸν ἰσχυρὸν δήσῃ). In this way, the narrative throws the spotlight on the binding of the strongman.

But what schema does the "strongman" call forth? Within the parable (second-degree narrative) the connection is clear, since the episode contains only one actor, namely, Satan. From this perspective, v. 27 implies that Jesus (ὁ ἰσχυρότερος, 1:7) has bound (at the temptation, 1:13?) Satan (τὸν ἰσχυρὸν, 3:27) and is carrying off his vessels (τὰ σκεύη αὐτοῦ, cf. 1:15, 27, 34, 39; 3:11).[64] But further support of this view can be found in the first-degree narrative. In the section that relates the setting for this parable, the one who "enters a house" is Jesus.[65] Nevertheless, at the first-degree level of narrative a competing schema also emerges. While vv. 28–30 create an awkward change after Jesus' parable in the second-degree narrative, these verses fit quite well in the first degree narrative.[66] Mark tries to smooth the transition with an anachronistic explanatory ὅτι clause: ὅτι ἔλεγον, Πνεῦμα ἀκάθαρτον ἔχει. In this "wink" to the reader, he recalls the charge of demon possession that induced Jesus' parable. But this charge is immediately preceded by the disparaging assessment of Jesus' mental state made by his family.[67]

64. Σκεῦος produces at least two lexical frames: a general sense, "possessions," or a more restricted sense, "vessels." In the schema that sees Jesus as the one who binds the strongman, the latter seems the more appropriate, since the references cited are primarily instances of the deliverance of those who were formerly "vessels" for the unclean spirits.

65. This is true even if the less probable variant ἔρχονται is original. Jesus is not only part of this group but also its leader.

66. Tolbert, *Sowing the Gospel*, 100.

67. Fowler (*Let the Reader Understand*, 200) describes Mark's use of the phrase οἱ παρ᾽ αὐτοῦ as "artful ambiguity." From the standpoint of narrative sequence, all the reader knows about this group is that they have some special relation to Jesus, either "companions/associates," or "relatives." Fowler argues that this ambiguity holds the reader in suspense until the end of the scene where Jesus' "associates" are discovered to be his family (201).

Furthermore, immediately prior to that, the reader encounters an internal prolepsis regarding the betrayal of Judas (3:19).

Each of these frames suggests Jesus as the referent of the "strongman." Moreover, the parable itself is bounded on the other end by another reference to Jesus' family that reflects a degree of distance between him and them (3:31). Thus, vv. 21 and 31 form an *inclusio* that highlights the division within Jesus' "house" and makes identification of Jesus with the "strongman" even more plausible.[68] The schema that sees Jesus as the strongman who is being bound reads more than a touch of irony in Jesus' words: καὶ ἐὰν οἰκία ἐφ᾽ ἑαυτὴν μερισθῇ, οὐ δυνήσεται ἡ οἰκία ἐκείνη σταθῆναι (3:25).

Both frames for the strongman find support in the Markan narrative. In his typical fashion, the author presents multiple schemata that the reader can use as grids to interpret the subsequent narrative material. Jesus is the first referent of ἰσχυρός (1:7–9) but later, Satan (3:23–27). The polyvalence causes the reader to ambivalate between the two frames. The Satan-as-bound-strongman schema eventually supersedes (Jesus is "loosed" by resurrection), but only after further oscillation.

One noticeable cue suggesting Satan as the strongman who is bound, is found in the pericope of the Gerasene demoniac (5:1–20). The analepses in vv. 3–5 supply details that, though unnecessary from the standpoint of logical flow, nevertheless encourage the reader to process the incident of the demoniac begun in 5:1 with the strongman schemata as a backdrop. The main verbs of these verses (εἶχεν, ἐδύνατο, δεδέσθαι, διεσπάσθαι, συντετρῖφθαι, ἴσχυεν, ἦν κράζων . . . κατακόπτων) signal the narrative pause,[69] while the position and content of the intrusion prime the reader to process the incident in light of the strongman schema.

According to this pericope, a man bound spiritually (ἐν πνεύ–ματι ἀκαθάρτῳ, 5:2) is presented *at the beginning of the pericope* as one too powerful to be bound physically (cf. 5:3, καὶ οὐδὲ ἁλύσει οὐκέτι οὐδεὶς ἐδύνατο αὐτόν δῆσαι and 5:4, καὶ οὐδεὶς ἴσχυεν αὐτὸν δαμάσαι). At the end of the pericope, however, this same man has been so spiritually loosed that he does not require physical binding. This transformation has been effected by the simple command of Jesus

---

68. It should also be noted that in 15:1 Jesus is handed over to Pilate "bound."

69. The tenses suggest actions in process in the story world, but the narration of them stops.

(ὁ ἰσχυρότερος, 1:7) narrated in 5:8: ἔξελθε τὸ πνεῦμα τὸ ἀκάθαρτον ἐκ τοῦ ἀνθρώπου. The man's action (ἔδραμεν καὶ προσεκύνησεν αὐτῷ, 5:7) and repeated fearful pleadings (καὶ παρεκάλει αὐτὸν πολλὰ ἵνα μὴ αὐτὰ ἀποστείλῃ ἔξω τῆς χώρας, 5:10)[70] together with the entreaty of the demons (καὶ παρεκάλεσαν αὐτὸν λέγοντες· πέμψον ἡμᾶς εἰς τοὺς χοίρους, ἵνα εἰς αὐτοὺς εἰσέλθωμεν, 5:12) suggest a schema in which Jesus is the stronger man (ὁ ἰσχυρότερος, 1:7) who has bound the strongman, Satan (= SM$_1$), who had bound the strongman, the demoniac (= SM$_2$), and had plundered his house.

But the strongman schema does not cease oscillating with the story of the Geresene demoniac. In two later episodes, the narrator leaves clues that point to Jesus. In these cases, however, the literary link is the notion of "binding" rather than the idea of a strongman. This makes the association more subtle, but hardly less potent.

The first of these incidents finds John the Baptist "bound" in Herod's prison (6:17). The parallels between John and Jesus have already been noted. The binding of John thus makes the binding of Jesus a viable possibility for the reader, and this is precisely what the reader discovers at 15:1. Jesus is the bound strongman!

The narrative suggests the Jesus-as-strongman schema as early as 3:27, overturns it at 5:1–20, and revisits it at 6:5 and 6:17. At 15:1, in the same manner that Jesus is handed over to Pilate, the narrator hands Jesus over to the reader—physically bound. The situation for Jesus appears ominous. But earlier the narrator has left clues that the outcome will be positive. On three previous occasions Jesus has predicted his passion *and* resurrection (8:31; 9:31; 10:33–34). He predicted his return as Son of Man (13:26) and spoke of drinking the fruit of the vine in the kingdom of God (14:25).

But the narrator may have left another hint of Jesus' ultimate victory. Mark 11:1–11 is the only other place in the Gospel where the binding motif occurs. Here, however, the binding relates not to a strongman, but to a colt. Why the story about a colt? True, it may relate a prediction of Jesus that is immediately fulfilled (assuming Jesus had not previously made arrangements with the colt's owner) and thus, like Jesus' prophecy regarding the fig tree that also receives swift fulfillment, gives the reader more assurance that Jesus' predictions about his fate will also come to

---

70. The man probably feared that he would have been treated more cruelly by the "stronger man."

pass. Nevertheless, its primary significance lies in its re-presentation of the binding motif, its addition of the "loosing" element, and its position in the narrative chain.

In Mark 11:2, Jesus tells the disciples that they will find a having-been-bound colt (πῶλον δεδεμένον) and commands them to loose it (λύσατε). In v. 4, the disciples find the having-been-bound colt (πῶλον δεδεμένον), and they are loosing it (λύουσιν αὐτόν). The binding-loosing references end in v. 5, where bystanders ask: τί ποιεῖτε λύοντες τὸν πῶλον? The participle is modal; hence the question should be rendered, "What are you doing by loosing that colt?"[71] At the story level, the query is simple enough; at the narrative level, however, it may evoke a different schema: "What is the narrative doing by loosing the colt?"

Mark 11:1–11 thus introduces a binding-loosing motif. Two items are especially significant. First, the binding-loosing sequence ends with loosing. The sequence of verbs is diagramed as follows:

binding → loosing → binding → loosing → loosing

More important, however, is the fact that the sequence is placed in the context of Jesus' triumphal entry into Jerusalem. As such, it is a harbinger of Jesus' ultimate victory.

The "binding the strongman" parable immediately follows two charges against Jesus: (1) that he is out of his mind; and (2) that he is in league with Satan. The first is the more significant for our context since it arises from Jesus' family. This juxtapositioning gives Jesus' words about the "divided house" a double entendre and introduces a possible schema for Jesus as the bound strongman. The loosing of the Gerasene demoniac (5:1–20) shows Satan as the bound strongman. The binding of John (6:17) hints at Jesus. Jesus bound before Pilate (15:1) indicates Jesus. The binding of Jesus sees its strongest imagery at the crucifixion (15:24), though the term "binding" is absent. The picture is one of complete powerlessness. This, however, only heightens the reader's relief when the Jesus-as-bound-strongman schema is decisively overturned by the announcement of Jesus' resurrection (16:6–7).

The binding-loosing grid helps the reader make sense of the turns in Jesus' life. At the outset of the narrative, Jesus is the "mightier one." He demonstrates authority over disease, demons, and natural law. Yet

---

71. Taylor (*Mark*, 455) renders the original: "What do you mean by loosing the colt?"

with respect to humanity, he always operates from a position of weakness: he invites, but does not coerce; he teaches, but only to "those who have ears to hear"; he commands, but leaves people free to disobey. Jesus rejects the "things of men" perspective in goal and methodology: He does not seek his own aggrandizement and does not control others by force. With respect to abusive power, Mark's Jesus offers neither rebellion ("Render to Caesar . . ." 12:17) nor apocalypse ("This Gospel must first be preached," 13:10).[72]

The Herod-Baptist Episode: Mark 6:14–29

Mark 6:14–29 is the most obtrusive anachrony in the Gospel. Several features support this. The Herod-Baptist account is the only story in Mark's Gospel not directly about Jesus;[73] it does not bear any obvious link with the primary narrative; its language reflects a higher degree of refinement than the Gospel as a whole;[74] it forms a discrete narrative since it includes a beginning, a complication, and a denouement;[75] it interrupts the story of the sending and return of the Twelve, creating a disjuncture on both ends;[76] and most importantly, it is unique in its handling of narrative order: "nowhere else in Mark does the narrator transpose story order so radically over such a short stretch of narrative text."[77]

Before examining the significance of the narrative sequence of events within the Herod-Baptist story, let us consider the import of the story's placement within the larger frame of the Gospel. That the account of the Baptist's demise is given more narrative space in Mark than

72. On this, see Senior, "'Swords and Clubs.'"

73. See, e.g., Kee, *Community*, 55; Nineham, *Mark*, 172; Schweizer, *Mark*, 132; Taylor, *Mark*, 310; and Cranfield, *Mark*, 208.

74. Kee, *Community*, 55; Camery-Hoggatt, *Irony in Mark's Gospel*, 144. Lohmeyer (*Evangelium des Markus*, 117–18) notes, among other things, the absence of historical presents, the frequency of aorists, imperfects, and genitive absolutes and the use of numerous Markan παξ λεγόμενα (Kee [*Community*, 191n20] provides a list of these words).

75. Camery-Hoggatt, *Irony in Mark's Gospel*, 144.

76. This, of course, is not the only instance of intercalation in Mark's Gospel. Kee (*Community*, 54), for example, catalogues eight such occurrences.

77. Funk, *Poetics of Biblical Narrative*, 196. Although Funk provides a scheme for comparing the chronological order of the events of the Herod intercalation with the order in which they are imparted in the narrative, he makes little comment on the significance of this transposition.

in any of the other Gospels, suggests its special significance for Mark.[78] Nevertheless, the summary fashion in which the disciples' ministry is related has led some to conclude that the Herod-Baptist story was placed between the sending and return of the Twelve to fill the gap resulting from the lack of specific details about this ministry.[79] Pushed to the extreme, this line of reasoning regards the account simply as a shocking— and perhaps fanciful—story used to simulate the passing of time.[80]

The primary concern here, however, is not with Mark's motive for including the Herod—Baptist story, but rather with the role this story plays in the reading transaction. The most widely recognized function of the account of the Baptist's demise is its anticipation of Jesus' passion. James Edwards describes the parallels between the death of the Baptist and the death of Jesus:

> Mark clearly intends to show that as John was the forerunner of Jesus' message and ministry, so too is he the forerunner of his death. John is righteous and suffers silently, and the same will be true of Jesus. Both Herod and Pilate are Roman officials, both are vacillating and pusillanimous in the face of social pressure, and both condemn innocent men to death.[81]

Nevertheless, as Edwards rightly points out, this understanding of 6:14–29 does not explain its placement between the sending (6:7–13) and the return (6:30) of the Twelve. Mark has postponed the conclusion (only one verse!) to his account of the disciples' first missionary venture until after the Herod—Baptist account. How does this effect the reader's processing of the text? Let us examine the narrative more closely to see how this narrative technique plays itself out.

As noted earlier, the Herod—Baptist story interrupts a story already in progress. Robert Fowler describes this narrative configuration as an "intercalation or sandwich arrangement, wherein one episode is

---

78. Hurtado, *Mark*, 94.

79. This is the approach taken by Cranfield (*Mark*, 206) and Taylor (*Mark*, 307), and perhaps less directly by Nineham (*Mark*, 172).

80. Nineham (*Mark*, 173) describes the Herod-Baptist story as "a popular report, frequently inaccurate, and with something of the character of the fairy tale."

81. J. Edwards, "Markan Sandwiches," 205–6. Note also Nineham (*Mark*, 173): "The fate of the forerunner is a presage of the fate of the successor"; Cranfield (*Mark*, 208–9): "the passion of the Forerunner [is] a pointer to the subsequent passion of the Messiah"; Schweizer (*Mark*, 132): "[the Baptist's execution] is at the same time a prophecy of man's opposition to Jesus and of Jesus' future destiny."

split in two and another episode tucked between the split halves."[82] This technique provides a way of describing nonsequentially events that happen simultaneously.[83] However, since the time covered in the framing episode and the framed episode is in both cases indefinite, a clear connection of simultaneity is difficult to detect. Fowler suggests a more discernable function: it provides the reader with a paradigm for filling narrative gaps:

> By his use of intercalation, the narrator reveals his own awareness of the dynamic of creating and filling gaps, which is exactly what the narrator himself is doing in the act of intercalating: he is simultaneously creating and filling a gap in his own story. Thus, the narrator is not only issuing an implicit challenge to read two episodes simultaneously, each in the light of the other, but also implicitly training the reader in the general practice of perceiving and filling gaps in narrative.[84]

Thus, the Herod—Baptist episode (framed story) is intended to be read in light of the account of the disciples' first missionary venture (framing story), and vice versa.

In this narrative sandwich, the framed story is not grammatically connected to the framing story. The referent of the verb ἤκουσεν is left unstated. Most translations assume the referent to be the ministry activity of the disciples ("King Herod heard *about this*"), since it immediately precedes in the context. But Jesus alone is the clear focus of thought in this verse. Isolated from this context, what Herod hears would more naturally be reports about Jesus himself ("King Herod heard *about him*"). This would be true if the verse followed a statement directly about Jesus.

The displacement of the account of the Baptist's demise prompts asking where this story would have been placed had strict adherence to chronology been the author's primary concern. The gap between 1:15 and 16 offers the best answer. First, after John's general baptizing activity (1:4), prophecy of the coming Mightier One (1:7–8), and baptizing of

---

82. Fowler, *Let the Reader Understand*, 143. Fowler lists seven generally recognized intercalations in Mark. See also idem, *Loaves and Fishes*, 164; Dewey, *Markan Public Debate*, 20–23; and Edwards, "Markan Sandwiches."

83. Another way, of course, is to supply a temporal phrase such as "at the same time X was occurring, Y was taking place," or, to cite a time-worn expression, "meanwhile, back at the ranch."

84. Fowler, *Let the Reader Understand*, 144.

Jesus (1:9), he makes no other appearances on the Markan stage. Second, the Herod-Baptist account (6:14–29) indicates that John was in prison at the time of his death. This makes 1:14–15, which analeptically relates John's imprisonment, an appropriate insertion point for the account of the Baptist's demise. Third, placing the Herod—Baptist account after 1:15 eliminates a huge narrative gap regarding the details surrounding John's imprisonment.

In this arrangement, the ambiguity regarding what Herod heard disappears since Jesus is the sole active agent before the phrase Καὶ ἤκουσεν ὁ βασιλεὺς Ἡρῴδης (6:14). The direct mention of Jesus' name in 1:14 (ἦλθεν ὁ Ἰησοῦς εἰς τὴν Γαλιλαίαν κηρύσσων τὸ εὐαγγέλιον τοῦ θεοῦ) also makes more natural the occurrence of the pronoun (αὐτοῦ) in the explanatory γάρ clause φανερὸν γὰρ ἐγένετο τὸ ὄνομα αὐτοῦ (6:14b). Finally, Jesus' proclamation regarding ἡ βασιλεία τοῦ θεοῦ in 1:15 would certainly catch the ear of "King" Herod.

Thus, the Herod-Baptist account fits well into the immediate context of the gap between Mark 1:15 and 16.[85] But how does its placement here accord chronologically with the remainder of the narrative? Though the Baptist's role as an active agent in Mark's narrative ends abruptly at 1:9, three references to him (excluding the banquet scene of 6:14–29) follow the allusion to his imprisonment in 1:14: the controversy over fasting (2:18–20), the question of popular opinion regarding Jesus' identity (8:27–29), and the controversy over the source of Jesus' authority (11:28–33).

Fitting the Herod-Baptist account in Mark 1 poses no chronological problems for the subsequent references to John the Baptist. Mark 8:28 assumes the Baptist's death (cf. 6:14, 16). Mark 11:30 speaks of John's baptism in the past tense (τὸ βάπτισμα τὸ Ἰωάννου ἐξ οὐρανοῦ ἦν ἢ ἐξ ἀνθρώπων;). Jesus' statement in 2:19 that fasting is inappropriate ἐν ᾧ ὁ νυμφίος μετ' αὐτῶν ἐστιν implies John's absence (prison or death?) from his disciples, since his disciples *are* fasting.[86]

Since the Herod-Baptist account fits chronologically between 1:15 and 16, what is the effect of its displacement to 6:14 on the reader? In terms of the overall narrative structure, delaying the presentation of the

---

85. If some linking of Jesus traditions predated Mark's Gospel (an *Urmarkus*? or a standardized outline of Peter's preaching?), this may have been the original placement of the Herod-Baptist episode.

86. See Cranfield, *Mark*, 109; Taylor, *Mark*, 209.

Baptist's death until 6:14–29 keeps the reader in suspense regarding his fate.[87] The fasting of John's disciples (2:18) reminds the reader of this "loose end." In the shadow of Jesus' comment that "the attendants of the bridegroom are not able to fast while the bridegroom is with them" (2:19), the suspense regarding the Baptist builds; his "absence" can be schematized as imprisonment, but it also holds the possibility of death.

After an episode highlighting the dishonor that Jesus himself received from relatives and hometown friends (6:1–6a), Jesus briefs his disciples on their missionary task (6:6b–11). His instructions include a forewarning of their rejection. In 6:12–13, the narrator describes the missionary activity of the Twelve: healing, exorcizing, and preaching that people should repent.[88] With that the stage is set for the reader to encounter the Baptist's demise. In this way, the narrator links the fate of the Baptist to the fate of the disciples.

The Herod-Baptist story derives rhetorical power not only from its position in the episode sequence of the Gospel as a whole, but also from the sequence of events within the episode itself. Comparing the narrative sequence with other possible arrangements of the same events often corroborates conclusions regarding the effect of a particular sequence of events. The chronological order, as seen in the first part of this section, can be used to advantage. However, a caveat is necessary: reproducing the chronological framework that accommodates every event of a narrative is almost always a speculative enterprise, particularly susceptible to the *post hoc, ergo propter hoc* fallacy. The information presented in the text is the primary evidence from which the chronological frame can be deduced. But, as argued in chapter 2, the whole of a story can never be told and the reader is therefore required to fill in many gaps. In the absence of narrative clues that suggest otherwise, the reader will fill the gaps by assuming a causal connection. A comparison of the chronological and narrative frames of the Herod-Baptist story is instructive (see Table 3 at the end of this chapter).

With some events the chronological order is clear-cut. For example, Herodias's grudge against the Baptist and her desire to kill him (4) must

---

87. Suspense is felt not only by a reader unfamiliar with the Baptist's fate; even a reader familiar with the general story will wonder when his death will be narrated and what significance the narrator will attach to it.

88. Jesus' prediction (1:17) that he would make Simon and Andrew (and presumably the rest of the disciples) "fishers of men" receives uptake here.

surely follow the Baptist's rebuke of Herod for having his brother's wife (3). In other cases, however, the chronology is far less certain: did Herod hear John gladly (1) before his marriage to Herodias (2) and John's subsequent imprisonment (6), or did Herod have occasion to listen to John only after John was imprisoned? While complete accuracy is unlikely, obvious departures from a chronology can be identified and their effects on the reader described.

According to the chronological scheme, the reader's first impression of Herod is positive. Herod pays attention to what the Baptist is doing and enjoys listening to him. But his marriage to his brother's former wife incurs the Baptist's rebuke. The Baptist's rebuke incites Herodias's anger and desire for revenge. Yet Herod fears (and respects?) the Baptist and tries to protect him from the wiles of Herodias. Herod's reluctance to do the Baptist harm pervades the narrative, even at the point where the Baptist is imprisoned.

The narrative speeds up with the account of Herod's birthday banquet (only one day in *story time*) that ends, much to the reader's shock, in the Baptist's brutal execution. The episode shifts gears a final time with the circulation of rumors as to Jesus' identity and culminates with Herod's fearful conclusion: "John, the man I beheaded, has been raised from the dead!"

The narrative sequence proceeds along a different course. It opens with Herod hearing news. But the actual content of the reports is not stated. This narrative device evokes the question, "What did Herod hear?" The processing of this narrative information begins from outside the Herod-Baptist story. The reader carries forward the immediately preceding episode of the disciples' missionary activity and so constructs a schema in which Herod hears something about Jesus, his disciples, and their preaching/healing/exorcism ministry.

Within the Herod-Baptist episode, the only clue as to what Herod heard is provided analeptically by an explanatory γὰρ clause (φανερὸν γὰρ ἐγένετο τὸ ὄνομα αὐτοῦ) that immediately follows. Since Jesus' name is not mentioned in the preceding episode, the reader must disambiguate the αὐτοῦ. This action is not particularly challenging since Jesus is the central figure of Mark's story and since the third-person masculine pronoun is singular.[89] Nevertheless, the indirect reference to Jesus has

89. Cf. Taylor, *Mark*, 308. According to Taylor, vv. 14–16 rule out the mission of the Twelve as a schema for what Herod heard since they are concerned with Jesus alone.

the effect of throwing the spotlight on the two primary characters of the episode: Herod and John the Baptist.

Comparing the chronological and narrative orderings of the events in the Herod-Baptist story shows that if the narrator's purpose is to bait the reader's suspense until the climactic moment, he has ordered his material as clumsily as one who delivers a joke's punchline too early. The chronologically structured narrative keeps the reader in suspense regarding the fate of the Baptist almost until the axe falls. In Mark's presentation, however, the reader learns of the Baptist's beheading before the curtain rises on Herod's birthday banquet. The first of the circulating rumors regarding Jesus' identity (6:14b) dispassionately informs the reader of the Baptist's death. Herod's opinion of Jesus (6:16) supplies the means. The actual execution is anticlimactic, to say the least.[90]

More specifically, moving the narrative element "Jesus' name becomes known" (7) from its chronological position (column 1, #7) before Herod's banquet to the earlier part of the narrative (column 2, #7) takes Jesus off the stage earlier and throws a spotlight on Herod and John. Moving the element "Herod hears John and likes to listen to him" (column 1, #1) to the position immediately preceding the banquet scene (column 2, #1) makes Herod's action against the Baptist look all the more foolish. In the narrative sequence, John has Herod rapt in his message of morality one day, and Herod has John wrapped in a burial shroud the next.

The contrast between Herod and John is the primary element of this interrupting scene. The two differ considerably, especially regard-

---

For Taylor (ibid.), "it is the ministry and mighty works of Jesus throughout Galilee" that best describe what Herod heard. Nevertheless, placement of this story immediately after the disciples' mission keeps this schema before the reader, and is reinforced at the story's conclusion where the reader encounters the missionary report that concludes the framing story.

90. Schweizer (*Mark*, 133) argues that the placement of Herod's opinion after the opinions of the general populace indicates "that it is the question about Christ which interests Mark, and not Herod's uneasy conscience." That the references to John's being raised (ἐγήγερται, 6:14 and ἠγέρθη, 6:16) form an *inclusio* highlighting the inner material could be used in support of Schweizer's view. But this is not as simple as Schweizer makes it. Certainly, the question of Jesus' identity is an important Markan theme. But it plays no major role in the Herod-Baptist story. In fact, Jesus is completely absent from the story after Herod's opinion is related. Rather, Herod's opinion functions to create the gap that the remainder of the story attempts to fill.

ing their orientation to power. This contrast is dealt with in more detail below, but first we consider the role of Jesus in the pericope.

The narration of the rumors regarding Jesus' identity serves three notable functions in the episode: (1) it causes the reader to reaccess schemata relating to Jesus' identity; (2) it causes the reader to reconsider the connections between Jesus and the Baptist; and (3) it matter-of-factly informs the reader of the Baptist's death.

The identity of Jesus has been fixed for the reader well before the Herod-Baptist scene. The designation "Messiah" and "Son of God" (1:1), the affirmation of divine sonship by a voice from heaven (1:11), the recognition of Jesus as "Holy One of God" and "Son of God" by the evil spirits (1:24; 3:11), the demonstration of his divinity by forgiving sins (2:7–12), and the affirmation of Jesus as "Son of man" who is "Lord of the Sabbath" (2:28) leave little ambiguity regarding Jesus' identity. Thus, the false speculations about Jesus (vv. 14–16) strengthen the narrator-reader bond and nurture the reader's trust in the narrator as a reliable guide.

Herod's confusion between Jesus and John is perfectly understandable in light of the similarity of their message: both preached the necessity of repentance. Nevertheless, the reader does not share Herod's perplexity. The roles of Jesus and John have already been distinguished. The reader knows that John was the forerunner of Jesus in his appearance for public ministry. Now that the Baptist has been executed, the narrative prompts the question: will John also play the role of Jesus' forerunner in his death?

Camery-Hoggatt maintains that the "understated way [Mark] reports the macabre events leading up to the execution of John the Baptist" indicates the use of irony.[91] He finds one cue for this irony in "the dissonance between the content of the story—which is horrifying—and the tenor of the story—which is understated and dispassionate."[92] That the major actant in the story is Herod, while John, in typical Markan fashion, has only a passive role, supports Camery-Hoggatt's contention that the primary irony of the episode lies in the actions of Herod:

---

91. Camery-Hoggatt, *Irony in Mark's Gospel*, 77. The author sees irony operating in this episode in two other ways. He points first to the fact that Herod did not hold the title "king," but rather "tetrarch" and suggests that Mark may be intending ridicule by his use (overuse?) of "king" to describe Herod. The second display of irony lies in the contrast between Herod and the Baptist; Herod, who is "trumped up to be more than he is" and John, who is "understated but powerful" (ibid., 145).

92. Ibid., 145.

> The old king has been out-foxed.... He executes John to save face, but in that act exposes his debauchery. The head on the platter is a burlesque of the feast. It is the king's own head, blood-splattered, ghastly, gagging on the monstrosity he has created.[93]

The linking of constructions in which question-raising information is followed by an explanatory statement of cause or reason signaled by γάρ, ὅτι, or διά causes the reader to realize gaps in the narrative just before they are filled by the information in the explanatory statement.[94] In this way, the narrator guides the reader to the experience intended by the episode.

The opening line of the episode, Καὶ ἤκουσεν ὁ Βασιλεὺς Ἡρῴδης (6:14), as we have already seen, prompts the question, "What did Herod hear?" The γάρ clause suggests the content to be something related to Jesus. The next phrase, καὶ ἔλεγον ὅτι Ἰωάννης ὁ βαπτίζων ἐγήγερται ἐκ νεκρῶν (6:14b), prompts the question, "Why were some saying that Jesus was John the Baptist raised from the dead?" The following causal clause διὰ τοῦτο ἐνεργοῦσιν αἱ δυνάμεις ἐν αὐτῷ (6:14c) supplies the answer.

The suggestions that Jesus is Elijah or one of the prophets are not followed by causal clauses; but Herod's opinion, ὃν ἐγὼ ἀπεκεφάλισα Ἰωάννην, οὗτος ἠγέρθη (6:16), raises two questions: "Why does Herod think that Jesus is the Baptist resurrected?" and "Why did Herod behead John?" The causal clauses that follow incrementally fill the gaps. The γάρ clause that immediately follows, Αὐτὸς γὰρ ὁ Ἡρῴδης ἀποστείλας ἐκράτησεν τὸν Ἰωάννην καὶ ἔδησεν αὐτὸν ἐν φυλακῇ (6:17a), itself suggests another question: "Why did Herod have John imprisoned?" The next clause, διὰ Ἡρῳδιάδα τὴν γυναῖκα Φιλίππου τοῦ ἀδελφοῦ αὐτοῦ (6:17b), supplies a partial answer, but leaves unclear the connection with Herodias. The narrator makes another partial revelation by bringing in Herod's marriage to his brother's former wife: ὅτι αὐτὴν ἐγάμησεν (6:17c). The next γάρ clause, ἔλεγεν γὰρ ὁ Ἰωάννης τῷ Ἡρῴδῃ ὅτι οὐκ ἔξεστίν σοι ἔχειν τὴν γυναῖκα τοῦ ἀδελφοῦ σου (6:18), allows the reader to retroactively piece together the reason for

---

93. Ibid., 145–46.

94. See Fowler, *Let the Reader Understand*, 92–101. Fowler treats these explanatory statements as "explicit commentary by the narrator" and argues that the inside views that they reflect "often supply clear, direct, and indisputable guidance for the reader" (125).

John's imprisonment: John rebuked Herod for marrying Herodias; Herodias was angered; Herod imprisoned John to appease Herodias.

Verse 19 confirms this schema and shows the intensity of Herodias's anger: ἡ δὲ Ἡρῳδιὰς ἐνεῖχεν αὐτῷ καὶ ἤθελεν αὐτὸν ἀποκτεῖναι (6:19a, b). The commentary on the initial results of Herodias' desire to kill the Baptist (καὶ οὐκ ἠδύνατο) causes the reader to consider what is standing in her way. Mark's sequencing of the story leaves no doubt in the reader's mind that Herodias will get her wish; the only uncertainty is related to how it will be brought about. Again a γὰρ clause guides the reader: ὁ γὰρ Ἡρῴδης ἐφοβεῖτο τὸν Ἰωάννην, εἰδὼς αὐτὸν ἄνδρα δίκαιον καὶ ἅγιον, καὶ συνετήρει αὐτόν, καὶ ἀκούσας αὐτοῦ πολλὰ ἠπόρει, καὶ ἡδέως αὐτοῦ ἤκουεν. Herod protected John because he feared him. But this prompts the question, "Why did Herod fear John?" If the participle εἰδὼς is used causally, Herod feared John because he knew that John was a righteous and holy man.

Less than halfway into the story, the narrative makes a drastic change in speed that does not decrease until the Baptist's body is in a tomb. The previous events imply a considerable duration of time (circulation of rumors about Jesus, John's repeated rebukes of the illicit marriage, Herodias' nursing a grudge, and Herod's listening to John). In contrast, the banquet scene ostensibly lasts one day. The episode thus rushes to conclusion at breakneck speed.

Several features signal this shift in narrative speed. Firstly, beginning with the banquet scene, the events are linked primarily by καὶ in paratactic fashion. After the explanatory comment in 6:20, only one causal phrase appears. Even here its position requires less processing time. Since it precedes its referent (διὰ τοὺς ὅρκους καὶ ἀνακειμένους οὐκ ἠθέλησεν ἀθετῆσαι αὐτήν, Mark 6:26), it fills the gap before the reader realizes a gap was present. Secondly, the large proportion of dialogue tends to equalize story time and narrative time. Thirdly, of the twelve imperfect tense verbs in the entire episode, not one occurs after v. 20.[95] Finally, the banquet section gives no indication of the passage of time between events; each seems to come right on the heels of the other. Mark 6:25 highlights the celerity with which Herodias'

---

95. Vv.14–20 contain twenty-three verbs in the indicative mood. The tenses are distributed as follows: imperfect (12), present (3), aorist (7), perfect (1). By contrast, vv. 21–29 contain nineteen indicative verbs: imperfect (0), present (1) aorist (15), perfect (1), and future (2).

daughter commences (εὐθύς) and executes (μετὰ σπουδῆς) her obe-
dient response to her mother's desires. The remaining events follow in
staccato rhythm: the king orders the executioner to bring John's head;
the executioner beheads John and gives the severed head to Herodias'
daughter; Herodias' daughter presents John's head to her mother; and
John's disciples take his body and lay it in a tomb.

This temporal shift turns a spotlight on the factors that brought
about the Baptist's death and relegates the actual details of his death
to the shadows. The bizarre banquet scene is merely the catalyst that
provides the opportunity (signaled by 6:21a: Καὶ γενομένης ἡμέρας
εὐκαίρου) for the heinous intentions against John to be carried out. The
underlying reason for John's demise is his rebuke of Herod's adulterous
marriage to Herodias, an especially audacious, indecorous act in light of
Herod's influential position of power. Seen from Herodias' perspective,
a locust-eating, desert-dwelling religious fanatic clad in camel's hair is
calling a king into account for his actions.

Herod, however, fears to harm John. By imprisoning him, he not
only tries to appease his wife's anger but also prevents John from amass-
ing a greater following that could lead to insurrection.[96] With John
bound in prison, Herod has no need for his execution. Thus, the plot
requires a catalyst to force Herod's hand, and the banquet scene with its
provocative dance handily fills this role.

The sequencing of the narrative information regarding Herod
makes him a fitting illustration of the thorny ground from the Parable of
the Sower.[97] Herod's opinion regarding Jesus, "John, the man whom I beheaded . . . ," follows the popular opinion that "John the Baptist has been
raised from the dead." Thus, the reader's initial shock at learning the fact
of John's death occurs before Herod's opinion supplies knowledge of the
means of his death. The worst part of Herod's deed is stated at the outset.
The remainder of the episode helps the reader to sense some pity for
Herod. At John's condemnation of Herod for having his brother's wife,
Herodias—not Herod—"nurses a grudge" against the Baptist; Herod's
reaction is one of respect. Moreover, when Herod realizes he has been

---

96. The narrator gives Herod's knowledge of John's righteous and holy character as
the reason for Herod's fear (i.e., reverential awe) and portrays Herod as "outfoxed" into
executing the Baptist by his daughter's untimely request. Josephus (*Antiquities* 18.5.2)
claims that Herod executed the Baptist for fear he would lead a rebellion.

97. See Tolbert, *Sowing the Gospel*, 158.

tricked, he is extremely grieved and only reluctantly and remorsefully (6:26) consents to execute John.

Nevertheless, in spite of inclinations toward sympathy for Herod, the reader sees him in a negative light. In the end, Herod alone bears responsibility for the Baptist's gruesome death. He hears John gladly (cf. 4:7, 18), but the word sown in him is choked by his concern for position and reputation (cf. 4:19). He is willing to sacrifice up to half his kingdom for "entertainment," but unwilling to sacrifice his reputation—let alone his life—to enter God's kingdom. He thinks the "things of men."

John, on the other hand, plays the role of the sower. Apart from his condemnation of Herod's marriage, John has a typically passive role on the Markan stage: he is arrested, bound, and imprisoned; his head is removed and used in a degrading manner; and his body is laid in a tomb. He sows the word, but the "reward" he receives is execution. His fate at the hands of a Roman tetrarch foreshadows the fate of Jesus at the hands of a Roman governor.[98] Throughout the episode, John operates from a position of powerlessness. John thinks the "things of God."

The content of the Baptist's conversations with Herod is not narrated, but can be inferred from what the reader has seen to be the prophet's essential message: a baptism of repentance for the forgiveness of sins (1:4). This element firmly links the Herod-Baptist episode with its framing story (the missionary activity of the Twelve) at the point of interruption since the disciples are proclaiming the same message. The account of Herod and John is also linked to its framing story at the end-point, although the reader must deduce the connection. The lifeless body of one wordsower is placed in a tomb just as the Twelve are gathering around (συνάγονται) Jesus to give account of their word-sowing. Thus, the sandwich foreshadows not only the suffering and death of Jesus but also the persecution of anyone who follows after him.

---

98. The narrative lays stress on Herod as a minister of governmental authority, rather than as an individual. Except for the opening (6:14), the title "king" is not used until the banquet scene (6:22); after this the name "Herod" is not used. In this way, the episode prepares the reader for the disciples' (and the reader's?) impending conflict with the governmental authorities—an external prolepsis predicted by Jesus (10:39; 13:9–13) but not narrated.

The Follower's Reward: Mark 10:29–30

Following Jesus is a pivotal theme of Mark's Gospel (see Table 4 at the end of this chapter).[99] One of the earliest clues to its importance is an observation related to narrative order: the second action of Jesus related in the narrative is the invitation he extends to Simon and Andrew, δεῦτε ὀπίσω μου (1:17). Significantly, however, the narrator makes no mention of compensation.

That Simon and Andrew follow Jesus without any promise of reward augments the "powerful Jesus" schema which the narrator proleptically initiates in 1:7,[100] but it also creates a narrative gap regarding what motivates their acceptance of Jesus' offer. At this point in the narrative, the only pertinent material that the reader can draw upon to fill the gap is Jesus' first action of the narrative: his proclamation concerning the kingdom of God.

Filling this gap, however, is a complex process, since the narrator nowhere defines the expression "kingdom of God." Jesus himself alludes to its mystery (4:11). The open-endedness of the phrase provides fertile territory for distinguishing the "things of God" and "things of men" perspectives. The narrator, of course, wants the reader to process "kingdom of God" according to the "things of God," and he has left a number of clues to enable the reader to decode it in this way.

---

99. See Best, *Following Jesus*; Beavis, "Women as Models"; Dewey, "Point of View"; Donahue, *Theology and Setting*; Malbon, "Fallible Followers"; idem, "Disciples—Crowds—Whoever"; Robbins, *Jesus the Teacher*; Stock, *Call to Discipleship*; Tannehill, "Disciples in Mark"; and Weeden, *Mark*. In all but two of the eighteen occurrences of ἀκολουθέω in Mark (9:38 and 14:13), Jesus is the one followed. In 9:38 the disciples rebuke an anonymous man for exorcising demons because he was not following them, but this is strongly overturned by Jesus (vv. 39–40). In 14:13, Jesus tells the disciples to follow a man carrying a jar of water, but this in no way indicates that a long-term relationship was in mind. Malbon ("Fallible Followers," 30) deems "followers" and "followership" more appropriate terms than "disciples" and "discipleship."

100. For Camery-Hoggatt (*Irony in Mark's Gospel*, 101), the noteworthy element about the disciples' response is that "these four men drop everything to follow Jesus *without knowing who he is*. Nothing yet narrated could have prepared them for this moment. Thus, when they respond so readily, they do so on the force of the call alone. In this way, the focus is shifted slightly from the fishermen's immediate and unquestioning response to the authoritative personality who can evoke such a response" (emphasis original). Note also that 1:17 is linked with 1:7 by the phrase ὀπίσω μου. In 1:7 the Baptist announces ἔρχεται ὁ ἰσχυρότερος μου ὀπίσω μου. In 1:17 Jesus invites Simon and Andrew: δεῦτε ὀπίσω μου.

Mark employs the expression "kingdom of God" fourteen times, and most of the contexts in which these are found provide material for developing a "things of God" schema for it. For example, Mark 1:15 and 9:47 relate the concept to repentance and faithfulness; the parables in Mark 4 suggest that the kingdom is God's deed, present in embryonic form and ever expanding as people respond positively to God's word; 12:34 describes the kingdom as loving God and one's neighbor; and 14:25 speaks of the future aspects of God's kingdom.

The linking of the "following" motif with the "kingdom of God" concept (1:15–18) can be traced through the remainder of the narrative, as a comparison of the schemata attached to both shows. The recognition scene (8:27–9:1) is a watershed for the "following" motif. To this point in the narrative, all occurrences of ἀκολουθέω inform the reader *that* people are following Jesus. Beginning with this episode, however, the emphasis falls on *how* people are to follow Jesus (e.g., denying the self, 8:34ff; sacrificing for others, 10:21; trusting Jesus, 10:52; obeying Jesus, 14:13; staying close to Jesus, 14:54; caring for the needs of others, 15:41). The parallels between the requirements for following Jesus and the requirements for entrance into God's kingdom are unmistakable. Yet all of these contexts leave the reward unspecified.

Mark 10:13–32, however, is quite another matter. Except for 1:14–20 (where the gap regarding reward first arises), this section has the distinction of being the only other place in the narrative where the "following" and "kingdom of God" motifs are so closely linked. The emphasis on the kingdom of God is obvious. The phrase "kingdom of God" occurs five times in the space of only twelve verses. The "following" motif protrudes in Jesus' response to the rich man, καὶ δεῦρο ἀκολούθει μοι (10:21) and in Peter's confident assertion ἰδοὺ ἡμεῖς ἀφήκαμεν πάντα καὶ ἠκολουθήκαμέν σοι. The difference between 10:13–32 and 1:14–20 is the discussion on rewards.

In Mark 10:29–30, the narrator relates Jesus' direct statements regarding rewards for those who follow him:

[29] ἔφη ὁ Ἰησοῦς· ἀμὴν λέγω ὑμῖν, οὐδείς ἐστιν ὃς ἀφῆκεν οἰκίαν ἢ ἀδελφοὺς ἢ ἀδελφὰς ἢ μητέρα ἢ πατέρα ἢ τέκνα ἢ ἀγροὺς ἕνεκεν ἐμοῦ καὶ ἕνεκεν τοῦ εὐαγγελίου, [30] ἐὰν μὴ λάβῃ ἑκατονταπλασίονα νῦν ἐν τῷ καιρῷ τούτῳ οἰκίας καὶ ἀδελφοὺς καὶ ἀδελφὰς καὶ μητέρας καὶ καὶ τέκνα καὶ

ἀγροὺς μετὰ διωγμῶν, καὶ ἐν τῷ αἰῶνι τῷ ἐρχομένῳ ζωὴν αἰώνιον.

The context that houses this homily on the disciple's reward provides an excellent example of the narrative technique of priming. Again, the narrative sequence is significant.

The words of Jesus in 10:29–30 are precipitated by an analepsis that extends to the beginning of the narrative: Peter exclaims, ἰδοὺ ἡμεῖς ἀφήκαμεν πάντα καὶ ἠκολουθήκαμέν σοι. This directs the reader back to 1:18 (καὶ εὐθὺς ἀφέντες τὰ δίκτυα ἠκολούθησαν αὐτῷ). Removed from its present context, Peter's assertion seems to be a simple statement of fact. In the context of 10:13–32, however, Peter's comment comes in response to Jesus' assessment of the failure of the rich man. This sets the reader up for a shocking element in Jesus' teaching on rewards.

The episode begins in 10:13 where the disciples are rebuking people for bringing their children to Jesus. Jesus' response, τῶν γὰρ τοιούτων ἐστιν ἡ βασιλεία τοῦ θεοῦ (10:14), shows the focus of this passage to be the kingdom of God, the identical theme where the gap regarding rewards for discipleship first occurred (1:17). Here, however, the narrative deals with requirements for entrance into the kingdom. Specifically, Jesus tells the disciples that the kingdom can be *received only as a child.* His instructive words illustrate the polyvalent nature of language as discussed in chapter 2 and thus require disambiguation.

The phrase ὡς παιδίον accesses a number of schemata for the reader. Among the more likely are such attitudes as "simple trust," "not counting on one's own merits," and "not regarding status." None of these is absolutely ruled out by the context. Therefore, owing to the interference caused by this overcoding, the reader carries all these notions through the episode until the narrator highlights the specific aspect that the reader is to embrace.

Mark has left conspicuous clues that indicate that status is the primary issue. In a society where wealth is viewed as a sign of righteousness, Jesus' statement about the inability of wealth to procure entrance to God's kingdom (10:25) is a clear indication of the powerlessness of status *vis-à-vis* entering the kingdom of God. Additionally, the section ends with a phrase that underscores (and undermines) the issue of status: πολλοὶ δὲ ἔσονται πρῶτοι ἔσχατοι καὶ οἱ ἔσχατοι πρῶτοι (10:31). This assertion captures the reader's attention not only because it interrupts the flow of the narrative but also because it interrupts a timeworn pattern of thinking the "things of men."[101] Is this a continuation of Jesus' homily or the narrator's direct comment to the reader?

At 10:17 the narrator links the "kingdom of God" with the notion of eternal life. The anonymous man's question to Jesus (τί ποιήσω ἵνα ζωὴν αἰώνιον κληρονομήσω) shows "inherit" to be an inappropriate rendering of κληρονομέω.[102] Inheritance is predicated upon an individual's status as an heir, not on something he or she does. This particular man is inquiring as to how he might acquire eternal life.[103] He thus views eternal life as a reward for some type of behavior (thinking the "things of men"). Jesus responds by quoting commandments from the Decalogue. Interestingly, he mentions only those commandments that deal with human relationships,[104] and he makes one change in the order: the commandment to honor one's parents is moved from first place to last. The order in which these commandments are cited is significant in that they are increasingly less likely to have been kept perfectly. Cranfield rightly notes that these commandments are

> the answer to the question about eternal life, not because a man can keep them and so earn eternal life, but because, if he honestly tries to keep them, he will be brought to recognize his bankruptcy and prepared to receive the kingdom of God as a little child.[105]

When Jesus required the man to sell all his possessions and give the proceeds to the poor, he attached the promise that the man would have treasure in heaven. This keeps the reward schema in the foreground. The two clauses are joined by a simple καί connective. The natural inference is to supply a causal relationship. But why would this act of philanthropy result in eternal life? The schema continues to build: sacrifice now and enjoy rich dividends later.

---

101. This statement fits more conveniently between 10:15–16 or after 10:25. The fact that it is delayed until 10.31 keeps the reader wondering as to the exact meaning of entering the kingdom "as a child." The abruptness of its appearance and its lack of direct connection with the preceding words of Jesus prevent the reader from bypassing its message.

102. Contra Taylor, *Mark*, 426.

103. BDAG, s.v. "κληρονομέω," cites Mark 10:17 as an example of the meanings "acquire," "obtain," "come into possession of."

104. Cranfield (*Mark*, 328) suggests, "it is by a man's obedience to the [commandments regarding the divine-human relationship] that his obedience to the latter [commandments regarding human relationships] must be outwardly demonstrated."

105. Ibid.

The man's refusal to comply indicates that he had failed the first commandment. He had let his wealth usurp the place intended for God. His money had become his idol. For him, parting with all his money would have been the act of proclaiming Yahweh as his God.

Now the reader must deal with Peter's confident acclamation. After Jesus stresses the impossibility of one who trusts riches to enter the kingdom of God, Peter confidently asserts: "Behold, *we* have left everything and have followed you." Peter was affirming that the disciples had done what the rich man had failed to do. The hook has been firmly implanted. The reader has been programmed to expect (with Peter) that since the disciples had fulfilled Jesus' command to the rich man, they would receive the reward that he forfeited.[106]

Jesus' first words in response to Peter confirm and heighten the reader's expectation. The lengthy enumeration of things abandoned to follow Jesus (which places children next to property) increases suspense and draws the lines along which the anticipated reward will be multiplied. According to Tannehill, the extravagance of the multiplication factor is the first indication that something strange is about to happen in the text. He supports his claim by insisting that a hundredfold reward would imply a "materialist's bonanza" and a "population explosion."[107] But this overlooks Jesus' frequent use of (and the reader's familiarity with) hyperbole. The multiplication factor of the reward accords well with the schemata already associated with the "kingdom of God" and "following" motifs. Instead, the first clue to a twist in the saying occurs with the phrase ἐν τῷ καιρῷ τούτῳ, which moves a step beyond the typical expectation of rewards in the afterlife. Jesus promises a reward νῦν ἐν τῷ καιρῷ τούτῳ.

The promise of reward "in this age" allows the reader to construct a schema that describes a kind of golden age on earth. This schema holds through the parallel list of rewards described by Jesus, but is overturned when the reader encounters the phrase "with persecutions." Tannehill has observed that the phrases that frame the list of rewards ("in this age" and "with persecutions") influence the reward schema:

> The phrase "with persecutions" is especially jarring. It is reserved until the end of the clause. The reader may get this far with his expectation of a simple and glorious reward, but he can go no

106. Tannehill, *Sword of His Mouth*, 149.
107. Ibid., 150.

farther. Without this frame the reader could only think of having houses, brothers, etc., in the same sense in which he had them before. However, the frame makes this view impossible. The reward cannot belong to some materialistic heaven nor to some miraculous period of peace and prosperity on earth. It belongs to the Christian's life now in the midst of persecution. The meaning that seemed to be implied has proved impossible. The reader's expectation has been frustrated and he must grope for a new meaning. The perceptive reader will soon see that the Evangelist is talking about what the disciple shares within the fellowship of the church.[108]

Thus, the narrator has capitalized on the reader's expectation of reward. The "hundredfold" multiplication of what was sacrificed suggests a grand materialistic reward ("things of men"). "With persecutions" presents an anomaly to this schema and thus calls for retrospection and repair. In the ordinary life of the church, family is no longer defined by birth but by obedience to the will of God (cf. 3:35); private ownership is replaced by communal sharing ("things of God").

The narrator finally delivers Jesus' promise of eternal life ἐν τῷ αἰῶνι τῷ ἐρχομένῳ, but his text has primed the reader to understand this promise from the "things of God" point of view. The preceding movement of the text debunks the reader's certainty that he or she has left everything and thus is due some great reward.[109] Eternal life (sharing in the kingdom of God) is the byproduct of following Jesus, not a payment for services rendered, nor a prerogative of social rank.

The Anonymous Woman: Mark 14:3–9

The placement of this section between the religious leaders' resolve to do away with Jesus (14:1–2) and their discovery of a means to that end (14:10–11) has often been noted.[110] Of concern here is the temporal aspect of this framing device and its resultant rhetorical effects.[111]

---

108. Ibid.

109. Ibid., 152.

110. See, e.g., Taylor, *Mark*, 530; Nineham, *Mark*, 370; Cranfield, *Mark*, 415; Fowler, *Loaves and Fishes*, 165; idem, *Reader*, 143; and Tolbert, *Sowing the Gospel*, 274.

111. Barton ("Mark as Narrative," 231) notes: "The story of the anointing woman in vv. 3–9 is framed by stories of evil men, in vv. 1–2 and 10–11. The effect of this framing is to pose a striking contrast. . . . Instead, it is a nameless woman who does what is right."

Robert Fowler describes this sandwich arrangement as "narrative sleight of hand, a crafty manipulation of the discourse level that creates the illusion that two episodes are taking place simultaneously."[112] In this way the reader is encouraged to read each incident in the light of the other.

Both the framed and framing episodes focus on the decision regarding Jesus. The connection with the parable of the sower and the soils is clear. Each of the characters illustrates the effect of soil type on sown seed. The religious leaders' immediate rejection of Jesus parallels the path along which seed was devoured by birds before it had a chance to take root. The iterative and conative imperfect (ἐζήτουν, 14:1; cf. 3:2, 6; 11:18; 12:12ff; 15:3) reinforces the steadfastness of their attitude of rejection.

In the closing section of the framing episode, Judas's immediate reception but ultimate failure typifies the rocky soil on which seed springs up quickly, but just as quickly perishes because it has no root. The account of Judas's appointment to apostleship does not directly state the immediacy of his response (contrast Simon, Andrew, James and John), but such is certainly implied. As a paradigm of those who accept Jesus' call to discipleship but ultimately fail him, Judas is a synecdoche for the disciples as a whole, although the reader only later discovers their failure.[113]

The thorny ground represents a group of individuals in the framed episode. In this case, however, the referents are described by the anonymous τινες. Nevertheless, their connection with the thorns is made apparent by their fixation on the monetary value of the perfume. What is ἡ ἀπάτη τοῦ πλούτου (4:19)? Is it the belief that giving money to the poor will extricate them from their poverty? This much is clear: when it comes to the episode's focus on the proper response to Jesus, this group surely is concerned with "other things" (4:19).

The good soil finds its paragon in the heroine of this pair of episodes, an unidentified woman who, in marked contrast to the religious leaders who *kept seeking* a way to destroy Jesus, anoints Jesus' head.[114] The

---

112. Fowler, *Let the Reader Understand*, 143–44.

113. The Twelve are specifically linked to Judas by his designation as ὁ εἷς τῶν δώδεκα (14:10).

114. "It is striking how many stories within the story have to do with women" (Barton, "Mark as Narrative," 231). For recent works that focus on women as disciples in Mark see, e.g., Malbon, "Fallible Followers"; idem, "Poor Widow"; Beavis, "Women as Models"; Schierling, "Women as Leaders"; Schmitt, "Women in Mark's Gospel," 228–33; Grassi, *Hidden Heroes*; idem, "Secret Heroine."

narrative gap regarding the motivation behind her act is partially filled by Jesus' response to the other guests: ὅ ἔσχεν ἐποίησεν· προέλαβεν μυρίσαι τὸ σῶμά μου εἰς τὸν ἐνταφιασμόν. This exemplary use of what she had at her disposal recalls the offering of the impoverished widow who put into the temple treasury πάντα ὅσα εἶχεν (12:44).[115] Taylor observes a dissimilarity in the accounts, namely, in 14:3–9 the woman's action does not consist of "giving all she has, but rendering the only service within her power."[116]

What is the nature of the service that this unnamed woman renders? In the ancient Near East, anointing was a common practice with a variety of purposes, of which four shed light on the anointing schema supported by the text: religious consecration, cosmetology, hospitality, and burial preparation.[117]

When the reader encounters the woman's action, he or she constructs a schema for it by testing the various linguistic nodes associated with the act. As we have seen in chapter 2, context (in particular, what immediately precedes in the narrative order) exerts a controlling influence on the linguistic nodes accessed by the reader. Here, the banquet setting evokes a script that primes the reader to process the woman's action as the hospitable custom of anointing the head of a guest. The costly perfumed ingredient, however, calls for retrospection and repair, since guests were normally anointed with readily available and inexpensive olive oil. In contrast, prostitutes typically used heavily perfumed

---

115. Both accounts contrast the piety of a woman with the treachery of the religious leaders. But see Wright, "Widow's Mites," 262. In an argument that Malbon ("Fallible Followers," 38) rightly appraises as "more ingenious than convincing," Wright rejects the more defensible view that the story of the widow's offering provides a vivid contrast between the sacrificial *giving* of the poor widow (12:41–44) and the merciless *taking* of the scribes (12:38–40). In view of Jesus' condemnation of the scribes (12:40) and prediction of the temple's destruction (13:2), Wright sees Jesus' assessment of the poor widow's gift as "downright disapproval"—not of the woman herself but of the religious leaders whose value system induced her action. The problem with taking Jesus' comment on the widow's gift as condemnation of the religious leaders is that the contrast that Jesus draws in 12:33–34 is between the *giving* of the πολοὶ πλούσιοι and the *giving* of the poor widow. Jesus is not addressing the scribes on this point. He is emphasizing the extent of the widow's devotion. To be sure, the religious leaders' proclivity to take advantage of such loyalty is noted in 12:40, but this is not the issue in 12:41–44. Thus, it is appropriate to see Jesus' attitude toward the widow's gift as approbatory and, as such, a potent contrast to the *taking* of the scribes.

116. Taylor, *Mark*, 532.

117. See Trevor, "Oil"; Thompson, "Ointment"; Huey, "Oil"; idem, "Ointment."

oils for cosmetic purposes, and this may cast a shadow on the woman's character.[118]

The fact that Jesus' *head* was anointed allows, but does not require, the view that the act had the religious significance of anointing Jesus as king/Messiah. Jesus has already been identified as the Messiah by the narrator (1:1) and Peter (8:29). Additionally, the "little Apocalypse" does speak of the coming of false messiahs (13:22) and so puts the notion of Messiah in close proximity to the woman's application of ointment to Jesus' head. Nevertheless, the text gives no indication that the *woman* understood her role in this way.

Attention then focuses on the monetary value of the ointment and the extravagance of using it to anoint a guest. The unnamed guests argue that the perfumed oil could have been sold and the money given to the poor; if her intention was to extend common courtesy, cheap oil could have been used. In overturning their rebuke, Jesus asserts that the woman has anointed his body for burial. This, then, is the schema that the narrator wishes the reader to attach to the woman's action. Again, however, the language of the text does not clearly indicate that the woman had the burial of Jesus in mind when she broke the alabaster flask and poured its contents on Jesus.[119]

Thus, the significance of the woman's act of anointing has been extended beyond its storyworld support. Herman Waetjen, for example, describes the Bethany anointing thus: OT prophets anointed kings in order to signify their divine election to ascend the throne and exercise sovereignty over Israel. This unnamed woman has assumed the role of prophet, but in order to anoint Jesus as the Messiah in death....

> Up to this point in the narrative none of Jesus' disciples appears to understand his unusual messiahship. None of them grasps who or what he really is, except this unnamed woman who bursts into a men's banquet, performs her ministry, and then disappears.[120]

118. The impropriety of her uninvited intrusion into a men's banquet may lend support to this view.

119. See BDAG, s.v. "προλαμβάνω." Where the temporal force of pro- is present, προλαμβάνω conveys either (1) "do something before the usual time" or (2) "take it upon oneself to do something." The second case would imply that the woman knew she was anointing Jesus' body for burial. The ambiguity makes this position tenuous.

120. Waetjen, *Reordering of Power*, 205. Waetjen goes as far as to say that the Bethany woman is "the only one in the Gospel who understands the distinctive character of Jesus' messiahship (205 n. 169).

Likewise, Joseph Grassi writes:

> In contrast to Peter's misunderstanding, the Bethany woman
> anoints Jesus' head and understands who he is. The anointing re-
> calls the similar prophetic designation of kings or anointed ones
> in the Scriptures (1 Sam 10:1; 16:13). Yet she does this in view of
> Jesus' death, which Peter and the disciples found so difficult to
> accept (8:33–34; 9:33).[121]

While the notion of Jesus' suffering Messiahship indeed echoes throughout the narrative, assigning this insight to a character in the story world
when there is no clear indication of this in the text is not justifiable.

The distinction between story world and narrative world allows us
to see how the narrator has again treated the reader as an insider, that
is, as one with access to information that the characters themselves do
not possess. This pair of episodes draws a striking contrast between the
woman's act of devotion ("the things of God") and Judas's act of treachery ("the things of men"). The unnamed woman is shown to be a true
disciple who "gives up money for Jesus and enters the house to honor
him (14:3–9)"; the Apostle Judas is revealed as an adversary who "gives
up Jesus for money and leaves the house to betray him (14:10–11)."[122]

The "things of men" and "things of God" perspectives differ at a critical point. For the former, the highest virtues are power and social status;
for the latter, the only virtue is obedience to the will of God. Discipleship
is predicated on action criteria, not status criteria.[123] Thinking "the
things of men" involves using others to achieve one's desires; thinking
"the things of God" involves using one's resources to serve others. The
narrative sandwich in 14:1–11 provides an illustration of both.

The position of this story in the narrative's chain of episodes plays
a large role in its significance for the reader. Stephen Barton argues
convincingly that the woman's action foreshadows Jesus' passion and
resurrection. For Barton, the narrator places the story of the anointing
woman at the beginning of Jesus' passion because

> he wants to cast the anonymous woman as a Christ-figure. Her
> extravagant love expressed in an act of self-giving which provokes

---

121. Grassi, *Hidden Heroes*, 37.

122. Malbon, "Fallible Followers," 40.

123. Barton, "Mark as Narrative," 231.

conflict, is an anticipation in the narrative of what will happen to Jesus himself.[124]

Thus, in Mark 14:3–9, an anonymous woman is identified by her marked parallel with Jesus: *she* acts self-sacrificially, experiences rejection and humiliation, and is vindicated by Jesus; *Jesus* acts self-sacrificially, experiences rejection and humiliation, and is vindicated by the empty tomb. The woman appears as a model disciple:

> Unlike Peter, she denies herself for Jesus's sake. In contrast to the rich man, she sacrifices her valued possessions. When reproached, she remains silent.... Her action shows ... the faith and vigilence of a true follower (cf. 13:33), able to distinguish *chronos* (ordinary time: "For you always have the poor with you") from *kairos* (special time: "but you will not always have me").[125]

That the model disciple in 14:3–9 is an anonymous woman is significant. The low social rank of women in the ancient world is well known. In this episode, however, Jesus praises the woman and hints that the men should learn from her example.[126] Thus, the narrative again overturns the notion of status and illustrates Jesus' statement (or the narrator's commentary?) that "many who are first will be last, and the last first" (10:31).[127]

The Crisis of Decision: Mark 14:53–72

In spite of the consistency with which Jesus proclaims, commends, and demonstrates thinking "the things of God," his efforts fail to produce the desired results in his own disciples. Up to the recognition scene in

124. Ibid., 232.

125. Ibid., 233.

126. Cf. the hemorrhaging woman (5:25–34), whose response to Jesus teaches a synagogue ruler an important lesson in faith. Women frequently illustrate seed ἐπὶ τὴν γῆν τὴν καλὴν σπαρέντες. Tolbert (*Sowing the Gospel*, 292) notes that "with the blatant exception of Herodias and her daughter (6:17–25), female characters throughout the Gospel have consistently embodied the good earth type." Meyers (*Binding the Strong Man*, 280) notes that, apart from Jesus, only women render διακονία in Mark's Gospel (1:31; 15:41). Cf. also the Syro-Phoenician woman (7:24–30), the poor widow (12:41–44), the anointing woman (14:3–9), and the women attending the crucifixion (15:40–41).

127. Meyers (*Binding the Strong Man*, 280) notes that the women in Mark's Gospel almost always appear without husbands. He assumes the Bethany woman is unmarried and hence has even lower status than a married woman.

8:27–29, the problem concerns their understanding of who Jesus is. After this point the issue is their failure to follow Jesus' example. The Twelve frequently display their affinity for the "things of men": they must be coaxed to pray (9:29; 14:38), they are status-minded (9:34; 10:13, 37, 41), and they are exclusive (9:38). Peter, their frequent spokesman, rebels against Jesus' resolve to suffer (8:32) and attempts to forestall Jesus' suffering by prolonging the glory of the transfiguration (9:5). These men have indeed sacrificed their livelihoods to follow Jesus (10:28), but are they willing to sacrifice their lives (8:35)? This is the acid test.

Mark 14:53–72 places Peter and Jesus in a similar position, where their decision regarding the "things of God" carries its highest stakes. Although the forensic features of Jesus' inquest are entirely lacking in the interrogation of Peter, for the reader, both Peter and Jesus are on trial. That the rest of the disciples have already chosen to "save their lives" (8:35) by deserting Jesus at Gethsemane (14:50) makes Peter's function in the present context more critical. Peter represents the reader's last opportunity to identify with the disciples as a follower of Christ.

The narrative, however, leaves little doubt as to the outcome of Peter's "trial," since Jesus so clearly and emphatically predicted his failure (σὺ σήμερον ταύτῃ τῇ νυκτὶ πρὶν ἢ δὶς ἀλέκτορα φωνῆσαι τρίς με ἀπαρνήσῃ, 14:30), and since Jesus' prior predictions have been consistently accurate. The effect of this is to focus the reader's attention on Jesus' faithfulness to the "things of God" under threat of death. A closer examination of the literary context shows that narrative sequence plays an important role in producing this effect.

The scene opens with the temple officers leading Jesus to the place where the religious leaders had convened (v. 53). Immediately the spotlight shifts to Peter sitting with the guards in the high priest's courtyard (v. 54). Then, just as abruptly, the spotlight is redirected to the scene of Jesus' interrogation (vv. 55–65), after which attention is again shifted to the courtyard where Peter's three progressively more emphatic denials of Jesus take place. A more natural order would place v. 55 immediately after v. 53 and move v. 54 immediately before v. 66. As it is, however, the interweaving of these trial scenes creates the impression that they are happening simultaneously and invites the reader to read each in light of the other.

Placing Peter in the high priest's courtyard before the narration of Jesus' trial encourages the reader to interpret the trial as a paradigm for later trials that the disciples (and the reader?) will face. The reader is inclined to process the text in this fashion since Jesus earlier predicted such trials (13:9–11) and since ἠκολούθησεν αὐτῷ (14:54) recalls the "following" motif.[128]

These trial scenes exhibit a fair amount of the verbal and situational irony that characterizes the entire narrative.[129] Throughout this Gospel the disciples have been, as Tolbert puts it, "victims of constant and increasingly broad doses of situational irony."[130] The reader thus becomes increasingly less inclined to identify with the disciples.

While irony victimizes outsiders, its more significant function is to strengthen the rapport between the narrator and the reader.[131] In the case of Mark's Gospel, irony also draws a tighter bond between the reader and Jesus, since Jesus' viewpoint is virtually identical to the narrator's. The text coaxes the reader to reject the "things of men" perspective found in the disciples and to accept the "things of God" viewpoint shared by the narrator and Jesus. The reader must choose. Herein lies the most profound irony to which the reader falls victim: Jesus and Peter are interrogated, but the one presently on trial is the reader!

THE READER AS FOLLOWER

Narrative sequence plays a large role in conveying the narrator's ideology. In particular, the sequential arrangement of narrative information about a character influences the reader to view him as either as "a good fellow with some human frailties" or "an ugly customer surprisingly possessed

128. Although Peter is following the group that has arrested Jesus, the singular αὐτῷ emphasizes that he is following Jesus.

129. See esp. Camery-Hoggatt, *Irony in Mark's Gospel*, 171–74.

130. Tolbert, *Sowing the Gospel*, 103. They are ignorant of Jesus' identity after Jesus stills the storm (4:41), even though Jesus explained *everything* to them privately (4:34); they are befuddled about how Jesus will feed four thousand (8:1–9) when they previously participated in his feeding of a larger crowd with less provisions (6:35–44); they worry about having only one loaf (8:14–21) after Jesus has just fed the second multitude (8:1–9) and miss the connection of leaven with moral blindness (Camery-Hoggatt, *Irony in Mark's Gospel*, 154, writes: "How ironic it is that the disciples—possessors of the mystery of the kingdom—should fail even to understand the warning against blindness!"); Peter's rebuke of Jesus (8:32) aligns him, not with God, but with Satan; and James and John unknowingly request to occupy the crosses that will stand on either side of Jesus (10:37; cf. 15:29).

131. See Booth, *Rhetoric of Irony*, 28.

of a few attractive or redeeming traits."[132] This phenomenon is especially important in Mark's Gospel since the narrator's ideology is identical to that of his central character, Jesus, and since all other characters in the narrative are judged according to their alignment with or deviation from the narrator's (= Jesus') ideology.

Mark's narrative capitalizes on a reader's tendency to identify with characters who most closely share his or her situation. The initially positive depiction of the disciples secures the reader's attachment to these men and leads the reader to experience the events of the story world from their perspective.[133] The presentation is positive wherever the disciples live out the values shared by Jesus and the narrator (τὰ τοῦ θεοῦ).[134] As the narrative progresses, however, the disciples' repeated failure to adopt the values of Jesus functions to distance the reader from them. In spite of this, "something of the initial identification remains,"[135] creating ten-

132. These expressions are from Sternberg, *Expositional Modes*, 96.

133. According to Tannehill ("Disciples in Mark," 392–93), Mark "composed his story . . . in order to speak indirectly to the reader through the disciples' story." Addressing reader-character identification, Dewey ("Oral Methods of Structuring Narrative in Mark," 42–43) cites Petersen ("'Point of View' in Mark's Narrative") as holding that the reader identifies with Jesus (43n54). But this observation rests on a categorical error that overlooks an important distinction. Petersen does indeed affirm that the reader "identifies" with Jesus. But his analysis in indicates a concern with point of view (97) or ideological standpoint (107), not with what I have labeled "reader-character identification": "Through this commonality of psychologically internal points of view, and with the support of the plotting of the story by which one actor is rendered central, the narrator is aligned—if not identified—with the central actor. Together, the distribution of points of view and the plotting of the story lead the reader to identify with, and trust, not only the narrator, but also the central actor" (102). Petersen's analysis does speak of the reader's identification with Jesus, but he speaks strictly in terms of a shared point of view. A reader need not identify with a character simply because he or she happens to share the same point of view. Readers identify with characters who most closely share their situation. The uniqueness of Jesus makes unlikely any strict identification of him with the reader. The disciples are far more likely candidates for this role.

134. Dewey ("Point of View," 103) argues that Mark's reader identifies both with the disciples and with Jesus in that he or she shares the *situation* of the disciples, but the *values* of Jesus. The initial identification is close since the disciples adopt and act on the values of Jesus.

135. Tannehill ("Disciples in Mark," 392) supports this by affirming that the reader and the disciples still share a similar situation. However, this phenomenon may also be attributed to the "primacy effect." Menakhem Perry ("Literary Dynamics," 57) writes: "The reader retains the meanings constructed initially *to whatever extent possible*, but the text causes them to be replaced. The literary text, then, *exploits* the 'powers' of the primacy effect, but ordinarily it sets up a mechanism to oppose them, giving rise, rather,

sion in the reader—disciple bond. In Sternberg's phraseology, the reader
views the disciples as "good fellow[s] with some human frailties"—but
the frailties are serious. Tannehill assesses how the tension generated by
the negative shift in the disciples' characterization effects the reader:

> This tension between identification and repulsion can lead the
> sensitive reader beyond a naively positive view of himself to
> self-criticism and repentance. The composition of Mark strongly
> suggests that the author, by the way in which he tells the disciples'
> story, intended to awaken his readers to their failures as disciples
> and call them to repentance.[136]

The unflattering portrayal of the disciples in Mark's Gospel can be
explained as an attempt to teach by negative example. Theodore Weeden,
for example, explains the negative portrayal of the disciples in Mark's
Gospel as a polemic against a *Theios-Aner* Christology, which focused
on signs and wonders and rejected the self-sacrificial aspect of discipleship. Tannehill rightly faults Weeden for not taking sufficient account of
the positive features of the disciples' characterization.[137] Yet Tannehill
himself makes far more use of the disciples' foibles than their virtues.
The disciples are primarily examples of what true followers of Jesus are
not to be. Their failure prompts the reader to critical self-evaluation and
repentance.[138] Nevertheless, Tannehill differs from Weeden in admitting
the possibility of the disciples' restoration; for Weeden, their failure is
irremediable.[139]

---

to a recency effect. Its terminal point, the point at which all the words that have hitherto
remained 'open' are sealed, is the decisive one" (emphasis his).

136. Tannehill, "Disciples in Mark," 393.

137. Ibid., 394. Cf. Malbon ("Fallible Followers," 33): "The entire Markan pattern
of characterization is . . . more complex. The disciples are not simply the 'bad guys.'"
For Malbon the flight of the disciples "indicates that they are fallible, not that they are
non-followers" (43).

138. Tannehill ("Disciples in Mark") emphasizes that the reader "must choose between the attitudes of Jesus and those of the disciples" (402) and must "disentangle
himself from [the disciples]" (403).

139. Tannehill (ibid., 403–4) writes: "The Gospel holds open the possibility that
those who deserted Jesus will again become his followers, reinstating the relationship established by Jesus' call." Weeden (*Mark: Traditions in Conflict*, 50–51) charges:
"Mark is assiduously involved in a vendetta against the disciples. He is intent on totally
discrediting them. He paints them as obtuse, obdurate, recalcitrant men who at first
are unperceptive of Jesus' messiahship, then oppose its style and character, and finally
totally reject it. As the coup de grace, Mark closes his Gospel without rehabilitating the
disciples."

Peter's denial climaxes the increasingly negative portrayal of the disciples in their role as models of followership. Because the reader has experienced the entire narrative through the viewpoint of the narrator (= Jesus), his or her abandonment of the disciples is inevitable; since the disciples have forsaken Jesus, the reader forsakes the disciples.[140]

Yet the reader still gropes for a model of true followership. This provokes retrospection and anticipation. Several minor characters, less prominent but more faithful to τὰ τοῦ θεοῦ, have already made cameo appearances on the Markan stage: (the four pallet-bearers, 2:3–5; Jairus, 5:22–24a, 35–43; the hemorrhaging woman, 5:24b–34; Syrophoenician woman, 7:24–30; Bartimaeus, 10:46–52, the poor widow, 12:41–44; the anointing woman, 14:3–9).[141] In case the reader has not reaccessed these, the narrative provides—subsequent to Peter's denial—still other models for followership.

After the last of the Twelve exits the stage, Mark's narrative tantalizingly presents several minor characters for the reader's evaluation. Most of these disappear from the stage as abruptly as they arrive. Pilate (15:1–15) has an opportunity to align himself with Jesus, but political expediency (v. 15) chokes his apparent desire to spare Jesus' life (v. 9). Simon (v. 21) follows Jesus to the site of crucifixion, but this is under compulsion. An anonymous man (v. 36) offers Jesus sour wine (to ease his suffering?), but punctuates his gesture with ridicule.

After Jesus dies (v. 37) and the temple curtain is torn (v. 38), a centurion (v. 39) affirms Jesus to be God's Son, but the ambiguity of the anarthrous expression υἱὸς θεοῦ allows the confession to be merely a recognition of heroic status ("son of a god") or pious character ("a godly man"). None of these characters unequivocally models true followership. But the final performers in Mark's drama much more closely approximate the ideal disciple. These personae are narratively configured so as to draw special attention from the reader.

Jesus' humiliating death on the cross overturns worldly notions of status and power. The appearance of a group of women as the only Markan witnesses to this event is, therefore, appropriate for convey-

---

140. "The reader who was at first content to view the disciples as reflections of his own faith and who may have continued to hope for a happy ending to their story must now try to disentangle himself from them, which will mean choosing a path contrary to their path" (Tannehill, "Disciples in Mark," 403).

141. Rhoads and Michie (*Mark as Story*, 129–35) apply the label "little people" to characters of this type.

ing the narrator's ideology. The fact that these women outdistance the Twelve should not strike the reader as incredible, because the narrator has carefully laid the groundwork for this moment.[142] As Boomershine observes:

> All aspects of the characterization of the women—the extended inside views, the positive norms of judgment in relation to their actions, the overall atmosphere and mood—create a steady intensification of appeals for identification with women.[143]

Several features underscore the significance of the women's role. The fact that their appearance immediately follows the failure of the disciples and the nefarious treatment of Jesus in the trial and crucifixion makes their faithful followership all the more striking.[144] Their link with the beginning of the narrative (and Jesus' ministry; cf. 1:9) by the reference to Galilee also indicates their importance.[145] Their activity is reported in discipleship terminology (διακονέω, ἀκολουθέω, 15:41). Finally, they are the last figures on the Markan stage when the final curtain falls.

Sandwiched between the wholly positive portrayal of the women (15:40–41) and their wholly unexpected failure in 16:8, Mark inserts a scene that features another positive model of followership: Joseph of

---

142. Cf. Malbon's critique ("Fallible Followers," 40–41) of Winsome Munro ("Women Disciples in Mark?"): "While there may be 'little preparation for the women who appear at the death and burial of Jesus and at the empty tomb' in the sense of literal and straightforward narrative anticipation, the same cannot be said in terms of metaphorical and allusive narrative dimensions. Individual women characters have previously exhibited in particular actions the active faith and self-denying service of followership. . . ." (Malbon quotes Munro, 230).

143. Boomershine, "Mark 16:8," 232.

144. Cf. Tolbert (*Sowing the Gospel*, 292): "[The women] appear all the better because they follow the disciples' nadir, enduring where the Twelve have not." Some would fault the women for witnessing the crucifixion ἀπὸ μακρόθεν, but see Malbon, "Fallible Followers," 43, who reads *presence* with Jesus as a sign of followership and remaining *at a distance* as an indication of fallibility—for Peter in the courtyard of the high priest (14:54) and for the women at Golgotha (15:40).

145. To use Genette's terminology (*Narrative Discourse*, esp. 40–56), the reference to the women in 15:40–41 is an "internal" (within the time of the story), "homodiegetic" (deals with the same line of action as the first narrative), "repeating" (fills in a missing element from a period that the narrative generally covers) "analepsis" (retrospection) whose "reach" (temporal distance) spans the entire plotted life of Jesus and whose "extent" (length of story) almost covers the entire narrative. Malbon ("Fallible Followers," 41) notes that Mark's singular usage of this feature in 15:40–41 "increases its significance."

Arimathea. The appearance of Joseph at this point in the narrative is significant for at least two reasons. The first has to do with the narrator's description of his character; the second with the role he plays in the narrative.

The narrator describes Joseph with only two pieces of information (15:43): (1) he is a "prominent council member" and (2) he is "waiting for the kingdom of God." The first is important for its evidence that Jesus' following was not limited to the poor, ignorant masses. The second is crucial in that it reinforces the connection between following Jesus and citizenship in God's kingdom.

But the role that Joseph performs is just as vital to the narrative's overall effect as the description of his character. In burying Jesus, Joseph performs an action that the disciples of John did for their teacher, but which Jesus' own disciples failed to do. The nobility of Joseph's caring for Jesus burial is highlighted even more starkly when compared with the actions of Judas: unlike Judas who gives up Jesus for money, Joseph gives up money for Jesus. Thus, in Joseph, as in the anointing woman (14:3–9) and the women who "cared for [Jesus'] needs" (15:41), the narrator offers the reader a more stable model of followership than the Twelve.

Even before the Joseph scene closes, the women reenter the stage (15:47) in preparation for the narrative's final scene. In the end, the general portrayal of the women parallels that of the disciples. Both begin on a positive note and end in failure. Yet they differ in an important aspect: whereas the disciples' failure is made more comprehensible by various premonitory signals, nothing prepares the reader for the disobedience and flight of the women. Their characterization has been positive throughout the narrative, a feature fresh in the reader's mind, since he or she only learns this via the analepsis in 15:41.

Once again, the sequencing of events heightens the reader's expectation that the women will remain firm in their commitment to Jesus. Purchasing spices (giving money for Jesus) and caring for Jesus' body are acts that model true followership.[146] The women's flight is strategically

---

146. Some argue that the women's intention to anoint Jesus' body displays lack of faith in Jesus' resurrection predictions. But nowhere *in the narrative* do women hear Jesus' three-day prediction. See Malbon's argument in "Fallible Followers," 43–44: "It seems unlikely, then, that the Markan narrator and implied reader would expect the women followers to anticipate or understand the resurrection with no forewarning" (44). The ὑμῖν οϕ καθὼς εἶπεν ὑμῖν (16:7) could include the women, but the very ambiguity speaks against it being taken in this way.

positioned at the last sentence of the narrative where it has the greatest impact on the reader.

Any reading of Mark's Gospel must come to grips with the "supremely enigmatic and provocative narrative comment" relating the flight and silence of the women.[147] The form of the sentence relating this information indicates that the narrator anticipated the reader's surprise at the actions of the women and sought to explain them.[148] Boomershine cogently argues that "the norms associated with the women's flight and silence are totally negative":

> The connotations of the women's flight are determined by the earlier narration of the flight of the disciples and the young man where the same verb, ἔφυγον, is used (14:50–52). The disciples' flight is presented as a scandalous act and is associated with the shame of the young man's running away naked. Since this turning point in the narrative includes the only prior use of the word, the women's flight is unavoidably associated with the disciples' action. It is set, therefore, in a strongly negative context.
>
> The women's silence is even more inappropriate. The angelic young man commanded them to go and tell the disciples. The news of Jesus' resurrection is incomparably good news and the possibility of the disciples' seeing Jesus in Galilee is associated with joy. The women's silence is, therefore, the exact opposite of the angel's command and dashes the expectations of joyful reunion that Mark has established. It is the most blatant form of disobedience to a divine commission. Therefore, since the norms associated with the command of an angel are positive, the women's silence is unequivocally and unambiguously wrong. It is a shocking reversal of expectations.[149]

Although the preceding narrative information has stamped the women's actions with a strongly condemnatory tone, the narrator offers an explanation for their flight (εἶχεν γὰρ αὐτὰς τρόμος καὶ ἔκστασις) and their silence (ἐφοβοῦντο γάρ). The condemnation functions to alienate the reader from the women, but the explanations invite

147. The phrase is found in Boomershine and Bartholomew, "Narrative Technique," 217.

148. Boomershine and Bartholomew (ibid., 215) list twenty-two Markan usages of γάρ that explain confusing or surprising events related in the previous sentence. They further show two instances where a γάρ clause concludes a Markan episode and "leaves several strings hanging out which invite the audience to do some work" (217).

149. Boomershine, "Mark 16:8," 229.

sympathetic attachment. Since the narrator condemns the women's *response* rather than the women themselves, "a high degree of identification is maintained."[150] Thus, the reader hears the announcement of Jesus' resurrection from the women's perspective.[151] With the women, the reader is presented a choice: proclaim the resurrection of Jesus or remain silent. Boomershine describes the effect of the ending:

> The ending concretizes, therefore, the powerful conflict between responsibility and fear that is implicit in the commission to announce the resurrection.
>
> The intended meaning of the ending is, therefore, the total effect of the ending. The ending is designed to be an experience of conflict between the scandal of silence and the fear of proclamation. In response to the shock of realization that the response of silence is utterly wrong, the story appeals for the proclamation of the resurrection regardless of fear. In the silences surrounding the climactic short statements of 16:8 and the surprising ending, Mark invites his audience to reflect on their own response to the dilemma that the women faced.[152]

Boomershine's evaluation is particularly defensible in that it accounts for the affective appeal recently shown to be a major focus of ancient literature.

Malbon sees the women's silence in the context of its function within the "outward movement of the text from author to reader." In her view, Mark's narrative emphasizes that followership is neither exclusive nor easy. Failures are inevitable, but not justifiable. The responsibility of followership continues even in the face of failure. Where one has fallen silent another must speak. The existence and content of Mark's narrative testifies to it:

> The women characters follow Jesus after the disciples flee; the narrator tells Jesus' story after the women's silence; it remains for the hearer/reader to continue this line of followers.[153]

---

150. Ibid., 232–33.

151. Ibid., 232.

152. Ibid., 237.

153. Malbon, "Fallible Followers," 45.

CONCLUSION

From a strictly literary perspective, this chapter's analysis corroborates Mark's fondness for what Robert Fowler has labeled a "rhetoric of indirection."[154] The numerous instances of ambiguity (e.g., the identity and function of the "messenger" and "strongman") and polyvalence (e.g., the intended schema for ἀρχή,[155] ἁλιεῖς ἀνθρώπων,[156] τὰ τοῦ θεοῦ, τὰ τῶν ἀνθρώπων,[157] and ὡς παιδίον)[158] indicate that anyone wishing to understand Mark's narrative faces some thought-provoking challenges.

The selective nature of language is witnessed in the narrative gaps that Mark admits. Some of these are left open (e.g., the precise call issued to disciples other than Simon and Andrew); some are filled only after much narrative time (e.g., the question of rewards for responding to the call); and some are immediately filled (e.g., the numerous explanatory γάρ, ὅτι, and διά clauses).

Language's linear attribute assures that Mark's reader will be transported through his narrative in a restricted sequence. This path influences the reader to make specific connections between the characters and events of the narrative. The predictions of Isaiah and John, together with their immediate fulfillments, influence the reader to expect that the open-ended aspect of Jesus' subsequent prediction (perhaps the arrival of God's kingdom, but certainly the promise to make the disciples "people-fishers") will similarly come to pass.

To this should be added Mark's intercalating technique, which directs the reader to read one event in light of another (e.g., the Herod-Baptist episode, 6:14–29), which is sandwiched between the sending out (6:7–13) and return (6:30) of the Twelve; Jesus' disruption of temple-business (11:15–19), which is positioned between the cursing (11:12–14) and destruction (11:20–21) of the fig tree; and the story of the anonymous woman who anointed Jesus (14:3–9), which falls between the religious leaders' resolve to do away with Jesus (14:1–2) and their discovery of a means to that end (14:10–11).

154. Fowler, *Let the Reader Understand*, 155.

155. Among the possibilities are "beginning," "elementary principles," "origin," "first cause," "ruler," "authority," and "sphere of influence."

156. Literally "fishers of men."

157. I.e., "the things of God/the things of men."

158. I.e., "as a little child."

Narrative sequence plays an important role in the unfolding of the narrator's ideology. The narrative that emphasizes following Jesus requires itself careful followership from its reader. Indeed, its function bears a striking resemblance to that of Jesus' parables: only those whose worldview is open to change will see beneath the *text* ("the surface meanings of the dialogue") and apprehend the *subtext* ("the underlying connotative meanings").[159]

The Gospel of Mark presents challenging illustrations of the "things of God" and "things of men" perspectives. The opposition between the two is evidenced not only in Jesus' conflict with the religious leaders but also in the disciples' obduracy. Jesus is clearly the narrative's focal point. He is the quintessence of the "things of God" and the one everyone (including the reader) is encouraged to emulate. Yet the uniqueness of Jesus precludes direct reader identification.

Nevertheless, Mark's narrative does offer several reader-identifiable personae who model the "things of God" perspective. These individuals[160] and groups[161] are socially and narratively marginal. Of Mark's cast, two character groups are the most strategically significant: the Twelve and the women who followed Jesus.[162] Mark's sequential development of the characterization of these groups induces the reader to identify with the characters themselves yet condemn their failure. In doing so, the reader is encouraged to analyze his or her own life situation in light of these models and adopt the narrator's ideology. This action is described straightforwardly as thinking the "things of God" and pictured metaphorically as "following Jesus" and "entering the kingdom of God."

The sequential arrangement of events in Mark's narrative also overturns worldly notions of power. Jesus did not coerce people to ac-

159. This distinction, formulated by Miller (*Word, Self, and Reality*, 46–47), is employed by Camery-Hoggett in the subtitle of his monograph on Markan irony (*Irony in Mark's Gospel*) and discussed on its opening page.

160. Some are named e.g., John the Baptist, Jairus, Bartimaeus, Joseph of Arimathea, the two Marys and Salome (function as a group), and Peter, James, and John (often function with the Twelve or as a subgroup thereof); some are anonymous, e.g., the demon-possessed man, the hemorrhaging woman, the Syrophoenician woman, the poor widow, and the anointing woman.

161. Some are defined narrowly, e.g., the Twelve, Peter-James-John, Mary-Mary-Salome; and others loosely, e.g., four pallet-bearers, unnamed exorcists, children, and women.

162. The uniqueness of Jesus' person and of John's role as eschatological prophet makes it unlikely that a first-century reader would identify with either of them.

cept God's rule; he suffered for them. In suffering, God invites humanity to participate in his kingdom. To think the "things of God" is to follow Jesus; to follow Jesus is to go the way of the cross (8:34–38); and to go the way of the cross is the only way to enter God's kingdom. Citizenship in the kingdom of God requires abandoning a self-serving, status-seeking, power-oriented strategy of living and following instead a self-sacrificial, seed-sowing, service-oriented program of action.

TABLE 1*: Processing the "Messenger" of Mark 1:2:
Reader Unfamiliar with the Hebrew Scriptures

[1] Beginning of the gospel about Jesus Christ, the Son of God.
JESUS = SoG

[2] It is written in Isaiah the prophet: "I will send my messenger ahead of you, who will prepare your way—
I (=N)   *MESSENGER (=J)*   *YOU (=R)*

[3] "a voice of one calling in the desert, 'Prepare the way for the Lord, make straight paths for him.'
voice   *(you=R)*   *YHWH*

[4] And so John came, baptizing in the desert region and preaching a baptism of repentance for the forgiveness of sins.
JOHN [†]

[5] The whole Judean countryside and all the people of Jerusalem went out to him. Confessing their sins, they were baptized by him in the Jordan
JOHN

[6] John wore clothing made of camel's hair, with a leather belt around his waist, and he ate locusts and wild honey.
JOHN

[7] And this was his message: "After me will come one more powerful than I, the thongs of whose sandals I am not worthy to stoop down and untie.
Me/I   *mightier one (=?J)*

[8] I baptize you with water, but he will baptize you with the Holy Spirit.
I   *YOU (=R)*   *HE (=M.O.=?J)*   *SPIRIT*

[9] At that time Jesus came from Nazareth in Galilee and was baptized by John in the Jordan.
JOHN   *JESUS (=M.O.!)*

[10] As Jesus was coming up out of the water, he saw heaven being torn open and the Spirit descending on him like a dove.
JESUS   *SPIRIT*

[11] And a voice came from heaven: "You are my Son, whom I love; with you I am well pleased."
VOICE (=GOD)   *You=SON (=J!)*

*SOG=Son of God; N=narrator; J=Jesus; R=reader; M.O.=mightier one.
†Identification of the messenger with Jesus is overturned here.

TABLE 2*: Processing the "Messenger" of Mark 1:2: Reader Familiar with the Hebrew Scriptures

---

[1] Beginning of the gospel about Jesus Christ, the Son of God.

> Jesus = SoG

---

[2] It is written in Isaiah the prophet: "I will send my messenger ahead of you, who will prepare your way—

I (=Y)	MESSENGER (=?A)	YOU (=?M=?J)
	(=?E)	(=?Y=?J)
	(=?J)	(=?R)

---

[3] "a voice of one calling in the desert, 'Prepare the way for the Lord, make straight paths for him.'

> voice   (you)   Lord

---

[4] And so John came, baptizing in the desert region and preaching a baptism of repentance for the forgiveness of sins.

> *John*

---

[5] The whole Judean countryside and all the people of Jerusalem went out to him. Confessing their sins, they were baptized by him in the Jordan

> John

---

[6] John wore clothing made of camel's hair, with a leather belt around his waist, and he ate locusts and wild honey.

> John

---

[7] And this was his message: "After me will come one more powerful than I, the thongs of whose sandals I am not worthy to stoop down and untie.

> *ME/I*   *MIGHTIER ONE (=?J)*

---

[8] I baptize you with water, but he will baptize you with the Holy Spirit.

> I   He (=M.O.=?J)   Spirit

---

[9] At that time Jesus came from Nazareth in Galilee and was baptized by John in the Jordan.

> *JESUS (=M.O.!)*   *JOHN*

---

[10] As Jesus was coming up out of the water, he saw heaven being torn open and the Spirit descending on him like a dove.

> Jesus   Spirit

---

[11] And a voice came from heaven: "You are my Son, whom I love; with you I am well pleased.

> *VOICE*   (=Y)   *YOU=SON (=J!)*

---

*SOG= Son of God; A=angel; M=Moses; E=Elijah; Y=Yahweh; J=Jesus; R=reader.

TABLE 3: The Herod-Baptist Episode: A Comparison of Chronological Order with Narrative Order

Chronological Order	Narrative Order
1. Herod hears John and likes to listen to him (6:20b, c).	15. Herod hears [activity of Jesus and disciples?] (6:14a).
2. Herod marries Herodias (6:17b).	7. Jesus' name becomes known (6:14a).
3. John rebukes Herod for marring Herodias (6:18).	14. Rumors circulate regarding Jesus' identity (6:14b–15).
4. Herodias nurses a grudge and wants to kill John (6:19).	16. "John, whom I beheaded, has been raised from the dead!" (6:16).
5. Herod fears John and protects him (6:20a).	6. Herod has John arrested, bound, and imprisoned (6:17a).
6. Herod has John arrested, bound, and imprisoned (6:17a).	2. Herod marries Herodias (6:17b).
7. Jesus' name becomes known (6:14a).	3. John rebukes Herod for marring Herodias (6:18).
8. Herod's birthday banquet (6:21).	4. Herodias nurses a grudge and wants to kill John (6:19).
9. Herodias' daughter dances for "king" Herod (6:22a).	5. Herod fears John and protects him (6:20a).
10. Herod promises up to half his kingdom (6:23).	1. Herod hears John and likes to listen to him (6:20b, c).
11. Herod has John beheaded (6:27).	8. Herod's birthday banquet (6:21).
12. John's head brought on platter (6:28).	9. Herodias' daughter dances for "king" Herod (6:22a).
13. John's disciples place his body in tomb (6:29).	10. Herod promises up to half his kingdom (6:23).
14. Rumors circulate regarding Jesus' identity (6:14b–15).	11. Herod has John beheaded (6:27).
15. Herod hears [activity of Jesus and disciples?] (6:14a).	12. John's head brought on platter (6:28).
16. "John, whom I beheaded, has been raised from the dead!" (6:16).	13. John's disciples place his body in tomb (6:29).

TABLE 4: "Follow" in Mark

1:18	καὶ εὐθὺς ἀφέντες τὰ δίκτυα ἠκολούθησαν αὐτῷ.
2:14	ἀκολούθει μοι.
2:14	καὶ ἀναστὰς ἠκολούθησεν αὐτῷ.
2:15	ἦσαν γὰρ πολλοὶ καὶ ἠκολούθουν αὐτῷ.
3:7–8	Καὶ ὁ Ἰησοῦς μετὰ τῶν μαθητῶν αὐτοῦ ἀνεχώρησεν πρὸς τὴν θάλασσαν, καὶ πολὺ πλῆθος ἀπὸ τῆς Γαλιλαίας [ἠκολούθησεν], καὶ ἀπὸ τῆς Ἰουδαίας 8καὶ ἀπὸ Ἱεροσολύμων καὶ ἀπὸ τῆς Ἰδουμαίας καὶ πέραν τοῦ Ἰορδάνου καὶ περὶ Τύρον καὶ Σιδῶνα πλῆθος πολὺ ἀκούοντες ὅσα ἐποίει ἦλθον πρὸς αὐτόν.
5:24	καὶ ἀπῆλθεν μετ᾽ αὐτοῦ. καὶ ἠκολούθει αὐτῷ ὄχλος πολὺς καὶ συνέθλιβον αὐτόν.
6:1	Καὶ ἐξῆλθεν ἐκεῖθεν καὶ ἔρχεται εἰς τὴν πατρίδα αὐτοῦ, καὶ ἀκολουθοῦσιν αὐτῷ οἱ μαθηταὶ αὐτοῦ.
8:34	εἴ τις θέλει ὀπίσω μου ἀκολουθεῖν, ἀπαρνησάσθω ἑαυτὸν καὶ ἀράτω τὸν σταυρὸν αὐτοῦ καὶ ἀκολουθείτω μοι.
9:38	διδάσκαλε, εἴδομέν τινα ἐν τῷ ὀνόματί σου ἐκβάλλοντα δαιμόνια καὶ ἐκωλύομεν αὐτόν, ὅτι οὐκ ἠκολούθει ἡμῖν.
10:21	ὕπαγε, ὅσα ἔχεις πώλησον καὶ δὸς [τοῖς] πτωχοῖς, καὶ ἕξεις θησαυρὸν ἐν οὐρανῷ, καὶ δεῦρο ἀκολούθει μοι.
10:28	ἰδοὺ ἡμεῖς ἀφήκαμεν πάντα καὶ ἠκολουθήκαμέν σοι.
10:32	Ἦσαν δὲ ἐν τῇ ὁδῷ ἀναβαίνοντες εἰς Ἱεροσόλυμα, καὶ ἦν προάγων αὐτοὺς ὁ Ἰησοῦς, καὶ ἐθαμβοῦντο, οἱ δὲ ἀκολουθοῦντες ἐφοβοῦντο.
10:52	καὶ εὐθὺς ἀνέβλεψεν καὶ ἠκολούθει αὐτῷ ἐν τῇ ὁδῷ.
11:9	καὶ οἱ προάγοντες καὶ οἱ ἀκολουθοῦντες ἔκραζον·
14:13–14	ἀκολουθήσατε αὐτῷ 14καὶ ὅπου ἐὰν εἰσέλθῃ εἴπατε τῷ οἰκοδεσπότῃ ὅτι ὁ διδάσκαλος λέγει·
14:54	καὶ ὁ Πέτρος ἀπὸ μακρόθεν ἠκολούθησεν αὐτῷ ἕως ἔσω εἰς τὴν αὐλὴν τοῦ ἀρχιερέως καὶ ἦν συγκαθήμενος μετὰ τῶν ὑπηρετῶν καὶ θερμαινόμενος πρὸς τὸ φῶς.
15:40–41	καὶ Μαρία ἡ Μαγδαληνὴ καὶ Μαρία ἡ Ἰακώβου τοῦ μικροῦ καὶ Ἰωσῆτος μήτηρ καὶ Σαλώμη, 41αἳ ὅτε ἦν ἐν τῇ Γαλιλαίᾳ ἠκολούθουν αὐτῷ καὶ διηκόνουν αὐτῷ, καὶ ἄλλαι πολλαὶ αἱ συναναβᾶσαι αὐτῷ εἰς Ἱεροσόλυμα.

Total Occurrences: 18	Words in Book: 11313

4

Narrative Sequence in Chariton's *Chaereas and Callirhoe*

In the narrative time of the romance, the relationship between the separate elements of the action must always be a matter of "first" and "then"; what takes place *simultaneously* in the fictional time must be transformed into a *linear* succession in the narration.

—Hägg, *Ancient Greek Romances*

INTRODUCTION

A S THE DISCUSSION IN chapter 2 has shown, any legitimate assessment of a narrative's effect on a reader cannot entirely divorce the element of sequence from other equally important textual and extratextual components of the narrative exchange.[1] René Wellek and Austin Warren, who react strongly against early literary criticism's "over-emphasis on the conditioning circumstances rather than on the works themselves," nevertheless acknowledge "some kind of dependence of literary ideologies and themes on social circumstances."[2]

---

1. Textual components include, e.g., genre, style, and vocabulary (lexical field). Participants (author, text, and audience), precipitating circumstances, and purpose are among the extratextual components. All are important for determining the schemata that various words or phrases would call to the reader's mind. Since the hierarchical ordering of schemata is based on the reader's experience (Collins and Loftus, "Spreading-Activation Theory"), and since the act of reading produces a confrontation between the reader's world and the literary world molded by the author, awareness of a work's sociological milieu is vital.

2. Wellek and Warren, *Theory of Literature*, 139, 109. For the authors' discussion of the sociocultural component, see 94–109. While these scholars urge caution regarding conclusions drawn from a text's background, they rightly acknowledge that "literature occurs only in a social context, as part of a culture, in a milieu" (105).

Contemporary reader-response narratologists recognize the complementary relationship between textual and extra-textual components. Of course, the reader's world and the world of the text do not wholly coincide. Nevertheless, as Douglas Edwards affirms:

> By comparing an author's narrative against the backdrop of outside material (literary conventions, myths, genres, and historical circumstances), one can view the author's transformation of such material . . . ; one sees the author's view of reality, his *Weltanschauung*.[3]

To discover the narrator's cues and assess how readers process textual information requires a basic understanding of the socio-literary milieu in which the text arose. The following discussion on the background and characteristics of the Greek novel argues that *Chaereas and Callirhoe* is subversive literature in form and content. The remainder of the chapter illustrates the contribution that the sequencing of narrative events makes in conveying the narrator's ideology.

BACKGROUND AND CHARACTERISTICS
OF THE GREEK NOVEL

Chariton's *Chaereas and Callirhoe* is one of five works that form the canon of ancient love-and-adventure romance novels.[4] This select body of literature has been characterized as "extended fictitious narrative in prose,"[5] and while the description does not strike the modern ear as strange, for the ancients such a format represented a distinct departure from accepted literary practice.[6] Gareth Schmeling writes:

> Imaginative literature in Greece and Rome rode the vehicle of poetry until sometime in the second-first century b.c. when, at one level at least, a part of it switched to prose. This change from

---

3. Edwards, "Acts of the Apostles," 19–20.

4. The other four are Xenophon Ephesius's *An Ephesian Tale*, Achilles Tatius's *Leucippe and Clitophon*, Longus's *Daphnis and Chloe*, and Heliodorus's *An Ethiopian Story*.

5. Reardon, "Theme, Structure." The phrase is found on pp. 3–4.

6. Pervo (*Profit with Delight*, 104) affirms that "the use of prose for Greek novels constituted a decisive break with the tradition of verse as the medium for entertaining fiction."

poetry to prose for fiction is one of the most significant developments for ancient, medieval, and modern literatures.[7]

By narrating a ficticious story in a prose format, the Greek novelists departed from ancient literary convention that held poetry to be the only acceptable medium for fiction. "Prose fiction," as Schmeling describes it, "stood as a ... bastard in ancient literature, an embarrassment, a genre that somehow did not seem to belong."[8]

The marriage of ficticious narrative with prose format at least partly caused the Greek novels to be scorned by the literary intelligentsia of their day. This narrative technique could suggest that these works were aimed at a much broader, less educated, and lower-classed audience.[9] However, it could also reflect an intentionally subversive polemic aimed at the intelligentsia.

The depreciatory assessment of the Greek novels extends into modern times. Erwin Rohde's pioneering study of 1876, *Der griechische Roman und seine Vorläufer*, added scholarly support to the unflattering view bequeathed by antiquity. Misunderstanding of the novels' *Entstehungszeit* (see below) led Rohde to view these works as "degenerate imitation[s] of good literature."[10] This assessment held sway for nearly a century.

Until recently, scholarly interest in this literary corpus confined itself to questions regarding the origin of the genre and the dates of composition of its various representatives. Karl Plepelits's appraisal suggests that Chariton's *Chaereas and Callirhoe* may supply answers to these queries:

> Chariton's *Callirhoe* is not only with high probability the oldest completely-contained novel of world-literature—the contents

7. Schmeling, *Chariton*, 27.

8. Ibid., 28. Many scholars identify this overt challenge to the literary status quo as the reason the Greek novels were covered for more than a millenium by the dust of scholarly disinterest.

9. Perr (*Ancient Romances*, 4–5) claims ancient romances were regarded with scorn by educated men "when they were regarded at all." They were "stereotyped as melodrama for the edification of children and the poor-in-spirit" and "ignored or despised as trivial by the prevailing literary fashion of the time." Perry described the romance-genre as "latter-day epic for Everyman" (48). Reardon (*Form of Greek Romance*, 8) affirms the ancient scholars' disinterest in Chariton's novel since, as he put it, "very few copies of [*Chaereas and Callirhoe*] were ultimately shelved anywhere, other than in Egyptian garbage dumps."

10. Pervo, *Profit with Delight*, 88.

speak for the middle of the first century a.d. as a date of origin
. . .—but among the ancient Greek novels perhaps also the most
worthy of reading.[11]

Appropriately, therefore, the present investigation analyzes *Chaereas
and Callirhoe vis-à-vis* its date of composition and relation to the origin
of the novel genre. Included in its scope, however, are other external
questions (specifically, authorship and readership) as well as features
related to the text itself (e.g., literary characteristics, purpose, characters,
and storyline).

Date of Composition

Temporally locating the debut of Chariton's (first?) novel is an important
enterprise. Attempts to do so have not resulted in unanimity.[12] Rohde's
1876 publication placed Chariton's novel in the fifth or sixth century
CE.[13] As early as 1930, however, B. E. Perry challenged this notion, arguing for a date "well back into the second [century CE]."[14] Other scholars
have adduced subsequent discoveries of papyrus fragments and various linguistic arguments to push this date back as far as the first century BCE.[15] Nevertheless, the emerging consensus puts Chariton's novel
around the middle of the first century CE, making it the earliest extant
Greek romance novel.[16]

11. The original reads: "Charitons *Kallirhoe* ist nicht nur mit hoher Wahrscheinlichkeit
der älteste vollständig erhaltene Roman der Weltliteratur—die Indizien sprechen für
die Mitte des I. Jahrhunderts n. Chr. als Entstehungszeit . . . —sondern unter den antiken griechischen Romanen vielleicht auch der lesenswerteste" (Plepelits, *Kallirhoe*, 1;
translation mine). Plepelits's abbreviated title for Chariton's novel reflects his view that
the original title did not mention Chaereas. Perhaps the strongest support for this lies in
the author's last words, where Chaereas's name is conspicuously absent: "Τοσάδε περὶ
Καλλιρόης συνέγραψα" ("So many things I have published concerning Callirhoe";
8.8.16).

12. Chariton may also have authored *Metiochus and Parthenope* and *Chione*. See
Hägg, "Parthenope Romance Decapitated?"; and Reardon, "Form of Ancient Greek
Romance," 208.

13. Rohde, *Der griechische Roman und seine Vorläufer*.

14. Perry, "Chariton and His Romance," 93 n. 1.

15. See Hägg, *Novel in Antiquity*; and idem, *Narrative Technique*, 15. For linguistic
arguments, see Papanikolaou, "Zur Sprache Charitons," 7–8.

16. E.g., Perry, *Ancient Romances*, 344; Reardon, "Greek Novel," 294n10; Plepelits,
Kallirhoe, 1; Schmeling, *Chariton*, 55; and, with some reserve, Heiserman, *The Novel
Before the Novel*, 75.

This backward shift in dating has effected a more commendatory assessment of Chariton's work. Taking *Chaereas and Callirhoe* as a product of the fourth or fifth century prompted Rohde to see in it many deficiencies measured against the Sophistic norm. Affirming the novel's first-century CE origin elicits greater appreciation for its novelties.

Authorship

Several strands of evidence have been adduced to provide extratexutal corroboration for Chariton's self-proclaimed authorship of *Chaereas and Callirhoe*. Numerous scholars (e.g., Reardon, Plepelits, Perry, and Schmeling) point to a Chariton disparagingly mentioned in Philostratus's *Letter 66*. B. E. Perry judges it "very probable that the Chariton addressed by Philostratus in Epistle 66 is the author of *Chaereas and Callirhoe*." And Schmeling notes archaeological evidence that a "Chariton" and an "Athenagoras" were citizens of Aphrodisias.[17]

The case for identifying the Chariton described in Philostratus's letter and inscribed on the artifact from Aphrodisias with the self-identified author of *Chaereas and Callirhoe* is admittedly tenuous.[18] The possibility that other Greeks used the name Chariton is certainly not remote. In view of this difficulty, Brigitte Egger contends that apart from the autobiographical references found in Chariton and Heliodorus, "all other information on the novelists . . . is more or less [?] fictitious."[19] Philostratus's *Letter 66* and the inscription at Aphrodisias remain the only links to the authorship of *Chaereas and Callirhoe*.[20]

Origin of the Greek Novel

The origin of the Greek novel has been vigorously debated.[21] B. E. Perry reacts strongly to Rohde's evolutionary understanding of the novel's development:

17. Reardon, *Form of Greek Romance*, 46; Plepelits, *Kallirhoe*, 1; Perry, "Chariton and His Romance," 97 n. 7; and Schmeling, *Chariton*, 17.

18. Schmeling (*Chariton*, 17) describes this as "the fly in our carefully prepared ointment."

19. Egger, "Women in the Greek Novel," 1n2.

20. For an overview of recent scholarly opinion on authorship and dating of the Greek novels see esp., Johne, "Übersicht über die antiken Romanautore"; and Treu, "Der antike Roman."

21. For a concise historical and critical survey of scholarly hypotheses regarding the origin of the Greek novel, see Pervo, *Profit with Delight*, 86–114.

> The first romance was deliberately planned and written by an individual author, its inventor. He conceived it on a Tuesday afternoon in July.[22]

Perry argues that new literary forms emerge "only as the willful creations of men made in accordance with a conscious purpose."[23]

Graham Anderson charges that Perry's view is as fundamentalist as Rohde's is scientific. For Anderson, neither Perry nor Rohde takes proper account of the influences of other genres: Perry focuses on the individual author; Rohde on the developmental movement from "non-novels" through a series of "not-quite-novels" that culminated in the Greek novel.[24] Neither of these positions satisfies Anderson, who not only refuses to see the Greek novelists as inventors but also denies them any significant creative role. Arguing that "the material of Graeco-Roman novels was already 'ancient storytelling,'"[25] he views the Greek novelists as translators whose task was "to *accommodate* narrative material [specifically that of early Sumerian texts] to a new cultural context."[26]

The evidence in Sumerian literature of plotlines similar to those found in the Greek novels disallows neither the influence of earlier Greek genres on the Greek novels nor the novelties of the Greek novels themselves, Anderson's arguments notwithstanding. Scholars point to numerous similarities with earlier Greek genres. Sophie Trenkner, for

---

22. Perry, *Ancient Romances*, 175.

23. Ibid., 9.

24. Anderson, *Novel in the Graeco-Roman World*, 25.

25. Ibid., 26. Anderson adds that "the decision to write the first Greek novel was the decision to communicate to a Greek readership what was already there, without neces-sarily any decision about its form" (26). "It is as the artful retelling of ancient tales, rather than the random invention of ephemera, that ancient prose fiction may best be understood and enjoyed" (2).

26. Ibid., 27; emphasis added. What Anderson means by "accommodate" may be illustrated by his comparison of Greek (*Chaereas and Callirhoe*) and Sumerian (*Enlil and Ninlil*) child-legitimizing scenes: "Ninlil's bargain to redeem her child from being born in the lower world is rather like a business transaction at a sperm bank, with the lady laying down the terms, and instant intercourse to conclude the bargain. In Chariton's version the lady insists on her noble position; but the idea of intercourse as such . . . is rejected; respectable marriage is demanded. . . . In Ninlil's case . . . we are told simply that [the man] kissed her and slept with her. For Chariton the mention of copulation even between husband and wife is scarcely conceivable; the nearest he gets to it is when he makes Callirhoe hold the picture of her lost husband to her pregnant belly: the theme of physical contact with the first lover is ingeniously preserved, but with the maximum of modesty" (ibid., 107).

example, identifies themes of love, adventure, trickery, chance (as prime mover of human destiny), and self-sacrifice in Euripidean tragedy, middle comedy, and new comedy.[27]

Schmeling identifies influences of epic ("journey" as a motivational device, formulae, plot-summaries), drama (five-act structure, theatre scenes, comparison of courtroom scene to theatrical performance [5.8.2]), historiography (similarities with Xenophon's *Cyropaedia*, similarities with guidelines given to Lucceius for writing a tragic history of Cicero's life), and love elegy (thematic parallels with a number of Alexandrian love elegies).[28]

The Greek novels' connections with historiography are particularly significant.[29] In *Chaereas and Callirhoe*, for example, the author begins his work in the manner of a classical historian: providing his name, residence, and position (Χαρίτων Ἀφροδισιεύς, Ἀθηναγόρου τοῦ ῥήτορος ὑπογραφεύς).[30] Furthermore, several scholars have noted numerous historical references and allusions sprinkled throughout Chariton's novel.[31] According to Hägg, Chariton tried to "create that titillating sensation peculiar to historical fiction, which is the effect of mix-

---

27. Trenkner, *Greek Novella*.

28. Schmeling, *Chariton*, 42–59. For the view that the Greek novels evolved from love elegies, see esp. Giangrande, "On the Origins."

29. Hägg (*Novel in Antiquity*, 112) considers historiography to be the deepest influence on the Greek novels. Perry (*Ancient Romances*, 78) argues that "their outward form and décor was that of historiography." He notes that "historical persons and events are much more prominent in [Chariton's] book than in any extant romance known to have been written in the second century or later" (343 n. 1).

30. "Chariton of Aphrodisias, secretary of the lawyer Athenagoras" (translation mine). Unless otherwise noted, translations of Chariton's Greek are mine. Such renderings relate what in my judgment are the most likely denotations of the vocabulary and syntax, at the expense of stylistic "woodenness." For a smooth, readable English translation more attuned to dynamic equivalence, see Reardon, ed., *Collected Ancient Greek Novels*, 21–124. For the present study, translations taken from Reardon are followed by "[R]." To avoid confusion with reference and content notes, translation notes will begin with "Tr.:"

31. See esp. Perry, "Chariton and His Romance," 100–102 n. 11, who mentions the following either as actual historical figures or as possible allusions to historical figures: Hermocrates, the Syracusan general; Artaxerxes Mnemon and his wife, Statira; Ariston, the father of Chaereas; Dionysius; and Rhodogyne. Perry claims that "in Chariton legend and history have determined in a greater degree than in any of the other extant erotic romances, not only the choice of *dramatis personae*, but also the character of the episodes and of the style" (100).

ing openly fictitious characters and events with historical ones."[32] These features suggest historiography's influence on the Greek novel.

Of corresponding significance is the Greek novels' connection with the love elegy. In spite of their various sub-themes (e.g., travel, adventure, intrigue), the Greek novels are fundamentally love stories[33] that share a similar narrative framework:

> Boy and girl of aristocratic background fall in love, are separated before or shortly after marriage and subjected to melodramatic adventures that threaten their life and chastity and carry them around much of the eastern Mediterranean. Eventually love and fortune prove stronger than storms, pirates and tyrants and the couple is reunited in marital bliss.[34]

The introduction and conclusion to Chariton's novel illustrate especially well the influences of historiography and love elegy and highlight the latter as the author's primary interest. Although Chariton introduces himself in a form characteristic of the classical—but not contemporary—historians, he describes his work's purpose in terminology that signals instead the posture of a "deliberate and unconcealed novelist":[35] πάθος ἐρωτικὸν ἐν Συρακούσαις γενόμενον διηγήσομαι.[36] His closing statement, τοσάδε περὶ Καλλιρόης συνέγραψα,[37] also displays the tension between historiography and love story: συγγράφω refers to the composing of a factual account in prose and typically was used by historians; the name Καλλιρόη ("beautiful-flowing [river]") suggests love poetry.[38]

The love story *per se* cannot rightly be listed among the innovations made by the Greek novelists. Indeed, numerous stories about love relationships and their concomitant intrigues preceded them. Nevertheless,

---

32. Hägg, "Beginnings of the Historical Novel," 176.

33. So Giangrande, "Origins of the Greek Romance," 142; and Anderson, *Novel*, 2.

34. Bowie, "Literature of the Empire," 684.

35. Hägg, "Beginnings of the Historical Novel," 174. Hägg claims that Chariton's purpose in adopting the introductory phraseology of classical historiography is "to communicate . . . the spirit of the very age in which the plot is set."

36. Tr: I am going to relate a detailed account of a passion of love which took place at Syracuse.

37. Tr: I have published such great things concerning Callirhoe (8.8.16).

38. Hägg, "Beginnings of the Historical Novel," 174.

the particular love story offered by the Greek novels differs substantially from its antecedents.

Michael Muchow analyzes the pre-novel love stories and classifies them according to three types: stories of *passionate love*, stories of *love leading to marriage*, and stories of *marital fidelity*.[39] Stories of passionate love are characterized by sexual desire that is almost always aroused at first sight, occasionally unrequited, frequently culminated by rape or seduction, and never fulfilled by marriage.[40] Stories of love leading to marriage focus on the machinations necessary to affect the marriage of the hero and heroine. The heroine is usually of lower status (e.g., a courtesan or slave) and the hero's father often must be tricked into allowing the marriage. Stories of marital fidelity typically begin with a married couple, say little about the circumstances that led to their marriage, and center on the efforts of one spouse (usually the woman) to remain chaste. The stories usually end unhappily with the death or suicide of one or both of the spouses.[41]

According to Muchow, the Greek novels are innovative in two ways: they combine three types of love story into a single story and establish an equality between the hero and the heroine. Both features are evident in Chariton's *Chaereas and Callirhoe*, though here the heroine in fact upstages the hero.[42]

Although Chariton combines certain elements from each of the three types of love story categorized by Muchow, he does not utilize each type to the same degree nor adopt every element from any one of them. He includes the "love at first sight" motif typical of passionate love stories, but has none of their rape or seduction elements. He utilizes the premarital intrigue common in "love leading to marriage" stories, but gives this element only a minute fraction of narrative space and creates a heroine who outranks his hero. He retains the chastity struggles essential to stories of marital fidelity, but puts his couple on an ontological and moral par—in fact, the hero is more sexually faithful than the heroine—and ends his story happily.

39. Muchow, "Passionate Love," 3.

40. Ibid.

41. Muchow cites examples of these stories and provides a brief description of them in his Appendix B (ibid., 239–51).

42. "The emergence of the female hero and her central role in the story is entirely innovative, as far as we can tell" (Egger, "Women," 45).

Even in light of textual features that suggest the influence of various literary genres, the origins of the Greek novel remain under a shadow of uncertainty. Similarities in literary form supply only a partial answer; the novel required a catalyst. Summarizing the position of B. E. Perry, Arthur Heiserman identifies that catalyst as "a single human being, the man who first committed what no self-respecting literary man in antiquity would have dared write—the bastard prose medley of drama, epic, and history that is romance."[43]

Heiserman surveys the etiologies that have been suggested and sees a sense in which all are correct. He explains the variety of theories as "deriv[ing] from differing conceptions of literary form, of literary tradition, and of the things we call romances."[44] Pervo's conclusion to the matter is instructive:

> Although each of the theories advanced to explain the origins of the ancient novel has contributed to its understanding, no one of them is fully convincing. The novel is too complex a phenomenon to be reduced to a single impetus....
>
> The standard Greek novel thus came into being as a result of the changes wrought by Hellenism. Non-Greek prototypes probably played an important role. The environment was most likely Hellenized, rather than Hellenic. Varieties of older sources were *transformed, translated,* or simply *incorporated* in accordance with the *spirit* and *taste* of the age and the *goals* and *audience* of a particular novelist. No one theory serves to account for so diverse and productive a phenomenon.[45]

Notwithstanding the uncertainties of origin, awareness of the novel's similarities to and differences from already established genres provides a means of ascertaining how the original readers processed the various schemata evoked by the text.

Literary Characteristics

Chaereas and Callirhoe is written in straightforward, everyday, middle-class Greek. This facilitates the forward movement of his plot, since the reader is rarely required to reread sentences in order to make sense of

---

43. Heiserman, *Novel before the Novel*, 92.

44. Ibid., 93.

45. Pervo, *Profit with Delight*, 101–2; emphases added. These items are discussed below, specifically in connection with Chariton's novel.

the story.[46] Although the language is simple,[47] it is highly emotive and "charged with pathos and drama."[48] "Chariton . . . loses few opportunities for emotional and rhetorically moulded outbursts."[49]

If Chariton's language is calculated to engage the reader's emotions, his style is equally so. The copius use of proleptic narrative *asides*, for example, stimulates the reader's curiosity and creates a sensation of suspense.[50] Chariton frequently pauses in the telling of his story in order to speak directly to the reader. In some of these instances, the narrator announces in advance the outcome of a certain sequence of events. Chariton utilizes this technique in such a way that the reader's curiosity, rather than being squelched by learning an outcome in advance, is aroused and, more importantly, refocused.

Hägg's analysis is particularly insightful for the discussion of proleptic authorial asides. He catagorizes Chariton's narrative anticipations in two ways; the first has to do with their scope, and the second (what he designates as "a fourth aspect") concerns the perspective from which they are given:

> First, there is a wide range of possibilities between, on the one hand, an explicit and detailed statement of the outcome of the present episode or even of the whole romance and, on the other, a vague hint of the general direction of the action or of a happy/ unhappy ending. Secondly, the anticipation may include more or less extensive parts of the story—just a single episode or the whole romance. Thirdly, the event anticipated may be what comes next in the narration—the anticipation is thus an introductory statement, a 'heading', the starting-point of a chain of events— or the reader may have to wait a considerable time before the anticipation is fulfilled. . . .

46. Hägg, *Novel in Antiquity*, 106; Schmeling, *Chariton*, 24–25.

47. Rohde (*Griechische Roman*, 528) contrasts the *Bombast* and vain *Feierlichkeit* of Heliodorus and the intolerable *Gewitzel* and glittering *Phrasenfunkeln* of Achilles Tatius with the *einfache und klare sprache* of Chariton.

48. Reardon, *Form of Greek Romance*, 24.

49. Bowie, "Literature of the Empire," 685.

50. Narrative "asides" are instances where the narrator speaks directly to the reader. The information he conveys is generally not available to the characters in the story. This puts the reader in a privileged position, providing a special vantage point from which he or she can evaluate the actions and attitudes of the story's characters. It also enhances the possibilities for irony.

> …A fourth aspect will be exploited.… I refer to the classifica-
> tion into, on the one hand, anticipations uttered by the narrator
> himself on his own authority and, on the other, those integrated
> into the action as part of the characters' speeches, thoughts, etc.
> or otherwise brought to their knowledge (oracles etc.).[51]

Most of the narrator's proleptic asides either introduce the immediately following scene or convey a "vague hint of the general direction
of the action."[52] In both cases, the reader's curiosity is piqued; he or she
knows something about the *what* but little about the *how*. In this way, the
narrator focuses the reader's attention on the various elements that bring
about the turns in the plot.

Proleptic narratorial asides that explicitly reveal detailed information about the outworking of the plot are rare in Chariton. The clearest
example is found in the introduction to book 8 (8.1.2–5):

> ἔμελλε δὲ ἔργον ἡ Τύχη πράττειν οὐ μόνον παράδοξον,
> ἀλλὰ καὶ σκυθρωπόν, ἵνα ἔχων Καλλιρόην Χαιρέας ἀγνοή
> σῃ καὶ τὰς ἀλλοτρίας γυναῖκας ἀναλαβὼν ταῖς τριήρεσιν
> ἀπαγάγῃ, μόνην δὲ τὴν ἰδίαν ἐκεῖ καταλίπῃ οὐχ ὡς ᾿Αριά
> δνην καθεύδουσαν, οὐδὲ Διονύσῳ νυμφίῳ, λάφυρον δὲ τοῖς
> ἑαυτοῦ πολεμίοις . . . . ἠλέησεν αὐτὸν ᾿Αφροδίτη καὶ ὅπερ
> ἐξ ἀρχῆς δύο τῶν καλλίστων ἥρμοσε ζεῦγος, γυμνάσασα
> διὰ γῆς καὶ θαλάσσης, πάλιν ἠθέλησεν ἀποδοῦναι. νομί
> ζω δὲ καὶ τὸ τελευταῖον τοῦτο σύγγραμμα τοῖς ἀναγινώ
> σκουσιν ἥδιστον γενήσεσθαι· καθάρσιον γάρ ἐστι τῶν ἐν
> τοῖς πρώτοις σκυθρωπῶν. οὐκέτι λῃστεία καὶ δουλεία καὶ
> δίκη καὶ μάχη καὶ ἀποκαρτέρησις καὶ πόλεμος καὶ ἅλωσις,
> ἀλλὰ ἔρωτες δίκαιοι ἐν τούτῳ καὶ νόμιμοι γάμοι. Πῶς
> οὖν ἡ θεὸς ἐφώτισε τὴν ἀλήθειαν καὶ τοὺς ἀγνοουμένους
> ἔδειξεν ἀλλήλοις λέξω.[53]

---

51. Hägg, *Narrative Technique*, 214. To the two types classified under the fourth aspect; Hägg adds a third: "anticipations on the divine level." These are almost exclusively
given by the narrator's direct comments to the reader.

52. Ibid.

53. Tr: Fortune was about to do a work not only contrary to all expectation but
also sad: Chaereas, would have Callirhoe and not be aware of it; and taking the other
men's wives on board the trireme, he would take them home and leave there only his
wife—not as sleeping Ariadne, and not for Dionysius as *her* bridegroom, but as spoils
of war for his enemies. ³But Aphrodite considered *this* terrible, for she was already being reconciled to him. Originally she was sorely angered because of his inappropriate
jealousy. He had received from her the most beautiful gift, which not even Alexander
Paris *received*, and he treated the gift outrageously. But since Chaereas honorably made

The effect of this prolepsis is two-fold: It eliminates the distraction caused by uncertainty about the story's final outcome (Ἀφροδίτη] πάλιν ἠθέλησεν ἀποδοῦναι;[54] no more hardships, only ἔρωτες δίκαιοι ανδ νόμιμοι γάμοι);[55] and it directs the reader's attention to the characters' psychological and emotional reactions to the movements of the plot.

That Chariton is only remotely concerned with the outward happenings that make up his plot is evident from the meager proportion of narrative space he devotes to the action proper. His narrative is an unequal mixture of scene and summary, in which scene overwhelmingly predominates.[56] Although summary makes up only about ten percent of the narrative, this small portion of the text contains almost all of the novel's action.[57] Chariton's interest, then, lies not in the events themselves, but, as Hägg puts it, in the "psychological interaction between the characters and the reactions of the individual to the outward happenings."[58]

---

ammends to Eros, having been caused to wander from west to east through innumerable sufferings, Aphrodite had mercy on him; thus, after she harassed on land and sea the couple she had joined at the beginning—two of the most beautiful people—she decided to give them back *to each other* again. [4]And I think this last book will be very pleasing to the readers, for it is a catharsis from the sad events of the first part. No longer piracy and slavery and court trial and strife and starvation and war and capture, but in this *book* proper loves and legitimate marriages. [5]Thus I will tell you how the goddess illuminated the truth and revealed the unrecognized ones to each other.

54. Tr: [Aphrodite] decided to reunite *them* again.

55. Tr: Proper loves and legitimate marriages.

56. "Scene" refers to the mimetic type of narrative, i.e., the reader is *shown* the events as they are happening. "Summary" describes diegetic narrative, i.e., the reader is *told* that the events are happening or have happened. Some of the earliest modern scholars to note this distinction are Liddell (*Some Principles of Fiction*, 67); Friedman ("Point of View," 1161–62); Booth (*Rhetoric of Fiction*, 3–20); Stanzel, *Typische Formen des Romans*, 3–4, 11–13); and Hägg (*Narrative Technique*, esp. 87–111). Friedman, Stanzel, and Hägg cite evidence that the distinction goes back to ancient times (Plato, *Republic*, 392e–394c; Aristotle, *Poetics*, 3, 24 [1448a, 19–28; and 1460a, 7–11]; Quintilian, *Institutio Oratoria*, 7.3.61–71). "Showing" and "telling" have become common foci of recent narrative-critical studies.

57. Reardon ("Theme, Structure," 11) describes the interplay of scene and summary in *Chaereas and Callirhoe* as a repeating pattern of "rapid narrative summarizing a sequence of events," followed by a slowing of the narrative tempo from which materializes a scene displaying "the actions, thoughts, utterances of an important character at an important juncture of events."

58. Hägg, *Narrative Technique*, 92. For Reardon ("Theme, Structure," 20), "what [Chariton] wants to present as important [is] his characters' psychological reactions as set in the emotional *sequence* of events" (emphasis original).

In *Chaereas and Callirhoe* plot is primarily a means of portraying the characters' psychologies. Proleptic asides reveal *what* will happen and recapitulatory plot synopses (also in the format of narrative asides) recall *what* did happen, but Chariton invites the reader to consider *how* the plot turns and *how* the characters respond to these circumstances.

Chariton's narrative asides are not confined to proleptic and analeptic references. The narrator often interrupts the telling of his story to interject information to which only the reader is privy.[59] These brief interludes typically introduce a philosophizing comment about life or supply insight into the attitudes, hopes or desires of one or more of the characters. The reader's privileged perspective gives her or him a special bond with the narrator and makes possible the exploitation of irony. For Perry, Chariton's readers are "in the same exalted position as the spectators of an ancient tragedy; they see all the factors involved in the action and are thereby able to appreciate its ironies."[60]

A telling illustration of Chariton's use of irony is found in a dialogue between Callirhoe and the brigand Theron (1.13.7–11). In the immediately preceding scene (1.13.1–6), Chariton *shows* Theron making arrangements with Leonas for the sale of Callirhoe to Dionysius. Now, in what amounts to a character-generated prolepsis (already adjudged false

59. This technique is an example of what Meir Sternberg (*Poetics of Biblical Narrative*, 163–64) labels "reader-elevating" strategies . Using shared information (i.e., who shares the narrator's knowledge of specific story details) as the evaluative criterion, Sternberg distinguishes "reader-elevating strategies from their polar opposite, "character-elevating" strategies, and from a third, mediating, approach which he calls "evenhanded" strategies: "The two 'elevating' strategies mark polar extremes, the one's superior intelligence figuring as the other's victim of irony. Within the reader-elevating configuration, the discrepancies in awareness are so manipulated in our favor, at the expense of the characters, that we observe them and their doings from a vantage point practically omniscient. . . . The character-elevating procedure reverses this discrepancy. Through a piecemeal release of material, it propels the reader from initial ignorance (or at best mystification) to ultimate surprise, usually two-pronged because it springs on us both new facts and, no less inglorious, some character's long-standing awareness of them" (164–65).

60. Perry, *Ancient Romances*, 143. As Sternberg (*Poetics of Biblical Narrative*, 164) puts it: "The narrator's disclosures put us in a position to fathom [the characters'] secret thoughts and designs, to trace or even foreknow their acts, to jeer or grieve at their misguided attempts at concealment, plotting, [and] interpretation." Forexamples of irony in *Chaereas and Callirhoe*, see Perry, "Chariton and His Romance," 124–27. For Perry, irony is a "good index to the intellectual and artistic temperament." He affirms: "If we measure Chariton by this classical standard, we shall find him far superior to his colleagues" (124).

by the narrator), Theron attempts to fool Callirhoe into believing he will eventually take her back to her homeland.

Here (1.13.10) Chariton gives the reader inside information into Callirhoe's understanding of the situation: ἤδη γὰρ πωλουμέ–νη ἠπίστατο, τῆς δὲ πάλαι εὐγενείας τὴν πρᾶσιν εὐτυχεστέραν ὑπελάμβανεν, ἀπαλλαγῆναι θέλουσα λῃστῶν.[61] With this narrative aside, Chariton has set the stage for the stinging irony of Callirhoe's response: Καὶ χάριν σοι φησὶν ἔχω, πάτερ, ὑπερ τῆς εἰς ἐμὲ φιλαν–θρωπίας· ἀποδοῖεν δὲ ἔφη πᾶσιν ὑμῖν οἱ θεοὶ τὰς ἀξίας ἀμοιβάς.[62] Indeed, the starvation death of Theron's crew (3.3.18) and Theron's torturous impalement (3.4.18) confirm the accuracy of this character-generated prolepsis.

Chariton's preponderant use of scene gives his narrative a lively mimetic style,[63] and its effect on the reader is of singular importance. Watching an event as it is happening is more directly and deeply affective than hearing about it after the fact. Nevertheless, intensity, of itself, is neither positive nor negative. Indeed, Plato and Aristotle differed in their assessment of the value of mimesis; the former took it to be dangerous, while the latter lauded its therapeutic possibilities. Aristotle would have hailed Chariton's achievement:

> [Chariton] plays on the emotional effect that directly presented drama can create, by moving rapidly from "scene" to "scene," by presenting his Callirhoe living before our eyes, in pathetic mono-logue and vivid, theatrically charged personal crisis.[64]

Purpose

Suggestions as to Chariton's purpose are many and varied. Perry sees Chariton's novel as purely secular entertainment; Reardon, as a myth of the isolated individual in Hellenistic society; Schmeling, as an aretalogy

---

61. Tr: For she already knew that she was being sold, but desiring to be delivered from the pirates, she considered the sale more fortunate than her former noble status (1.13.10).

62. Tr: "Thank you, father [sir]," she said, "for your benevolence to me." And, she said, "May the gods grant you all the deserved repayment" (1.13.10).

63. Chariton's style is characterized thus by Perry ("Chariton and His Romance," 109n23). Perry summarizes several passages in which this mimetic style is particularly apparent (109, 121, 123).

64. Reardon, *Form of Greek Romance*, 71.

and thank offering to Aphrodite; Merkelbach, as a *mysterientext*; and Anderson, as a Hellenistic operetta.[65]

The entertaining quality of *Chaereas and Callirhoe* does not establish reader amusement as Chariton's primary intention.[66] This claim does not denigrate entertainment *per se*. Rather, it disputes the extent to which entertainment answers the question of Chariton's purpose. Arguing for entertainment as Chariton's motivating concern leaves unexplained the novel's purpose *qua* entertainment.

To be sure, not all forms or instances of entertainment accomplish the same goal. In general, however, entertainment fixes an audience's attention on a created world that differs from yet overlaps with the real world. Where it differs it offers escape; where it overlaps it offers identification; and taken together it promotes psychological solidarity and catharsis.[67]

The literary characteristics displayed in *Chaereas and Callirhoe* provide insight into the author's purpose. The largely mimetic style and selective "inside views" support the hypothesis that Chariton wants his reader to identify with the novel's protagonists and vicariously experience their struggles and eventual triumph:

> Readers are encouraged to identify with or have sympathy for certain feelings, passions or modesties, and, conversely, not to condone, or even to reject, others. The characters to whom read-

65. Perry, *Ancient Romances*, 35, 45, 85; Reardon, "Aspects of the Greek Novel"; idem, "Greek Novel," 296–97; Schmeling, *Chariton*, 129; Merkelbach, *Roman und Mysterium*, 159, 339–40; Anderson, *Eros Sophistes*, 21.

66. "Ancient romances . . . need not be viewed as the equivalent of ancient comic books or soap operas" (Edwards, "Acts and Chariton," 83). Pervo (*Profit with Delight*, 96) rightly observes that "'pure entertainment' and 'for its own sake' are quite slippery terms with little real value in the history of literature." Even those scholars who see entertainment as the primary function of the Greek novels concede that some could have had religious import (Edwards, "Acts and Chariton," 107 n. 19). Pervo (*Profit with Delight*, 96) writes: "There is much room for debate about the religious message of this or that ancient novel, but no accurate picture of the Hellenistic and Roman eras can fail to take into account the significance of belief."

67. "In one sense, then, all novels have a message. In response to Perry's argument, one way of providing entertainment is through statement and restatement of the current message or messages" (Pervo, *Profit with Delight*, 98). For Frye (*Secular Scripture*, 186), the romances offer a dream world in place of normal experience. For Reardon ("Form of Ancient Greek Romance," 211), romance embodies "a picture of human life: a figure of human beings in life, undergoing its vicissitudes and arriving finally at salvation, in some form or other."

ers feel especially close tend to be those that the narrator "opens up" by "inside views," i.e. direct renderings of the feelings—*usually the central couple.*[68]

But whom does Chariton envision as his readers and what struggles does he seek to address? Since readers will identify with those characters with whom they share comparable particulars,[69] the text provides clues that enable the critic to construct a picture of the original audience and its concerns. Knowledge of social conditions gleaned from other sources supplements and sharpens the image.

As for the problems addressed in the novel, Reardon suggests the isolation of the Hellenistic individual in a world grown large, which induced the quest "for a god who will care for him personally, as an individual . . ."[70] Muchow posits a discontentment with the custom of arranged marriages.[71] Both of these conjectures reflect awareness of two major features of Chariton's romance, namely, the religious and erotic elements. The present analysis argues that Chariton specifically addresses the implied reader's feeling of powerlessness *vis-à-vis* the sociopolitical machinery of the first-century world and its emphasis on conformity to the strictures of respectable Hellenistic society.

Audience

To understand how Chariton's novel deals with the reader's feelings of isolation and impotence, we must first produce some picture—if only with wide brushstrokes—of the reader implied by this text.[72] Broadly

68. Egger, "Women," 326; emphasis original.

69. Another important factor in reader-identification is the allure of power, a key element of this chapter's thesis.

70. Reardon, "Greek Novel," 304.

71. Muchow, "Passionate Love," 35–63, 219.

72. On this see esp. Pervo's excursus "To Whom Were Ancient Popular Novels Addressed?" in *Profit with Delight*, 81–85). Some general understanding of the real reader's social context (and the text's historical context) is critical for understanding what effects the various narrative devices have on the implied reader (see Wilder, *Bible and Literary Critic*, 29–30). The present discussion attempts to identify the reader implied by the text itself. Nevertheless, attention to the historical context is not only inevitable but also expedient. Egger's thorough investigation of the Greek novels' female readership ("Women") employs the basic approach adopted in this study: *Rezeptionsästhetik*. She describes this methodology as "a theory of reading which both assigns an important role to the text itself and considers the historical conditions of its production as well as its reception" (21).

speaking, Chariton's text assumes a reader from the middle socioeconomic stratum of the first-century world: its vocabulary and syntax are distinctively *koiné*, and its fictional content is presented in a prose style. The former is significant since the classical style would have been the more appropriate choice for presenting a story set in the classical period. The latter is remarkable since up to that time poetry had been the only acceptable medium for fictional writing.

Both the *koiné* style and the prose format diminished the appeal of Chariton's novel for the literati, who regarded Greek romances as highly inferior texts (when they regarded them).[73] Had Chariton intended that his work appeal to an upper-class readership, the classical style would have been a wiser selection. If, however, his intent was not to impress but rather to challenge the establishment, his choice was well made and his effort must be judged successful. In any case, his novel surely found acceptance among those in the middle eschelons of Hellenistic society.

Nevertheless, as Pervo notes, the argument from style alone is hardly adequate. "Greater weight," he suggests, "must be attached to the use of literary citation and allusion, the imitation of classic scenes, and the employment of learned motifs."[74] Viewed from this perspective, Chariton's novel might appear to have in mind a highly educated and highly cultured audience:

> Chariton presents the strongest case. There are a number of quotes, the vast majority from Homer, two-thirds from the *Iliad*. In addition, a number of scenes are based upon Homeric models. Chariton also imitates the historians, especially Xenophon.[75]

But Pervo argues that the reader need not have submitted to the rigors of sophisticated academic training to be able to recognize the citations from Homer; a basic education—one that brought the ability to

---

73. Perry (*Ancient Romances*, 4–5) argues that the romances were either "ignored or despised as trivial by the prevailing literary fashion of the time." They were "stereotyped as melodrama for the edification of children and the poor-in-spirit." Egger ("Women," 10–11) notes and affirms the trend in recent scholarship that rejects this notion: "Modern scholarship has finally discarded the long-standing persuasion that the Greek novels were 'literature for the masses' or 'poor in spirit.' General agreement has been reached that their intended audience must have been largely 'bourgeois' or middle-to-leisure-class, and that the social borders of this main circle of recipients may be assumed to have been open more on the upper than on the lower fringe."

74. Pervo, *Profit with Delight*, 84.

75. Ibid.

read—would be sufficient for that. Moreover, he adds, even if readers miss Chariton's allusions, their interest or enjoyment will not be substantially diminished:

> Unlike some of the recherché works of the Second Sophistic, which cannot be appreciated without knowledge of the model being imitated, it is quite possible to read Chariton without recognizing his limited literary allusions. . . . Not even the "best" of the pre-Sophistic novels thus appears to require a highly cultured audience.[76]

A more specific assessment of the implied reader's socioeconomic level is difficult to substantiate. Nevertheless, in view of the low opinion of the romances and the high cost of books, a middle-class audience is more easily defendable than a higher or lower group.[77] Upper-class readers viewed the novels with disdain; middle-class readers could have at least envisioned the fall from and subsequent reattainment of success portrayed by Chaereas and Callirhoe; but Chariton's novel would have held little appeal for a reader from the lowest class, who would have been so far removed from "the good life" that its textual world could not have offered her or him any real hope.

The gender of the implied reader is a considerably more complex issue.[78] The question begs to be addressed since the narrative has two major characters—a hero and a heroine—sharing only at points the same plotline, each of whom may be viewed as the main character.[79] Does the text address one sex to the exclusion of the other? If so, which? If not, is either sex the primary target? What does the text do to the male and female reader, respectively and collectively?

---

76. Ibid.

77. For an interesting discussion on the production and acquisition of books in the first century and a helpful characterization of the "real readers" of Chariton's novel from a sociohistorical perspective, see Schmeling, *Chariton*, 30–34. For a more extensive treatment, see Knox, "Books and Readers," esp. 16–22.

78. For recent studies on the role of gender in the reading process, see, e.g., Miner, "Guaranteed to Please"; Flynn, "Gender and Reading"; and Crawford and Chaffin, "Reader's Construction."

79. Anderson (*Novel in the Graeco-Roman World*, 62–63) argues that Chaereas and Callirhoe be taken as "a *Liebespaar*, a single organism trying to unite itself." For Anderson, Chaereas is a puppet whose sole profile is that of consort to Callirhoe. Although he rightly observes the overshadowing of the hero by the heroine, there is merit in seeing the two as individual characters (see below).

That the majority of the novel revolves around Callirhoe certainly can be taken as a point in favor of a predominately female audience.[80] Moreover, the image of women reflected by the text is essentially positive.[81] The ideal woman is beautiful, chaste, and faithful unto death. Even where women play a negative role in the narrative, they are not denigrated because they are women. Further, women wield considerable power in Chariton's novel, though in subtle ways. When males in high political positions make decisions that have been influenced by female characters, the result is at times comical. Finally, most of the deities in the novel are female.

Nevertheless, none of these features necessarily substantiates the hypothesis of a female audience. The fact that the novel's main character is a woman may mean nothing more than that the male reader's attention is to be fixed on her. The feminine ideals of beauty, chastity, and fidelity may merely reveal a typically male perspective.[82] Women's power, at least in the case of Callirhoe, usually can be attributed to Eros working through the woman's beauty. And Chariton's female deities would appeal at least as much to male fantasies as to female.

Indeed, several features suggest that Chariton had a male audience in mind: the novel exhibits an essentially positive portrayal of stereotypical male actions and attributes;[83] male characters outnumber the

---

80. Egger ("Women," 45) argues that Callirhoe's central role in the novel is "entirely innovative." Apparently the later novelists followed suit, for female protagonists typically overshadow their male counterparts in the Greek novels in general. Egger notes: "It has become a notorious interpretive observation that the male protagonist tends to remain behind the heroine in both strength of character and interest to the reader" (175). Egger's dissertation focuses on the evidence for and the implications of a female readership for the Greek novels. She concludes: "If any of the five novelists can lay claim to the title of an author of women's fiction, it is surely Chariton" (401). Hägg (*Novel in Antiquity*, 95) writes: "It is tempting to think of the novel as the first great literary form to have had its main support among women." He suggests that female authors lie behind some of the novels that appear to be pseudonymous (96).

81. Egger ("Women," 170) characterizes Chariton as "a gynophile author who has not a single harsh word at all for any of his female characters."

82. This is a point that Hägg himself admits (*Novel in Antiquity*, 96).

83. For example, Hermocrates wanted Callirhoe to do reverence to Aphrodite in the temple, but *her mother* took her (1.1.5). Callirhoe's suitors view her as a trophy to be won (1.2.1). The narrator tells the reader that "*everyone* prayed to lie in bed beside [Callirhoe]" (5.5.9). Chaereas gives advice to an Egyptian soldier regarding how to deal with a woman: "Appeal to her, flatter her, make promises to her! Above all, let her think that she is loved!" (7.6.10). Throughout the novel Callirhoe is viewed by her suitors as a prize to be possessed, rather than someone with whom they may share a relationship.

female characters more than two to one[84] and are more prominent in the novel as active agents;[85] the plot structure traces a male's journey through the *rites de passage* (separation, isolation, death of the old, and symbolic rebirth);[86] direct intrusions of the narrator often reflect a male orientation;[87] and the narrator's reference to his readers in 8.1.4 bears a masculine inflection (νομίζω δὲ καὶ τὸ τελευταῖον τοῦτο σύγγραμμα τοῖς ἀναγινώσκουσιν ἥδιστον γενήσεσθαι).[88] In addition to these subtle literary features, a sociological factor may be considered: since education of females was limited, women probably constituted a much smaller percentage of the reading public.[89]

Nevertheless, like the arguments for a female audience, these factors, individually or collectively, do not constitute proof that Chariton's

---

84. Egger ("Women," 40-41) provides statistics for the five extant romance novels: "39 male versus 16 female members of the cast in Heliodorus; 27 versus 10 in Xenophon; 28 versus 7 in Achilles; 23 versus 10 in Chariton; 17 versus 10 in Longus." The average male-female ratio for all five novels is a little over 2.5:1.

85. Ibid., 172.

86. As Chaereas proceeds on this journey, he becomes "a new kind of hero, who fights only if he must, but who takes his place as a hero through gentleness, devotion to his mistress, social graces, and conformity to the ideals of a leisure class" (Schmeling, *Chariton*, 137).

87. See, for example, the narrator's direct address to the reader in 1.4.2: "... a woman is easy prey when she thinks she is loved." Cf. Egger's ("Women," 40n1) assessment: "Generally, the more 'mediated,' reflective forms of narrating in the Greek novel lead away from the female characters and the feminine perspective to a more male viewpoint, while the level of action and identification concentrates on them."

88. Tr: And I think this last book will be very pleasing to the readers (8.1.4).

89. Egger ("Women," 29–38) takes pains to cite evidence for the literary capabilities of females at the time of the novels' appearance. However, she describes the questions regarding "women's literacy, education and access to books" as "mostly unsolved" (30) and concludes that "it is difficult to speak about women's literacy with certainty" (31). "To facilitate the assumption of a female audience" she widens the scope of readership to include aural "readers," i.e., those who heard narratives performed orally (34–35). The strongest piece of evidence she offers is that within the Greek novels themselves "female reading and writing is a common feature" (36). This, she notes, stands in marked contradistinction to all of the works of classical tragedy wherein only one woman (Phaidra in Euripides' *Hippolytus*) knows how to write (36). Chariton provides a clear witness to female literacy in his heroine, Callirhoe, of whom he writes: λαβοῦσα δὲ γραμματί διον ἐχάραξεν οὕτως (8.4.4). Egger concedes that establishing that women (primarily of the leisure class) could read for enjoyment or entertainment does not necessarily prove that they did so (253). Nevertheless, it would demonstrate that females represent a potential audience for the novels.

Chaereas and Callirhoe assumes a predominately male audience.[90] Brigitte Egger's explanation for the grammatically masculine reference to Chariton's readers (8.1.4) is one possible argument that would at least allow for a substantial female readership:

> The grammatical subsumption of the feminine under the masculine gender, well-known to philologists and outlined as an ideoogical problem by modern feminist linguistics, is addressed in ancient legal texts, in which unequivocal definitions and identities are imperative. Thus, Servius says (*Dig.* 32, 62): *semper sexus masculinus etiam femininum sexum continet.*[91]

The impossibility of eliminating either sex from Chariton's audience invites one to consider whether this text ignores or exploits the gender of its readers, and, in the latter case, to identify and interpret the gender-specific invitations that the text extends to its reader.[92]

What finally can be said to characterize the author, the text, and the readers of *Chaereas and Callirhoe*? The author clearly is an innovative nonconformist, well versed in the classics, who most frequently assumes the role of a third-person omniscient narrator but occasionally addresses the reader from the first-person point of view.

Chaereas and Callirhoe is a mimetic, highly emotive, bastard-prose medley of drama, epic, love elegy, and history that is less interested in the events it portrays than in its characters' reactions to those events. As the earliest complete representative of its genre, it may be defined prescriptively as a

> relatively lengthy work of prose fiction depicting or deriding certain ideals through an entertaining presentation of the lives and experiences of a person or persons whose activity transcends the limits of ordinary living as known to its implied readers.[93]

90. Oral performance would have made Chariton's story accessible to a broad spectrum of society, not only along the lines of gender but on the socioeconomic level as well.

91. Egger, "Women," 18 n. 1. One could argue, however, that the need to state this explicitly in a forensic context may indicate that inclusion of the feminine in masculine references was not an a priori assumption.

92. "We have no reason to assume that late Greek 'popular' literature . . . was as gender-specific and gender-split as popular fiction is today. . . . I find it likely that they appealed to a male and a female audience" (Egger, "Women," 399).

93. Pervo, *Profit with Delight*, 105. Pervo looks at the Greek novel from three aspects: typical features, cultural function and setting, and structure. The typical features

Chariton's readers are moderately educated middle-class males and females who feel isolated and impotent in a world grown large, and who seek to define themselves in the context of the sociopolitical machinery of the Hellenistic world. Ultimately, they wish to acquire power and a sense of control for their lives. Using his narrative world and the world-view reflected in it, Chariton addresses this need.

THE IDEOLOGY OF CHARITON

In chapter 1, the work of several scholars was adduced to support the premise that narratives transport ideologies. For example, Norman Petersen, on the basis of his work on narrative sequence in Mark's Gospel, concludes that "the plotting of incidents" creates a "world of values as well as of events." Similarly, Menakhem Perry argues that one of functions of narrative order is to induce the reader to accept certain impressions or attitudes presented in a text. Robert Bergen likewise demonstrates that narrative order is a discourse-grammatical feature that can be used to determine the author's intention.[94]

Thus, we have likened the narrative text to a conductor's baton, suggesting that the text is the means by which the reader identifies the author's "ideological score." Chapter 3 applied this notion to the Gospel of Mark. Now we give attention to the ideological score presented in Chariton's *Chaereas and Callirhoe*.

Power is a subtle but ubiquitous element of Chariton's novel. Of the six categories that Pervo lists as features typical of the Greek novel, most relate in some way to power relationships: *patriotism*, individual-state; *politics*, individual-state and individual-individual; *religion*, individual-god and individual-state; *fidelity*, spouse-spouse and spouses-state; *status*, individual-state, individual-family and individual-individual; even

---

include *themes* (politics, patriotism, religion, wisdom, fidelity, and status), *motifs* (travel, adventure and excitement, warfare, aretalogy, court life and intrigue, rhetoric, and miscellany), and *modes* (marvelous, historical, sentimental, comic and satyric, realistic, diactic, missionary, pastoral, and tragic). Pervo views the cultural function and setting as an "escape from the drudgery and horror of the routine and a suggestion about how things might be better" (112) and notes five structural items: scene and summary alternated, stories interpolated within the main story, episodes linked, ideals communicated through characters, and sententious asides offered.

94. Petersen, "'Point of View,'" 108; Perry, "Literary Dynamics," 40; and Bergen, "Text as a Guide."

Pervo's *wisdom* category includes sapient utterances that touch on power relationships.[95]

Scholars of the Greek novels not only have identified isolation as "the predominant *Weltanschauung* of the social context in which they were produced (and originally read)," but also have found this sentiment to be expounded in and reflected by the texts themselves.[96] Indeed, isolation is underscored by one of the Greek novels' major motifs—travel:

> It is by no means an accident . . . if the heroes of the novel travel so much. . . . The novelists of our century are not unaware—nor were they—that the solitude of man never becomes more apparent than in travel, and by it.[97]

Isolation augments a sense of powerlessness. Chariton's readers saw themselves as helpless individuals in a world grown large, powerless "playthings of Fortune" searching for identity and a certain degree of self-determinability.[98]

These readers identify with the adventures and misadventures of the hero and heroine, for they too are on a quest for their identity.

Of the two protagonists, however, the heroine is preeminent as the one with whom the reader will identify. Callirhoe more precisely typifies the Hellenistic individual's spirit of isolation and condition of impotence. Both she and Chaereas are separated from family and homeland for most of the novel. Chaereas, however, often is surrounded by colleagues and always has the faithful Polycharmus at his side, whereas Callirhoe has no one. Both Callirhoe and Chaereas are moved about by Fate or the will of others, but Callirhoe more so. Practically every action she makes is a passive response to someone's (usually a male's) bidding. But Chaereas often evaluates evidence and makes his own decision to go here or there in his search for Callirhoe.

95. The categories are listed and expanded in Pervo, *Profit with Delight*, 105–6.

96. Egger, "Women," 231. Reardon ("Greek Novel," 296) notes: "Isolation seems indeed to be the central concern of the Greek novel."

97. Grimal, *Romans Grecs et Latins*, xiii, quoted in Reardon, "Greek Novel," 296 (translation mine). The original reads: "Ce n'est point un hasard . . . si les héros de roman voyagent tant. . . . Les romanciers de notre siècle n'ignorent pas, eux non plus, que jamais la solitude de l'homme n'apparaît mieux que dans le voyage, et par lui."

98. Perry (*Ancient Romances*, 48) writes: "The bigger the world the smaller the man. Faced with the immensity of things and his own helplessness before them, the spirit of Hellenistic man became passive in a way that it had never been before, and he regarded himself instinctively as the plaything of Fortune."

Callirhoe is the more exemplary model of isolation and power-lessness for another reason: she is a woman. Although the mobility of women in the reader's world has been debated,[99] in the classical milieu of the narrative world two social practices contributed to the isolation of women: segregation (separate living quarters for men and women) and seclusion (confinement of women to their homes). Callirhoe appears in public only on special occasions (Chaereas's "funeral," the trial in Babylon, and temple visits). She moves from her father's house to a tomb, from the tomb to a ship, from the ship to Dionysius's house. At the end of the novel Callirhoe does appear briefly at the theater, where the city celebrates the return their beloved couple, but she is taken home as soon as she has greeted the crowd.

Both Callirhoe and Chaereas are primarily "passive victims to the whims and fancies of fate … [who] can merely react to the will of figures of power whose domain they happen to enter."[100] In spite of their func-tional impotence, however, each has an ontological power—though it is latent for most of the novel.

The sequence in which Chariton relates information about the protagonists makes the reader quickly aware of their power potential, and by doing so solicits reader identification. The pair's initial (and most frequent) characterization relates their noble birth (social status) and unsurpassing physical appearance. The reader expects them to act with confidence and self-determinacy. What the reader gets, however, is pre-cisely the opposite.

---

99. Muchow ("Passionate Love," iv–v) argues that the narrative world closely ap-proximates the reader's world in this regard. Chariton's novel thus offers the reader an escape from the restrictiveness of arranged marriages. Egger ("Women," 391) takes exception: "the novels do indeed not describe contemporary reality, but are an attempt to recapture past conditions, at a time when these have actually changed considerably." Muchow's view can be challenged on both textual and extratextual grounds. Egger (392) offers evidence (chiefly Imperial Greek marriage laws) that suggests that women of the reader's world had "extensive rights in marital law." From a textual standpoint, the problem with Muchow's view is that the novel seems to support arranged marriages. True, Callirhoe and Chaereas are granted an exemption because of their exceptional beauty and nobility, but the message seems to be that they paid dearly for circumvent-ing this tradition: Callirhoe is violently kicked; Chaereas is almost crucified; both are sold as slaves; and both lose a son. Perhaps Callirhoe's choice of Dionysius' daughter as a bride for her son and Chaereas's choice of Polycharmus as a groom for his sister reflects their (and the narrator's) conclusion on the matter.

100. Egger, "Women," 321–22.

Chaereas is brought to the despair of suicide on several occasions and only musters the courage to take control of his destiny (embarking on what is ostensibly a suicide mission) near the end of the novel. The primacy effect holds the reader's hope that Chaereas will eventually perform heroically, and the reader is not disappointed.

Callirhoe's power resides solely in her sensual attraction. By it she influences the schemes of those with *de facto* authority and so alters the very course of history. But this power operates apart from her intentions; she never even attempts to use it for self-aggrandizement. Rather, Chariton presents his heroine as *mit macht aber machtlos*. Egger's description well illustrates the notion:

> The four most powerful men of the Persian empire, including the Great King himself, are lying at her feet; each of them directs all his energies and efforts toward securing her for himself; they risk their positions, power, lives, wars—she herself is not even permitted to decide where she wants to stay (Ch 4.8.9) . . . , let alone to choose with which of her two husbands she wants to live (6.1.1). . . . Erotically omnipotent, she is moved around, against her will, like "a piece of furniture" (ὡς σκεῦος, 1.14.9).[101]

By identifying with Callirhoe, the female reader vicariously participates in the erotic power of the heroine's sexual radiancy and the tremendous influence it exerts on males in positions of authority. More subtly, however, she is seduced into accepting the narrator's portrayal of women as operationally impotent by hidden messages that reaffirm women's social limitations and incapacity to act. Her only means of power is to influence males in power positions. If she fully adopts Callirhoe as her model, she will not use this influence for selfish ends, but to procure sanctioned love within the context of a respectable society.

By identifying with Chaereas, the male reader begins a fantasy life as the son of a nobleman. Endued with a stunningly handsome appearance fitted to a conspicuously athletic physique, he is awarded—through no effort of his own—the supreme prize: the most beautiful woman in the world. As quickly as he gains his trophy, however, he loses her. He then embarks on a campaign to get her back, a goal that requires him to surrender everything he has and be reduced to slavery. With the assistance of Fate and the encouragement of a friend, Chaereas finally adopts the

---

101. Ibid., 364.

posture of a classical hero, leading both an army and a navy in successive victories that result in reunion with his wife.

All writers must engage and retain their reader's interest. With the Greek novels this interest hinges in part on the reader's "approval of and involvement with the main characters."[102] The implied author's ideology is reflected in his or her attiudes toward the actions and attributes of the novel's characters. Narrative sequence plays a significant role in how these attitudes are conveyed to the reader. The remainder of this section suggests how male and female readers might process Chariton's novel. The final section of the chapter treats additional instances where narrative sequence influences the reader to accept Chariton's ideology of power.

The allure of power operates at the subconscious level in Chariton's novel. Chariton baits the reader with two common devices for gaining power: (1) association or identification with someone who already visibly displays power, and (2) acquisition of some prize that is highly valued by people with power. Each of these narrative maneuvers operates independently, yet both may function simultaneously. To complicate matters further, Chariton's novel is structured according to two plot lines that at points merge into one. The operation of these devices depends on the identity (particularly gender) of the implied reader and his or her position on the plotline. Having described the implied reader in general terms, we are now in a position to analyze how each of these strategies is utilized by the text.

The male reader is drawn into the narrative world of *Chaereas and Callirhoe* by the desire to obtain external evidences of power. Indeed, in the first sentence of the story proper the narrator introduces the prize: Callirhoe.[103] Callirhoe is described as "an amazingly wonderful girl" (1.1.1),[104] "the pride of all Sicily" (1.1.1), and "the astonishing spectacle" (1.1.2). Her beauty is described as "more than human" (1.1.2) and likened to that of Aphrodite, the goddess of love.

---

102. Ibid., 46.

103. Before this the author gives only his name, the city in which he resides, and a broad description of his work: "a passion of love that took place in Syracuse." For a discussion of Callirhoe, see Hägg, *Novel in Antiquity*, 6. Hägg notes that the name "Callirhoe" means "beautiful-flowing (spring)." This is undoubtedly significant for the story.

104. The expression is θαυμαστόν τι χρῆμα παρθένου. Χρῆμα here expresses something strange or extraordinary of its kind.

Callirhoe's aristocratic parentage, however, casts a shadow of impossibility over the male reader's fantasy of possessing her. Thus, although he is initially drawn into the text by the desire to possess this "divine vision," he is kept at a distance because of the difference in socioeconomic levels. The higher expression of power (possessing its accouterments) recedes from the male reader's grasp and he subconsciously selects the next best approach—that is, he seeks to identify himself with someone who either already has or is likely to obtain tangible evidences of power.

Chariton provides several characters that manifest the accoutrements of power and therefore present themselves as candidates for the person (or group) with whom the reader would most readily identify: Aphrodite (goddess of love), Eros (Aphrodite's son), Tyche (goddess of Fortune, Chance), Hermocrates (Callirhoe's father), Ariston (Chaereas' father), Callirhoe (heroine), and Chaereas ("hero").[105] Hermocrates and Ariston must be set aside at the outset since they are absent from most of the novel, but what about the others?

To be sure, the Greek pantheon was widely regarded as a power complex. Yet it is unlikely that anyone would directly identify with any of the gods since they were so clearly distinct from humans, and since their jealous and capricious nature made it risky to choose any one of them to the neglect of the others.

Aphrodite is the prime mover of the novel's action,[106] but the unparalleled beauty of Callirhoe is clearly the means by which the plot is orchestrated.[107] Callirhoe's beauty attracts her lover, Chaereas, as well as a host of other suitors; it stimulates the envy of the suitors and forms the motivation for their deception of Chaereas; it provokes jealousy to take its course in Chaereas's heart until it is consummated in the apparently fatal blow that he delivers to her; it makes her valuable booty for the

105. Chaereas is described as "hero" since he differs from the typical hero of the Greek classics. Schmeling offers a helpful comparison of Chaereas with the classical heroes in *Chariton*, ch. 6, "A New Kind of Hero."

106. Schmeling, *Chariton*, 21.

107. The novel is saturated with expressions that laud Callirhoe's beauty in superlative terms. Her beauty is "more than human" (1.1.2; 1.10.7), "worth a king's fortune" (2.4.7), "accompanied by dazzling light" (5.3.9), "more valuable than anything here [funeral offerings]" (1.9.6); it "would enslave the whole of Ionia" (2.7.1); it has "won all hearts" (5.1.8). Callirhoe is described as: "nature's masterpiece" (4.7.5), having the appearance of Helen (5.5.9). On many occasions she is actually taken to be a goddess (3.9.1), even Aphrodite herself (3.2.17; 4.7.5; 5.9.1). In addition to these references there is also a rather lengthy description of Callirhoe's beauty in 4.1.8–9.

pirates and prompts her being sold to Dionysius; it captures the desire of Mithridates and gives rise to his schemes to possess her; it allows jealousy to take its course in Dionysius and precipitates the trial before Artaxerxes; it captures the desire of Artaxerxes and incites his desire to possess her; and it enflames Chaereas's anger against Artaxerxes and moves him to takearms with the Egyptians in their war against him.

In spite of Callirhoe's unique beauty and prominence in the novel, however, she is an equally unlikely candidate for the character with whom the male reader might identify. Although her beauty affords her widespread admiration and a degree of influence that extends even to people of high position, it also causes her a great deal of problems— problems that she seems helpless to resolve. This overwhelming radi- ance, rather than helping her achieve her personal goals, in fact runs counter to them. Callirhoe's aristocratic background is a second strike against her in the implied reader's search for power by association. A third obstacle is the unlikelihood that a male reader would directly iden- tify with a female character.[108]

Yet Chariton does provide a character sufficiently close to the back- ground and social status of the implied reader to make identification with him the strongest option. He is Chaereas, the winner of Callirhoe's hand and the hero of the novel. Chaereas is the most appropriate char- acter for achieving identification with the male reader: he is male; he is comparatively low on the social scale; he is athletic; and he is "surpass- ingly handsome" (1.1.3).[109]

---

108. This assumption is based on the "sharing of particulars" concept of reader iden- tification. We should note, however, that other factors may induce a reader identifica- tion that cuts across the lines of gender. Though beyond the scope of the present work, this gender factor suggests an area for further investigation.

109. Assessing the economic stratum from which Chaereas comes is not a straight- forward matter. His father, Ariston, is described as "second only to Hermocrates in Syracuse" (1.1.3). Ariston and Hermocrates are political rivals. But how this translates into economic terms is not clear. To be sure, neither is at poverty level. The funeral offerings seem to indicate this, although we are not certain that all the offerings came from these two families alone. What is clear, however, is that Chaereas is consistently de- scribed as being on a lower economic stratum than Callirhoe and her numerous suitors. Ariston tries to dissuade his son: "Hermocrates ... has so many rich and royal suitors for her. You must not even try to win her, or we shall be publicly insulted" (1.1.9). Callirhoe's suitors refer to Chaereas as a "worthless pauper" (1.2.3). In another place, Chaereas ex- claims: "I know I am a negligible rival for Dionysius—foreigner that I am, poor." (5.10.7). Elsewhere he describes the situation that he and his most trusted friend, Polycharmus, are facing: "poor as we are and in a foreign country" (7.1.9). Finally, Artaxates, the most

We have already established that the sequence in which information is presented in a text can move the reader to accept the narrator's ideology. We now apply this notion to data that relates specifically to the implied reader's identification with Chaereas.

Initially, Chaereas is portrayed positively. At the fore are his "surpassingly handsome" appearance, athletic build, and "noble and generous disposition" (1.1.8). As a candidate for the hand of Callirhoe, however, Chaereas is presented as the dark horse. Although his physical appearance and kind disposition make him the choice of the common people,[110] he is contrasted with the "many rich and royal suitors" who also have focused their designs on Callirhoe. After much persuasion, Hermocrates gives in to the pleas of the people and awards his daughter to Chaereas. Against the odds, Chaereas wins the prize and makes a tighter bond with the reader possible.

The positive portrayal of Chaereas becomes tainted, however, when in a fit of anger sparked by jealousy he delivers a blow to Callirhoe that apparently results in her death. This act initiates the narrator's increasingly unflattering portrayal of Chaereas.[111] Only near the conclusion of the novel, where he finally assumes the role of the classical hero, leading an army and a navy in victory and regaining his beautiful Callirhoe, is he ultimately redeemed. With Chaereas, the male reader has endured the slings and arrows of outrageous Fortune and emerges victoriously from the story. But he has not merely regained the prize; instead, he now sees the prize in a new light.

The female reader is likewise drawn into the narrative world of *Chaereas and Callirhoe* by the attraction of power. Unlike her male counterpart, she is able to accept the text's invitation to identify with Callirhoe. Callirhoe's overwhelming beauty, together with the power it

---

trusted servant of Artaxerxes, refers to Chaereas as a "poor islander" (6.5.3). While it is true that many of these descriptions come from those hostile to Chaereas, and that Chaereas is poor because he left most of his wealth at home, these descriptions nevertheless have the rhetorical function of decreasing the socioeconomic distance between him and the reader.

110. That he is the choice of the common people also strengthens the reader's identification with him.

111. When Chaereas is compared with the hero of the classics, he fails on many counts. He does not take an active role, either in the search for the grave robbers or in the search for Callirhoe. Although he begins these searches with fervor, he frequently must be restrained from self-destruction and coaxed into pursuit.

has over even the highest-ranking personages, make her a prime candidate for the female reader's identification. Moreover, her aristocratic parentage, rather than being an obstacle to be overcome (as for the male reader), is an ideal toward which she strives.

The portrayal of Callirhoe is consistently positive throughout the novel. Not only is she outwardly attractive, but also her words and actions display an inward beauty and strength of character.[112] Even when this "masterpiece of nature" (τὸ μέγα τῆς φύσεως κατόρθωμα, 4.7.5) is reduced to the level of slavery, her behavior accords with the highest standards of decorum. Indeed, her master's restrained passion for her serves only to underscore her unwavering propriety: "[Dionysius] could find no remedy for his passion: gifts would not serve, for he could see that she was proud, nor threats of force, for he was convinced that she would prefer death to violence" (2.8.1).

The greatest challenge to Callirhoe's dignity comes with the discovery of her pregnancy. However, when the heroine's loyalty to her husband is pitted against the life of their unborn child, motherly love triumphs over marital fidelity. In opting to marry Dionysius and raise the child as his, Callirhoe assumes the role of a passive agent and surrenders her honor.[113] This voluntary setting aside of her own interests highlights the heroine's character and allows a closer identification by the implied reader.

What precisely does Chariton intend by this presentation? His protagonists once had power and status through their family connections. Tragedy brings them loss of identity and powerlessness. The female reader has little trouble maintaining a close association with Callirhoe throughout the narrative. This relationship allows her to experience vicariously the loss and recovery of that which the heroine held most dear: life with her beloved.

---

112. In the bathing scene at Dionysius's estate Chariton describes the reaction of the slaves to Callirhoe's beauty: "... although when she was clothed they admired her face as divinely beautiful, when they saw what her clothes covered, her face went quite out of their thoughts" (2.2.2). When the slaves brought Callirhoe her clothes, she refused, requesting instead a slave's tunic. Rather than use her beauty to manipulate, she accepts her lot with grace. A few scenes later Chariton describes Callirhoe's reaction to a crowd of people who "followed Callirhoe spontaneously, as though she had been elected queen for her beauty": "[she] was embarassed and did not know what to do ..." (2.3.9).

113. Schmeling (*Chariton*, 99) remarks: "An aristocratic princess would have chosen suicide for herself and death for her foetus ..."

In the symbolic world of Chariton, a woman's beauty is her only source of power. It should only be used to procure sanctioned marriage, not actual social authority. Because of its powerful effect on men and possible harmful consequences, a woman's beauty should not be publicly displayed. For her own safety, she should remain faithful to her husband and confined to her room.

Egger adduces evidence to show that "real-life women readers of the novels were far more emancipated than the protagonists of these books."[114] Thus, Chariton's novel is subversive to his contemporary socioliterary context; by presenting a positive view of women's seclusion and segregation, and the custom of arranged marriages, Chariton solicits a return to the social mores of classical times.

NARRATIVE SEQUENCE AND CHARITON'S IDEOLOGY

This section attempts to show how Chariton's use of narrative time moves the reader to accept the ideology reflected in his text. Like Mark, Chariton uses analepses and prolepses to signal points that he especially wants his readers to note. Unlike Mark, who requires his readers to wade through a host of gaps and ambiguities and assemble the narrative puzzle for themselves, Chariton does much of the readers' cognitive work for them, preferring to solicit their emotional identification with his protagonists—and their participation in the protagonists' story.

Setting the Stage: 1.1.1–1.1.4

Chariton's opening paragraph sets the stage for the entire novel. It outlines the story's general theme (1.1.1, πάθος ἐρωτικὸν, 1.1.3, ὁ δὲ Ἔρως ζεῦγος ἴδιον ἠθέλησε συμπλέξαι, 1.1.3),[115] introduces the protagonists (1.1.1, Καλλιρόη and 1.1.3, Χαιρέας) and supplies the hook that draws the reader into the narrative world. The hook is the allure of power and status. The evidence for this is found in both the initial characterization of Hermocrates and the link of the protagonists to their fathers.

---

114. Egger, "Women," 394.

115. Tr: Passion [or calamity?] caused by love (1.1.1); But Eros desired to unite [συμπλέξαι] his own couple (1.1.3). The verb συμπλέκω primarily means "to plait or twine together." However, it was also used in the sense of being locked together in sexual intercourse. Thus, a mild sexual allusion is possible here. Nevertheless, Chariton typically is discreet about matters of sex.

Chariton wastes no time in introducing his main characters. Although Hermocrates is the subject of the first sentence of the narrative proper, he is upstaged here—as in the rest of the novel—by his daughter, Callirhoe, who also adumbrates every other character in the novel. While Chariton elaborates on the appearance of Callirhoe and its captivating effect, he limits the characterization of Hermocrates at this point in the narrative to one piece of information: He is the military commander renowned for defeating the Athenians.[116] The singularity of this characterization and its position as the first element of the narrative proper focus the reader's attention on power and status.

In the patriarchal world of Chariton's characters (and readers!), the locus of authority and power in the family was the father. It is significant, therefore, that the background that Chariton chooses to provide for his protagonists relates them strictly to their fathers and completely ignores their mothers.[117] In the fathers, the narrator extends the sphere of power beyond the family to the political arena (ἦν ἐν αὐτοῖς πολιτικὸς φθόνος, 1.1.3).[118] Moreover, these particular fathers represent high social status in that they are the leading citizens of Syracuse.

Chariton's decision to introduce the female protagonist before the male protagonist immediately establishes her as the more important figure.[119] Callirhoe has an established place in Chariton's story as the daughter of a powerful aristocratic war general. Chaereas only has a place in the narrative in the context of suitors for Callirhoe. Thus, the sequencing of narrative information in the opening section of *Chaereas and Callirhoe* suggests power as the novel's primary motif and Callirhoe as its primary character.

116. Although Chariton does give considerable narrative space to Callirhoe in the opening paragraph, all of his comments about her emphasize one characteristic, viz., her beauty. As we have seen, Callirhoe's unparalleled physical appearance is the driving force behind virtually every movement of the plot.

117. In Chariton's novel mothers are "never shown as acting alone or in an extended scene" (Egger, "Women," 124). Mothers rarely appear on the stage in the Greek novels. Whenever they play a significant part in the narrative (which in *Chaereas and Callirhoe* they do not), they invariably are cast in a negative light. As Egger (339) expresses it, "motherhood is a cliché addressed on the verbal level, but not corroborated by scenes on the plot level (apart from a few recognition scenes)."

118. Tr: There was a political rivalry between them.

119. Nothing in the remainder of the narrative ever overturns this notion.

The narrator's statement at the end of this segment (φιλόνεικος δὲ ἐστιν ὁ Ἔρως καὶ χαίρει τοῖς παραδόξις κατορθώμασιν· ἐζήτησε δὲ τοιόνδε τὸν καιρόν, 1.1.4),[120] since it follows his comment that the protagonists' fathers readily would have made an marriage alliance with anyone rather than each other, functions proleptically as a general heading for the subsequent narrative, or at least that portion of the narrative up to and including the protagonists' marriage.[121] The anticipation is vague; it supplies no details as to how this will happen, but it does strongly suggest that Callirhoe and Chaereas will eventually marry.

The anticipation in 1.1.4 thus gives the reader some clue *that* the marriage will take place, but does not explain *how* the obstacle of the fathers' disapproval will be overcome. Thus, the reader's attention is focused on the necessity of the fathers' approval and how it is brought about. The pleadings of the citizenry of Syracuse in a regular assembly (1.1.11–13) are sufficient to persuade Hermocrates to allow the marriage. In this way, Callirhoe and Chaereas are granted an exemption from the standard practice of arranged marriage. Their marriage based on love violates society's norms, but does so with its approval.

After the reader has processed enough of the subsequent narrative data to discover how the fathers' approval is obtained, the result becomes an interpretive lens through which he or she views the remainder of the novel. The practice of arranged marriage has been circumvented; what will be the result?

Chaereas Deceived: 1.2.1–1.6.5

The wedding scene closes on a note of rejoicing: πάντες δὲ Καλλιρόην μὲν ἐθαύμαζον, Χαιρέαν δὲ ἐμακάριζον (1.1.16).[122] Chariton likens

---

120. Tr: Now Eros is contentious and enjoys success against the odds; he sought a suitable time as follows.

121. Hägg (*Narrative Technique*, 215–17) distinguishes three types of anticipation in the Greek novels: "authorial," "divine," and "human." He cites the novel's opening statement as an example of authorial anticipation and the statement of Eros's intention in 1.1.4 as an example of the divine type. Nowhere in the novel, except perhaps 6.4.5, do divine beings (e.g., Ἀφροδίτη, Τύχη, Ἔρως) speak directly. Their thoughts and intentions are mediated through the narrator's voice. This distinguishes them from Hägg's third type, "human" anticipations ("character-generated" is preferable).

122. The contrast drawn by the μὲν ... δὲ construction is significant; everyone is *admiring* (worshipping) Callirhoe, but *congratulating* Chaereas. Chaereas is the winner

his protagonists' nuptial festivities to the wedding of Peleus and Thetis and uses that analogy in an anticipatory heading that punctuates the wedding scene with an ominous tone: πλὴν καὶ ἐνταῦθά τις εὑρέθη βάσκανος δαίμον, ὥσπερ ἐκεῖ φασὶ τὴν Ἔριν (1.1.16).[123] The presence of a βάσκανος δαίμων, specifically paralleled with Ἔριν (goddess of discord), foreshadows the protagonists' marital problems, but leaves the reader clueless as to how this might happen.

Chaereas is the victim of two attempts at deception. The first scheme proceeds as follows. The rejected suitors, formerly rivals, form an alliance and elect a leader, "the tyrant of Acragas," who devises a plan to destroy Chaereas's marriage through jealousy.[124] During a night when Chaereas is at his parents' home tending to his ill father, the spurned suitors stealthily approach the newlywed's quarters and plant evidence of a riotous party. By this they hope to deceive Chaereas into believing that Callirhoe had been unfaithful to him. The plan is successful to that point; Chaereas is filled with jealousy and accuses Callirhoe. Callirhoe, however, easily convinces Chaereas of her innocence.

In the narration of this first deception, the reader hears *that* the scheme will involve jealousy three times before the narrator describes the outworking of the plan (1.2.1, 5, 6). The harm the suitors intend to bring to Chaereas is hinted at in 1.2.4 (θάνατον τῷ νυμφίῳ) and predicted in 1.2.5 (ἐπαγγέλλομαι διαλύσειν τὸν γάμον ἐφοπλιῶ γὰρ αὐτῷ Ζηλοτυπίαν, ἥτις σύμμαχον λαβοῦσα τὸν Ἔρωτα μέγα τι κακὸν διαπράξεται).[125] Since these prolepses are on the lips of characters in the story, they do not possess the same reliability as narratorial prolepses. In fact, the failure of the first plot leaves the reader wondering whether or not this marriage will be broken apart. Thus, a major element of the story begins to appear: can marriage based on love survive?

---

of the prize; but Callirhoe is the prize. Callirhoe is inherently worthy of praise; Chaereas is worthy of praise by virtue of his association with Callirhoe.

123. Tr: But a certain evil spirit was found here, just as Strife reportedly was there.

124. Every member of the group was minded to kill Chaereas (1.2.4: ἀλλὰ ἀνό-νητον αὐτῷ γενέσθω τὸ ἆθλον καὶ τὸ γάμον θάνατον τῷ νυμφίῳ ποιήσωμεν; "But let the prize become unprofitable for him; let us make the marriage death for the bridegroom"), except the man from Acragas. His plan to trick Chaereas into losing Callirhoe by his own doing persuaded each of them.

125. Tr: Death to the bridegroom (1.2.4); I promise to break up the marriage. I will set against him Jealousy, who, taking Love as ally, will produce a great calamity (1.2.5).

Chariton introduces the suitors' second scheme with an anticipatory phrase that serves as a heading for the next section but supplies no details about it (1.4.1).[126] The effect of this type of narrative anticipation is to throw the plot forward. Here the reader learns that another deception is imminent. The plot is moved forward by engaging both curiosity as to how the deception will be played out and suspense as to what its results will be.

In the second scheme, Chaereas is tricked into believing that he is actually witnessing Callirhoe's lover unlawfully enter his home. The "director of this drama" selected two "actors" for the deception; one to play the part of a lover and the other to prepare Chaereas for the staged event.[127] The latter engages Chaereas's attention and curiosity in much the same way that the narrator has been captivating his reader, namely, by making a proleptic statement that serves as a heading for the immediately ensuing scene: δός οὖν μοι σχολάζοντα σεαυτὸν καὶ ἀκούσῃ μεγάλα πράγματα ὅλῳ τῷ βίῳ σου διαφέροντα (1.4.4).[128]

The effect of this prolepsis is to make both the reader and Chaereas captives of their own curiosity and thus underscore the importance of the μεγάλα πράγματα (great matters) when the narrator subsequently gives content to the expression. The content given expresses a fear concomitant with marriage based on love: the infidelity of one's partner.[129]

---

126. Chariton frequently employs this technique. Cf. 1.1.4; 1.1.16; 1.2.6; 1.6.5; 1.14.1; 2.7.1; 2.8.3–4; 3.2.17; 3.3.8; 3.3.10; 3.3.12; 3.4.10; 3.9.8; 4.2.5; 5.1.2; 5.2.9; 5.10.10; 7.1.3; 7.2.6; 7.6.6; 8.1.2; 8.1.4–5.

127. These terms are the narrator's own designations for the man from Acragas (ὁ δημιουργὸς τοῦ δράματος, 1.4.2) and the participants in his scheme (ὑποκριτής, 1.4.2). They illustrate the connection of Chariton's novel with Greek drama. Chariton notes the display of emotions made by one of the actors in this scene: εἶτα συναγαγὼν τὰς ὀφρῦς καὶ ὅμοιος γενόμενος λυπουμένῳ μικρὸν δέ τι καὶ δακρύσας . . . ("then he frowned, assumed a sad expresssion, and even let a tear drop from his eye" [R], 1.4.5.).

128. Tr: Present yourself to me when you have leisure and you will hear important matters that will make a difference in your whole life.

129. Both the heroine and the hero fear losing their partner to another lover. Chaereas's immediate assumption of Callirhoe's unfaithfulness in the suitor's first scheme and the ease with which he is convinced of her infidelity in the second scheme illustrate this fear on the hero's part. For the heroine, see Callirhoe's tomb soliloquy where she addresses her beloved as follows: οὐκ ἔδει σε ταχέως θάψαι Καλλιρόην οὐδ' ἀληθῶς ἀποθανοῦσαν. Ἀλλ' ἤδη τάχα τι βουλεύῃ περὶ γάμου ("It was not necessary to bury Callirhoe so quickly, even if she had truly died. But perhaps you are already making plans for marriage," 1.8.4).

Callirhoe and Chaereas marry because their physical attraction to each other is too powerful to healthily be resisted. But what happens if one of the partners encounters someone more beautiful? If physical attraction is a sufficient justification for marriage, could it not logically be used to justify infidelity? Chaereas's fear of infidelity is clearly what makes the second scheme succeed. In this way, the narrator has identified a weakness of marriage based on love. The protagonists' marriage faces threats to its survival from its inception.[130]

The narration of the second scheme to deceive Chaereas contains another character-initiated prolepsis. Here the narrator places it on the male protagonist's lips. Chaereas asks to see evidence of Callirhoe's unfaithfulness, not to assure himself of her guilt (he has already accepted that) but to have better reason for killing himself; he promises that he will spare her even though she is acting unlawfully (1.4.7). The apparently fatal blow that he delivers to Callirhoe in the next scene overturns his prediction and shows him to be an unreliable guide for the reader. The reader thus depends more heavily on the commentary of the narrator, whose predictions have never been proven false.

Chaereas's act of violence also creates a disruption in the male reader's identification with Chaereas. If the narrator intends the male reader to live his story through Chaereas, he must recapture the reader's sympathy for him. Chaereas's repentant attitude and deep remorse accomplish this to a degree, but in a larger sense, he is not fully reinstated until the end of the novel.

Callirhoe at the Mercy of Pirates: 1.7.1–1.14.10

Chariton introduces this section with his typical proleptic heading: τὸ δὲ δοκοῦν εἰς τιμὴν τῆς νεκρᾶς γεγονέναι μειζόνων πραγμάτων ἐκίνασεν ἀρχήν (1.6.5).[131] In addition to moving the plot forward, this particular prolepsis illustrates Chariton's fondness for providing logical motivations for the turns in his plot. Here the elaborate funeral offerings

---

130. Chaereas's violence against Callirhoe is first narrated in 1.4.12 and brought before the reader again by means of the brief analepsis at 1.8.3: τότ᾽ οὖν ἀνεμνήσθη τοῦ λακτίσματος καὶ δι᾽ ἐκεῖνο πτώματος, μόγις δὲ καὶ ἐκ τῆς ἀγωνίας ἐνόησε τάφον ("Then she remembered the kick and the fall it caused; and gradually she became aware of *her position in* the tomb *which was brought about* by the struggle").

131. Tr: That which seemed to have been done for honoring the dead girl set in motion the beginning of even greater events.

set in motion a series of "greater events." Again, the ambiguity of the terminology engages the reader's curiosity and entices her or him to read on to discover what happened.

When Theron, the leader of the pirates, discovers the resuscitated Callirhoe, he is first minded to kill her.[132] In a brief analepsis that intensifies the reader's sympathy for her plight, Callirhoe pleads for Theron to have mercy on "the girl who did not receive mercy from husband or parents." This statement joins the narrator's analepsis earlier in this section (1.8.3, τότ 'οὖν ἀνεμνήσθη τοῦ λακτίσματος)[133] as an indictment against Chaereas. But with what are the heroine's parents charged? Perhaps she blames them too for burying her so quickly. Or could it be that she faults their choice of a husband who would abuse her?[134]

After Theron realizes the value of Callirhoe's beauty, he judges that it would be more profitable to keep her alive and in good condition for sale (1.9.6). Thus, his stated intention to take Callirhoe back to her parents (1.9.7, θέλω γὰρ αὐτὴν ἀποδοῦναι τοῖς γονεῦσιν)[135] and his direct promise to her to do so (1.13.9, ἐπανιὼν δὲ παραλήμψομαι καὶ μετὰ πολλῆς ἐπιμελείας ἄξω λοιπὸν εἰς Συρακούσας)[136] aggravate his already roguish characterization.

Chariton takes pains to show that Callirhoe is powerless to extricate herself from Theron's scheme. Callirhoe addresses her father in a brief analeptic soliloquy that highlights the most important aspect of his characterization, namely, his military prowess, and uses it to chide him for not saving her: πάτερ, ἐν ταύτῃ τῇ θαλάσσῃ τριακοσίας ναῦς Ἀθηναίων κατεναυμάχησας ἥρπασε δὲ σου τὴν θυγατήρια κέλης μικρὸς καὶ οὐδέν μοι βοηθεῖς (1.11.2).[137] As the daughter of Syracuse's

132. Chariton plays up the fact that Callirhoe's life, though spared from her violent injury, is still in grave danger (cf. her reaction to seeing the gleam of Theron's sword, 1.9.5).

133. Tr: Then she remembered the kick . . .

134. The narrator specifically states (1.1.14) that Callirhoe was not aware of the assembly at which the populace of Syracuse persuaded her father to go against his inclinations and accept Chaereas as his son-in-law. Even if she learned of this later—and this is not narrated—her recently discovered plight may be influencing her to consider her marriage as "arranged" and blame her parents for it.

135. Tr: I wish to bring her back to her parents.

136. Tr: On the return I will pick you up, and thereafter with utmost care I will take you to Syracuse.

137. Tr: Father, in this very sea you defeated three hundred Athenian warships, now a little boat has snatched away your daughter, and you do nothing to help me.

most famous general, Callirhoe has power but cannot make use of it; as the most beautiful woman in the Hellenistic world, she has power of attraction but is powerless to chart her own course in life.[138]

Callirhoe's predictive blessing on Theron and his band of brigands (ἀποδοῖεν δὲ ἔφη πᾶσιν ὑμῖν οἱ θεοὶ τὰς ἀξίας ἀμοιβάς, 1.13.10)[139] is loaded with sarcasm and functions as a prolepsis regarding the fate of these evildoers. The implication is that misfortune will come to the pirates, but the reader is left in suspense as to how.

Chariton closes book 1 with another analeptic soliloquy by his heroine (1.14.6–10). The key elements of this flashback are: her lover's kick, her apparent death, her stay in the tomb, her time with the pirates, and her sale as a slave. The analepsis functions to remind the reader of the major movements of the plot to this point. More importantly, however, it emphasizes (1) that her course is never self-determined and (2) that she is powerless to change the situation. Chariton's heroine is always at someone's mercy; first her father, then the pirates, and now the Ionian aristocrat, Dionysius.

Callirhoe Weds Dionysius: 2.1.1–3.2.17

Chariton links the opening of book 2 with the close of book 1 by a shared situation-motif. At the end of book 1, Callirhoe, bemoaning her circumstances, is finally overcome by sleep. At the beginning of book 2, Dionysius, bemoaning his circumstances, awakens from sleep.

Dionysius's chief steward, Leonas, finds his master still in bed. At this point the narrator begins an analepsis that explains that Dionysius, distraught with grief over his wife's death, had practically confined himself to his bedroom as if his wife was still with him.

The dream that Dionysius subsequently relates to Leonas appears to continue in an analeptic mode. Ostensibly a flashback of his first wedding, the dream nevertheless contains irregular features that suggest something more; the woman Dionysius identifies as his wife is "indeed

---

138. Egger, "Women," 398, contends that "the leading notion of femininity in [the Greek novels] is the strong narcissistic fantasy of women's emotional and erotic omnipotence linked with their actual powerlessness." This is a point well illustrated by Callirhoe, but mostly later in the novel. While her physical attractiveness has already saved her from death at the hands of the brigands, the narrator has not yet begun his parade of men in power positions who are taken captive by Callirhoe's beauty.

139. Tr: May the gods grant all of you the deserved repayment.

taller and more excellent" (μείζονά τε καὶ κρείττονα, 2.1.2). While his master is relating the dream, Leonas interrupts and relates analeptically his encounter with and purchase of Callirhoe. He prefaces his story, however, with an anticipatory heading that converts Dionysius's dream to a prolepsis: μέλλεις ἀκούειν ταῦτα, ἃ τεθέασαι (2.1.3).[140] Thus, Leonas presents Callirhoe as the fulfillment of Dionysius's proleptic dream.

Callirhoe's prayer to Aphrodite in 2.2.7–8 contains an analepsis and prolepsis. The analepsis credits the goddess with having introduced the couple, but charges that she has not protected them from misfortune. The prolepsis consists of a request that the heroine will attract no other man after Chaereas. The reader is not required to wait for the outcome of this request. The narrator directly states πρὸς τοῦτο ἀνένευσεν ἡ Ἀφροδίτη and adds καὶ πάλιν ἄλλον ἐπολιτεύετο γάμον, ὃν οὐδὲ αὐτὸν ἔμελλε τηρήσειν (2.2.8).[141] Thus, the narrator has made it quite obvious in advance that Callirhoe will eventually marry Dionysius and that their marriage will not survive.[142] Once again, the reader knows in advance the *that* but is ignorant of the *how*. This is the narrator's way of emphasizing the factors that bring the marriage about and those that lead to its demise.

The first meeting of the pair destined for temporary marriage is indeed orchestrated by Aphrodite. The narrator lets the reader know this by means of an analepsis in his order of presentation. At the suggestion of Leonas, Dionysius is on his way to the country to visit his estate. Here the narrator interrupts with the reason Callirhoe is going to be at Aphrodite's temple: ἡ δὲ Καλλιρόη τῆς νυκτὸς ἐκείνης θεασαμένη τὴν Ἀφροδίτην ἠβουλήθη καὶ πάλιν αὐτὴν προσκυνῆσαι (2.3.5).[143]

---

140. Tr: You are about to hear the things that you dreamed.

141. Tr: Aphrodite denied this *request* . . . and again she was planning another marriage that she was not even going to preserve.

142. Hägg (*Narrative Technique*, 220) describes this type of anticipation: "They are often very vaguely put and serve as a kind of mystification, enough to arouse the curiosity but not meant to give any specific information: I, 1,16 πλὴν καὶ ἐνταῦθά τις εὑρέθη βάσκανος δαίμων . . . ('And again a certain evil spirit was found there' [hinting at the intrigues of the suitors]). The connection with the immediately following part of the narrative is sometimes made explicit by adding a phrase like II, 8, 3 ἄξιον δὲ ἀκοῦσαι τὸν τρόπον ['the means is worthy of hearing'] or III, 3, 8 μάθοι δ᾽ ἄν τις ἐκ τῶν γενομένων ['knowledge anyone *can derive* from what happened']."

143. Tr: That night Callirhoe contemplated Aphrodite and decided to worship her again.

Callirhoe is therefore praying in the temple when Dionysius enters and mistakes her for the goddess herself.

In their later interview of Callirhoe, Dionysius turns to Leonas and utters a prediction that the reader already knows to be true (ἔλεγόν σοι … ὅτι οὐκ ἔστι δούλη· Μαντεύομαι δὲ ὅτι καὶ εὐγενής, 2.5.6)[144] and that Callirhoe subsequently confirms for her interrogators (Ἑρμοκράτους εἰμὶ θυγάτηρ, 2.5.10).[145] The rest of her story is a synopsis (and a truncated one at that) of the plot thus far.[146] It is a logical and chronological concatonation of the narrative's key events (viz., the heroine's fall, apparent death, costly funeral, capture by pirates, and sale to Leonas).[147]

The paucity of detail and consistently chronological presentation make more obvious to the reader the element that Callirhoe has chosen not to include in her account, namely, her marriage to Chaereas. In case the reader has overlooked the omission Chariton immediately adds: πάντα εἰποῦσα μόνον Χαιρέαν ἐσίγησεν (2.5.11).[148] While this statement fills the narrative gap created by the analepsis, it nevertheless creates a narrative gap of its own.

Specifically, the narrative arrangement in 2.5.10 causes the reader to consider why Callirhoe might have done such a thing. To be sure, her marriage to Chaereas is not an item that she is likely to have forgotten. Is she trying to protect herself? Perhaps she wants to avoid false conclusions that might be drawn from her husband's jealous actions. Or does she subconsciously desire Dionysius?

Whatever the precise reason, Callirhoe's omission of all details related to Chaereas (specifically, the marriage and the apparently fatal kick) and the absence of Chaereas in the events leading up to her introduction to Dionysius encourage the reader to view Dionysius as the more fitting marriage candidate for Callirhoe. Chaereas is not only offstage; he is ef-

---

144. Tr: I told you she wasn't a slave.... I predict that she is even of noble birth.

145. Tr: I am Hermocrates's daughter.

146. Part of the reason for its brevity is "its position early in the romance before there is so much to recapitulate" (Hägg, *Narrative Technique*, 256).

147. The order of events in the analepsis matches the sequence found in the primary narrative. Hägg (ibid., 256–57) provides a brief concordance that pairs the details in Callirhoe's account with their locations in the primary narrative.

148. Tr: She told them everything; only about Chaereas did she remain silent.

fectively beyond the reader's purview. In this arrangement, the positive descriptions of Dionysius are more likely to win the reader over.

The enticement begins. Chariton lets the reader overhear a bystander describing Dionysius to Theron: ξένος εἶναί μοι δοκεῖς ἢ μακρό–θεν ἥκειν, ὃς ἀγνοεῖς Διονύσιον πλούτῳ καὶ γένει καὶ παιδείᾳ τῶν ἄλλων Ἰώνων ὑπερέχοντα, φίλον τοῦ μεγάλου βασιλέως (1.12.6).[149] To this terse, but highly complimentary introduction Chariton adds more praises of Dionysius through other characters (e.g., Leonas: διονύσιος ἀνὴρ δικαιότατός ἐστι καὶ νομιμώτατος, 2.5.2)[150] as well as direct narratorial commentary (e.g., ἀνὴρ γὰρ βασιλικός, διαφέρων ἀξιώματι καὶ παιδείᾳ τῆς ὅλης Ἰωνίας, 2.1.5; ἦν δὲ καὶ φύσει καλός τε καὶ μέγας καὶ μάλιστα πάντων σεμνὸς ὀφθῆναι, 2.5.2).[151]

Chariton's presentation of Dionysius moves beyond physical attractiveness (which Chaereas shares) to include such qualities as compassion, maturity, sophistication, sociopolitical savvy, tact, charm and commitment to the heroine's welfare.[152] According to Egger, the reason for Dionysius's superiority is that "the narrator grants him too many inside views (about his emotions, intentions, fears) and extended scenes together with the heroine to keep him in the secondary position easily."[153] Egger contrasts the narrator's treatment of Chaereas and Dionysius:

> Chaereas' relationship with the heroine is not much developed beyond a few standard phrases and topic monologues in the fast-moving first book (before they get married within three Budé pages, have their first fight within five, and are separated within eight), whereas Dionysius' perspective is particularized at length.[154]

The truncated nature of the account that Callirhoe gives Dionysius not only causes the reader to consider the missing element (Callirhoe's marriage to Chaereas) but also marks for the reader's special attention

149. Tr: You seem to me to be a foreigner or to have come from a great distance; you do not know Dionysius who is above all other Ionians in wealth, nobility, and culture—a friend of the Great King.

150. Tr: Dionysius is a just man and an observer of the law.

151. Tr: For he is a kingly man, preeminent in reputation and culture in all Ionia; he was by nature handsome, tall, and most of all dignified in appearance.

152. Egger, "Women," 193.

153. Ibid., 194.

154. Ibid.

the details that are included. These items are significant because they reaffirm, and hence reinforce, Callirhoe's stock power-characterization.[155] Her aristocratic parentage is the platform from which she relates her brief autobiography. This power image is augmented by the description of her father as a military general (ἑρμοκράτους εἰμὶ θυγάτηρ, τοῦ Συρακοσίων στρατηγου, 2.5.10)[156] and underscored by Dionysius in his conversation with Leonas in the following scene: οὐκ ἀκούεις Ἐρμοκράτην τὸν στρατηγὸν τῆς ὅλης Σικελίας ἐγκεχαραγμέ– νον μεγάλως, ὃν βασιλεὺς ὁ Περσῶν θαυμάζει καὶ φιλεῖ, πέμπει δὲ αὐτῷ κατ' ἔτος δωρεά ὅτι Ἀθηναίους κατεναυμάχησε τοὺς Περσῶν πολεμίους (2.6.3).[157] Propriety, of course, explains her silence regarding her primary attribute (beauty), but Dionysius's words of comfort which immediately precede her self-description clearly allude to it: Οὐδὲν γὰρ περὶ σεαυτῆς ἐρεῖς τηλικοῦτον, ἡλίκον ὁρῶμεν. Πᾶν ἐστί σου σμικρότερον λαμπρὸν λαμπρὸν διήγμα (2.5.9–10).[158]

In 2.8.3, Chariton introduces a proleptic narratorial aside that sets up what may well be the most significant analepsis in the novel. He has just praised Callirhoe's seemingly invincible fidelity to Chaereas. Now he adds:

Κατεστρατηγήθη δ' ὑπὸ τῆς Τύχης, πρὸς ἣν μόνην οὐδὲν ἰσχύει λογισμὸς ἀνθρώπου· φιλόνεικος γὰρ ἡ δαίμων, καὶ οὐδὲν ἀνέλπιστον παρ' αὐτῇ. καὶ τότ' οὖν πρᾶγμα παρά δοξον, μᾶλλον δὲ ἄπιστον κατώρθωκεν· ἄξιον δὲ ἀκοῦσαι τὸν τρόπον. (2.8.3)[159]

---

155. This is, of course, the diegetic characterization. The heroine is mimetically portrayed as powerless.

156. Tr: I am the daughter of Hermocrates, the Syracusan general. See also 3.1.6: ἐγώ, φησίν, οἰκίας οὖσα τῆς πρώτης ὢν Σικελίᾳ ... ("'I,' she said, 'am from the first household in Sicily'").

157. Tr: Haven't you heard about Hermocrates, the general of all Sicily, who has a great record, whom the king of Persia praises and loves and sends gifts every year because he defeated the Athenians, the enemies of Persia.

158. Tr: For nothing you will say about yourself *could be* as wonderful as the greatness we see. Every tale is less magnificent than you yourself.

159. Tr: Fortune outwitted her, though; Fortune, against whom alone human calculation has no power. For Fortune relishes victory, and anything may be expected of her. So now she brought about an unexpected, indeed incredible, state of things. How she did it is worth hearing. [R]

Thus, the narrator indirectly informs the reader *that* Callirhoe's fidelity to her husband will be broken; again the suspense—and therefore the emphasis—centers on *how* (τὸν τρόπον) this will take place.

Fortune plotted against the heroine's sexual discretion. The τροπός (that is, "means") is revealed in the analepsis that follows:

> ἐρωτικὴν γὰρ ποιησάμενοι τὴν πρώτην σύνοδον τοῦ γά
> μου Χαιρέας καὶ Καλλιρόη, παραπλησίαν ἔσχον ὁρμὴν
> πρὸς τὴν ἀπόλαυσιν ἀλλήλων, ἰσόρροπος δὲ ἐπιθυμία τὴν
> συνουσίαν ἐποίησεν οὐκ ἀργήν. ὀλίγον οὖν πρὸ τοῦ πτώ
> ματος ἡ γυνὴ συνέλαβεν. (2.8.4)[160]

The surprise incurred by encountering Callirhoe's pregnancy at this point in the story focuses the reader's attention on this narrative datum.[161] Since the heroine's pregnancy is not a minor detail, the reader will not dismiss the postponement of its presentation as merely resulting from the narrator's forgetfulness; instead she or he will attempt to discover its significance.

The sequential arrangement of narrative material again facilitates the reader's processing of the heroine's pregnancy. Indeed, the next scene shows that the pregnancy explains how Callirhoe's fidelity to Chaereas will be breached. This clue is heralded by a proleptic shift in narrative time; Plangon predicts that νικήσει σωφροσύνην γυναικὸς μητρὸς φιλοστοργία (2.9.1).[162]

Plangon's task is to influence Callirhoe to marry Dionysius. Callirhoe's pregnancy will force her to choose between marriage or slavery. She would sooner accept the latter—or even death—than betray Chaereas.[163] Either of the former alternatives would involve the same consequences for her child. As Plangon suspected, a mother's affection conquers a wife's chastity and Callirhoe agrees to marry Dionysius.

160. Tr: After Chaereas and Callirhoe were married, their first contact was passionate; they had an equal impulse to enjoy each other, and matching desire had made their union fruitful. So just before her fall Callirhoe became pregnant. [R] Note: Blake's text mistakenly gives ποιησόμενοι.

161. The reader learns of Callirhoe's pregnancy even before the heroine herself. As one manifestation of Chariton's penchant for giving the reader privileged inside information, this specific sequencing of narrative data functions to strengthen the narrator-reader bond and procure the reader's acceptance of the ideology reflected by the text.

162. Tr: The affection of a mother will conquer the fidelity of a wife.

163. Callirhoe actually threatens suicide if Dionysius would choose to make her his concubine: ἀπάγξομαι μᾶλλον ἢ ὕβρει δουλικῇ παραδώσω τὸ σῶμα (3.1.6).

In the course of her deliberation, Callirhoe speaks proleptically in a monologue addressed to her unborn son (2.9.5). She predicts that he will sail to Sicily, find his *father* and *grandfather*, and tell them her whereabouts.[164] As a result of the child's efforts, a fleet will sail from Sicily to save her and restore her to Chaereas.

This prolepsis, like many other character-generated prolepses in Chariton's novel, does not prove to be wholly accurate. In keeping with the novel's power orientation, the child does turn out to be male.[165] Yet nowhere in the narrative does he sail to Sicily. In fact, he all but disappears from the story after this scene.[166] A fleet will sail from Sicily and eventually Callirhoe will be rescued. But neither the child nor the fleet will be directly responsible for the heroine's salvation.[167]

The narrator stresses the role of the child in Callirhoe's decision (see, e.g., 2.11.4, οὐ δι᾽ αὐτὴν ἀλλὰ διὰ τὸ βρέφος ἐπείθετο ζῆν and 3.2.13, οὐκ ἂν ἐπείσθην σὲ ὀμόσαι καὶ τὸν σὸν υἱόν, εἰ μή με προΰδ—ωκε τοῦτο τὸ βρέφος).[168] Having examined the issue from this per-

---

164. Males are the ones who have the power and resources to come to Callirhoe's aid.

165. Callirhoe never considers the possibility that the child would be female. This may reflect a male orientation. The assumption that the child is male could be understood as mere hypothesizing or wishful thinking. To override this notion Chariton places the suggestion of a male child on the lips of another character, not Chaereas himself but a vision of him (2.9.6). In any case, a male child indicates a recognition that the locus of power and authority to bring about change resides with males. Further evidence of an interest in power and status is found in 2.9.5 where the the heroine draws an analogy between her son and male figures recognizable from mythology (Zethus and Amphion) and history (Cyrus). Zethus and Amphion are twin sons who were exposed at birth, saved from death, and later recognized as the rightful rulers of Thebes. Cyrus is probably Cyrus the Great, the historical founder of Persia whose life followed a similar sequence of events.

166. He appears briefly in a scene with his mother at a temple of Aphrodite, and he is mentioned as a consolation prize for Dionysius. Even if he sails to Sicily sometime external to the narrative world, he would not have to inform Callirhoe's father of her whereabouts since she and Chaereas are restored to their homeland at the novel's end.

167. Mention of the Sicilian fleet does provide the reader with a concrete object of hope. Introducing this possible means of rescue in advance sets up the reader to process the actual launch of the fleet as something that will directly reunite the separated lovers. The fleet's destruction (3.7.3) dashes this hope and the reader must seek out another. This sequencing of narrative material causes the reader to participate emotionally in the vississitudes experienced by the novel's protagonists.

168. Tr: She was persuaded to live, not for her own sake but on account of the baby (2.11.4); I would not have been persuaded to call you and your son as witnesses to my oath, if this baby had not betrayed me (3.2.13).

spective, Callirhoe fearfully chooses what she deems to be the lesser of two evils. Thus, the circumstances surrounding Callirhoe's marriage to Dionysius portray a heroine erotically powerful (her unparalled physical appearance brings a prominent authority figure to his knees),[169] yet pragmatically powerless (she lacks the authority and capacity to act or exist apart from external compulsion).

The Pirates' "Reward": 3.3.1—3.4.18

Broadly speaking, this entire section is analeptic. What makes it so is the linear nature of language that requires that any presentation of multiple events (even those events that happen simultaneously in fictional time) be given in a linear sequence. Simultaneous events cannot intelligibly be simultaneously narrated, either in an oral or written medium. The undisguised authorial intrusion in 3.2.17 informs the reader that the events she is about to encounter happened at the same time as those she has just processed: ἀλλ᾽ ἐνεμέσησε καὶ ταύτῃ τῇ ἡμέρᾳ πάλιν ὁ βάσκανος δαίμων εκεῖνος· ὅπως δὲ, μικρὸν ὕστερον ἐρῶ. βούλομαι δὲ εἰπεῖν πρῶτον τὰ γενόμενα ἐν Συρακούσαις κατὰ τὸν αὐτὸν χρόνον (3.2.17).[170]

When Chariton's hero and heroine are separated, they no longer share the same line of action.[171] The narrator must decide which line to

---

169. When Dionysius learns that Callirhoe has agreed to marry him, his strength is depleted to such an extent that he is taken for dead (Ἐξεπλάγη πρὸς τὸ ἀνέλπιστον ὁ Διονύσιος καὶ ἀχλὺς αὐτοῦ τῶν ὀφθαλμῶν κατεχύθη, παντάπασι δὲ ὢν ἀσθενὴς φαντασίαν παρέσχε θανάτου ["At this unexpected news Dionysius was thunderstruck. Mist covered his eyes; he went limp all over and presented a deathlike figure"] [R], 3.1.3). This *Scheintod* is a common feature in the Greek novels, and particularly *Chaereas and Callirhoe* (cf. Callirhoe's apparent death, 1.5.1).

170. Tr: But again, even on this day that evil spirit spewed. I will tell how a little later, but first I want to talk about the things that transpired in Syracuse during the same time.

171. The lines do not merge again until 8.1.7. The protagonists are "separated from each other for 80% of the narrative time; 7% precedes the separation, and 13% is left after the reunion. Thus, the dominating central part is, in principal, divided into two main lines of action" (Hägg, *Narrative Technique*, 140). Chariton builds a pattern of alternation between two lines of action of which the hero and heroine alternately are the center. Yet as Hägg stresses, the lines of action are seldom completely distinct: "The narrative concentrates here and there on other persons than Chaereas and Callirhoe, giving the same type of direct, inside information on behaviour and thoughts for each charcter chosen as temporary centre.... Thus, the romance is never experienced as a rhythmical alternation between the adventures of two separate persons but as a constant zigzagging

relate first. The question this raises for the present context is: how does the order in which these lines of action are presented function rhetorically *vis-à-vis* the narrator's ideology?

The point at which the primary line of action separates is the heroine's funeral (1.6.5). Callirhoe's death would lead the reader to expect the remainder of the narrative to center around Chaereas, perhaps showing how this event affected his character or impelled him on a quest for revenge against the perpetrators of his deception.[172] By introducing another character, Theron, and describing his scheme to rob the tomb, the narrator leaves the reader anticipating the reappearance of Chaereas. This sequencing heightens the reader's shock when the protagonist who reappears is not Chaereas but Callirhoe (τὰ δὲ περὶ Καλλιρόην δει–νοτέραν ἄλλην ἐλάμβανε παλιγγενεσίαν, 1.8.1).[173]

Relating the heroine's line of action first is agreeable to the reader since people typically side with the victim. But this narrative decision has another, more far-reaching effect: it induces the reader to view Chaereas more sympathetically. Several features support this conclusion. First, according to this sequencing, the reader learns immediately that Callirhoe has not died. She or he is more apt to forgive Chaereas since the results of his offense are not as grave as first supposed. Second, the antecedent position of the Callirhoe line mitigates the reader's view of Chaereas by elaborating on the treachery of the brigands since it emphasizes the cruelty of their deception rather than the violence of Chaereas's kick.[174] Finally, in the proposal of the first brigand the narrator teasingly pres-

---

between a greater number of individuals, all parts of the *same* superior line of action" (153–54). Hägg also notes the presence of concrete "bridges" (e.g., messengers, letters, etc.) and motifs ("regret/longing" and "searching") that integrate the two lines (148).

172. Chaereas learned the truth even before Callirhoe's funeral (ἔτι δὲ καιομένων καὶ τεμνομένων αὐτῶν ἔμαθε τὴν ἀλήθειαν ["while they were being burned and *otherwise* tortured, he learned the truth *about her*"], 1.5.2).

173. Tr: Now the things about Callirhoe; she received another mighty rebirth!

174. Callirhoe herself exonerates Chaereas from his spontaneous act of violence toward her (1.8.4). In the conversation with Dionysius in which she confesses her identity and relates the events that led to her sale, she attributes her loss of consciousness to a "sudden fall" (ἐξ αἰφνιδίου πτώματος, 2.5.10) but says nothing about Chaereas's kick, which caused it. Even though the motive behind her silence about the kick was the concealment of her marriage to Chaereas, her description reminds the reader of the event in a way that supports the reader's sympathy for Chaereas.

ents the possibility of a swift and happy ending to the story (ἀποδοῦναι δὲ τὴν Καλλιρόην ἀνδρὶ καὶ πατρὶ, 1.10.2).[175]

The order in which the Callirhoe and Chaereas lines are presented engages and retains the reader's sympathetic identification with these central characters. Both are victims of the suitors' jealousy and the brigands' greed.

When the Chaereas line resumes at 3.3.1, the hero is embarking on a search for his beloved Callirhoe. All human effort proves ineffectual, but Fortune orchestrates an encounter with Callirhoe's captors. The pirates receive, as Callirhoe proleptically promised (1.13.10), their "just rewards"—the crew through starvation (3.3.18), and their captain, Theron, through crucifixion (3.4.18).

Chaereas Sold: 3.5.1—3.10.8

In this section, Chaereas and Dionysius each learn of the other's existence. Chaereas first discovers that Callirhoe has remarried. Prostrating himself at the foot of a temple statue of Aphrodite, he reminds the goddess of her role in introducing him to Callirhoe (analepsis!) and requests that she give her back to him (prolepsis?). Upon arising, he sees a golden statue of Callirhoe. The position of this event in the narrative sequence of the episode invites the reader (and Chaereas) to take this as a sign that Aphrodite has heard his prayer and will reunite the lovers.

Without the aid of information that Theron could have provided, Chaereas continues his search. While anchored in a secluded spot, his trireme is attacked and burned by a detachment of Persians according to a plan instigated by a smooth piece of espionage on the part of Dionysius's steward Phocas. Along with other survivors of the ship's destruction—and partnered specifically with his ever faithful friend Polycharmus—Chaereas is sold into slavery. For Chaereas, the reversal in status and power is dramatic; from aristocratic commander of a Syracusan naval detachment to a slave. His change of fortune from aristocrat to slave parallels that of the heroine.

Chaereas's appearance to Callirhoe in a dream (3.7.4) segues to the Callirhoe line of action and provides the occasion where Dionysius learns of Chaereas. When in her sleep Callirhoe calls out to her first husband, Dionysius hears the name "Chaereas" for the first time.

---

175. Tr: To return Callirhoe to *her* husband and *her* father.

Callirhoe's statement that Chaereas's chains signify his death could be taken as foreshadowing the hero's death; however, as the reader has seen, character-generated prolepses, unlike those that come directly from the narrator, are not always reliable. The preceding scene adds some doubt since it describes Chaereas and Polycharmus in chains of *slavery* (3.7.3, ἐκεῖ δὲ πέδας σύροντες παχείας εἰργάζοντο τὰ Μιθριδάτου).[176] Moreover, in the following scene, the narrator mentions that Callirhoe herself entertained the possibility that her dream had been deceptive (3.7.7). Nevertheless, Callirhoe's interpretation of Chaereas's chains adds to the reader's suspense by keeping the possibility of the hero's death before the reader.[177]

The narrator tugs at the reader's emotions by periodically introducing circumstances or statements that suggest the possibility of Chaereas's death. The most direct statement falls in 3.9.10: χαιρέας τέθνηκεν.[178] Again, however, this information cannot be accepted at face value, since it is related through one of the characters, namely, Phocas.

Dionysius questions Phocas regarding two foreigners (Chaereas and Polycharmus) who were worshipping at the temple of Aphrodite. Phocas tries to soften the blow of what will be distressing news for Dionysius by first assuring him of a happy ending:

> Φαῦλον μὲν, εἶπεν οὐδὲν ἐστιν, ὦ δέσποτα, μεγάλων γὰρ ἀγαθῶν φέρω σοι διηγήματα· εἰ δὲ σκυθρωπότερά ἐστιν αὐτοῦ τὰ πρῶτα, διὰ τοῦτο μηδὲν ἀγωνιάσῃς μηδὲ λυπηθῇς, ἀλλὰ περίμεινον, ἕως οὗ πάντα ἀκούσῃς· χρηστὸν γὰρ ἔχει σοι τὸ τέλος. (3.9.8)[179]

Nevertheless, his efforts fail; Dionysius faints when Phocas reports the arrival of a Sicilian trireme carrying ambassadors sent to demand the return of Callirhoe. As soon as Dionysius revives, Phocas changes the

176. Tr: And there, dragging thick chains, they were working the land of Mithridates.

177. Chariton frequently shows death as an imminent possibility for Chaereas, e.g., his many temptations to suicide, his military exploits, and most dramatically his near crucifixion (4.3.5).

178. Tr: Chaereas died.

179. Tr: "It is nothing bad, O master," he said, "for I bring you news of great good. If the first *part* of it is sad, don't grieve or agonize, but wait until you hear everything. For the last *part* has pleasure for you."

intended order of events of his story and begins with the happy ending, χαιρέας τέθνηκεν· ἀπόλωλεν ἡ ναῦς οὐδεὶς ἔτι φόβος (3.9.10).[180]

With Dionysius relieved, the narrator summarizes (analeptically) the details that Phocas shared with his master. The description, however, indicates that some on the ship had died, but others had been captured. The fact that some had survived as prisoners, as Dionysius later points out to Phocas (3.9.12), leaves open the possibility that Chaereas is still alive. Dionysius, recognizing that his hold on Callirhoe will be more secure if she is convinced that Chaereas is dead, demands that the knowledge of the survivors be hidden from her. The reader knows his plan is successful since Callirhoe's analeptic summary of Chaereas's misfortunes (3.10.6–8) charges Aphrodite with killing her own suppliant (σὺ καὶ Χαιρέαν εἰς Μίλητον ἤγαγες φονευθῆναι καὶ ἐμὲ πραθῆναι, 3.10.8).[181]

Men of Power Compete for the Prize: 4.1.1—4.7.8

In book 4, Chariton shows that his heroine's incomparable beauty attracts and influences men of the highest social rank and political authority. To be sure, the theme of Callirhoe's beauty is not confined to this section. Here, however, her physical appearance is given its most magnificent accolades. What is emphasized is the effect that her beauty has on men of great political power. As athletes compete for a victory trophy, high-ranking civil leaders compete for Callirhoe's love.

The first figure to be moved to action by Callirhoe's beauty is Dionysius. Callirhoe has a dream in which she saves Chaereas from the burning trireme (analepsis). Haunted with the possibility that Chaereas might be alive, Callirhoe is becoming emaciated (τρυχομένην). Dionysius reasons that a physical burial will help bury her memory of Chaereas and thus prompts her to oversee the construction of a tomb for him. Inside information provided by a direct narratorial intrusion indicates that the motive behind this plan has more to do with the selfish concerns of Dionysius (μὴ ἄρα τι καὶ τοῦ κάλλους αὐτῇ παραπόληται, 4.1.2)[182] than a pure concern for Callirhoe's well being. Thus, Callirhoe's beauty motivates Dionysius to construct a tomb for Chaereas.

---

180. Tr: Chaereas has died; the ship is destroyed; nothing fearful remains!
181. Tr: You led Chaereas to Miletus to be murdered and me to be sold.
182. Tr: Lest some of her beauty be eroded.

Among the almost entire population of Ionia who had come to Chaereas's mock funeral were two political dignitaries: Mithridates of Caria and Pharnaces of Lydia. The narrator states that the alleged motive for their attendance was to honor Dionysius, but in reality they were drawn by the reports of Callirhoe's beauty (4.1.8). Judging from the narrator's description of the heroine's appearance on that occasion, these rulers were not disappointed:

Τότε δὲ καὶ τῆς δόξης εὑρέθη κρείττων· προῆλθε γὰρ μελα—
νείμων, λελυμένη τὰς τρίχας· ἀστράπτουσα δὲ τῷ προσώ
πῳ καὶ παραγυμνοῦσα τοὺς βραχίονας ὑπὲρ τὴν Λευκώ
λενον καὶ Καλλίσφυρον ἐφαίνετο τὰς Ὁμήρου. οὐδεὶς μὲν
οὖν οὐδὲ τῶν ἄλλων τὴν μαρμαρυγὴν ὑπήνεγκε τοῦ κά
λλους, ἀλλ' οἱ μὲν ἀπεστράφησαν, ὡς ἀκτῖνος ἡλιακῆς
ἐμπεσούσης, οἱ δὲ καὶ προσεκύνησαν. ἐπαθόν τι καὶ παῖδες.
Μιθριδάτης δὲ, ὁ Καρίας ὕπαρχος, ἀχανὴς κατέπεσεν,
ὥσπερ τις ἐξ ἀπροσδοκήτου σφενδόνη βληθείς, καὶ μόλις
αὐτὸν οἱ θεραπευτῆρες ὑποβαστάζοντες ἔφερον.[183]

The narrator later reinforces the debilitating effect that Callirhoe's beauty has upon prominent political powers. Mithridates returns to Caria in a far worse condition than when he came to Miletus, ὠχρός τε καὶ λεπτός, οἷα δὴ τραῦμα ἔχων ἐν τῇ ψυχῇ θερμόν τε καὶ δριμύ and τηκόμενος δὲ ὑπὸ τοῦ Καλλιρόης ἔρωτος (4.2.4–5).[184] Pharnaces, governor of Lydia and Ionia, gladly heard Dionysius's complaint against Mithridates mainly because of his burning passion for Callirhoe (... τὸ δὲ πλέον διὰ τὸν ἔρωτα· καὶ γὰρ αὐτὸς ἐκάετο τῆς Καλλιρόης, 4.6.2).[185] Even the King of Persia, Artaxerxes, on the strength of her reputation for beauty, summons her to appear with Dionysius (4.6.7–8).

183. Tr: On that day she looked even lovelier than she was reputed to be. She appeared dressed in black, with her hair let down; with her shining countenance and her arms bared she looked more beautiful than Homer's goddesses of the "white arms" and "fair ankles." In fact no one present could stand the radiance of her beauty. Some turned their eyes away, as if the sun's rays had fallen on them; some even fell to the ground in worship; even children were affected. Mithridates, the governor of Caria, was speechless with astonishment. He fell to the ground like someone struck unexpectedly by a slingshot, and his attendants could scarcely hold him up (4.1.8–9). [R]

184. Tr: Pale-yellow and weak, because he had a burning, piercing wound in his heart; and wasting away through love for Callirhoe.

185. Tr: ... but primarily because of love, for he himself was inflamed with passion for Callirhoe.

While Callirhoe's beauty is shown to debilitate rulers, almost every analepsis in this book highlights the misfortunes of Chaereas and and his comrade Polycharmus. Both of these men name Callirhoe as the cause of their afflictions. Polycharmus highlights the reversal of fortune endured by his friend Chaereas (4.3.1-4). Chaereas's complaint to Callirhoe (4.3.10) stresses his slavery, manual labor, and near crucifixion. His letter to Callirhoe (4.4.7-10) mentions the burning of the trireme, his sale by barbarians, his near execution, and his painful discovery of her marriage. Even Mithridates alludes to the trouble Chaereas and Polycharmus have had (4.4.2, 4.4.4).

Polycharmus's defense before Mithridates (4.3.1-4) is particularly significant since it both highlights the afflictions of the hero and points to the heroine as cause. The passage below is broken up into segments marked by sequential numbers in brackets. The concordance that follows the passage pairs (using "=") these numbered segments to corresponding parts of the primary narrative (designated by book and section).

[1]ἡμεῖς, οἱ δύο δεσμῶται, Συρακόσιοι γένος ἐσμέν. [2]ἀλλ᾽ ὁ μὲν ἕτερος νεανίσκος πρῶτος Σικελίας δόξῃ τε καὶ πλού– τῳ καὶ εὐμορφίᾳ ποτέ, ἐγὼ δε εὐτελὴς μέν, [3]συμφοιτητὴς δὲ ἐκείνου καὶ φίλος. 3.2 [4]καταλιπόντες οὖν τοὺς γονεῖς ἐξεπλεύσαμεν τῆς πατρίδος, ἐγὼ μὲν δι᾽ ἐκεῖνον, [5]ἐκεῖνος δὲ διὰ γυναῖκα Καλλιρόην τοὔνομα, ἥν, δόξασαν ἀποτεθνηκέ– ναι, [6]ἔθαψε πολυτελῶς. [7]τυμβωρύχοι δὲ ζῶσαν εὑρό– ντες [8]εἰς Ἰωνίαν ἐπώλησαν. [9]τοῦτο γὰρ ἡμῖν ἐμήνυσε δημοσίᾳ βασανιζόμενος Θήρων ὁ λῃστής. 3.3 [10]ἔπεμψεν οὖν ἡ πόλις ἡ Συρακοσίων τριήρη καὶ πρέσβεις τοὺς ἀνα– ζητήσοντας τὴν γυναῖκα. [11]ταύτην τὴν τριήρη νυκτὸς ὁρμοῦσαν ἐνέπρησαν βάρβαροι καὶ τοὺς μὲν πολλοὺς ἀπέ– σφαξαν, ἐμὲ δὲ καὶ τὸν φίλον δήσαντες ἐπώλησαν ἐνταῦθα. [12]ἡμεῖς μὲν οὖν σωφρόνως ἐφέρομεν τὴν συμφοράν· ἕτεροι δὲ τινες τῶν ἡμῖν συνδεδεμένων, οὓς ἀγνοοῦμεν, διαρρή ξαντες τὰ δεσμὰ φόνον εἰργάσαντο [13]καὶ σοῦ κελεύ– σαντος τὴν ἐπὶ τὸν σταυρὸν ἠγόμεθα πάντες. 3.4 [14]ὁ μὲν οὖν φίλος οὐδὲ ἀποθνήσκων ἐνεκάλει τῇ γυναικί, προήχθην δὲ αὐτῆς μνημονεῦσαι καὶ τῶν κακῶν αἰτίαν εἰπεῖν ἐκείνην, [15]δι᾽ ἣν ἐπλεύσαμεν. (4.3.1)[186]

186. Tr: We, the two prisoners, are Syracusans by birth. [2]But the other man is the foremost young man of Sicily in honor, wealth, and beauty of form; I am worthless, [3]that man's fellow-pilgrim and friend. (3.2) [4]We left our parents and sailed away from our homeland—I *left* on his account; [5]he *left* because of his wife Callirhoe, whom, having thought she had died, [6]he gave an expensive funeral. [7]Grave robbers found her alive and

1.	3.7.3	Chaereas and Polycharmus taken captive.
2.	1.1.3	Chaereas's rank and appearance narrated.
3.	1.5.2	Polycharmus prevents Chaereas from commiting suicide; friendship narrated.
4.	3.3.8	Chaereas sails for Callirhoe and returns with Theron.
	3.5.8–9	Chaereas and Polycharmus sail *"because of Callirhoe."*
5.	1.5.1	Callirhoe mistaken for dead.
6.	1.6	Callirhoe's funeral narrated.
7.	1.9	Tomb robbers find Callirhoe alive.
8.	1.14.5	Callirhoe sold in Ionia.
9.	3.4.13–14	Theron questioned under torture.
10.	3.5.8–9	Trireme sent *to find Callirhoe.*
11.	3.7.3	Trireme burned by Persians; Chaereas and Polycharmus taken captive and sold to work Mithridates's land.
12.	4.2.1–4	Chaereas and Polycharmus work on Mithridates land.
	4.2.5	Co-workers murder their overseer.
13.	4.2.6	Chaereas and Polycharmus condemned to crucifixion.
14.	4.2.7	Chaereas silently goes to place of execution; Polycharmus *blames Callirhoe.*
15.	3.5	*Search for Callirhoe.*

The above arrangement exposes incongruities between the recapitulatory complex and the primary narrative when viewed from the perspective of narrative sequence. Since the primary narrative adheres strictly to a chronological presentation, Polycharmus's account retrogresses at three points. These occur at junctures 1–2, 4–5, and 14–15. The latter two of these three transitional points fault at Callirhoe as the reason for the expedition and subsequent trials of Polycharmus and his friend. Thus,

---

[8]sold her in Ionia. (3.3) [9]The evil pirate Theron under torture disclosed this *information* to us. [10]Therefore, the city of Syracuse sent a trireme and group of ambassadors to search for the woman. [11]At night barbarians burned this trireme while at anchor and killed many men. They bound me and my friend and sold us there. [12]We bore the misfortune with self-control, but certain other men who were bound with us, whom we do not know, broke their bonds and committed a murder. [13]and you commanded that everyone be led away and *placed* upon the cross. (3.4) [14]My friend did not speak against his wife, even as he was dying, but I was led to remember her and to speak that evil cause because of whom we sailed.

Callirhoe's beauty has proven to be debilitating even to her lover (and his friend).

Moreover, segment 10 also relates that the trireme was sent to rescue "the woman" (τὴν γυναῖκα). Since Polycharmus has already used Callirhoe's name in segment 5, his substitution of a generalizing term may reflect anger and resentment. This certainly is evident in 4.2.7 (διὰ σὲ, φησίν, ὦ Καλλιρόη, ταῦτα πάσχομεν).[187]

The recapitulatory complex in 4.3.1–4 owes its basic structure to the inquiries of Mithridates that it answers: (a) τίς εἶ; (b) καὶ πόθεν; (c) καὶ πῶς ἦλθες εἰς Καρίαν; (d) καὶ διατὶ σκάπτεις δεδεμένος; and (e) μοι διήγησαι περὶ Καλλιρόης καὶ τίς ὁ φίλος (4.2.15).[188] Segments 1–3 respond to Mithridates's inquiry as to their identity and land of origin (questions *a* and *b*). Segments 4–10 explain how the comrades ended up at Caria (question *c*). And segment 11 reveals what brought them to slave labor (question *d*).

Mithridates's primary interest (question *e*; μάλιστα, 4.2.15), however, was Callirhoe; Polycharmus's "friend" is added almost as an afterthought. As noted earlier, Callirhoe is named (segment 5) and alluded to (segment 10) as the cause of the comrades' trouble. But Mithridates apparently still considers the possibility of a second woman with the same name as Callirhoe (cf. 4.2.11), even though Polycharmus quickly identified the Callirhoe of whom he spoke as "the daughter of the general Hermocrates" (4.2.12).

It appears that Mithridates does not identify the Callirhoe mentioned in segment 5 with the daughter of Hermocrates until segment 15, where Polycharmus identifies his friend's wife (i.e., the Callirhoe of segments 4–14) with the one whose name he evoked when his execution was about to take place. Mithridates finally makes the connection and identifies Chaereas as Polycharmus's friend and compatriot. Realizing that with Chaereas back in the picture Dionysius's hold on Callirhoe will be less secure, Mithridates cons Chaereas into writing a letter that will mix the heroine's emotions between her two husbands and give his own advances more chance for success.

---

187. Tr: "Because of you, O Callirhoe," he said, "we are suffering these things."

188. Tr: (a) "Who are you?" (b) "From where have you come?" (c) "How did you come to Caria?" (d) "Why are you digging as a one who has been bound?" and (e) "tell about Callirhoe and who your friend is."

Power is an important element in this section. Dionysius is described as the most powerful of the Ionians (δυνατώτατος Ἰώνων, 4.6.4). Pharnaces and Mithridates hold high political offices; the latter holds love and power to be the two greatest blessings (4.7.2).[189] Callirhoe's beauty exerts a strong influence on men in key power positions. Nevertheless, she does not consciously use that power for her own advantage. Instead, she passively responds to the will of men in authority.

Chaereas is shown as powerless; practically all of the flashbacks to earlier events highlight his weaknesses and sufferings. Even one who he believes is championing his cause is against him. In his letter to Callirhoe, he refers to Mithridates as his benefactor, but the reader knows that Mithridates's *help* is motivated by his designs on Callirhoe.

The Love Letter: 4.4.7–10

Chaereas's letter to Callirhoe, written at the suggestion of Mithridates, exhibits a peculiarity that calls for an additional attention. Most of the novel's recapitulatory complexes relate the events in chronological sequence. Chaereas's letter, however, breaks from this pattern:

4.4.7 καλλιρόῃ Χαιρέας· ζῶ, καὶ ζῶ διὰ Μιθριδάτην, τὸν ἐμὸν εὐεργέτην, ἐλπίζω δὲ καὶ τὸν σόν· ἐπράθην γὰρ εἰς Καρίαν ὑπὸ βαρβάρων, οἵτινες ἐνέπρησαν τριήρη τὴν καλήν, τὴν στρατηγικήν, τὴν τοῦ σοῦ πατρός· ἐξέπεμψε δὲ ἐπ' αὐτῆς ἡ πόλις πρεσβείαν ὑπὲρ σοῦ. τοὺς μὲν οὖν ἄλλους πολίτας οὐκ οἶδ' ὅ τι γεγόνασιν, ἐμὲ δὲ καὶ Πολύ–χαρμον τὸν φίλον ἤδη μέλλοντας φονεύεσθαι σέσωκεν ἔλεος δεσπότου. 4.4.8 πάντα δὲ Μιθριδάτης εὐεργετήσας τοῦτό με λελύπηκεν ἀντὶ πάντων, ὅτι μοι τὸν σὸν γάμον διηγή–σατο· θάνατον μὲν γὰρ ἄνθρωπος ὢν προσεδόκων, τὸν δὲ σὸν γάμον οὐκ ἤλπισα. ἀλλ' ἱκετεύω, μετανόησον. κατασπέν–δω τούτων μου τῶν γραμμάτων δάκρυα καὶ φιλήματα. 4.4.9 ἐγὼ Χαιρέας εἰμὶ ὁ σὸς ἐκεῖνος ὃν εἶδες παρθένος εἰς Ἀφροδίτης βαδίζουσα, δι' ὃν ἠγρύπνησας. Μνήσθητι τοῦ θαλάμου καὶ τῆς νυκτὸς τῆς μυστικῆς, ἐν ᾗ πρῶτον σὺ μὲν ἀνδρός, ἐγὼ δὲ γυναικὸς πεῖραν ἐλάβομεν. ἀλλὰ ἐζηλοτύ–πησα. τοῦτο ἴδιόν ἐστι φιλοῦντος. δέδωκά σοι δίκας. ἐπρά–θην, ἐδούλευσα, ἐδέθην. 4.4.10 μή μοι μνησικακήσῃς τοῦ λακτίσματος τοῦ προπετοῦς· κἀγὼ γὰρ ἐπὶ σταυρὸν ἀνέ–βην διὰ σέ, σοὶ μηδὲν ἐγκαλῶν. εἰ μὲν οὖν ἔτι μνημονεύσε–

---

189. Mithridates depicts political authority (ἡγεμονία) as a glorious burial shroud (ἐντάφιον ἔνδοξον). This suggests that to him this is the most important goal in life.

ιας, οὐδὲν ἔπαθον· εἰ δὲ ἄλλο τι φρονεῖς, θανάτου μοι δώ–
σεις ἀπόφασιν.[190]

Several structural features of this letter are worthy of mention: It begins *in medias res*; it contains two sections of analeptic details separated by a plea for restoration (the former section begins in reverse chronological order and concludes chronologically, and the latter section, with the exception of one event, is presented chronologically); and it ends with a second plea for restoration.

By beginning with the fact that he was exported for sale (ἐπράθην, φρομ πέρνημι), Chaereas makes an immediate point of identification with Callirhoe. The rhetorical function of the two protagonists overlaps here. Both demonstrate a dramatic change of status from aristocrat to slave. The reader can almost hear the heroine's response: "He's going through what I'm going through—only worse." The immediately following allusion to the burning of the trireme and its former glory days also adds to the depiction of a fall from power. Thus, the emotion of pity is aroused from the start.

With the narrative detail of the near execution, the account moves to a time subsequent to Chaereas's capture and sale. From here the recapitulation moves chronologically to Chaereas's discovery of Callirhoe's second marriage. The first analeptic section concludes with Chaereas's plea for restoration.

The second recapitulatory section temporally retrogresses to events prior to those that initiated the first; in fact these events reach all the

190. Tr: (4.4.7) From Chaereas to Callirhoe. I am alive, alive thanks to Mithridates, my benefactor—and yours, I hope. I was taken to Caria and sold by barbarians who set on fire that splendid trireme that was your father's flagship—the state had sent off a delegation in it, to recover you. I do not know what has happened to the other Syracusans, but my friend Polycharmus and I were on the point of being executed when our master took pity on us and we were spared. (4.8) But all of Mithridates' kindness is counteracted by the distress he has caused me in telling me of your marriage. Death I expected—I am human; but I never thought to find you married. Change your mind, I beseech you—this letter of mine is drenched with the libation of my tears and kisses! (4.9) I am your Chaereas—that Chaereas you saw when you went to Aphrodite's temple as a virgin, that Chaereas who caused you sleepless nights! Remember our bridal chamber and that night of initiation—when you first knew a man, and I a woman! You will say I showed jealousy. That is the mark of a man who loves you. I have made amends to you: I was sold, enslaved, put in chains. (4.10) Do not harbor malice against me for kicking you, in my temper—in my turn I ascended the cross because of you and did not say a word against you. Oh, if you should still remember me, my sufferings are nothing; but if you are minded otherwise, you will be passing sentence of death on me! [R]

way to the beginning of the novel. They recall the couple's first meeting near the temple of Aphrodite (ἐκεῖνος ὃν εἶδες παρθένος εἰς Ἀφροδίτης βαδίζουσα, 4.4.9)[191] and their first celebration of marital love (τοῦ θαλάμου καὶ τῆς νυκτὸς τῆς μυστικῆς, ἐν ᾗ πρῶτον σὺ μὲν ἀνδρός, ἐγὼ δὲ γυναικὸς πεῖραν ἐλάβομεν, 4.4.9).[192] These are the most positive events that the couple shares.[193]

Chaereas's letter does not paint a completely rosy picture of the couple's relationship; it mentions one surely negative feature—but even this is done in a mitigating way. After describing their *coup de foudre* and their initial celebration of marital love, Chaereas admits to experiencing jealousy. This he excuses, however, as an identifying mark of one who loves (τοῦτο ἴδιόν ἐστι φιλοῦντος). He follows that with allusions to his descent into slavery (ἐπράθην, ἐδούλευσα, ἐδέθην), which as he argues, expiates his offenses toward Callirhoe (δέδωκά σοι δίκας).[194]

Chaereas even mentions the nearly fatal blow that he delivered to Callirhoe. Again, however, the narrative presentation extenuates his crime. The positioning of the kick element disrupts the otherwise chronological sequencing of the second recapitulatory section, a feature that tends to give it prominence. This arrangement, however, places it between two narrative elements that relate Chaereas's suffering; the first displays his sale, slavery, and enchainment, and the second his near crucifixion. Sandwiched between these graphic descriptions of suffering, the violent act appears to have been expiated.[195] Thus, at least one of the

191. Tr: That one whom you, as a virgin proceeding to Aphrodite's *temple*, saw . . .

192. Tr: [Remember] the bridal chamber and that night of initiation—when you first knew a man, and I a woman! [R]

193. The wedding celebration and accompanying first kiss (1.1.14–16) are the couple's only other positive experiences that Chaereas does not mention in the letter.

194. Tr: I was sold; I did slave labor; I was bound; I have given you justice.

195. Even the description of the act encourages Callirhoe's (and the reader's) sympathy. He refers to the blow as an act of προπετοῦς, that is, a rash, out-of-control act, which would be devoid of premeditated malice. Chaereas calls on Callirhoe not to bear a grudge against him. Here also he is careful not to give offense. The statement does not imply that Callirhoe presently harbors these feelings. μὴ with the aorist subjunctive as an imperative forbids the inception of some action. Robertson (*Grammar*, 890) gives an excellent illustration from Acts 18:9: μὴ φοβοῦ, ἀλλὰ λάλει καὶ μὴ σιωπήσῃς. He describes the implications of the tenses as follows: "He had been afraid, he was to go on speaking, he was not to become silent." Chaereas was imploring Callirhoe not to even begin to hold a grudge against him. Chaereas goes too far, however, when he offers his final defense. His argument is essentially that since he willingly ascended a cross because of her (διὰ σέ) and did not lay blame (σοὶ μηδὲν ἐγκαλῶν) to her, she should

rhetorical functions of the letter is to increase the reader's sympathy for Chaereas.

Chaereas's letter is the *causa causans* for the trial in Babylon. Dionysius intercepts the letter and assumes it has been written not by Chaereas (whom he presumed dead) but by Mithridates (as a ploy to make Callirhoe more vulnerable to seduction). He complains to his superior, Pharnaces, who, because of political rivalry with Mithridates, gladly brings the matter before their superior, Artaxerxes. The Great King, himself enchanted by the rumors of Callirhoe's beauty, happily summons all parties involved (even Callirhoe herself!) to his court to rule on the matter. All adds up to a test case for passionate love in respectable society.

Beauty and a Beast: 5.1.1–5.10.10

Babylon is the sight of the forthcoming trial in which Dionysius accuses Mithridates of attempting to overpower his wife. It also is the stage for a beauty contest. Callirhoe's beauty, the motivating force of the novel, makes both events a matter for public concern. When Callirhoe irrefutably outshines Rhodogune, the most beautiful woman the Persians have to present, the latter, convinced of her inferiority to the heroine, refuses to enter even a *nolo contendere* plea. Callirhoe is the uncontested winner. Now the question returns: who will win Callirhoe?

The first of Chariton's two major narratorial recapitulatory complexes occurs at the beginning of book 5.[196] This summary review sets the stage for the trial in Babylon, providing a synopsis of every major plot element that has taken place to this point. So thorough is its coverage that one could well make sense of the rest of the novel on the basis of the information contained in this recapitulation alone:[197]

> 5.1.1[1] Ὡς μὲν ἐγαμήθη Καλλιρόη Χαιρέᾳ [2] Καλλίστη γυναικῶν ἀνδρὶ καλλίστῳ, [3] πολιτευσαμένης Ἀφροδίτης τὸν γάμον, [4] καὶ ὡς δι᾽ ἐρωτικὴν ζηλοτυπίαν Χαιρέου πλήξαντος αὐτὴν [5] ἔδοξε τεθνάναι, [6] ταφεῖσαν δὲ

---

likewise not hold a charge against him. It is clear, however, that Callirhoe was not the cause of Chaereas's misfortunes in the same way that he was of hers.

196. The other occurs at the beginning of book 8 where it prepares the reader for the recognition scene on Aradus.

197. Admittedly, the reader's emotional involvement in the story would be less intense.

πολυτελῶς [7] εἶτα ἀνανήψασαν ἐν τῷ τάφῳ [8] τυμβωρύ
χοι νυκτὸς ἐξήγαγον ἐκ Σικελίας, [9] πλεύσαντες δὲ εἰς
Ἰωνίαν [10] ἐπώλησαν Διονυσίῳ, [11] καὶ ἐτὸν ἔρωτα τὸν
Διονυσίου [12] καὶ τὴν Καλλιρόης πρὸς Χαιρέαν πίστιν [13]
καὶ τὴν ἀνάγκην τοῦ γάμου διὰ τὴν γαστέρα [14] καὶ τὴν
Θήρωνος ὁμολογίαν [15] καὶ Χαιρέου πλοῦν ἐπὶ ζήτησιν
τῆς γυναικὸς [16] ἅλωσίν τε αὐτοῦ καὶ πρᾶσιν εἰς Καρίαν
μετὰ Πολυχάρμου τοῦ φίλου, 5.1.2 [17] καὶ ὡς Μιθριδάτης
ἐγνώρισε Χαιρέαν μέλλοντα ἀποθνήσκειν [18] καὶ ὡς ἔσ–
πευδεν ἀλλήλοις ἀποδοῦναι τοὺς ἐρῶντας, [19] φωράσας
δὲ τοῦτο Διονύσιος ἐξ ἐπιστολῶν διέβαλεν αὐτὸν πρὸς
Φαρνάκην, [20] ἐκεῖνος δὲ πρὸς βασιλέα, [21] βασιλεὺς δὲ
ἀμφοτέρους ἐκάλεσσεν ἐπὶ τὴν κρίσιν, —ταῦτα ἐν τῷ πρό
σθεν λόγῳ δεδήλωται· τὰ δὲ ἑξῆς νῦν διηγήσομαι.[198]

One of the more noticeable aspects of this passage is the limited
number of words that are used to recall events that comprise either an
action/description (segments 2, 4, 5, 7–9, and 11–13), an entire scene
(segments 1, 6, 10, 14–17, 20, and 21), or a sequence of scenes (segments
3, 18, and 19). Hägg describes the formation of typical recapitulations as
follows: "An originally detailed scene or sequence of scenes is reduced to
a verb or a *nomen actionis*, sometimes (esp. in the direct speech) supple-
mented with a few specifying adjuncts."[199]

The author, then, takes blocks of narrative material and compresses
them into a word (cf. 3.9.11) or phrase that carries the gist of an event,
scene, or scene-sequence. To be sure, the reader has already formed his or
her own gist of these chunks of narrative material. However, by forming
recapitulations in this way, the narrator supplies the gist that he wishes
the reader to bring to the primary narrative following the recapitulation.

198. Tr: (5.1.1) How Callirhoe, the most beautiful of women, married Chaereas,
the handsomest of men, by Aphrodite's management; how in a fit of lover's jealousy
Chaereas struck her, and to all appearances she died; how she had a costly funeral and
then, just as she came out of her coma in the funeral vault, tomb robbers carried her
away from Sicily by night, sailed to Ionia, and sold her to Dionysius; Dionysius's love
for her, her fidelity to Chaereas, the need to marry caused by her pregnancy; Theron's
confession, Chaereas's journey across the sea in search of his wife; how he was captured,
sold, and taken to Caria with his friend Polycharmus; (1.2) how Mithridates discovered
his identity as he was on the point of death and tried to restore the lovers to each other;
how Dionysius found this out through a letter and complained to Pharnaces, who reported it to the King, and the King summoned both of them to judgment—this has all
been set out in the story so far. Now I shall describe what happened next. [R]

199. Hägg, *Narrative Technique*, 267.

Thus, the narrator influences both how the reader understands the previously encountered narrative material and how the reader will process the subsequent narrative material.

The sequential arrangement of these gists also influences how the reader will process the narrative material. For the most part, the order in which the events are recounted in the recapitulation in 5.1.1 matches the order of their appearance in the primary narrative—even where the recapitulation could have deviated from the order in the primary narrative without departing from a strictly chronological presentation (specifically, the point where the story line separates into two lines of action).[200] The recapitulation traces the plot line of the primary narrative, presenting first Callirhoe's line and then Chaereas's when, in fact, the narrator overtly states that the events related in each line happened during the same period (3.2.17). That Chariton chooses to give precedence to the Callirhoe line of action in both the primary narrative and the recapitulation underscores the heroine as the novel's central character.

In spite of its overall chronological presentation, the recapitulation offers one slight temporal discontinuity. The physical attractiveness of the couple (segment 2) and the designs of Aphrodite in arranging the marriage (segment 3) are narrated before the wedding (segment 1) in the primary narrative.

Since deviations from the chronological pattern call to the reader's attention the narrative element/s disjointed by it, the couple's beauty and the power of Aphrodite are again underscored. Specifically, segment 2 functions to reinforce a gist that by this point in the narrative has been firmly established. Segment 3 similarly reinforces an original gist, but makes a significant alteration. In the primary narrative, the one who schemes for the couple's union is Eros (ὁ δὲ Ἔρως ζεῦγος ἴδιον ἠθέλησε συμπλέξαι . . . . φιλόνεικος δὲ ἐστιν ὁ Ἔρως καὶ χαίρει τοῖς παραδόξοις κατορθώμασιν· ἐζήτησε δὲ τοιόνδε τὸν καιρόν, 1.1.3);[201] Aphrodite's temple merely serves as the locale for their initial meeting.[202]

200. Ibid., 248.

201. Tr: But Eros desired to unite [συμπλέξαι] his own couple. . . . But Eros is contentious and likes successes *that run* contrary to expectations; thus, he sought a suitable occasion as follows (1.1.3).

202. Muchow ("Passionate Love," 106–19) explains the appropriateness of this location for the couple's first meeting. He notes several items are germane to Chariton's novel: (1) religious festivals were among the rare occasions when a young girl was permitted to leave the house; (2) meeting in broad daylight before witnesses assures

The recapitulation, however, credits Aphrodite with this work (πολιτε—υσαμένης Ἀφροδίτης τὸν γάμον, 5.1.1).[203]

In naming Aphrodite as the agent behind the couple's marriage, the narrator makes explicit that which the reader has been lead to suspect from the beginning, namely, that Aphrodite is the real power behind the entire plot. Eros and Fate are paralyzed when she decides to intervene. Edwards summarizes the purpose of Chariton's novel:

> It affirms and confirms the power and significance of Aphrodite over all aspects of the world order especially the machinations of fate and social upheaval (represented by pirates, wayward politicians, disruption of proper marriage, separation from family, friends, country, and spouse). In addition, it makes clear the power of Aphrodite before the political order: even the mightiest are susceptible to her power.[204]

The protagonists acknowledge Aphrodite's power over their lives. Callirhoe's beauty overpowers men of power, but she herself is powerless to control the effects of her beauty. She grants that Aphrodite is responsible for her beauty, yet sees it as a curse. Although Chaereas never asked Aphrodite to grant him Callirhoe for a wife, he does profess that it was she who in fact did so.[205]

Temporal rearrangements are not the only evidence for authorial guidance. Hägg writes:

> If it is natural that the chronology of the events in the primary narrative should be followed in the recapitulation, it is also evident that the differences between narrative and recapitulation

---

the reader that the heroine is a virgin since no one would suspect the young lady of impropriety or the young man of seduction (meetings at houses or night festivals typically connote sexual intrigue); (3) experiencing *le coup de foudre* at a religious festival points to the divine instigation and approval of the protagonists' love; and (4) festivals brought a temporary relaxation of social norms and thus "provided the ideal setting for the protagonists to be released from traditional marriage practices" (118).

203. Tr: The marriage by Aphrodite's administration. Cf. 2.2.8. This passage clearly shows Aphrodite as the one responsible for bringing about Callirhoe's marriage to Dionysius. Note esp. the presence of Palin, which infers that Aphrodite also was responsible for Callirhoe's first marriage.

204. Edwards, "Acts and Chariton," 97–98.

205. See Chaereas's analeptic cry in 3.6.3. In that same scene, a temple attendant analeptically affirms that it was Aphrodite who made Callirhoe mistress over them all. This is another way of saying that she brought about the marriage of Callirhoe and Dionysius. Callirhoe also credits Aphrodite with giving her Chaereas (3.2.12).

must lie in the *selection* of events to be recapitulated and in the *amount of detail* that is admitted.[206]

The recapitulation in 5.1.1–4 is also significant when viewed from this perspective. The events are restricted to those that "actually forward the action and are necessary for understanding the plot."[207] In this respect, the review section moves the reader rapidly through the major turns in the plot. This then serves as the background information for processing the trial narrative that follows.

In addition to those items that have already been mentioned in the context of sequence, the positive (or at worst neutral) portrait of all the actants except Chaereas should be mentioned. By direct authorial commentary, the primary narrative indicates that Mithridates had his own designs on Callirhoe (4.4.1). But in the narrator's summary review, the governor of Caria appears as a benefactor concerned simply to restore the protagonists to each other (segment 18).

Dionysius does not always appear in an admirable light in the primary narrative either. Although his initial characterization is highly laudatory, he tends thereafter to display a self-centered perspective. When Callirhoe tells her story he weeps—ostensibly for Callirhoe, but in truth for himself—since he was not getting her for himself (2.5.12). His prayer to Aphrodite (3.8.3–6) is clearly self-centered. In 4.1.2, he is concerned to see Callirhoe wasting away in mourning for Chaereas, "because of course he was afraid her beauty might suffer." The narrator also reports that he discouraged Callirhoe's choice for the site of Chaereas's tomb because "he wanted to keep that spot for himself" (4.1.5). The recapitulation, however, mentions only his love for Callirhoe (segment 11).

The narrator's plot review in 5.1.1–4 tends to minimize the negative characteristics of the contenders for Callirhoe's heart. Even Chaereas, the only character to have a negative aspect related here, is at least partially redeemed by the allusions to his arduous search for Callirhoe and his sale into slavery.

The narrative material introduced by the recapitulatory summary in 5.1.1–4 emphasizes insecurity. Crossing the Euphrates is, for the protagonists, entering a foreign world. Callirhoe's analeptic monologue addressed to Fortune stresses her descent to the depths of barbarian

---

206. Hägg, *Narrative Technique*, 248; emphasis original.
207. Ibid.

lands (5.1.6). The narrator indicates that Callirhoe's renown has made Dionysius insecure (5.2.7). And the Persian women are threatened by Callirhoe's beauty.[208]

The trial narrative also showcases power elements. The Persians try to secure Callirhoe's favor because they expect that she will soon acquire great power (5.1.8). A rare narrative pause describes the courtroom and its places for leaders of various ranks (5.4.5–6). Callirhoe refers to herself as "Hermocrates's daughter" (5.5.4), a description echoed by the Great King Artaxerxes who also mentions her father's naval victory over Athens (5.8.5). Dionysius admits he cannot rival Mithridates in power and resources (5.6.4). And Chaereas hopelessly capitulates in the face of Dionysius's greater resources.

In retrospect and prospect: Mithridates's trial starts out investigating his attempt to possess Callirhoe and ends up considering who deserves to possess her. Everybody in Babylon is debating these matters; the lawcourt is made a synecdoche for the entire city: ὅλη ἡ Βαβυλὼν δικαστήριον ἦν (5.4.4).[209] And the narrator exploits the opportunity to show the populace choosing sides (5.4.1–4). Both plaintiff and defendant present their cases, which include summary accounts of what has transpired earlier in the narrative. Mithridates is acquitted since he produces Chaereas and proves that he did not forge the letter to Callirhoe.[210]

The king then assumes the responsibility of determining which of Callirhoe's husbands has the more legitimate claim to her. Both men fear a negative outcome. Dionysius blames Aphrodite and considers having the child intercede with his mother on behalf of his father (καὶ νῦν ἄπελθε καὶ ἱκέτευσον ὑπὲρ τοῦ πατρός, 5.10.4).[211] Chaereas, reckoning himself to be out-powered by Dionysius, is, by Polycharmus, saved from suicide (again!)—this time, at the last minute and by forcible restraint.

208. The brief analeptic statement that introduces what the narrator describes as a beauty contest is found in 5.3.1: ὃς καὶ πάλαι μὲν πάντες ἐθαύμαζον ἐπὶ τῷ κάλλει ("indeed, since long ago, everybody was wondering at *her* beauty").

209. Tr: All Babylon was a courtroom.

210. Irony is present here, since the reader knows what Chaereas does not, namely, that Mithridates really did have designs on Callirhoe, even though he did not forge the letter.

211. Tr: Now go and beg on your father's behalf. Dionysius also is a victim of irony, since the reader knows that this request, taken at face value, would have the child intercede with his mother on behalf of Chaereas.

Finally, three brief character-generated prolepses in this book foreshadow a positive outcome for the novel's protagonists. Plangon interprets proleptically Callirhoe's analeptic dream of her and Chaereas on their wedding day (5.5.5–6). Mithridates predicts that Dionysius will lose Callirhoe (5.7.7). And Statira, the Great King's wife, predicts Callirhoe will be awarded the husband she wishes (5.9.3).

Bedlam in Babylon: 6.1.1—6.9.8

Book 6 opens with the entire populace of Babylon "up in the air" (μετέ ρος, 6.1.1)[212] over the king's imminent decision by which they expected either Chaereas or Dionysius to be adjudged the legitimate husband of Callirhoe. "Tomorrow is Callirhoe's marriage," they exclaim. But like many such character-generated prolepses in the novel, this prediction proves to be inaccurate (6.2.3).

The narrator recounts the supporting and opposing arguments for each of the candidates. These summaries of what the people were saying reiterate plot elements given in many previous analepses. The arguments for Chaereas include their marriage, mutual love, father's blessing, and burial, but say nothing about Chaereas's kick, which caused the near death. Dionysius's side, however, argues that Chaereas killed Callirhoe (a claim that both readers and characters know is not true). His supporters argue that he paid money for Callirhoe in order to save her from murder at the hands of pirates (readers, at least, know this is not true) and married her. What they see as the strongest point in Dionysius's favor, namely, that he shares a child with her, is clearly seen as ironic by the reader. This point really supports Chaereas's claim (though none of these characters knows this); Chaereas is not the murderer of Callirhoe, but he is the father of her child.

In the reader's assessment of these arguments, Chaereas emerges the winner. And as it happens, he is the people's choice as well; Dionysius is supported only by Persians from the highest eschelons of their society (6.2.1). Surely the reader cannot miss the irony here. When the choice was between Mithridates and Dionysius, the aristocrats rejected Dionysius, who was the choice of the common people (δημaτικὸν εὔνουν, 5.4.1).

---

212. The translation "up in the air" is Reardon's rendering (*Collected Ancient Greek Novels*, 89). Cf. Molinié's "*en attente*" (*Roman de Chairéas et Callirhoé*, 151), which gives the sense of expectancy, and Plepelits's "*in gespannter Erwartung*" (*Kallirhoe*, 116), which stresses the notion of tenseness or suspense.

In both cases, the people of wealth, rank, and power sided with the more affluent, higher stationed, more powerful candidate.

Of even greater import than this bedlam in the marketplace is the bedlam reigning in the king's heart. Here the narrator basks in paradox. Callirhoe's journey has brought her in contact with men of successively higher rank. The Persian king Artaxerxes represents the apex of human power. Nevertheless, this powerful king is himself overpowered. The perpetrator of the coup is Eros.

Several brief references in book 6 emphasize the king's power. The king himself alludes to belief in the divinity of royalty when he refers to the Sun as his ancestor (6.1.10). The king's splendor is displayed during a hunt (6.4.1–9). His authority is emphasized in 6.7.6 when Artaxates reminds Callirhoe of how quickly Queen Statira jumped to obey the king's command (6.7.5). This reinforces the narrator's comment that no one may argue when the king issues a command (6.7.3). Artaxates, having discovered (almost to his harm) the king's intention to resist Eros, flatteringly tells him he can win the battle against the god (δύνασαι γὰρ, ὦ δέσποτα, σὺ μόνος κρατεῖν καὶ θεοῦ, 6.3.8).[213]

As powerful as he is, even the Great King is no match for Eros. Artaxerxes's passion for Callirhoe is so strong that he decides to postpone the trial date thirty days so he will be able to see her longer. He claims the gods appeared to him and demanded sacrifice (6.2.2), but since the content of this analepsis is not found anywhere in the primary narrative and since the king's desire to postpone the trial has been narrated (6.1.12), the reader will suspect the king of lying. Thus, the king has sacrificed principle for love.

The king's helplessness before Eros appears vividly in his sacrifices to this god and in his prayers to Aphrodite soliciting her assistance (καὶ πολλὰ παρεκάλεσσεν Ἀφροδίτην, ἵνα αὐτῷ βοηθῇ πρὸς τὸν υἱόν, 6.2.4).[214] But Eros is the king's persistent adversary. The king called a royal hunt to help him forget his passion for Callirhoe; instead his fervor increased. The reason is supplied analeptically by the narrator: συνεξῆλθε γὰρ ἐπὶ τὴν θήραν ὁ Ἔρως αὐτῷ (6.4.4).[215]

213. Tr: For you are able, O master—and you alone—to conquer even a god.

214. Tr: And he earnestly entreated Aphrodite in order that she might help him against her son.

215. Tr: For Eros went out on the hunt with him.

Later, in what may be the only occasion in the novel where a god speaks directly, Eros calls to the king's mind the thought of what it would be like to see Callirhoe with exposed legs, bared arms, flushed face, and heaving breasts (6.4.5).

Love's relentless pursuit reappears at 6.7.1:

Πάλιν δὲ νυκτὸς γενομένης ἀνεκάετο καὶ ὁ Ἔρως αὐτὸν
ἀνεμίμνησκεν οἵους μὲν ὀφθαλμοὺς ἔχει Καλλιρόη, πῶς δὲ
καλὸν τὸ πρόσωπον. τὰς τρίχας ἐπήνει, τὸ βάδισμα, τὴν
φωνήν· οἵα μὲν εἰσῆλθεν εἰς τὸ δικαστήριον, οἵα δὲ ἔστη,
πῶς ἐλάλησε, πῶς ἐσίγησε, πῶς ἠδέσθη, πῶς ἔκλαυσε.[216]

This prompts the king to put more pressure on Artaxates to persuade Callirhoe to respond to his desires. Only the outbreak of rebellion in Egypt, a rare *deus ex machina*, temper's the king's passion and spares Callirhoe from a decision carrying fatal consequences.

As for Chaereas, the emphasis is on his repeated attempts to escape the domination of superior powers by suicide. When the king postpones the trial, Polycharmus again has to step in to prevent him from starving himself (Χαιρέας δὲ οὐχ ἥπτετο τροφῆς, οὐδὲ ὅλως ἤθελε ζῆν, 6.2.8).[217] Chaereas's despair is so great that he regards with disdain his friend's efforts to prevent him from taking his own life (εἰ δὲ φίλος ἦς, οὐκ ἂν ἐφθόνεις μοι τῆς ἐλευθερίας ὑπὸ δαίμονος κακοῦ τυραν—νουμένῳ· πόσους μου καιροὺς εὐτυχίας ἀπολώλεκας, 6.2.9).[218]

Chaereas then follows with a speech (itself in chronological order) in which he protests the times Polycharmus prevented his suicide, namely, after his acquittal of Callirhoe's death (1.6.1–2), after he learned of Callirhoe's marriage to Dionysius (4.3.8), and after the trial of Mithridates and Dionysius (5.10.6–10). Even after this very speech, Polycharmus must do everything but tie him up in order to prevent him from taking his own life with his sword (6.2.11). Thus, Chaereas also is portrayed as overpowered.

---

216. Tr: And again when evening had come he became inflamed with passion and Eros reminded him of what *beautiful* eyes Callirhoe had, how beautiful her face was. He praised her hair, her walk, her voice; how she entered the courtroom, how she stood, how she spoke, how she held her peace, how she blushed, how she wept.

217. Tr: Chaereas was not touching food; he did not even desire to live at all.

218. Tr: If you were my friend, you would not begrudge one being tormented by an evil spirit, namely, me, *the opportunity for* freedom.

Even the heroine despairs at the power wielded against her. The general mood at the thirty-day religious festival proclaimed by the king is joyous. The narrator notes only three exceptions: πάντων δὲ ἐν θυμηδίας ὄντων μόνοι τρεῖς ἐλυποοῦντο, Καλλιρόη, Διονύσιος, καὶ πρὸ τούτων Χαιρέας, 6.2.5.[219] That Callirhoe is mentioned first in this list and treated first in the subsequent discussion illustrates the heroine's central place in the novel.

Book 6 presents two scenes (6.5.1–10; 6.7.5–13) where Callirhoe is tempted to surrender to the king's desires. In each of these scenes, the enticements are presented through an intermediary, Artaxates, who there functions as the king's love ambassador. Both display an ideology of power.

A narratorial prolepsis (6.4.10) prefaces the first "temptation" scene and prepares the reader for Artaxates's failure to convince Callirhoe. More importantly, however, the narrator supplies the reason for Artaxates's joyful acceptance of the task: he thought it would earn him political clout (καὶ Ἀρταξάτης δὲ ἔχαιρε νομίζων πρὸς ὑπηρεσίαν ὑπεσχῆσθαι, βραβεύσειν δὲ λοιπὸν ἅρμα βασιλικόν, 6.4.10).[220]

A preoccupation with power is evident in Artaxates's approach to Callirhoe. He seems to pride himself on his ability to tell people what they want to hear, and he constantly looks for ways to wield his diplomatic skills for personal profit (6.3.7–8; 6.4.7–8; 6.4.10; 6.5.7; 6.7.11). Consumed with the desire for power, he assumes that Callirhoe is motivated by the same concern. He concedes that she has been blessed with extraordinary beauty, but argues that she has not received any great benefit from it:

> Τὸ διὰ γῆς πάσης ἔνδοξον καὶ περιβόητον ὄνομα μέχρι σήμερον οὐκ εὗρεν οὔτ' ἄνδρα κατ' ἀξίαν οὔτ' ἐραστήν, ἀλλ' ἐνέ πεσεν εἰς δύο, νησιώτην πέντα, καὶ ἕτερον, δοῦλον βασιλέ— ως· τί σοι γέγονεν ἐκ τούτων μέγα καὶ λαμπρόν; ποῖον χώ— ραν ἔχεις εὔφορον; ποῖον κόσμον πολυτελῆ; τίνων πόλεων ἄρχεις; πόσοι δοῦλοί σε προσκυνοῦσι; γυναῖκες Βαβυλώ— νιαι θεραπαινίδας ἔχουσι πλουσιωτέρας σου. (6.5.3–4)[221]

219. Tr: Now everyone was in a rejoicing mood; only three were grieving: Callirhoe, Dionysius, and—above all—Chaereas.

220. Tr: Artaxates was in high spirits too; he thought that he had undertaken a valuable service and would be holdng the reins at court from now on. [R]

221. Tr: Your name is known and famous over the world; but up till now it has not got you a husband or lover worthy of you—it has lit on two men, one a poor islander,

Artaxates attempts to entice Callirhoe with the king's power (. . . τὸν μέγαν βασιλέα, τὸν δυνάμενόν σοι Μίλητον αὐτὴν καὶ ὅλην Ἰωνίαν καὶ Σικελίαν καὶ ἄλλα ἔθνη μείζονα χαρίσασθαι, 6.5.7).[222] But her complete disregard for his power position (as well as the king's) leaves him standing agape (ἀχανής, 6.5.10).

Outdone in his first attempt, Artaxates tries to turn away the king's passion for Callirhoe. The king, however, is helpless before Eros and commands Artaxates to persuade Callirhoe on his behalf. On this occasion the king's most trusted servant impresses on Callirhoe the full extent of the king's power in this situation. He stresses both the rewards for furnishing what the king wants (δῶρα λήψῃ τὰ κάλλιστα καὶ ἄνδρα ὃν θέλεις, 6.7.7)[223] and the consequences of withholding it (πείσῃ ἄκουσα ἃ πάσχουσιν οἱ βασιλέως ἐχθροί, μόνοις γὰρ τού– τοις οὐδὲ ἀποθανεῖν θέλουσιν ἔξεστι, 6.7.7).[224]

Callirhoe is unmoved by the threat even of death. She responds with a rapid recall of her past sufferings, concluding with the worst: that she is near Chaereas and cannot see him (6.7.9). When Artaxates refers to Chaereas as a "slave of Mithridates," Callirhoe lists (analeptically for the reader) Chaereas's power qualifications (6.7.10).

The reader is certain the heroine will not be persuaded by the arguments of Artaxates—that is, until his final warning: "Stop looking at yourself alone; think about Chaereas who is running the risk of dying a lamentable death, for the king will not tolerate being surpassed in love" (6.7.13). A narratorial analepsis with an immediate reach concludes the scene and affirms the possibility that Callirhoe may succumb: "But Callirhoe took his final words to heart." Fortunately, the report of rebellion in Egypt delivers the heroine in the hour of her most difficult test.

The king and his faithful servant Artaxates operate from a power position. These men desire *willing* obedience to the king's desires, but,

---

the other a slave of the King. What great or glorious benefit has come to you from them? What fertile land do you own? What costly jewels? What cities do you rule over? How many slaves bow down before you? Women in Babylon have servants who are wealthier than you. [R]

222. Tr: . . . the Great King, who is able to give you as presents Miletus itself and all Ionia and other nations greater than these.

223. Tr: You will receive the most beautiful gifts—and the husband whom you desire.

224. Tr: Surely you have heard about the things which enemies of the king suffer; for these alone it is not permitted to die, even if they desire it.

as the book progresses, they give the impression that they may settle for obedience. Both Chaereas and Callirhoe are threatened by the desires of the king.

Saved by a War! 7.1.1–7.6.12

The king's attention is now occupied by the war. Dionysius, reasoning that courageous performance on the battlefield will influence the king to decide the case of Callirhoe's husband in his favor (6.9.3), assumes a position in the front ranks (6.9.2). To ensure the recovery of his wife, however, the principled Dionysius (2.5.3; 2.11.6; 3.2.4) resorts to a deception.[225] The perfect tenses underscore the analeptic nature of the event itself as well as the telling of it:

Ἐξιὼν ἐπὶ τὴν μάχην κατέλιπε τὸν ἀπαγγελοῦντα πρὸς Χαιρέαν ὅτι βασιλεὺς ὁ Περσῶν χρείαν ἔχων συμμάχων πέπομφε Διονύσιον ἀθροῖσαι στρατιὰν ἐπὶ τὸν Αἰγύπτιον καὶ, ἵνα πιστῶς αὐτῷ καὶ προθύμως ἐξυπηρετῆται, Καλλιρόην ἀπέδωκε. (7.1.4)[226]

The reader knows that Artaxerxes did enlist the support of Dionysius for his campaign to crush Egypt's rebellion. Nevertheless, the narrative that precedes this analepsis makes clear that Dionysius was not under special invitation, nor was the decision to join in the war effort his own idea. To be sure, he went with his own aspirations. But he also went under compulsion (Ἴων γὰρ ἦν καὶ οὐδενὶ τῶν ὑπηκόων μένειν ἐξῆν, 6.9.1).[227]

A more flagrant prevarication, however, is Dionysius's report that the king has already named him as Callirhoe's husband.[228] In case the reader misses this lie (perhaps assuming the king had decided in Dionysius's favor but the narrator neglected to mention it until now), the

225. Actually, this is not his first use of deception. In 4.10 he led Callirhoe to believe that Chaereas was dead by keeping from her the knowledge that some of the men on the Syracusan trireme had been captured alive. In light of this, the reader is able to see irony in his accusing Mithridates of pretending that Chaereas was alive (5.6.7).

226. Tr: When he went out to the battle, he left someone who announced to Chaereas that the King of Persia had had need of allies and had commissioned Dionysius to gather soldiers against Egypt. And, so that he would faithfully and wholeheartedly assist him to the utmost, he had given *him* Callirhoe.

227. Tr: For he was an Ionian and none of the subjects were permitted to remain.

228. This does not happen until Dionysius proves himself in battle (7.5.15).

narrator exposes the deception in commenting on Chaereas's reaction to the message: ταῦτα ἀκούσας Χαιρέας ἐπίστευσεν εὐθύς· εὐεξαπά– τητον γὰρ ἄνθρωπος δυστυχῶν, 7.1.4).[229] Thus, the reader's sympathy for Dionysius wanes.

Although the reader is not fooled by Dionysius's deception, Chaereas is. Believing that the king has already decided against him, he again is minded to commit suicide—this time in a way that will shame the king for his unfair judgment (7.1.6). This intention, though not strictly an analepsis, recalls for the reader the numerous times Chaereas has been driven to the point of self-destruction. On this occasion, however, Chariton gives the scenario a new twist: Polycharmus supports his decision and agrees to die with him!

Although he is willing to die with his friend, Polycharmus disagrees with the method Chaereas has in mind. Shedding their own blood at the palace gates would shame the king, but it would hardly effect his repentance. Instead, he urges that the two should die while attempting to inflict noticeable damage on the king. In arguing for this option, Polycharmus is suggesting that they die actively rebelling against the king's abuse of power rather than passively exposing it.

Chaereas is not persuaded. He compares the king's power (τὸν κύ ριον τηλικούτων καὶ τοσούτων ἐθνῶν καὶ δύναμιν ἔχοντα, 7.1.9)[230] with their lack of power (ἡμεῖς οἱ δύο μόνοι μόνοι καὶ πένητες καὶ ξένοι, 7.1.9).[231] But Polycharmus offers a reasonable plan. He suggests joining the Egyptian forces and using their resources against the Great King. Chaereas is convinced. Having behaved unheroically since the beginning of the novel, he experiences an immediate transformation.[232] Polycharmus has fulfilled his most valuable narrative function; hereafter it is Chaereas who makes the decisions.[233]

---

229. Tr: When Chaereas heard these things, he believed *them* immediately; for an unfortunate man is easily mislead.

230. Tr: The lord of so great and so numerous nations, who has power.

231. Tr: We two are alone and poor and foreigners.

232. The immediacy of Chaereas's transformation is displayed by the phrase introducing Chaereas's response: οὔπω πᾶν εἴρητο ἔπος καὶ Χαιρέας ἀνεβόησε Σπεύ– δωμεν, ἀπίωμεν, ("All the counsel was not yet spoken but Chaereas cried out: 'Let's hurry! Let's go!'" 7.1.11).

233. However, he does accept the wise counsel of Callirhoe in the final book (8.2.5).

In commending their services to the Egyptian king, Chaereas emphasizes his connections with power; he recalls his noble birth and his association with Hermocrates, the famous Syracusan war hero (7.2.3). He concludes his speech with a quotation from Homer that marks his transition to the classical hero:

> No, let me not die without effort, without glory, but after some great exploit that even our descendents will know about![234]

This attitude is described and demonstrated throughout the hero's brief military career. The narrator notes his quest for respect (7.2.6) and the attainment of it (7.5.11); his prowess in battle (7.4.6); and stability under pressure (7.4.9).

Face to face with difficult obstacles, the new Chaereas speaks with confidence and translates that speech into action. He predicts success against Tyre four times (7.3.4; 7.3.5; 7.3.10; 7.3.11). The fact that these prolepses find immediate fulfillment creates a more powerful image of Chaereas in the reader's mind.

The fall of Tyre to the Egyptians prompted Artaxerxes to free his fighting forces from anything that would impede rapid movement. Callirhoe, who has a smaller role in this book than in any other section of the novel, thus ended up on the island of Aradus with queen Statira and the rest of the king's "possessions." Callirhoe herself becomes part of the booty. At a (ubiquitous) temple of Aphrodite she again laments her miserable circumstances (7.5.2–5). Here, geographical separation is emphasized.

Because of Chaereas's success against Tyre, he is offered the command of Egypt's navy. In making the offer, the king recalls Hermocrates's victory over the Athenians (7.5.8), the most recurrent analepsis in the novel. Chaereas accepts the task in true heroic fashion.

The resulting naval battle occurs on the same day as the land battle. The narrator's decision to relate the land battle first interrupts the Chaereas section. The effect of this is to postpone the results of Chaereas's naval battle. Will he have the same success as his father-in-law?

The section framed by the preparations for the naval battle (7.5.6–11) and the battle itself (7.6.1–2) throws a spotlight briefly on

---

234. *Iliad*, 22. 304–5. Chaereas's statement echoes the last words uttered by Hector before his fatal combat with Achilles. Translation and note are from Reardon, *Collected Ancient Greek Novels*, 102.

Dionysius. Because of his decisive routing of the Egyptian land forces, Dionysius wins the title of "king's benefactor" and the hand of Callirhoe in marriage.

When the narrative thread of the naval battle is resumed, the narrator spends little time on its description. The account begins with its outcome: Chaereas is victorious!

A few details indicating the ease of conquest follow. After the battle, Chaereas and his crew sail to Aradus and, encountering no resistence, capture the king's possessions.

Among the captives is Chaereas's beloved Callirhoe, although he himself is not aware of it. Thinking he was addressing the queen behind a closed door, an Egyptian guard tried to calm her fears by telling her that his master (whose name he does not mention) would treat her kindly and even marry her. On hearing another marriage proposal, the heroine requests death.

At this point, the portrayal of Chaereas has reached its zenith while that of Callirhoe has sunken to its nadir. He is full of power; she is powerless.[235] The stage is set for the hero to rescue the damsel-in-distress.

All's Well That Ends Well! 8.1.1–8.8.16

The final section of a novel naturally has a greater potential for recapitulation than foreshadowing because more narrative material lies behind than ahead. Chariton's book 8ight realizes this potential. Indeed, it is framed by two recapitulatory complexes, the first, narratorial, at the beginning (8.1.1), and the second, character-generated, at the end (8.7.6–8.8.11).

The first of these analeptic complexes is noteworthy because of its reach: all of the events selected for recall are drawn from book 7. This fact cannot escape the reader's notice, since the narrator directly points it out:

> Ὡς μὲν οὖν Χαιρέας ὑποπτεύσας Καλλιρόην Διονυσίῳ
> παραδεδόσθαι, θέλων ἀμύνασθαι βασιλέα πρὸς τὸν Αἰγύ–
> πτιον ἀπέστη καὶ ναύαρχος ἀποδειχθεὶς ἐκράτησε τῆς
> θαλάσσης, νικήσας δὲ κατέσχεν Ἄραδον, ἔνθα βασιλεὺς καὶ

---

235. In the absence of a ruler with higher authority than the Great King, even her beauty cannot avail for her.

τὴν γυναῖκα τὴν ἑαυτοῦ καὶ πᾶσαν τὴν θεραπείαν ἀπέθετο
καὶ Καλλιρόην, ἐν τῷ πρόσθεν λόγῳ δεδήλωται. (8.1.1)²³⁶

Book 8 thus opens by recapping the events that display Chaereas in the role of a classical hero. He is actively taking charge of his own destiny.

Chariton follows this analepsis with a god-generated anticipation (Hägg's "divine" type):

Ἔμελλε δὲ ἔργον ἡ Τύχη πράττειν οὐ μόνον παράδοξον,
ἀλλὰ καὶ σκυθρωπόν, ἵνα ἔχων Καλλιρόην Χαιρέας ἀγνοή
ση καὶ τὰς ἀλλοτρίας γυναῖκας ἀναλαβὼν ταῖς τριήρεσιν
ἀπαγάγῃ, μόνην δὲ τὴν ἰδίαν ἐκεῖ καταλίπῃ οὐχ ὡς' Ἀριά
δνην καθεύδουσαν, οὐδὲ Διονύσῳ νυμφίῳ, λάφυρον δὲ τοῖς
ἑαυτοῦ πολεμίοις. (8.1.2)²³⁷

Following, as it does, the positive, "hero to the rescue" sense of 8.1.1, this information gives the reader an emotional letdown. Nevertheless, by now the reader has learned that this kind of narrative anticipation is not certain of fulfillment. It represents one possible (in this case, disappointing) outcome. But since the narrator has not validated it, a spark of hope remains.

The reader hopes for a refutory word from the narrator. What immediately follows, however, is a narrative segment that begins as an analepsis and concludes as a prolepsis:²³⁸

Ἀλλὰ ἔδοξέ τι δεινὸν Ἀφροδίτη· ἤδη γὰρ αὐτῷ διηλλά—
ττετο, πρότερον ὀργισθεῖσα χαλεπῶς διὰ τὴν ἄκαιρον
ζηλοτυπίαν, ὅτι δῶρον παρ' αὐτῆς λαβὼν τὸ κάλλιστον,

236. Tr: How Chaereas, suspecting that Callirhoe had been handed over to Dionysius, determined to avenge himself on the King and so went over to the Egyptian side; how he was appointed admiral and gained control of the sea; how after his victory he seized Aradus, where the King had placed his own wife for security, and along with her all his train and Callirhoe too—all of that has been described in the previous book. [R]

237. Tr: Fortune was about to do a work not only contrary to all expectation but also sad: Chaereas, would have Callirhoe and not be aware of it; and taking the other men's wives on board the trireme, he would take them home and leave there only his *wife*—not as sleeping Ariadne, and not for Dionysius as *her* bridegroom, but as spoils of war for his enemies.

238. This analepsis gives only general statements about the protagonists' sufferings: the arena (wandering from west to east); the cause (Chaereas's jealousy); and the cure (Chaereas's honorable ammends to Love). The lack of details here makes these elements the gist that the reader carries to the remainder of the narrative. Further, since Aphrodite brought the pair together in the first place, this goddess-generated prolepsis has greater likelihood of fulfillment, even without a direct confirmation by the narrator.

οἷον οὐδὲ Ἀλέξανδρος ὁ Πάρις, ὕβρισεν εἰς τὴν χάριν.
ἐπεὶ δὲ καλῶς ἀπελογήσατο τῷ Ἔρωτι Χαιρέας ἀπὸ δύ—
σεως εἰς ἀνατολὰς διὰ μυρίων παθῶν πλανηθείς, ἠλέησεν
αὐτὸν Ἀφροδίτη καὶ ὅπερ ἐξ ἀρχῆς δύο τῶν καλλίστων
ἥρμοσε ζεῦγος, γυμνάσασα διὰ γῆς καὶ θαλάσσης, πάλιν
ἠθέλησεν ἀποδοῦναι. (8.1.3)[239]

But this also is a god-generated prolepsis and therefore represents
one possible (in this case, encouraging) outcome. Although less necessary since Aphrodite is the central divine figure of the novel, the reader
now seeks—and immediately finds—a confirmatory word from the
narrator:

Νομίζω δὲ καὶ τὸ τελευταῖον τοῦτο σύγγραμμα τοῖς ἀναγ—
ινωσκουσιν ἥδιστον γενήσεσθαι· καθάρσιον γάρ ἐστι τῶν
ἐν τοῖς πρώτοις σκυθρωπῶν. οὐκέτι λῃστεια καὶ δουλεία
καὶ δίκη καὶ μάχη καὶ ἀποκαρτέρησις καὶ πόλεμος καὶ ἅλ—
ωσις, ἀλλὰ ἔρωτες δίκαιοι ἐν τούτῳ καὶ νόμιμοι γάμοι.
πῶς οὖν ἡ θεὸς ἐφώτισε τὴν ἀλήθειαν καὶ τοὺς ἀγνοουμέ
νους ἔδειξεν ἀλλήλοις λέξω. (8.1.4–5)[240]

The narrator promises that all terrible events are past and that the
remainder of his story deals only with proper loves (ἔρωτες δίκαιοι)
and prescriptive marriages (νόμιμοι γάμοι).[241] The psychological highs

239. Tr: But Aphrodite considered *this* terrible, for she was already being reconciled
to him. Originally she was sorely angered because of his inappropriate jealousy. He had
received from her the most beautiful gift, whom not even Alexander Paris *received*,
and he treated the gift outrageously. But since Chaereas honorably made ammends to
Eros, having been caused to wander from west to east through innumerable sufferings,
Aphrodite had mercy on him; thus, after she harassed on land and sea the couple she
had joined at the beginning—two of the most beautiful people—she decided to give
them back *to each other* again.

240. Tr: And I think this last book will be very pleasing to the readers, for it is a
catharsis from the sad events of the first part. No longer piracy and slavery and court
trial and strife and starvation and war and capture, but in this *book* proper loves and
legitimate marriages. [5]Thus I will tell you how the goddess illuminated the truth and
revealed the unrecognized ones to each other.

241. The adjectives δίκαιος and νόμιμος are quite similar in meaning. Both involve
conformity to social custom, rule, or law (see Liddell and Scott, *Greek-English Lexicon*,
429, 1179; Schrenk, "δίκαιος, et. al.," 2:182–84; and Seebass and Brown, "Righteousness,
Justification," 3:353, 358, 930). Nevertheless, the following distinctions have been proposed: "*amours permises et mariage légitime*" [permissible loves and lawful marriage]
(Molinié, *Roman de Chairéas et Callirhoé*, 182); "*wahre Liebe und rechtmässige Ehe*"
[proper loves and lawful marriages] (Plepelits, *Kallirhoe*, 141). In light of the arranged
marriages of Polycharmus to Chaereas's sister (who appears only here, 8.8.12) and

and lows experienced throughout the novel are compressed in the last book into a briefer section of narrative material, thus enhancing the effect. After 8.1.4, the emotional roller-coaster ride is over. But the recaptulatory complex at the end of the novel allows the reader to retrace the protagonists' journey.

An important character-generated prolepsis (8.1.8) sets up the fulfillment of the narrator's proleptic promise to tell how *the goddess* arranged the protagonists' reciprocal recognition (8.1.5). Believing that he is talking to a woman he does not know, Chaereas assuringly says, Ἕξεις δὲ ἄνδρα, ὃν θέλεις (8.1.8).[242] Callirhoe, the narrator claims, recognized her lover's voice; the reader, however (and perhaps the heroine herself), also recognizes the familiarity of Chaereas's words. They are the exact words of comfort that Statira spoke to Callirhoe when she was awaiting the Great King's decision regarding her two husbands (5.9.3).[243] Thus, the narrator swiftly has lived up to his promise to reveal the recognition scene and in advance has credited Aphrodite with arranging the encounter.

Each of the lovers desires to learn of the other's experiences, and the occasion of their sharing (8.1.14–17) offers another analeptic review of the novel's key events. Several items are significant for the present context. Firstly, that Callirhoe's story is recounted first reflects her central role. Secondly, Callirhoe's story is restricted to outlining her sufferings and demonstrating her chastity. Chastity is her only victory, and even this is somewhat tainted by her relationship with Dionysius. Thirdly, although the narrator reports that Chaereas "told *everything* accurately" (καὶ πάντα ἀκριβῶς διηγήσατο . . .), the reader hears nothing negative. The narrator fills the gap left by the vague πάντα ("everything") with a phrase that points to Chaereas's heroic achievements (ἐναβρυνό– μενος τοῖς κατορθώμασιν)[244] and Chaereas himself mentions only his

---

Callirhoe's son to Dionysius's daughter (8.4.6), the narrative may be arguing for a return to the traditional marriage customs of the classical period (note that in the former case Chaereas solicits the *people's* approval and that in neither case are the spouses-to-be consulted in the matter).

242. Tr: You will have the husband whom you desire.

243. Cf. Also the despairing words that Chaereas addresses to Callirhoe as he prepares to hang himself: ἔχε ὃν θέλεις, 5.10.8). Although ἄνδρα is not expressed here, it is clearly implied by the context.

244. Tr: Taking pride in his successes.

heroic activity (πεπλήρωκα γῆν καὶ θάλασσαν τροπαίων, 8.1.17).[245]
Thus, this analeptic section highlights Callirhoe's chastity and Chaereas's heroic demeanor.

Chaereas's letter to king Artaxerxes also displays a power approach:

> Σὺ μὲν ἔμελλες τὴν δίκην κρίνειν, ἐγὼ δὲ ἤδη νενίκηκα παρὰ τῷ δικαιοτάτῳ δικαστῇ· πόλεμος γὰρ ἄριστος κριτὴς τοῦ κρείττονός τε καὶ χείρονος. οὗτός μοι Καλλιρόην ἀποδέ—δωκεν, καὶ οὐ μόνον τὴν γυναῖκα τὴν ἐμήν, ἀλλὰ καὶ τὴν σήν. οὐκ ἐμιμησάμην δὲ σου τὴν βραδυτῆτα, ἀλλὰ ταχέως σοι μηδὲ ἀπαιτοῦντι Στάτειραν ἀποδίδωμι καθαρὰν καὶ ἐν αἰχμαλωσίᾳ μείνασαν βασιλίδα ... (8.4.2–3)[246]

The μὲν . . . δὲ construction and the grammatically unnecessary personal pronouns σὺ ("you") and ἐγὼ ("I") highlight the Great King's disgrace and betray the hero's smoldering indignation. Chaereas leaves the impression that the king is helpless to retrieve his wife or possessions. It is only because of Callirhoe that he is returning them—and he expects something in return!

The letter clearly adopts a one-sided perspective. Chaereas does not mention, for example, that the Persians have won the war, nor that siding with the Egyptians was not his idea in the first place. Nevertheless, for Chaereas, the war had one goal, namely, take vengence on Artaxerxes in a way that he would remember. By capturing the city of Tyre, defeating the Persian navy, and stealing Statira (along with some of the king's other possessions), Chaereas accomplished what he had set out to do. Regaining Callirhoe was his unexpected bonus.

Book 8 concludes with an enormous recapitulation (See the excerpt at the end of this chapter) that outlines every significant plot turn in the novel. As a preliminary observation, one should note that Callirhoe, whose presence has dominated the novel, is conspicuously absent when *her* story is broadcast. She makes a cameo appearance at the theater long enough to greet the crowd and then is taken home

---

245. Tr: I have filled land and sea with trophies.

246. Tr: You were going to decide the case, but I have already been declared the winner by the fairest of judges: war is the best arbiter between stronger and weaker. War has given me back Callirhoe; and it has given me not only my wife but yours as well. But I am not as slow to act as you; I am restoring Statira to you rapidly, though you have not even asked for her return; she is undefiled, and even in captivity has remained a queen. [R]

where, according to the classical mindset and perhaps to Chariton himself, women belong. The recapitulation passes over her afflictions in a cursory fashion (8.7.7). From here on Chaereas occupies center stage; *her* story has become *his* story.

When examined in light of the primary narrative, the recapitulation displays several inconsistencies. Negative personality features and dishonorable motivations are smoothed over. Mithridates's passion for Callirhoe, for example, is presented as altruism with regard to Chaereas (8.8.4). Dionysius, who frequently has displayed a bottom-line egocentricity[247] is described solely in positive terms. He is wealthy, of noble birth, and of excellent reputation (8.7.9, 12); he didn't treat her as slave, but as the mistress of his household (8.7.10). Even when he brought her to the King's court, he made her the "wonder of all Asia" (8.8.6).

The image of Chaereas is subtly but noticeably enhanced in the recapitulation. The speech ends with a litany of the hero's achievements, for which he credits only himself. He does not think to mention, for example, that the idea and impetus for joining the Egyptians belong to Polycharmus (7.1.11). Similarly, he mentions his politically wise return of the Persian queen and the families of other Persian dignitaries (8.8.10), but never credits Callirhoe with the idea; he intended to give Statira to Callirhoe as a servant (8.3.1). These narrative omissions maintain the powerful image that the feats of book 7 originated.

Chaereas's image is also spared detraction by the way this analeptic summary handles his many temptations to capitulate to Fate. His intentions and attempts to commit suicide are concentrated at one spot in his review, rather than scattered throughout as they occurred in the primary narrative. Bunched together, they are more likely to obtain the reader's sympathy than criticism. Their position in the review's narrative chain intensifies the cathartic effect, since the mention of this despair immediately precedes the "critical moment" (εὐκαίρως) when fortune changes.

Furthermore, the recapitulation seems to aggravate the hero's afflictions in order to heighten the reader's sympathy. The description of his near crucifixion has him taken down from the cross at the point of death (8.8.4), whereas in the primary narrative he was just ascending his cross when his rescuers arrived (4.3.5).

---

247. Cf. 2.5.12; 3.8.3–4; 4.1.2, 5.

In the description of his experience as Mithridates's prisoner, Chaereas substitutes his name for the heroine's at a critical point. In the primary narrative, when Polycharmus is about to be tortured by Mithridates, he mentions *Callirhoe's* name; in the recapitulation, it is *Chaereas's* name that Polycharmus utters. This is another indication of Chaereas's primacy at this point in the novel.

Another important feature of this recapitulation is that it is entirely character generated. That is not to say that it is wholly generated by the same character; Chaereas is responsible for most of it, but Hermocrates also makes a contribution. And even the crowds "get into the act."

That Chaereas shares with Hermocrates the task of reviewing the novel's story line associates him with the Syracusan war hero's aura of power. References to Hermocrates and his victory over the Athenians are among the most frequent of Chariton's flashbacks.[248] Though not always a willing participant, Chaereas nonetheless has obtained qualifications of the classical hero.

Although the summary review is character generated, the narrator's presence as the teller of the tale is apparent at several points: ὁ δὲ Χαιρέας ἔνθεν ἑλὼν διηγεῖτο ("taking up from there, Chaereas began to relate," 8.7.9); θρῆνον ἐξέρρηξεν ἐπὶ τούτοις τὸ πλῆθος, εἶπε δὲ Χαιρέας ("at these matters, the crowd burst out in a dirge, but Chaereas said," 8.8.2), ὁ δὲ δῆμος ἐξεβόησε ("the people cried out"), and καὶ ὃς ἔλεγεν ("and he continued speaking"). After this narrator's presence is hidden.

The crowds indicate that Chariton wants the reader to experience the narrative as a whole. They urge Chaereas to relate the story in order and not to omit any important details (ἐρωτῶμεν, ἄνωθεν ἄρξαι, πάντα ἡμῖν λέγε, μηδὲν παραλίπῃς ["We beg you to begin from the beginning! Tell us everything! Don't omit anything!] 8.7.3; cf. λέγε πάντα, 8.8.2).

Unlike many of Chariton's analepses, this section contains several departures from the order of events in the primary narrative. In the recapitulation: (1) Calirhoe's funeral (1.6.1–5) is narrated before Chaereas's trial and acquittal (1.5.4–7);[249] (2) Chaereas's search (3.3.1–

---

248. The following are some of the references to Callirhoe's noble family status and her father's power: 1.1.1, 13; 1.6.4; 1.11.2; 1.14.10; 2.5.10; 2.6.3; 3.1.6; 3.2.2; 3.4.3, 18; 3.10.8; 5.8.7–8; 6.7.10; 7.5.8; 8.2.12; 8.6.10; and 8.7.2.

249. See Table 5, 8.7.6.

3.5.9) is narrated before Dionysius's purchase and marriage of Callirhoe (2.1.1–3.2.17);[250] (3) Chaereas's mock funeral (4.1.7) is narrated before the shipwreck and construction of his tomb (3.10.1–4.1.6);[251] and (4) Chaereas wins the sea battle and captures Aradus (7.6.1–4) before the Egyptian King dies (7.5.14).[252]

The position of Callirhoe's funeral in the narrative chain presented in the recapitulation is harder to explain than identify. Reardon cites Chariton's haste to finish his story as a possible explanation for other inconsistencies in this section, and perhaps this suggestion applies here.[253] Nevertheless, it may be placed before the murder trial here, because the reader knows now what he or she did not know then, namely, that Callirhoe is alive. In the primary narrative, the murder trial assures the reader that Callirhoe has dead; in the recapitulation, the funeral assures the reader that the murder trial was appropriate.

Chaereas's search must precede Dionysius's purchase and marriage of Callirhoe because Hermocrates, the speaker of the first part of this recapitulation, does not know these details. Nevertheless, the placement of the Chaereas line first may add to the overall switch in emphasis from Callirhoe to Chaereas, notwithstanding the logical necessity of this arrangement.

CONCLUSION

Chariton capitalizes on the reader's tendency to identify with the character or characters with whom he or she shares a common background and motivating situation. He focuses on the widespread experience of isolation and impotence in a world grown large, a feature that has left many of his contemporaries with the feeling that there is no use fighting the divine city hall. Through the protagonists the reader is able to relive the buffetings of fate that he or she has experienced and, more importantly, to share their triumph.

We have noted that many of the novel's temporal disjunctions and abberations from a strictly chronological presentation highlight the protagonists' powerlessness. As citizens of Aphrodisias, a Greek city in Asia

---

250. See Table 5, 8.7.7–12.

251. See Table 5, 8.8.3.

252. See Table 5, 8.8.9–10.

253. Reardon, *Collected Ancient Greek Novels*, 122 n. 135.

Minor that surrendered its independence to the Roman world order, Chariton's protagonists (and readers) seek to define themselves in the context of that new power. The defining center is the cult of Aphrodite.

While the unparalleled radiance of Callirhoe appears to instigate all of the major plot turns in the novel, the heroine's beauty is merely a tool at the disposal of Aphrodite. Aphrodite alone is ultimately responsible for the union, separation, and reunion of the protagonists as well as for all their sufferings in between. Although reminders of Aphrodite's preeminence are scattered throughout the novel (notably in the wide geographical distribution of her temples),[254] this fact is made clear to the reader in one sentence that begins analeptically and concludes proleptically: "Having harassed by land and sea the handsome couple she had originally brought together, she decided now to reunite them" (8.1.3). The novel thus offers the reader security, a sense of belonging, and even access to political power through identification with the cult of Aphrodite.

The central role of the female protagonist has import for Chariton's view of the role of women in Hellenistic society. Chariton presents females as more socially restricted than was the case in the reader's world. As powerful as her sensual attraction is, Callirhoe complains of being moved about against her will like a piece of furniture. Her beauty gives her powerful emotional control, but she never gains control over the men who hold the real authority. On several occasions the narrative hints at the insult involved in requiring a woman to be accessible to public view. A woman's place was in the home—in separate quarters! Thus, Chariton's novel subverts the contemporary view of the liberated woman.

The love motif addresses the issue of societal norms for respectable marriage. Chariton's protagonists are permitted to marry for love rather than familial conjugation. This practice was more common in the reader's world than in the classical setting that the novel affords. The protagonists' marriage was (in their world) an exemption from the respected practice of arranged marriage. Although one could argue that things worked out well for them in the end, one could also argue that they paid dearly for their privilege. Moreover, the fact that the heroine arranges a marriage for her son and the hero arranges a marriage for his sister seems to suggest that Chariton is supporting the traditional

---

254. Callirhoe herself embodies the power and presence of Aphrodite. On repeated occasions she is actually mistaken for the goddess herself.

marriage practices of classical times. In this respect too, Chariton's novel is subversive.

Chariton has provided his first-century Hellenistic reader with an entertaining story, and, at the same time, has imparted a worldview. His novel is subversive in form and content: it presents a fictional story in a prose medium and it argues for a return to the social, especially marriage-related, practices of the classical period. Security is found in the confines of traditional marriage. Power, especially in a political context, is found in association with the goddess Aphrodite.

TABLE 5: Chariton's Final Recapitulation

8.7.5. As for the first part of the story, the people themselves already know that—it was they themselves who brought about your marriage. ⁶We all know how you fell into unfounded jealousy because of the intrigue the rival suitors mounted, and how you groundlessly struck your wife, and how she was thought dead and given a costly funeral, and how when you were tried for murder you condemned yourself to death out of your own mouth because you wanted to die along with your wife; ⁷but the people realized that what had happened was involuntary on your part and acquitted you. As for what happened after that—how the tomb robber Theron broke into the tomb at night, found Callirhoe alive among the funeral offerings, put her on his pirate ship, and sold her in Ionia; how you went out to search for your wife, did not find her, but fell in with the pirate vessel at sea, ⁸and found all the rest of the pirates dead of thirst and only Theron still alive; how you brought him into the assembly and he was tortured and questioned and then crucified; how the city sent a ship and a delegation to bring back Callirhoe, and your friend Polycharmus volunteered to sail with you—all this we know. Now you tell us what happened after you sailed from here.

⁹Taking up the tale from there, Chaereas began his account. We crossed the Ionian Sea safely and landed on the estate of a citizen of Miletus called Dionysius, a man preeminent throughout Ionia for his wealth, lineage, and distinguished reputation; he was the man who had bought Callirhoe from Theron for a talent. ¹⁰Do not be afraid; Callirhoe did not become a slave! At once he made the woman he had bought for money the mistress of his own heart. Loving her as he did, he would not bring himself to force his affections on a freeborn woman, but he could not bear to send back to Syracuse the woman he loved. ¹¹When

Callirhoe realized that she was pregnant by me, she found herself compelled to marry Dionysius, because she wanted to preserve your fellow citizen; she disguised the child's parentage so that it should be thought that Dionysius was the father, and so that it should be brought up in a worthy manner. [12]Yes, Syracusans! There is growing up in Miletus one who will be a Syracusan; a wealthy one, and reared by a distinguished man—for Dionysius is indeed of distinguished Greek lineage. We should not grudge him his great inheritance!

8.8.1. This, of course, I learned only later. At the time, when I had landed on this estate, I saw only Callirhoe's statue in a temple, and that gave me great confidence. But during the night a band of Phrygian brigands made a lightning raid on the shore, set fire to our ship, slaughtered most of us, tied me and Polycharmus up, and sold us in Caria. [2]The crowd broke out in lamentation at this. Allow me to pass over in silence what happened next, said Chaereas. 'It is grimmer than the beginning of the story.' 'Tell us the whole story!' cried the assembled people. Chaereas continued. 'The man who bought us, a slave of Mithridates, the governor of Caria, ordered us to be put in chains and set digging. When some of the chain gang murdered their guard, Mithridates ordered us all to be crucified. [3]I was taken away. Polycharmus, on the point of being tortured, spoke my name, and Mithridates recognized it—while staying with Dionysius in Miletus he had been present at Chaereas's funeral— Callirhoe had heard about the ship and the brigands, thought I had been killed, and constructed a costly tomb for me. [4]So Mithridates at once ordered that I be taken down from the cross—I was practically finished by then—and put me among his closest friends; he was anxious to restore Callirhoe to me, and got me to write a letter to her. [5]But through the carelessness of Mithridates' agent in the matter Dionysius got hold of the letter himself. He did not believe I was alive; he did believe that Mithridates had designs on his wife, and he immediately wrote to the King, accusing Mithridates of adulterous intentions. The King decided to hear the case and summoned everyone to him. So we went up to Babylon. [6]Dionysius took Callirhoe with him and made her celebrated, the wonder of all Asia; Mithridates took me along with him; and when we got there we pleaded our cases in a great trial before the King. Well, he acquitted Mithridates at once and announced his intention of arbitrating between me and Dionysius over Callirhoe, whom he placed in the charge of Queen Statira in the meantime. [7]How often, Syracusans, do you think I determined to kill myself, separated from my wife? Except that Polycharmus, the only friend to remain faithful to me throughout, saved my life. Furthermore, the King had quite disregarded the case—he was passionately in love with Callirhoe. [8]But he could not win her, and he did not offer her violence. "At the critical moment there was a rebellion in Egypt; that started a great war, which however brought me great benefits. The Queen took Callirhoe with her, and I heard a false report—someone told me she had been awarded to Dionysius. To get my revenge on the King I went over to the Egyptians and brought off great feats: [9]by my own actions I subdued Tyre, which was very difficult to take; then I was appointed admiral, beat the Great King at sea, and captured Aradus, where the King had left the Queen for safety, along with the riches you have seen. [10]So I was able to set up the Egyptian king as lord of all Asia, only he was killed fighting in a separate battle where I was not present. Finally, I secured the Great King's friendship for you by making a present to him of his wife and by sending to the Persian nobles their mothers and sisters and wives and daughters. [11]I have brought back here with myself the best Greek troops and those of the Egyptians who wanted to come. Another fleet of yours will come from Ionia too, and it will be commanded by the descendant of Hermocrates." [R]

5

Conclusion

Mark as Hellenistic Popular Literature

Locating Mark in the ranks of Hellenistic popular literature does appear to account for [its simple, fairly crude, synthetic structure] and . . . helps to clarify the Gospel's links to elite forms of aretalogy, biography, and memorabilia.

—Tolbert, *Sowing the Gospel*

SUMMARY OF RESULTS

THIS INVESTIGATION BEGAN AS an attempt to deal with the apparently indiscriminate arrangement of the narrative material in the Gospel of Mark. It has shown that although the episodes that comprise Mark's story are seldom linked causally, a logic nevertheless underlies their arrangement. At least part of the reason that Mark's order presents such an obstacle to the modern interpreter is a failure to take the Gospel on its own terms.

Our analysis has argued that the Gospel of Mark is a rhetorical document. In situations where someone is trying to persuade others to accept a specific worldview or take a particular course of action, the modern reader (or hearer) expects the appeal to follow a well-outlined presentation in which each point follows logically from its antecedent and a summary statement brings them all together. The recipient's task is to follow the line of argument and accept both the premises and conclusions of the author (or speaker). The problem, as Joanna Dewey has rightly noted, is that "Mark is telling a story for a listening audience, not presenting a logical argument."[1]

The verdict of form criticism confirms that judging Mark's Gospel by modern standards of logical argumentation inevitably influences the interpreter to view it as a concatenation of disjointed pericopae. Contrariwise, the assessment of narrative critics reveals that taking the Gospel on its own terms, according to the rhetorical standards of its own day, esteems its structure for the powerful way it transmits the speaker's ideology. Again Dewey's comments are instructive: "Arguments may be clouded by the lack of a clear outline, but stories gain depth and enrichment [and, we should add, force] through repetition and recursion."[2]

The decision to read Mark's Gospel on its own terms led naturally to a consideration of its affinities to other contemporaneous literary works. Specifically, the stylistic similarities between Mark and the ancient novels focused our attention on Tolbert's thesis that the true home of Mark's Gospel is the popular literature of the Hellenistic world.[3] To test this association, we compared Mark to the earliest extant Hellenistic romance novel, Chariton's *Chaereas and Callirhoe*, using the index of narrative sequence to narrow the scope.

The selection of narrative sequence was impelled especially by the work of Sternberg and Perry, who demonstrate that the order in which narrative events are presented affects the meanings apprehended and/ or assembled by the reader.[4] This in turn led to considering how the temporal ordering of narrative events in Mark and Chariton transported the author's ideologies.

Although Hägg and Petersen identify a number of temporal anachronies in Mark and Chariton, they often leave unexplored the function of these specific disconcordances.[5] To answer this question our inquiry probed the field of cognitive science for recent research that specifically analyzes how the brain processes language. This data was combined with reading theories that not only take account of the general effect of narratives (persuasion, catharsis, entertainment, etc.) but also explore the characteristics of language itself (selectivity, ambiguity, polyvalence,

---

1. Dewey, "Mark as Interwoven Tapestry," 224.

2. Ibid.

3. Tolbert, *Sowing the Gospel*, 59–79.

4. Perry, "Literary Dynamics"; and Sternberg, *Expositional Modes*.

5. Petersen, *Literary Criticism*; and Hägg, *Narrative Technique*.

aurality, and linearity) and the role these elements play in processing a narrative text. These theories were then applied to the Gospel of Mark (ch. 3) and Chariton's *Chaereas and Callirhoe* (ch. 4).

The sequential arrangement of Mark's material and the temporal disjunctions found therein influence the reader to accept the narrator's (=Jesus' = God's) worldview, which essentially means replacing a self-serving, status-seeking, power-wielding strategy of living with a self-sacrificial, seed-sowing, service-oriented pattern of thinking and program of action.

Mark's reader is early attracted to Jesus by the powerful aura that surrounds him. He or she initially identifies with the disciples because of their immediate, unconditional response to Jesus' invitation. As the narrative progresses, however, the disciples' failure to apprehend and model Jesus' message makes the reader increasingly less comfortable in identifying with them. Thus, when the disciples abandon Jesus at the Garden of Gethsemane, the reader abandons the disciples as identity models. Following the lead of minor characters that Mark subsequently introduces (or, in some cases, reintroduces), the ideal reader analyzes her or his own life situation in light of these models and adopts the "things of God" perspective proclaimed and demonstrated by Jesus.

Since Chariton's novel addresses an audience that shares essential commonalities with Mark's readers, its similar focus on power is not surprising. Chariton plays upon his reader's situation in a rapidly expanding world and, in particular, upon the feelings of isolation and powerlessness at least partially induced by it, by appealing to the natural allure of power and status. Again narrative order influences Chariton's reader to accept the ideology presented by the text.

The initial presentation of the protagonists is wholly positive: Callirhoe is the most beautiful woman in the world, and Chaereas the most handsome man. This highly enviable characterization is enhanced in both cases by the characters' aristocratic background. Their fathers, Hermocrates and Ariston, are the two most prominent citizens of Syracuse.[6]

Although Chariton presents two viable candidates for reader identification, Callirhoe quickly emerges as the novel's central character. She is introduced before her male counterpart. Her father (Hermocrates) is

---

6. That nothing is said of their mothers is another indication of the novel's power orientation.

presented before Chaereas's father (Ariston) and characterized as more powerful.[7] And practically all of the novel's action revolves around her.

The protagonists' first-rate credentials prime the reader to expect them to act with poise and confidence, but this expectation is quickly and repeatedly overturned. In spite of the powerful influence of her radiant sexuality, the heroine is a passive victim of the desires of men in positions of authority.

Rather than seeing her physical attractiveness as an asset, Callirhoe faults it as the cause of all her trouble. She is abused because of her husband's jealousy; she is sold as a slave because of the pirates' greed; she is threatened by the sensual desires of political rulers (even the "Great King" Artaxerxes!); and she is forced to surrender marital faithfulness for motherly duty because her beauty incited the passion of the wealthy landowner Dionysius.

Chaereas loses his identificatory appeal when he is overtaken by jealousy and delivers an apparently fatal blow to Callirhoe. Despair of ever finding Callirhoe repeatedly brings him to the brink of suicide. Constant coaxings are required to spare his life and spur him to continue the search for his wife.

Only by heeding his commrade's suggestion to side with the Great King's enemy—a challenge that he accepts only because it means dying with honor—does Chaereas take an active role in his destiny. By outmaneuvering Artaxerxes, Chaereas successfully resists a hostile power and wins back his bride in heroic fashion.

Especially important to the novel's message is a character who, though frequently addressed, never speaks: the goddess Aphrodite. Although the heroine's beauty appears to be the exciting force behind almost all the major plot turns in the novel, this sexual radiance, along with the machinations of other deities, are merely tools in the hands of Aphrodite who ultimately directs the novel's course of events.

7. Hermocrates is a retired war general celebrated for his defeat of the Athenians, and this is one of the most frequently repeated analepses of the novel. Ariston often appears in situations of weakness. He is characterized as less affluent than Hermocrates (1.1.9); he falls from a ladder and is apparently near death (1.3.1); and he is ill at Callirhoe's funeral (1.6.3). While Hermocrates organizes an investigation into his daughter's disappearance and, in fact, participates in the search, Ariston plays no part at all in the efforts to find Callirhoe (3.3.8). As the second expedition is about to be launched, Ariston is portrayed as diseased and half-dead (3.5.4). Even at the novel's end, Ariston is upstaged by Hermocrates who, in the city theatre, shares with *Ariston's* son the task of recounting the whole story before the people of Syracuse.

Aphrodite alone is responsible for bringing the lovers' initial union, final reunion, and all the struggles in between. Chaereas indeed wins back his wife, but only after he visits a temple of Aphrodite, falls to his knees, credits the goddess for bringing Callirhoe to him, and begs her to give Callirhoe back to him (3.6.3).

The analepsis at the beginning of book 8 confirms that Aphrodite was responsible for the couple's union and for Chaereas's tribulation (8.1.3). She had given him the finest gift and he repaid her with arrogance. After his punishment, however, he made amends to Love, and Aphrodite decided to have pity on him. Thus, the section concludes with a prolepsis that indicates that Aphrodite is about to affect the couple's reunion.

The hero's tribulation is clearly explained. What is not mentioned, however, is the reason for the heroine's suffering. Perhaps her beauty evoked the jealousy of the gods. But this would be unusually cruel, for throughout the entire story Callirhoe, in spite of her sufferings, remains more faithful to Aphrodite than she was to Chaereas.

The apparent lack of motivation for the heroine's suffering suggests that the rationale behind the torments of both protagonists may be more mundane than heavenly. In *Chaereas and Callirhoe*, the narrator relates the story of a couple who married on the basis of love rather than familial conjugation. Chaereas and Callirhoe have circumvented the practice of arranged marriage, and have paid dearly for the exemption. The narrator has shown that this type of union is more susceptible to destruction by jealousy. In this way, he overturns what was becoming an accepted practice in his day and calls for a return to the safer, traditional marriage customs of the classical period.

Aphrodite, though herself silent throughout the narrative, is nevertheless a key player in Chariton's drama. It is she who orchestrates the entire story world. Chariton sends the clear message that all who wish life to work out in their favor must be at peace with Aphrodite. The work of Douglas Edwards has shown the importance of Aphrodite in linking Hellenistic society to the power of Imperial Rome.[8] Thus, the answers Chariton gives to the reader's feelings of insecurity and impotence are traditional marriage and association with the goddess Aphrodite.

---

8. Edwards, "Acts of the Apostles."

ON READING MARK AS HELLENISTIC
POPULAR LITERATURE

In spite of her recognition that the Gospel of Mark bears "striking *stylistic* similarities to the popular Greek ancient novel," Mary Ann Tolbert affirms: "*The Gospel of Mark is obviously not an ancient novel of the erotic type.*"[9] Tolbert's observation is important. Moreover, the results of the present investigation suggest that the textual evidence, specifically as it relates to narrative sequence, is insufficient to substantiate that Mark should be read as an ancient novel at all.[10]

To be sure, many stylistic and thematic similarities between the Gospel of Mark and Chariton's *Chaereas and Callirhoe* can be listed. Nevertheless, when one subjects these elements to closer scrutiny, even the similarities reveal significant differences.

Both Chariton and Mark reveal the influence of historiography. Their casts include historical individuals with whom their original readers were familiar.[11] Nevertheless, although both authors have adopted a historiographical format, their narratives operate in different historical domains. Chariton's novel takes place centuries before the time of his readers. This affords him absolute freedom to construct the details of his story in any way appropriate for his purposes. That he makes full use of this freedom is confirmed by the obvious historical blunders in his story.

In contrast, Mark's narrative world is less than a generation removed from his contemporaries. Although he clearly links his narrative to the distant past (cf. the prophecy of Isaiah), virtually all of the action of the story takes place in the recent past. Thus, the historical circumstances of Mark's narrative world more closely approximate the reader's world.

9. Tolbert, *Sowing the Gospel*, 65; emphases original.

10. Its genre is not identical to any of the complete ancient novels known at present. Nevertheless, Tolbert (*Sowing the Gospel*, 65) notes fragmentary evidence of a more biographical type of ancient novel: "If such a historical/biographical type of ancient novel existed, it would clearly be the generic home of the Gospels."

11. Cf. Mark (Isaiah; John; Jesus; Herod; Herodias; Pilate; the Twelve; Mary, the mother of Jesus; Mary, the mother of James, Joses and Salome; Mary Magdalene; and Joseph of Arimathea) and Chariton (Hermocrates; Artaxerxes; Statira; Dionysius; Athenagoras[?]; Ariston[?]; and Rhodogyne[?]).

Episodic plot structure is another stylistic feature that Mark's Gospel shares with Chariton's novel. Again, however, we note a difference in the way these episodes are pieced together. Chariton takes pains to show a logical (frequently temporal) connection between episodes. Linking phrases (typically of the form μεν . . . δέ) that summarize the action of the previous episode and set the stage for the following are common elements of his novel.[12]

Mark, however, rarely displays a causal connection between episodes and even less frequently states it explicitly. His narrative is more like a series of snapshots that have been arranged in an order designed to highlight certain themes or compare the responses of certain characters. The sandwiching of the Herod-Baptist episode in the middle of the disciples' evangelistic ministry is a vivid illustration of this technique.

Mark's episodic arrangement prompts addressing the larger question of narrative gaps in general. Chariton's concern for causal links typically leaves fewer narrative gaps than result from Mark's approach. We have argued that the Gospel of Mark and *Chaereas and Callirhoe* are rhetorical documents. The comments of the early rhetorician Demetrius (ca. first century BCE) are significant:

> Not everything should be given lengthy treatment with full details but some points should be left for our hearer to grasp and infer for himself. If he infers what you have omitted, he no longer just listens to you but acts as your witness, one too who is predisposed in your favor since he feels he has been intelligent and you are the person who has given him this opportunity to exercise his intelligence. In fact, to tell your hearer everything as if he were a fool is to reveal that you think him one.[13]

Judged according to this standard, Mark has a greater chance of persuading his reader than Chariton. In fact, this may partly explain the disdain with which Chariton's novel apparently was met.

Mark lays out the pieces of the puzzle and requires the *reader* to assemble the picture. Chariton, in contrast, does most of the reader's work. When Chariton wishes the reader to bring certain cognitive or affective elements to bear on a forthcoming episode, he usually explicitly states

---

12. Hägg (*Narrative Technique*, 147) cites the following references: 1.1.7; 1.5.1; 1.6.1; 1.9.1; 1.11.4; 1.13.7; 1.14.6; 2.3.5; 2.4.1; 2.6.1; 2.8.1; 2.9.1; 3.5.1; 4.2.4; 4.5.3; 5.5.1; 5.8.10; 5.10.6; 6.2.1; 6.2.8; 6.6.2; 8.5.1; 8.6.1; 8.7.3.

13. Demetrius, *Eloc.*, 221–22; quoted in Tolbert, *Sowing the Gospel*, 43.

those elements in the form of a recapitulation. Mark often includes only a signifier such as πάλιν in the episode to be processed. This requires the *reader* to reaccess the episode to which the πάλιν refers and bring the gist of it to bear on the current episode.

Similarities between Mark and Chariton also are apparent in terms of how each handles narrative time. Both exhibit a considerable number of analepses and prolepses. In general, however, Mark is oriented proleptically and Chariton analeptically.

In Mark, the most commanding prolepses relate to the prediction of Jesus' passion and resurrection. The contents of the Gospel beg the question: how did such a godly and powerful person come to such a terrible, untimely end? The narrative's answer to it is simply that Jesus' death was neither untimely nor the end.

The many prolepses related to Jesus' passion clearly show that the crucifixion did not take him by surprise; it was his intention all along. Moreover, that the prediction of his resurrection is often linked with the prediction of his passion emphasizes that Jesus' end was not really an end, but the transition to a new mode of existence. Clearly, the paradigmatic death of Jesus is the central focus of Mark's Gospel.

Chariton's emphasis on analepses directs his reader's attention more to the protagonists' struggles than the final outcome.[14] Although a few character-generated proleptic hints occur earlier in the novel, the narrator's prediction of a happy ending does not occur until the final book. Since character-generated prolepses have proven to be generally unreliable, the reader is not assured of the happy ending until the narrator affirms it in 8.1.3–4.

Nevertheless, Chariton does make judicious use of prolepses. Often these relate in vague terms the outcome of the next scene or series of scenes, leaving the reader free to focus on the character's reactions to the events that bring that outcome about. In a similar way, Mark's early and clear and repeated predictions of his story's outcome set the reader in a position above the characters, enabling them to see where Jesus' disciples miss the mark. Subtly the reader is then called to pick up where the disciples have failed.

Chariton's narrator shares the proleptic function with many of the characters in the novel. In Mark, the narrator limits this function almost

---

14. Does this help to make his point, namely, conform to traditional marriage and avoid similar tribulations?

exclusively to Jesus. Peter's affirmation that he would accept death before denying Jesus is the most striking exception in the Gospel. Since Peter's subsequent denial of Jesus overturns his prediction, this exception illustrates the rule that the only fully reliable predictions are those of the narrator (and Jesus, in the case of Mark).

Another feature common to both narratives is a protagonist who represents a deity. In Mark, Jesus is God's Son (1:11; 9:7; 13:32; 14:61–62), Son of Man (2:28; 8:38; 10:45; 13:26; 14:61–62), and Messiah (1:1; 8:29; 14:61–62). He exercises power over diseases, natural laws, and evil spirits. Chariton's heroine is frequently mistaken for the goddess Aphrodite, but the narrative makes clear that she is mortal. When Dionysius rebukes his steward for failing to recognize her deity, she retorts: "Stop making fun of me! Stop calling me a goddess—I'm not even a happy mortal!" (2.3.7).

Drama also figures significantly in Mark and Chariton. Both are scene-summary mixtures in which scene predominates. Thus, direct speech is a major part of the narratives. Most of this speech occurs in character dialogue. In Chariton, the protagonists seldom emerge the winners in confrontational dialogue. In Mark, the situation is dramatically the opposite. Jesus' dialogue with the Syrophonecian woman may be the only place where Jesus is bettered in debate.[15]

Chariton also includes a number of monologues, most of which take the form of prayers to Aphrodite. Monologues are almost nonexistent in Mark. Jesus' Gethsemane prayer (14:35–36) may be the sole exception. Mixing direct speech with narratorial commentary has the effect of placing the reader on the front row of the theater in the seat next to the director.

CONCLUSION

While the numerous stylistic similarities between the Gospel of Mark and Chariton's *Chaereas and Callirhoe* speak in favor of a common literary background, they are not enough to argue that the former should be read either as Hellenistic popular literature in general or as an ancient Greek novel in particular.

---

15. Jesus' response is probably an example of *peirastic* irony. That is, Jesus intentionally set up the dialogue as a test of the woman's faith. See Camery-Hoggatt, *Irony in Mark's Gospel*, 150–51.

This investigation has revealed that Mark's Gospel bears significant differences from Chariton's novel—even among the narrative techniques and stylistic similarities they share. Chariton's novel is, by the author's own definition, a love story (πάθος ἐρωτικὸς);[16] Mark's story is a gospel (εὐαγγέλιον). The tenor of these works betrays very different purposes.

Modern scholarship has long held entertainment to be the principal motivation behind the composition of the Greek novels. We have argued that "entertainment" does not specify clearly enough the novel's effect on the reader. In the case of Chariton, we have shown that the text transmits the author's ideology. Nevertheless, this does not require that pushing an ideology was the author's motive. On the contrary, the style, language, and general tenor of Chariton's novel betoken entertainment more than serious reflection.

The Gospel of Mark presents the opposite picture. Drama is present, but it is not exploited.[17] Mark's rhetoric of indirection, which requires the reader to put the pieces together for her- or himself, indicates the presence of a subject matter that calls for concentrated contemplation.

This particular narrative approach has proven to be a helpful way of looking at the narratives of Mark and Chariton and suggests direction for future research. The gender of the implied reader was given attention in the treatment of *Chaereas and Callirhoe* primarily because this narrative features both a male and a female protagonist operating in two intertwining story lines. Yet much remains undone in considering the implications of gender for Mark's implied reader. Furthermore, in noting the repetition of events when discussing analeptic and proleptic references, we have exposed some open terrain with regard to analyzing these narratives in terms of Genette's categories of "frequency" and "duration." Perhaps these kinds of analyses will shed light on the ideology reflected by these texts.

---

16. See Liddell-Scott, s.v. "ἐρωτικός" and "πάθος." ἐρωτικός is primarily "of, or caused by love." πάθος is "that which happens" (good or bad), but frequently this word carries negative overtones (unfortunate accident, misfortune, calamity). Thus, the expression πάθος ἐρωτικος could be rendered "a calamity caused by love" or "a passion of love." In moving through the text, the reader would probably think of it as first "a passion caused by love," then as "a calamity caused by love." Even the happy ending might not be enough to bring it back to its initial connotation.

17. This is evident in the author's restraint in describing the Herod-Baptist episode.

Bibliography

Abbott, V., and J. B. Black. *The Representation of Scripts in Memory*. Technical report. Department of Psychology, Yale University, 1980.

Achtemeier, Paul J. "'He Taught Them Many Things': Reflections on Marcan Christology." *CBQ* 42 (1980) 465–81.

Alonzo-Schoekel, Luis. "Hermeneutics in the Light of Language and Literature." *CBQ* 25 (1963) 371–86.

Alter, Robert. "How Convention Helps Us Read: The Case of the Bible's Annunciation Type-Scene." *Proof* 3 (May 1983) 115–30.

Anderson, Graham. *Eros Sophistes: Ancient Novelists at Play*. American Classical Studies 9. Chico, CA: Scholars, 1982.

———. *The Novel in the Graeco-Roman World*. Totowa, NJ: Barnes and Noble, 1984.

Anderson, Janice Capel. "Double and Triple Stories, The Implied Reader, and Redundancy in Matthew." *Semeia* 31 (1985) 71–89.

Anderson, John R. "Verbatim and Propositional Representation of Sentences in Immediate and Long-Term Memory." *JVLVB* 13 (1974) 149–62.

Anderson, Richard C., et al. "Frameworks for Comprehending Discourse." *AERJ* 14 (1977) 367–81.

Aune, David E. *The New Testament in Its Literary Environment*. LEC. Philadelphia: Westminster, 1987.

Bar-Efrat, Shimon. *Narrative Art in the Bible*. JSOTSup 70. Sheffield: Sheffield Academic, 1989.

Bartlett, Frederick. *Remembering*. Cambridge: Cambridge University Press, 1932.

Barton, Stephen C. "Mark as Narrative: The Story of the Anointing Woman (Mk 14:3–9)." *ExpTim* 102 (1991) 230–34.

Bauer, Walter. *A Greek-English Lexicon of the New Testament and Other Early Christian Literature*. Translated and edited by William F. Arndt and F. Wilbur Gingrich. Chicago: University of Chicago Press, 1957.

Beavis, Mary Ann. *Mark's Audience: The Literary and Social Setting of Mark 4:11–12*. JSOTSup 33. Sheffield: JSOT Press, 1989.

———. "The Trial Before the Sanhedrin (Mark 14:53–65) Reader Response and Greco-Roman Readers." *CBQ* 49 (1987) 581–96.

———. "Women as Models of Faith in Mark." *BTB* 18 (1988) 3–9.

Begg, Ian, and W. A. Wickelgren. "Retention Functions for Syntactic and Lexical vs. Semantic Information in Sentence Recognition Memory." *MemCog* 2 (1974) 353–59.

Belo, Fernando. *A Materialist Reading of the Gospel of Mark*. Translated by Matthew J. O'Connell. Maryknoll, NY: Orbis, 1981.

Bergen, Robert D. "Text as a Guide to Authorial Intention: An Introduction to Discourse Criticism." *JETS* 30 (September 1987) 327–36.

Best, Ernest. *Following Jesus: Discipleship in the Gospel of Mark*. JSNTSup 4. Sheffield: JSOT Press, 1981.

———. *Mark: The Gospel as Story*. Edinburgh: T. & T. Clark, 1983.

Bietenhard, Hans. "Beginning." In *NIDNTT* 1:164–69.

Bilezikian, Gilbert G. *The Liberated Gospel: A Comparison of the Gospel of Mark and Greek Tragedy*. Grand Rapids: Baker, 1977.

Boomershine, Thomas E. "Mark the Storyteller: A Rhetorical-Critical Investigation of Mark's Passion and Resurrection Narrative." Ph.D. diss., Union Theological Seminary, 1974.

———. "Mark 16:8 and the Apostolic Commission." *JBL* 100 (1981) 225–39.

Boomershine, Thomas E., and Gilbert Bartholomew. "The Narrative Technique of Mark 16:8." *JBL* 100 (1981) 213–23.

Booth, Wayne C. *The Rhetoric of Fiction*. Chicago: University of Chicago Press, 1961.

Boring, M. Eugene. "Mark 1:1–15 and the Beginning of the Gospel." *Semeia* 52 (1990) 43–83.

Bowie, E. L. "The Literature of the Empire." In *The Cambridge History of Classical Literature*, vol. 1, *Greek Literature*, edited by P. E. Easterling and B. M. W. Knox, 642–713. Cambridge: Cambridge University Press, 1985.

Bransford, John D., and N. S. McCarrell. "A Sketch of a Cognitive Approach to Comprehension." In *Cognition and the Symbolic Processes*, edited by Walter Weimer and David Palermo, 1:189–249. New York: Wiley, 1974.

Brewer, William F. "Memory for Ideas: Synonym Substitution." *MemCog* 4 (1975) 458–64.

Brewer, William F., and E. H. Lichtenstein. "Memory for Marked Semantic Features versus Memory for Meaning." *JVLVB* 13 (1974) 172–80.

Brown, Colin, general editor. *The New International Dictionary of New Testament Theology*. 4 vols. Grand Rapids: Zondervan, 1975–78.

Bultmann, Rudolf. *History of the Synoptic Tradition*. Translated by John Marsh. New York: Harper & Row, 1963.

Burch, Ernest W. "Tragic Action in the Second Gospel: A Study in the Narrative of Mark." *JR* 11 (1931) 346–58.

Buttrick, George A., editor. *The Interpreter's Dictionary of the Bible*. 4 Vols. Nashville: Abingdon, 1962.

Camery-Hoggett, Jerry. *Irony in Mark's Gospel: Text and Subtext*. SNTSMS 72. Cambridge: Cambridge University Press, 1992.

———. "Rhetoric of Text, Rhetoric of Sermon: A Reader-Response Approach to the Business of Preaching." Unpublished manuscript from the library of Southern California College, Costa Mesa.

Carey, M., et al., editors. *The Oxford Classical Dictionary*. Oxford: Clarendon, 1949.

Carpenter, Ronald H. "Stylistic Redundancy and Function in Discourse." *Language and Style* 3 (1970) 62–68.

Carrington, Philip. *The Primitive Christian Calendar: A Study in the Making of the Marcan Gospel*. London: Cambridge University Press, 1952.

Chariton. *Kallirhoe*. Translated by C. Lucke and K.-H. Schäfer. Leipzig: Reclam, 1985.

Chatman, Seymour. *Story and Discourse: Narrative Structure in Fiction and Film*. Ithaca, NY: Cornell University Press, 1978.

Cherry, Colin. *On Human Communication*. Cambridge: MIT Press, 1957.

Clark, Herbert, and Eve Clark. *Psychology and Language: An Introduction to Psycholinguistics.* New York: Harcourt Brace Jovanovich, 1977.

Collins, Allan, and Elizabeth Loftus. "A Spreading-Activation Theory of Semantic Processing." *PsyRev* 82 (1975) 407–28.

Collins, Allan., and M. Ross Quillian. "Retrieval Time from Semantic Memory." *JVLVB* 8 (1969) 240–47.

Colson, Francis H. "τάξει in Papias." *JTS* 14 (1912–13) 62–69.

Cranfield, C. E. B. *The Gospel according to Mark.* CGTC. Cambridge: Cambridge University Press, 1959.

Crawford, Mary, and Roger Chaffin. "The Reader's Construction of Meaning: Cognitive Research on Gender and Comprehension." In *Gender and Reading: Essays on Readers, Texts, and Contexts,* edited by Patrocinio P. Schweickart and Elizabeth A. Flynn, 3–30. Baltimore: Johns Hopkins University Press, 1986.

Culpepper, R. Alan. *Anatomy of the Fourth Gospel: A Study in Literary Design.* Philadelphia: Fortress, 1983.

———. "An Outline of the Gospel According to Mark." *RevExp* 75 (Fall 1978) 619–22.

Dehn, Günther. *Der Gottessohn. Eine Einführung in das Evangelium des Markus.* Hamburg: Furche, 1953.

Delling, Gerhard. "ἀρχη." In *TDNT* 1:479–86.

Derrett, J. Duncan M. *The Making of Mark: The Scriptural Bases of the Earliest Gospel.* Vol. 1: *From Jesus' Baptism to Peter's Recognition of Jesus as the Messiah.* Warwickshire: P. Drinkwater, 1985.

Dewey, Joanna. "Mark as Interwoven Tapestry: Forecasts and Echoes for a Listening Audience." *CBQ* 53 (1991) 221–36.

———. *Markan Public Debate: Literary Technique, Concentric Structure, and Theology in Mark 2:1–3:6.* SBLDS 48. Chico, CA: Scholars, 1980.

———. "Oral Methods of Structuring Narrative in Mark." *Int* 43 (1989) 32–44.

———. "Point of View and the Disciples in Mark." *SBLSP* 118 (1982) 97–106.

Dijk, Teun A. van. *Text and Context: Explorations in the Semantics and Pragmatics of Discourse.* Longman Linguistics Library. New York: Longman, 1977.

Dijk, Teun A. van, and Walter Kintsch. *Strategies of Discourse Comprehension.* New York: Academic Press, 1983.

Dodd, Charles H. "The Framework of the Gospel Narrative." *ExpTim* 43 (June 1932) 396–406.

Donahue, John R. *The Theology and Setting of Discipleship in Mark.* Milwaukee: Marquette University Press, 1983.

Eco, Umberto. *The Role of the Reader: Explorations in the Semiotics of Texts.* Bloomington: Indiana University Press, 1979.

Edwards, Douglas R. "Acts of the Apostles and Chariton's *Chaereas and Callirhoe*: A Literary and Sociohistorical Study." Ph.D. diss., Boston University, 1987.

Edwards, James R. "Markan Sandwiches: The Significance of Interpolations in Markan Narratives." *NovT* 31 (1989) 193–216.

Egger, Brigitte. "Women in the Greek Novel: Constructing the Feminine." Ph.D. diss., University of California, Irvine, 1990.

Enslin, Morton S. "The Artistry of Mark." *JBL* 66 (1947) 385–99.

Farrer, Austin. *A Study in St. Mark.* London: Dacre, 1951.

Faw, Chalmer E. "The Outline of Mark." *JBR* 25 (January 1957) 19–23.

Flynn, Elizabeth A. "Gender and Reading." In *Gender and Reading: Essays on Readers, Texts, and Contexts*, edited by Patrocinio P. Schweickart and Elizabeth A. Flynn, 267–88. Baltimore: Johns Hopkins University Press, 1986.

Fowler, Robert M. "A Critical Model of Reading." In *Let the Reader Understand: Reader-Response Criticism and the Gospel of Mark*, 41–58. Minneapolis: Fortress, 1991.

———. *Let the Reader Understand: Reader-Response Criticism and the Gospel of Mark*. Minneapolis: Fortress, 1991.

———. *Loaves and Fishes: The Function of the Feeding Stories in the Gospel of Mark*. SBLDS 54. Chico, CA: Scholars, 1984.

———. "Using Literary Criticism on the Gospels: Emerging Trends in Biblical Thought." *ChrCent* 99 (1982) 626–29.

———. "Who Is 'the Reader' in Reader-Response Criticism?" *Semeia* 31 (1985) 5–23.

Frei, Hans. *The Eclipse of Biblical Narrative: A Study in Eighteenth and Nineteenth Century Hermeneutics*. New Haven: Yale University Press, 1974.

Friedman, Norman. "Point of View in Fiction: The Development of a Critical Concept." *PMLAA* 70 (1955) 1160–84.

Friedrich, Gerhard. "εὐαγγελίζομαι." In *TDNT* 2:707–737.

Frye, Northrop. *The Secular Scripture: The Study of the Structure of Romance*. The Charles Eliot Norton Lectures, 1974–75. Cambridge: Harvard University Press, 1976.

Funk, Robert W. *The Poetics of Biblical Narrative*. Sonoma, CA: Polebridge, 1988.

Genette, Gérard. *Narrative Discourse: An Essay in Method*. Translated by J. Lewin. Ithaca, NY: Cornell University Press, 1980.

Gerhardsson, Birger. *Memory and Manuscript: Oral Tradition and Written Transmission in Rabbinic Judaism and Early Christianity*. Copenhagen: Gleerup, 1961.

Giangrande, Giuseppe. "On the Origins of the Greek Romance." *Eranos* 60 (1962) 132–59.

Gombrich, Ernst H. *Art and Illusion: A Study in the Psychology of Pictorial Representation*. BSer 35. New York: Pantheon, 1960. Reprint, 2nd ed., Princeton: Princeton University Press, 1969.

Goppelt, Leonhard. *Theology of the New Testament*, vol. 1: *The Ministry of Jesus in Its Theological Significance*. Translated by John Alsup, edited by Jürgen Roloff. Grand Rapids: Eerdmans, 1981.

Graesser, Arthur C. *Prose Comprehension beyond the Word*. New York: Springer, 1981.

Grassi, Joseph A. *The Hidden Heroes of the Gospels: Female Counterparts of Jesus*. Collegeville, MN: Liturgical, 1989.

———. "The Secret Heroine of Mark's Drama." *BTB* 18 (1988) 10–15.

Green, Georgia M., and Jerry L. Morgan. "Writing Ability as a Function of the Appreciation of Differences between Oral and Written Communication." In *Writing: The Nature, Development, and Teaching of Written Communication*, vol. 2, edited by Carl H. Frederiksen and Joseph F. Dominic, 177–88. Hillsdale, NJ: Erlbaum, 1981.

Guelich, Robert. "'The Beginning of the Gospel'—Mark 1:1–15." *BR* 27 (1982) 5–15.

Gumpez-Cook, Jenny, and John J. Gumpez. "From Oral to Written: The Transition to Literacy." In *Writing: The Nature, Development, and Teaching of Written Communication*, vol. 1, edited by Marcia Farr Whitemann, 89–107. Hillsdale, NJ: Erlbaum, 1981.

Guthrie, Donald. *New Testament Introduction*. Downers Grove, IL: InterVarsity, 1970.

Guy, H. A. *The Origin of Mark's Gospel*. London: Hodder & Stoughton, 1954.

Hägg, Tomas. "The Beginnings of the Historical Novel." In *The Greek Novel: AD 1–1985*, edited by Roderick Beaton, 169–81. London: Croom Helm, 1988.

———. *Narrative Technique in Ancient Greek Romances*. Stockholm: Acta Instituti Atheniensis Regni Seuciae, 1971.

———. *The Novel in Antiquity*. Berkeley: University of California Press, 1983. Originally published in Swedish as *Den Antika Romanen*. Uppsala: Bokförlaget Carmina, 1980.

———. "The Parthenope Romance Decapitated?" *Symbolae Osloenses* 59 (1984) 61–91.

Havelock, Eric A. "Oral Composition in the *Oedipus Tyrannus* of Sophocles." *NLH* 16 (1984) 175–97.

———. *Preface to Plato*. Cambridge, MA: Belknap Press of Harvard University Press, 1963.

Hedrick, Charles W. "What Is a Gospel? Geography, Time, and Narrative Structure." *PRSt* 10 (1983) 255–68.

Heiserman, Arthur R. *The Novel before the Novel: Essays and Discussions about the Beginnings of Prose Fiction in the West*. Chicago: University of Chicago Press, 1977.

Hengel, Martin. *Studies in the Gospel of Mark*. Translated by John Bowden. Philadelphia: Fortress, 1985.

Hirsch, Eric D. *Validity in Interpretation*. New Haven: Yale University Press, 1967.

Holzberg, Niklas. *Der Antike Roman: Eine Einführung*. Artemis Einführungen 25. Munich: Artemis, 1986.

Hooker, Morna D. "Christology and Methodology." *NTS* 17 (1970–71) 480–87.

———. "On Using the Wrong Tool." *Th* 75 (1972) 570–81.

Horowitz, Rosalind, and S. J. Samuels, editors. *Comprehending Oral and Written Language*. New York: Academic Press, 1987.

Houck, Robert F. "Why New Testament Scholars Should Read Ancient Novels." Paper presented at the annual meeting of the Society of Biblical Literature, San Fransisco, 1992.

Hrushovski, Benjamin. *Segmentation and Motivation in the Text Continuum of Literary Prose: The First Episode of War and Peace*. Tel-Aviv: Porter Institute for Poetics and Semiotics, Tel-Aviv University, 1976.

Huey, F. B., Jr. "Oil." In *ZPEB* 4:513–15.

———. "Ointment." In *ZPEB* 4:515–18.

Hunt, Morton. *The Universe Within: A New Science Explores the Human Mind*. New York: Simon & Schuster, 1982.

Hurtado, Larry W. The Gospel of Mark in Recent Study." *Them* 14 (1989) 47–52.

———. *Mark*. NIBC. Peabody, MA: Hendrickson, 1983.

Hutchinson, Peter. *Games Authors Play*. London: Methuen, 1983.

Ingarden, Roman. *The Cognition of the Literary Work of Art*. Translated by Ruth Ann Crowley and Kenneth R. Olson. NUSPEP. Evanston, IL: Northwestern University Press, 1973. Originally published as *Vom Erkennen des literarischen Kunstwerks*. Tübingen: Niemeyer, 1968.

Iser, Wolfgang. *The Act of Reading: A Theory of Aesthetic Response*. Baltimore: Johns Hopkins University Press, 1978.

———. *Prospecting: From Reader Response to Literary Anthropology*. Baltimore: Johns Hopkins University Press, 1989.

Johne, R. "Übersicht über die antiken Romanautoren bzw.-werke mit Datierung und weitergeführter Bibliographie." In *Der antike Roman: Untersuchungen zur literarischen Kommunikation und Gattungsgeschichte*, edited by Heinrich Kuch, 198–230. Berlin: Akademie-Verlag, 1989.

Keck, Leander E. "The Introduction to Mark's Gospel," *NTS* 12 (1966) 352–70.

———. "Oral Traditional Literature and the Gospels: The Seminar." In *The Relationships among the Gospels: An Interdisciplinary Dialogue*, edited by William O. Walker Jr. San Antonio: Trinity University Press, 1978.

Kee, Howard Clark. *Community of the New Age: Studies in Mark's Gospel.* 1977. Reprint, Macon, GA: Mercer University Press, 1983.

Keegan, Terence J. *Interpreting the Bible: A Popular Introduction to Biblical Hermeneutics.* New York: Paulist, 1985.

Kelber, Werner H. "Gospel Narrative and Critical Theory." *BTB* 18 (1988) 130–36.

———. *The Kingdom of God in Mark.* Philadelphia: Fortress, 1974.

———. *The Oral and the Written Gospel: The Hermeneutics of Speaking and Writing in the Synoptic Tradition, Mark, Paul, and Q.* Philadelphia: Fortress, 1983.

Kennedy, George A. "Classical and Christian Source Criticism." In *The Relationships among the Gospels: An Interdisciplinary Dialogue*, edited by William O. Walker Jr., 125–55. San Antonio: Trinity University Press, 1978.

———. *New Testament Interpretation through Rhetorical Criticism.* Chapel Hill: University of North Carolina Press, 1984.

Kent, Thomas. "The Classification of Genres." *Genre* 16 (1983) 1–20.

Kingsbury, Jack Dean. *Matthew as Story.* Philadelphia: Fortress, 1986.

Kintsch, Walter, and Teun A. van Dijk. "Toward a Model of Text Comprehension and Production." *PsyRev* 85 (1978) 363–94.

Kittel, Gerhard, and Gerhard Friedrich, editors. *Theological Dictionary of the New Testament.* Translated by G. W. Bromiley. 10 Vols. Grand Rapids: Eerdmans, 1964–76.

Knox, Bernard M. W. "Books and Readers in the Greek World." In *The Cambridge History of Classical Literature*, vol. 1, *Greek Literature*, edited by P. E. Easterling and B. M. W. Knox. Cambridge: Cambridge University Press, 1985.

Köhler, Wolfgang. *Gestalt Psychology.* 1929. Reprint, New York: New American Library, 1947.

Krieger, Murray. *A Window to Criticism: Shakespeare's Sonnets and Modern Poetics.* Princeton: Princeton University Press, 1964.

Kümmel, Werner G. "Die Naherwartung in der Verkündigung Jesu." In *Zeit und Geschichte: Dankesgabe an Rudolf Bultmann zum 80*, 31–46. Tübingen: Mohr/Siebeck, 1964.

Lang, Friedrich G. "Kompositionsanalyse des Markus-evangeliums." *ZTK* 74 (1977) 1–24.

Liddell, Henry G., and Robert Scott. *A Greek-English Lexicon.* Oxford: Clarendon, 1940.

Liddell, Robert. *Some Principles of Fiction.* London: Cape, 1953.

Lightfoot, Robert H. *The Gospel Message of Mark.* London: Oxford University Press, 1950.

Linnemann, Eta. *Historical Criticism of the Bible: Methodology or Ideology?* Translated by Robert W. Yarbrough. Grand Rapids: Baker, 1990.

———. *Is There a Synoptic Problem?: Rethinking the Literary Dependence of the First Three Gospels.* Translated by Robert W. Yarbrough. Grand Rapids: Baker, 1992.

Lohmeyer, Ernst. *Das Evangelium des Markus.* Göttingen: Vandenhoeck & Ruprecht, 1953, 1970.

Longman, Tremper. "The Literary Approach to the Study of the Old Testament: Promise and Pitfalls." *JETS* 28 (1985) 385–98.

Lord, Albert Bates. "The Gospels as Oral Traditional Literature." In *The Relationships among the Gospels: An Interdisciplinary Dialogue*, edited by William O. Walker Jr., 33–92. Trinity University Monograph Series in Religion 5. San Antonio: Trinity University Press, 1978.

———. *The Singer of Tales*. Cambridge: Harvard University Press, 1960.

Mack, Burton L., and Vernon K. Robbins. "Chreia & Pronouncement Story in Synoptic Studies." In *Patterns of Persuasion in the Gospels*, 1–29. FF. Sonoma, CA: Polebridge, 1989.

———. *Patterns of Persuasion in the Gospels*. FF. Sonoma, CA: Polebridge, 1989.

Mailloux, Steven. *Interpretive Conventions: The Reader in the Study of American Fiction*. Ithaca, NY: Cornell University Press, 1982.

———. "Learning to Read: Interpretation and Reader-Response Criticism." *STL* 12 (1979) 93–108.

———. "Reader-Response Criticism?" *Genre* 10 (1977) 413–31.

Malbon, Elizabeth Struthers. "Disciples—Crowds—Whoever: Markan Characters and Readers." *NovT* 28 (1986) 104–30.

———. "Fallible Followers: Women and Men in the Gospel of Mark." *Semeia* 28 (1983) 29–48.

———. "The Poor Widow in Mark and Her Poor Rich Readers." *CBQ* 53 (1991) 589–604.

Mandler, J. M., and N. S. Johnson. "Remembrance of Things Parsed: Story Structure and Recall." *CogPsy* 9 (1977) 111–51.

Mansfield, M. Robert. *"Spirit and Gospel" in Mark*. Peabody, MA: Hendrickson, 1987.

Marrou, Henri I. *A History of Education in Antiquity*. Translated by George Lamb. New York: Sheed & Ward, 1956.

Matera, Frank J. "The Prologue as the Interpretative Key to Mark's Gospel." *JSNT* 34 (1988) 3–20.

McKnight, Edgar V. *Postmodern Use of the Bible: The Emergence of Reader-Oriented Criticism*. Nashville: Abingdon, 1988.

McLelland, James. "Stochastic Interactive Processes and the Effect of Context on Perception." *CogPsy* 23 (1991) 1–44.

Meagher, John C. *Clumsy Construction in Mark's Gospel: A Critique of Form- and Redaktionsgeschichte*. Toronto Studies in Theology 3. New York: Mellen, 1979.

———. "Die Form- und Redaktionsungeschickliche Methoden: The Principle of Clumsiness in the Gospel of Mark." *JAAR* 43 (1975) 459–72.

Merkelbach, Reinhold. *Roman und Mysterium in der Antike*. Munich: Beck, 1962.

Meyer, B. F. "Afterword." In *The Interrelations of the Gospels: A Symposium Led by M.-É. Boismard, W. R. Farmer, and F. Neirynck; Jerusalem 1984*, edited by David L. Dungan, 564–65. Macon, GA: Mercer University Press, 1990.

———. "Objectivity and Subjectivity in Historical Criticism." In *The Interrelations of the Gospels: A Symposium Led by M.-É. Boismard, W. R. Farmer, and F. Neirynck; Jerusalem 1984*, edited by David L. Dungan, 546–60. Macon, GA: Mercer University Press, 1990.

Miller, James E. *Word, Self, and Reality: The Rhetoric of Imagination*. New York: Dodd, Mead, 1972.

Miner, Madonne M. "Guaranteed to Please: Twentieth-Century American Women's Bestsellers." In *Gender and Reading: Essays on Readers, Texts, and Contexts*, edited by Patrocinio P. Schweickart and Elizabeth A. Flynn, 187–211. Baltimore: Johns Hopkins University Press, 1986.

Minsky, Marvin. "A Framework for Representing Knowledge." In *The Psychology of Computer Vision*, edited by P. H. Winston. New York: McGraw-Hill, 1975.

Molinié, Georges, editor and translator. *Le Roman de Chairéas et Callirhoé*. Collection des Univeristés de France. Paris: Belles Lettres, 1989.

Moore, Stephen D. "Narrative Commentaries on the Bible: Context, Roots, and Prospects." *FFFor* 3 (1987) 29–62.

Moulton, James H., and George Milligan. *The Vocabulary of the Greek New Testament Illustrated from the Papyri and Other Non-literary Sources*. 1914–30. Reprint, Grand Rapids: Eerdmans, 1974.

Muchow, Michael David. "Passionate Love and Respectable Society in Three Greek Novels." PhD diss., Johns Hopkins University, 1988.

Munro, Winsome. "Women Disciples in Mark?" *CBQ* 44 (1982) 225–41.

Myers, Ched. *Binding the Strong Man: A Political Reading of Mark's Story of Jesus*. Maryknoll, NY: Orbis, 1988.

Nineham, Dennis E. *The Gospel of Mark*. PGC. New York: Seabury, 1963.

Norman Petersen. "Story Time and Plotted Time in Mark's Narrative." In *Literary Criticism for New Testament Critics*, 49–80. GBS. Philadelphia: Fortress, 1978.

Novak, Michael. "Narrative and Ideology." *This World* 23 (Fall 1988) 66–80.

Ong, Walter J. *Interfaces of the Word: Studies in the Evolution of Consciousness and Culture*. Ithaca, NY: Cornell University Press, 1977.

———. *Orality and Literacy: The Technologizing of the Word*. New York: Methuen, 1982.

———. *The Presence of the Word*. New Haven: Yale University Press, 1967.

Papanikolaou, A. D. "Zur Sprache Charitons." Ph.D. diss., Köln, 1963.

Parsons, Mikeal C. "How Narratives Begin: A Bibliography." *Semeia* 52 (1990) 33–41.

———. "Reading a Beginning/Beginning a Reading: Tracing Literary Theory on Narrative Openings." *Semeia* 52 (1990) 11–31.

Perrin, Norman. *The New Testament, an Introduction: Proclamation and Parenesis, Myth and History*. New York: Harcourt Brace Jovanovich, 1974.

Perry, Ben E. *The Ancient Romances: A Literary-Historical Account of Their Origins*. Berkeley: University of California Press, 1967.

———. "Chariton and His Romance from a Literary-Historical Point of View." *AJP* 51 (1930) 93–134.

Perry, Menakhem. "Literary Dynamics: How the Order of a Text Creates Its Meanings." *PT* 1 (1979) 35–64, 311–61.

Pervo, Richard I. *Profit with Delight: The Literary Genre of the Acts of the Apostles*. Philadelphia: Fortress, 1987.

Pesch, Rudolf. *Das Markusevangelium*. Vol. 1. 3rd ed. HTKNT. Freiburg: Herder, 1984.

Petersen, Norman R. *Literary Criticism for New Testament Critics*. GBS. Philadelphia: Fortress, 1978.

———. "'Point of View' in Mark's Narrative." *Semeia* 12 (1978) 97–121.

Pierce, J. P. *Signals, Communication and Noise: The Nature and Process of Communication*. New York: Harper & Row, 1961.

Placher, William C. "Hans Frei and the Meaning of Biblical Narrative." *ChrCent* 106 (1989) 556–59.

Plepelits, Karl, translator. *Kallirhoe*. Bibliothek der griechischen Literatur 6. Stuttgart: Hiersemann, 1976.

Poland, Lynn M. *Literary Criticism and Biblical Hermeneutics: A Critique of Formalist Approaches*. AARAS 48. Chico, CA: Scholars, 1985.

Pritchard, John Paul. *A Literary Approach to the New Testament*. Norman: University of Oklahoma Press, 1972.

Reardon, Bryan P. Aspects of the Greek Novel." *GR* 23 (1976) 118–31.

———, editor. *Collected Ancient Greek Novels*. Berkeley: University of California Press, 1989.

———. "The Form of Ancient Greek Romance." In *The Greek Novel: AD 1–1985*, edited by Roderick Beaton, 205–16. London: Croom Helm, 1988.

———. "*The Form of Greek Romance*. Princeton: Princeton University Press, 1991.

———. "The Greek Novel." *Phoenix* 23 (1969) 291–309.

———. "Theme, Structure, and Narrative in Chariton." In *Later Greek Literature*, edited by John J. Winkler and Gordon Williams, 1–27. Yale Classical Studies 27. Cambridge: Cambridge University Press, 1982.

Reicke, Bo. "The History of the Synoptic Discussion." In *The Interrelations of the Gospels: A Symposium Led by M.-É. Boismard, W. R. Farmer, and F. Neirynck; Jerusalem 1984*, edited by David L. Dungan, 291–316. Macon, GA: Mercer University Press, 1990.

Rhoads, David. "Narrative Criticism and the Gospel of Mark." *JAAR* 50 (1982) 414–16.

Rhoads, David, and Donald Michie. *Mark as Story: An Introduction to the Narrative of a Gospel*. Philadelphia: Fortress, 1982.

Ricoeur, Paul. *Time and Narrative*. 3 Vols. Translated by Kathleen Blamey, Kathleen McLaughlin, and David Pellauer. Chicago: University of Chicago Press, 1984–88.

Rigg, H. A. "Papias on Mark." *NovT* 1 (1956) 161–83.

Rimmon-Kenan, Shlomith. *Narrative Fiction: Contemporary Poetics*. New York: Methuen, 1983.

Robbins, Vernon K. *Jesus the Teacher: A Socio-Rhetorical Interpretation of Mark*. Philadelphia: Fortress, 1984.

Robertson, A. T. *A Grammar of the Greek New Testament in the Light of Historical Research*. Nashville: Broadman, 1934.

Rohde, Erwin. *Der griechische Roman und seine Vorläufer*. 1876. Reprint, 4th ed., Hildesheim: Olms, 1960.

Rumelhart, David E. "Schemata: The Building Blocks of Cognition." In *Theoretical Issues in Reading Comprehension*, edited by Rand J. Spiro, B. Bruce, and William F. Brewer, 33–58. Hillsdale, NJ: Erlbaum, 1980.

Rumelhart, David E., and Andrew Ortony. "The Representation of Knowledge in Memory." In *Schooling and the Acquisition of Knowledge*, edited by Richard C. Anderson, Rand J. Spiro, and William E. Montague, 99–135. Hillsdale, NJ: Erlbaum, 1977.

Sachs, J. S. "Memory in Reading and Listening to Discourse." *MemCog* 2 (1974) 95–100.

Sanford, Anthony J., and Simon C. Garrod. *Understanding Written Language: Explorations of Comprehension beyond the Sentence*. London: Wiley, 1981.

Schank, R. C., and R. Abelson. *Scripts, Plans, Goals and Understanding: An Inquiry into Human Knowledge Structures*. Hillsdale, NJ: Erlbaum, 1977.

Schierling, Marla. "Women as Leaders in the Marcan Community." *Listening* 15 (1980) 250–56.

Schmeling, Gareth L. *Chariton*. Twayne's World Authors Series. New York: Twayne, 1974.

Schmitt, John. "Women in Mark's Gospel: An Early Christian View of Woman's Role." *TBT* 19 (1981) 228–33.

Schweickart, Patrocinio P., and Elizabeth A. Flynn, editors. *Gender and Reading: Essays on Readers, Texts, and Contexts*. Baltimore: Johns Hopkins University Press, 1986.

Schweizer, Eduard. *The Good News according to Mark*. Translated by Donald H. Madvig. London: SPCK, 1970.

Scribner, Sylvia, and Michael Cole. *The Psychology of Literacy*. Cambridge: Harvard University Press, 1981.

Seebass, Horst, and Colin Brown. "Righteousness, Justification." In *NIDNTT* 3:352–56, 358–65.

Senior, Donald. "'With Swords and Clubs...'—The Setting of Mark's Community and His Critique of Abusive Power." *BTB* 17 (1987) 10–20.

Sheeley, Steven. "The Narrator in the Gospels: Developing a Model." *PRSt* 16 (1989) 213–23.

Spiro, Rand J., Bertram C. Bruce, and William F. Brewer, editors. *Theoretical Issues in Reading Comprehension: Perspectives from Cognitive Psychology, Linguistics, Artificial Intelligence, and Education*. Hillsdale, NJ: Erlbaum, 1980.

Spoehr, Kathryn, and Stephen Lehmkuhle. *Visual Information Processing*. San Francisco: Freeman, 1982.

Standaert, B. *L'évangile selon Marc: Composition et genre littéraire*. Nijmegen: Stichting Studentenpers, 1978.

Stanzel, Franz K. *Typische Formen des Romans*. Göttingen: Vandenhoeck & Ruprecht, 1964.

Sternberg, Meir. *Expositional Modes and Temporal Ordering in Fiction*. Baltimore: Johns Hopkins University Press, 1978.

———. "Ideology of Narration and Narration of Ideology." In *Poetics of Biblical Narrative: Ideological Literature and the Drama of Reading*, 84–128. Indiana Leterary Biblical Series. Bloomington: Indiana University Press, 1985.

———. *The Poetics of Biblical Narrative: Ideological Literature and the Drama of Reading*. Indiana Leterary Biblical Series. Bloomington: Indiana University Press, 1985.

Stock, Augustine. *Call to Discipleship: A Literary Study of Mark's Gospel*. Wilmington, DE: M. Glazier, 1982.

Stroop, J. R. "Studies of Interference in Serial Verbal Reactions." *JEP* 18 (1935) 643–62.

Suleiman, Susan Rubin. "Redundancy and the 'Readable' Text." *PT* 1 (1980) 119–42.

Suleiman, Susan Rubin, and Inge Crosman, editors. *The Reader in the Text: Essays on Audience and Interpretation*. Princeton, NJ: Princeton University Press, 1980.

Sykes, Stephen. "The Grammar of Narrative and Making Sense of Life." *ATR* 67 (1985) 117–26.

Talbert, Charles H. *The Narrative Unity of Luke-Acts: A Literary Interpretation*, vol. 1: *The Gospel according to Luke*. FF. Philadelphia: Fortress, 1986.

Tannehill, Robert C. "The Disciples in Mark: The Function of a Narrative Role." *JR* 57 (1977) 386–405.

———. *The Sword of His Mouth: Forceful and Imaginative Language in the Synoptic Sayings*. 1975. Reprint, Eugene, OR: Wipf & Stock, 2003.

Tannen, Deborah. "Oral and Literate Strategies in Spoken and Written Discourse." In *Literacy for Life: The Demand for Reading and Writing*, edited by Richard W. Bailey and Robin Melanie Fosheim, 79–96. New York: Modern Language Association of America, 1983.

————. "Relative Focus on Involvement in Oral and Written Discourse." In *Literacy, Language, and Learning: The Nature and Consequences of Reading and Writing*, edited by David R. Olson, Nancy Torrance, and Angela Hildyard, 124–47. Cambridge: Cambridge University Press, 1985.

————. "What's in a Frame? Surface Evidence for Underlying Expectations." In *New Directions in Discourse Processing*, edited by R. O. Freedle, 137–81. Advances in Discourse Processes. Norwood, NJ: Ablex, 1979.

Taylor, Vincent. *The Gospel According to St. Mark.* 2nd ed. New York: St. Martin's, 1966.

Tenney, Merrill C., editor. *The Zondervan Pictorial Encyclopedia of the Bible.* 5 Vols. Grand Rapids: Zondervan, 1975.

Theissen, Gerd. *The Gospels in Context: Social and Political History in the Synoptic Tradition.* Translated by Linda M. Maloney. Minneapolis: Fortress, 1991.

Thompson, John A. "Ointment." In *IDB* 3:593–95.

Thorndyke, Perry W. "Cognitive Structures in Comprehension and Memory of Narrative Discourse." *CogPsy* 9 (1977) 77–110.

Thorndyke, Perry W., and Frank R. Yekovitch. "A Critique of Schema-Based Theories of Human Story Memory." *Poetics* 9 (1980) 23–49.

Todorov, Tzvetan. *Introduction to Poetics.* Translated by Richard Howard. Minneapolis: University of Minnesota Press, 1981.

Tolbert, Mary Ann. *Sowing the Gospel: Mark's World in Literary-Historical Perspective.* Minneapolis: Fortress, 1989.

Tompkins, Jane P., editor. *Reader-Response Criticism: From Formalism to Post-Structuralism.* Baltimore: Johns Hopkins University Press, 1980.

————. "The Reader in History: The Changing Shape of Literary Response." In *Reader-Response Criticism: From Formalism to Post-Structuralism*, edited by Jane P. Tompkins, 201–32. Baltimore: Johns Hopkins University Press, 1980.

Trenkner, Sophie. *The Greek Novella in the Classical Period.* Cambridge: Cambridge University Press, 1958. Reprint, New York: Garland, 1987.

Treu, K. "Der antike Roman und sein Publikum." In *Der antike Roman: Untersuchungen zur literarischen Kommunikation und Gattungsgeschichte*, edited by Heinrich Kuch, 178–97. Berlin: Akademie-Verlag, 1989.

Trevor, John C. "Oil." In *IDB* 3:592–93.

Trocmé Etienne. *The Formation of the Gospel according to Mark.* Translated by P. Gaughan London: SPCK, 1975.

Tulving, Endel, and C. Gold. "Stimulus Information as Determinants of Tachistoscopic Recognition of Words." *JEP* 66 (1963) 319–27.

Uspensky, Boris. *A Poetics of Composition: The Structure of the Artistic Text and Typology of a Compositional Form.* Translated by V. Zavarin and S. Wittig. Berkeley: University of California Press, 1973.

Vawter, Bruce. *On Genesis: A New Reading.* Garden City, NY: Doubleday, 1977.

Von Wahlde, Urban C. "Mark 9:33–50: Discipleship: The Authority That Serves." *BZ* 29 (1985) 49–67.

Waetjen, Herman C. *A Reordering of Power: A Socio-Political Reading of Mark's Gospel.* Minneapolis: Fortress, 1989.

Weeden, Theodore J., Sr. *Mark: Traditions in Conflict.* Philadelphia: Fortress, 1971.

Wellek, René, and Austin Warren. *Theory of Literature*. 3rd ed. New York: Harcourt Brace Jovanovich, 1970.

Wilcox, John T. *The Bitterness of Job: A Philosophical Reading*. Ann Arbor: University of Michigan Press, 1989.

Wilder, Amos N. *The Bible and the Literary Critic*. Minneapolis: Fortress, 1991.

Williams, James G. *Gospel against Parable: Mark's Language of Mystery*. BLS. Decatur, GA: Almond, 1985.

Winston, Patrick Henry. *Artificial Intelligence*. Reading, MA: Addison-Wesley, 1977.

Wittig, Susan. "Formulaic Style and the Problem of Redundancy." *Centrum* 1 (1973) 123–36.

Wittrock, Merlin C., C. Marks, and M. Doctorow. "Reading as a Generative Process." *JEP* 67 (1975) 484–89.

Wright, Addison G. "The Widow's Mite: Praise or Lament?—A Matter of Context [Mark 12:41–44; Luke 21:1–4]." *CBQ* 44 (1982) 256–65.

Wuellner, Wilhelm. "Where Is Rhetorical Criticism Taking Us?" *CBQ* 49 (1987) 448–63.

Index